Crime On Her Mind

Crime

Fifteen Stories

On Her Mind

of Female Sleuths from the
Victorian Era to the Forties

Edited and with Introductions

by MICHELE B. SLUNG

 Pantheon Books A Division of Random House, New York

Copyright © 1975 by Random House, Inc.

All rights reserved under International and Pan-American Copyright Conventions. Published in the United States by Pantheon Books, a division of Random House, Inc., New York, and simultaneously in Canada by Random House of Canada Limited, Toronto.

Library of Congress Cataloging in Publication Data
Slung, Michele B.   1947–   comp.
  Crime on her mind.
  Bibliography: pp. 379–80
  CONTENTS: Pirkis, C. L. The murder at Troyte's Hill.
—Sims, G. R. The man with the wild eyes.—Rook, C. The stir outside the Café Royal. [etc.]
  1. Detective and mystery stories, English. 2. Detective and mystery stories, American. 3. Women detectives—Fiction. I. Title.
PZ1.S6395Cr3 [PR1309.D4]   823'.0872   74-26201
ISBN 0-394-49573-X

Design by Irva Mandelbaum

Manufactured in the United States of America

First Edition

Permissions
Acknowledgments

Grateful acknowledgment is made to the following for permission to reprint various selections:

Curtis Brown Ltd. (London) and Gladys Mitchell: "Daisy Bell" by Gladys Mitchell. Reprinted from *Detective Stories of Today*, edited by Raymond Postgate (Faber & Faber Ltd., 1940).

Doubleday & Company, Inc.: "The Calico Dog" by Mignon Eberhart. Copyright 1934 by Mignon Eberhart. Reprinted from *The Cases of Susan Dare*.

Geoffrey M. Footner, Executor of the Estate of Gladys Footner Hall: "The Murder at Fernhurst" by Hulbert Footner. Reprinted from *The World's Best Detective Stories*, edited by Eugene Thwing (Funk & Wagnalls, 1929).

David Higham Associates, Ltd.: "The Mother of the Detective" by G. D. H. and M. Cole. Reprinted from *Mrs. Warrender's Profession* (William Collins & Sons Company Ltd.).

Hutchinson Publishing Group Ltd.: "The Murder at Troyte's Hill" by C. L. Pirkis. Reprinted from *The Experiences of Loveday Brooke, Lady Detective* (Hutchinson & Company Ltd., 1894).

For my parents, for Tom,
and for
Elise McStea Whitney

Contents

Acknowledgments

My largest debt is to Ira Wolff, whose generosity with his collection aided me immensely and gave me many hours of reading pleasure. I also wish to thank Allen J. Hubin for his encouragement and bibliographic aid, and the staff of the Mercantile Library of New York for their patient and enthusiastic service. I would also like to express my gratitude to Eleanor Sullivan and to Francis M. Nevins, Jr., W. O. G. Lofts, E. F. Bleiler, and David J. Goldin for helpful bits of information. And my personal thanks go to Claire S. Degener, Joan Brandt, Mary Jarrett, and Kathleen Macomber for their guidance of my project.

Introduction

One of the most heretical moments in the annals of crime-fiction scholarship came on January 31, 1941. It was on that date that Rex Stout, who had been invited as an honored guest, addressed a group of Holmesian devotees and scholars at a meeting of the New York chapter of the Baker Street Irregulars. His after-dinner speech was titled "Watson Was a Woman," and proved, to Stout's satisfaction at least, that the good doctor was, on his/her own textual evidence, a member of what was then still being disparagingly referred to as "the weaker sex." Though to some it might seem merely a clever spoof of Sherlockian studies, to the faithful it was nothing short of an outrage to hear Watson's sturdy sentiments interpreted as sentimentality, his manly self-sufficiency read as domesticity, and his loyal companionship transformed into wifely fidelity.

Needless to say, Stout departed that masculine sanctum sanctorum an excoriated pariah.

Yet, historically speaking, the great sleuth of Baker Street himself (leaving the issue of the sex of his roommate aside) was not without ancestresses; nor was he to lack female descendants. If Watson was *not* a woman (and it *is* a distinct possibility), still there were being created during the latter half of the nineteenth century a sizable number of women detectives who did not have to play second fiddle to a violin-playing eccentric but who were, minus deerstalker and cape, solving cases quite handily in their own right.

Though these early female characters represented in varying degrees the then emerging "modern" woman, they were all alike in eschewing domesticity in favor of detection, if only for long enough to give them a recordable career. Independent and audacious, skilled at disguise, and courageous in the face of danger, they set the stage for such diverse types as Nancy Drew, Miss Marple, and Modesty Blaise while reflecting the standards and prejudices, the tastes and aspirations, of the age. By the 1940s—when Stout dropped his teasing bombshell—the adventures of well over sixty women detectives had been chronicled, from Edwardian debutantes to ingenuous flappers, from elderly busybodies to hard-boiled molls.

In regard to the burning question, Just who was the *first* woman detective?—and when did she detect?—bibliographers of the genre have never quite reached a point of agreement on what year it was that Mrs. Paschal, considered by most the groundbreaker, saw the light. The usually acknowledged date is 1861, fully twenty-six years *before* Sherlock Holmes. Mrs. Paschal's creator bore the coy nom de plume "Anonyma," and the author's reticence was generally thought to be masking a writing syndicate rather than a single person. Copies of the original "yellowback" [1] are extremely scarce, which accounts for the controversy over the date of Mrs. Paschal's appearance, a battle that is still being waged by scholar-fans.

In his role as indefatigable historian and researcher into the archives of detectivedom, Ellery Queen adds another dimension to this skirmish. He iconoclastically denies the seniority of Mrs. Paschal and instead puts forward the claim of the Female Detective, the anonymous heroine of a book by the same name written by Andrew Forrester, Jr., and published in *1864*.[2]

---

[1] "Yellowback" was a nickname given to a type of cheap edition, usually bound in yellow paper or cloth, that was evolved around the middle of the last century for sale in railway bookstalls. Since these books were generally reprints and were often not dated, it is often difficult to determine even the approximate date of first publication of books that survive only in yellowback.

[2] Queen argues that the 1861 date for Mrs. Paschal's appearance is taken from a possibly inaccurate listing in Scribner's Catalogue Number 98, titled "Collection of Detective Fiction" and issued in 1935. Entry 48 in this catalogue describes the copy offered, with the title *The Experiences of a Lady Detective*, simply as "an early edition" of a book first published in 1861. Queen considers that *The Revelations of a Lady*

Rather than take sides, it would seem more fruitful to make use of the available descriptions of these coveted items and examine the background, personalities, and habits of these two Victorian ladies whose authors had them defy convention by their choice of profession.

When she joins the ranks of "the much-dreaded but little-known people called Female Detectives," Mrs. Paschal, an Englishwoman of good family and superior education, is a widow in her late thirties. Immodestly, she proclaims her intention to rely on the powers of her "vigorous and subtle" brain and her talents as an actress (a background which stood several other early women sleuths in good stead) to enable her to get to the truth of seemingly difficult cases.

Unlike her countrywoman, Forrester's nameless Female Detective has never been married (at least, Queen cites no evidence to the contrary); her origins and schooling are unspecified. That she speaks with the voice of frankness and authority is all that characterizes her. Like Mrs. Paschal, she opts for sleuthing as a means of warding off the undesirable (and far duller) state of genteel poverty. The only other similarity that can be extracted from the Queen description is a facility for acting, as the Female Detective confesses that she has often posed as a dressmaker or milliner, presumably in order to penetrate the inner reaches of a suspect's or witness's boudoir.

The Female Detective's insights into the usefulness of women investigators are, in general, sensible ones, for she perceives that criminals can be of either sex and "that the necessary detectives should be of both." Her pragmatism is further illustrated by her admission that while she is aware that "her trade is a despised one [she is] not ashamed of it." Only women, she reminds the reader, can successfully undertake certain types of cases and arrive at the correct solution. "But without going into particu-

---

Detective (1864) is actually the original collection of Mrs. Paschal stories—though it is referred to by most historians as a sequel to *Experiences*—and that the title *The Experiences of a Lady Detective* exists only on the title page of an 1884 reissue of *Revelations*. He cites British Museum records to support this claim, and also to show that the Female Detective appeared in 1864 *six months before* Mrs. Paschal.

lars," she states, "the reader will comprehend that the woman detective has far greater opportunities than a man of intimate watching, and of keeping her eye upon matters near which a man could not conveniently play the eavesdropper." Moreover, her experiences as a member of a "secret police" force have convinced her "that when a woman becomes a criminal she is far worse than the average of her male companions." [3]

Interestingly, since Mrs. Paschal too is connected with a police force (the Detective Department of the London Metropolitan Police), there were no women actually attached to the Metropolitan Police in London until 1883, when two women were appointed to oversee female prisoners. In 1905 a Miss McDougall received an official position, the duties of which combined the offices of social worker with those of wardress; eventually this position was designated "police matron." Real-life policewomen were expected to deal with prosaic and sordid cases of child prostitution, wife-beating, and the like, rather than the more "colorful" mail robberies and jewel capers assigned to Mrs. Paschal and her unacknowledged rival.[4]

Unfortunately for modern readers who have the chance of dipping into Mrs. Paschal's narratives, the stories have not stood up well to the test of time. There is very little in them that can be termed real detection. Critics have held them to be stylistically tedious, observing that Mrs. Paschal contents herself with following obvious clues and with putting the finger on easily identified villains. Nonetheless, because "Anonyma" makes use of what were to become standard conventions of the genre—forgery, blackmail, diabolical secret societies, the confusing existence of twins[5]—Mrs. Paschal, while her stories seem primitive today, deserves more than a casual nod of recognition. For those who are inclined to disparage her, let it be remembered that she

---

[3] *The Female Detective*, quoted in Ellery Queen, *In the Queen's Parlor* (New York: Biblo & Tannen, 1969), pp. 41–45.

[4] Chloe Owings, *Women Police* (New York: Frederick H. Hitchcock, 1925), pp. 2–3.

[5] Amnon Kabatchnik, "Retrospective Review," *The Armchair Detective* 7 (February 1974): 132.

appeared on the detective horizon a short twenty years (if the 1861 date is accepted) after Poe's "Murders in the Rue Morgue"—that most seminal story—and that thus she is certainly entitled to grandmotherly respect. Since so little is known about the Female Detective aside from Queen's citations, it seems suitable, if labels are necessary, to designate her as "great-aunt" to the sleuthing sisterhood so that she may take her rightful place next to the better-known Mrs. Paschal.

Between the years 1861 and 1901, no fewer than twenty women detectives made their appearance, the sobriquet "lady detective" often finding its way into the various titles. (This usage, in fact, followed a journalistic cliché of the times, for a quick glance through Victorian periodicals turns up any number of articles on lady fencers, lady photographers, lady farmers, lady guides, lady miners, lady graduates, and even lady balloonists.) Thus, one can read *The Experiences of Loveday Brooke, Lady Detective* (London, 1894), *The Adventures of a Lady Detective* (London, about 1890), or *Dora Myrl: The Lady Detective* (London, 1900). On the opposite side of the Atlantic, the fad was a bit slower to catch on, although a writer named Harry Rockwood produced a book called *Clarice Dyke, the Female Detective* (known only in an 1883 reprint edition).

This early crop of women sleuths was possessed of a collective sensibility that could indeed be best described as "ladylike." In fact, they were usually *over*endowed with feminine charms to compensate for their mannish profession. Though they were more at home in a drawing room than a smugglers' den or a thieves' kitchen, this is not to say they weren't willing to give low life a try in the pursuit of justice. It is simply that, combining a zest for adventure with an antipathetic but becoming reticence, the lady detectives were forced to trade on natural deductive abilities, or on what might be termed a practical application of their never-to-be-doubted "women's intuition," this quality eliciting alternate scorn and admiration from colleagues, clients, and criminals alike. The authors themselves seem never to be quite certain of their creations, intent as they are on playing up the novelty of such a peculiar figure, often abandoning her in mid-career and finishing her off, not at the Reichenbach Falls, but at the matrimonial altar, in order to reassure the Victorian public of her ultimate femaleness.

Sometimes, though, the man behind the lady detective was *far* behind her, either dead or disgraced. If the latter, it was not uncommon for the woman to have turned sleuth in order to clear the name of a husband or sweetheart, or to seek revenge. Many began their stints in just this manner.

Two turn-of-the-century heroines—Lois Cayley, the athletic adventuress, and Hilda Wade, the nurse with a photographic memory—went to great lengths and geographical distances to restore the honor of their men (the one, a fiancé; the other, a dead father). Wilkie Collins' 1875 novel *The Law and the Lady* is considered to contain an early attempt at the woman detective simply because the plot follows the protagonist's efforts to prove her husband innocent of the suspicion that he poisoned his first wife. A variation is Hagar Stanley, the dusky gypsy pawnbroker of Fergus Hume's *Hagar of the Pawn-Shop* (1899) who pursues her secondary career as a problem-solver while waiting for her lover to make his fortune and return to her. (Comely Mrs. Mollie Delamere, the "lady pearl-broker" of the 1899 novel of the same name, also combined mercantilism with some detection but was more importuned than attracted, finally avoiding such indelicate professional hazards by marrying an Australian millionaire.) Two later but still early women detectives, Lady Molly and Violet Strange, also illustrate this by-then familiar device, both using their sleuthing skills on behalf of men with whom they were involved.

The previously mentioned Clarice Dyke detected at the side of her husband, Donald. In a more unusual twist of fictional relationships, the author M. McD. Bodkin *wedded* his lady detective, Dora Myrl, to another of his creations, Paul Beck, known as "the Rule-of-Thumb" detective. In a novel aptly entitled *The Capture of Paul Beck* (1909), he made them first opponents, then lovers, and finally united them, eleven years after the introduction of that male sleuth and nine after the initial book featuring Miss Myrl. A later book introduced Paul, Jr., as *Young Beck: A Chip of the Old Block*; not unexpectedly, this boy sleuth followed in his parents' footsteps.

Extending the dates of this earliest period to include the years of the First World War, it becomes possible to observe the emergence of what were to be the firmly entrenched patterns and stereotypes of the entire body of detective literature. In nearly all respects, the conventions of the genre, from clues and corpses to red herrings and locked doors, are common to the adventures of the sleuths of both sexes, the major difference being that the overt femininity of the Mrs. Paschals and Lady Mollys is heavily emphasized, while the masculine traits of the Dupins and Holmeses are never made an issue. In regard to any characteristics peculiar to the woman sleuth, one sees that her similarities to the male are greater than her differences, and one can only fall back on the popular belief that many cases required "the woman's touch," with the ladies using this as their *raison d'être* and their trademark.

Whether they were police, private inquiry agents, or amateurs, the early women detectives tended to be involved with crimes of a straightforward nature—cases of murder or theft which they solved without the pyrotechnics of their more famous male counterparts. Keen analytical reasoning was not their forte, and they did not thrive on empiricism. The special qualifications of these heroines lay in their vivacious energy and brisk common sense, aided by their "female instincts." While on the scent, many of them were nonetheless accompanied or watched admiringly by a secondary character shaped on the model of Dr. Watson, and it is curious to note that a few of these figures were of the opposite sex from the heroine. Particularly worth singling out are Florence Cusack, who appeared in magazine stories at the turn of the century and whose cases were chronicled by an admiring medical man, and Hilda Wade, who ended her career in the arms of her recording comrade.

The first truly important innovation—one that was to have a

long-lasting effect on the portrayal of the woman detective—had occurred in 1897 with the appearance of Miss Amelia Butterworth, created by Anna Katharine Green. The aristocratic Miss Butterworth is a spinster whose social politesse and notions of decorum are at odds with her irrepressible nosiness; in other words, she is the prototype of the elderly busybody female sleuth. Humor is abundant as she bustles her way officiously through the two books that detail her "cases," her indifference to such inhospitable mutterings as "meddlesome old maid" presenting a distinct contrast to the winsome delicacy of the same author's later girl detective, Violet Strange.

In both novels, Miss Butterworth assists Mr. Ebenezer Gryce, the New York police detective who solved the Leavenworth case,[6] admitting that she comes to the world of criminal justice with no firsthand experience and acknowledging "for though I have had no adventures, I feel capable of them." During the course of *The Affair Next Door* (1897), Miss Butterworth questions rhetorically, with the unrepentant wisdom of hindsight, "Did they realize at first glance that I was destined to prove a thorn in the sides of everyone connected with this matter for days to come?" This frankly recalcitrant outlook is even more apparent in the opening passage of the sequel, *Lost Man's Lane* (1898), where she says in so many words that she has been stricken with the detective fever and is not going to be "satisfied with a single display of her powers."

Such enthusiasm would turn out to be the main characteristic of the similar "old maid" sleuths who, after a lapse of two decades, began to proliferate in the thirties. Miss Jane Marple is undoubtably the best known, although a host of lesser-known creations appeared as her contemporaries, including Miss Maud Silver, Ethel Thomas, Matilda Perks, Miss Rachel Murdock, Mrs. Warrender, and the incorrigibly obstreperous Hildegarde Withers, who enjoyed a relationship with Inspector Oscar Piper of the Manhattan police force quite like Miss Butterworth's with Mr. Gryce.

---

[6] *The Leavenworth Case: A Lawyer's Story* (1878) was the first book published by Anna K. Green. It earned her the title "mother of the detective novel."

In 1900, a journalist observed that "almost every profession has now opened its doors to women" and that "the days when the single woman had no prospect but to do domestic service, needlework, or teaching as a means of keeping body and soul together have gone, never to return." He went on to conclude that "it is not unlikely that the twentieth century will develop into a kind of golden age for women!" [7] Whether or not he was somewhat premature in his first statements, it is true that by the late teens the climate was changing. And in the field of detective fiction, at least, the Golden Age was indeed dawning.

The period of detective literature designated as "the Golden Age" spans the years 1918–1930, with a bit of leeway at both ends. Some historians of the genre regard it as the time of transition from the over-ornamented tales of mystery-romance to the more cleanly defined stories of detection-puzzle. Others see it simply as an era when ground rules were laid and smugly debated by writers and critics, adhered to by many writers, and wittily broken by others. Many of the greatest classics of the literature were produced during the Golden Age. Ironically, it has drawn fire from today's critics for its artificiality and lack of touch with reality, qualities with which the Golden Age authors thought they were dispensing.

Despite the trend toward naturalism and away from the romantic tradition, little change can be seen in the depiction of the women sleuths who appeared during the Golden Age; if anything, a few backward steps were taken, perhaps in reaction to the shifting societal patterns. One reason for this seeming anomaly might be that, despite the gradual erosion of traditional roles, society's ideas concerning women could not metamorphose at the same rate as could that creature of the imagination, the fictional detective, and that the unspoken tastes and preferences of the reading public were for the retention of illusion in heavy doses when it came to their heroines. This overcompensation appears the more startling because (bearing in mind the

[7] Bernard Owen, "Women Who Work: Various Ways of Making a Living," *The Harmsworth Magazine* 5 (August 1900–January 1901): 79.

limitations of the social codes of the nineteenth century) the earlier female detectives had been down-to-earth young women relatively unhampered by the romantic excesses. Throughout the gaslight period, it was sufficient romance *that they were women,* other exotic traits and flights of fancy being pretty much unnecessary.

The rise of the so-called "hard-boiled" school of mystery fiction and the gain in popularity of the "action" story coincided with the years of the Golden Age. Toughness and the ability to survive were the primary requisites for detectives in these pieces, but the fact was that authors could not easily imagine female characters in this manner. They found it simpler to keep the woman detective supplied with elaborate problems and perpetual curiosity rather than to equip her with moral indifference and overwhelm her with brutal beatings. As it had always been, so it was still hard to picture a woman face to face with a hardened criminal in a dark alley, and the authors opted out of this dilemma by pitting their heroines against domestic murderers and urbane villains instead of street thugs and hired killers. Throughout the Golden Age and the years immediately following, humor kept the female sleuth at arm's length and romance, in either of its meanings, kept her "safe."

Very few noteworthy heroine-investigators made their debuts during the Golden Age, although some of the period's most distinguished or enduring writers—Agatha Christie, Dorothy Sayers, Margery Allingham, Mary Roberts Rinehart, Mignon G. Eberhart—were women. Considering that Allingham never attempted a woman detective and that Harriet Vane is, for all her virtues, Sayers' fantasy of the intellectual woman rather than a sleuth, that leaves Miss Marple and "Miss Pinkerton" and Eberhart's Susan Dare to represent this stellar pantheon. Even including Patricia Wentworth's sedate Maud Silver, Gladys Mitchell's saurian Beatrice Bradley, Edgar Wallace's dainty Leslie Maughan of Scotland Yard, and Hulbert Footner's glamorous Madame Rosika Storey still makes a fairly poor showing for detective fiction's most celebrated dozen years, considering the deluge of female sleuths that was to appear between the years 1930 and 1940. It almost seems as if the question of dealing with a new kind of woman detective was shoved aside for the duration, until the internal changes in the genre and the external ones of the public world could catch up with each other. Although each of the above-mentioned characters—with the possible exception of Madame Storey—was to serve as a model, inspiring both subtle and not-so-subtle imitations, none of the originals and none of the copies were very far removed in spirit or conception from Mrs. Paschal, Loveday Brooke, Violet Strange, or Amelia Butterworth.

If the character of the fully developed woman sleuth eluded the writers of the genre during this period, another hybrid did not. One result of the golden years was to confuse the already disputed definitions of the categories "mystery" and "detection" by establishing as a firmly rooted subgenre the "HIBK" school of writing, a phrase coined by Ogden Nash and abbreviated from "Had I But Known," signifying the customary "backward intuition" of many heroine-*cum*-detectives. HIBK, with its origins in the Gothic mysteries and sensation novels of the nineteenth century, aligns itself on the side of clutter and flutter with immense disregard for a sleekly flowing narrative, causing purists who deplore it to be characterized (in some measure justly) by the epithet "misogynist."

Howard Haycraft, in *Murder for Pleasure*, a critical and historical compendium, gleefully reports a 1941 survey of detective-story readers who listed as prime bêtes noires "nosy spinsters . . . women who gum up the plot . . . super-feminine stories . . . heroines who wander around attics alone." [8] And as late as 1972, two critics pronounced HIBK an "indestructible fungus growth." [9] Nonetheless, acknowledging the purple tints of the melodramatic school that gave birth to HIBK, it would

[8] Howard Haycraft, *Murder for Pleasure* (New York: D. Appleton-Century Co., 1941; reprint ed., New York: Biblo & Tannen, 1972), p. 239.

[9] Jacques Barzun and Wendell Hertig Taylor, *A Catalogue of Crime* (New York: Harper & Row, 1972), p. 21.

seem as if this despised strain was a way, albeit a perverse one, to ease into the new naturalism. Granted, the writing often reeked of overperfumed ink; still, at the core was the attempt to put an everyday sort of woman (be she nurse, secretary, heiress, or impecunious orphan) into a suspenseful situation and let her curiosity take it from there.

However, to dwell on the HIBK heroines only complicates further the task of examining the woman detective. They were rarely if ever professional sleuths; rather, HIBK served as a broad passageway into the genre for the growing number of female amateur investigators. Perhaps "incidental investigators" would be a more accurate description, since most of the HIBK heroines were introduced in a single title and—except for stalwarts such as Leslie Ford's Grace Latham, who "had I but known'd" her way through a great many novels—never appeared in another. Eberhart's Nurse Sarah Keate is another HIBK sleuth who found herself involved in more than one case, while the various Midwestern heroines of Mabel Seeley and Mary Roberts Rinehart's disaster-prone socialites are typical of HIBK at its best and at its most trying.

The effect of HIBK was to diffuse the impact of the female detective on the literature, provoking sneering attacks on those heroines who did not set themselves up as private consultants but who "detected" because mysteries kept presenting themselves—at times, too coincidentally and conveniently—to hand. The extraordinary incidence of "convenient" murders and crimes is a charge that is often leveled by unfriendly critics at the entire detective genre, so that the specific shortcoming of HIBK might be best described as the attitude of determined foolhardiness which prevails.

In the succeeding years, women detectives became a regular and accepted part of the genre, the authors achieving some variety in their approaches while not swerving too radically from the established precepts—by no means an easy feat. Besides the plethora of elderly and middle-aged snoops mentioned earlier as coming to the forefront in the thirties, a number of younger women also found themselves involved with crime during this period. Ingenues like E. Phillips Oppenheim's Miss Lucie Mott and seemingly frivolous dilettantes such as Gilbert Frankau's Kyra Sokratescu appeared between the covers of books, while many other youthful female sleuths—Sally "Sherlock" Holmes Lane, for example—saw the light in popular periodicals. Rex Stout himself made a stab at the young woman detective, introducing in *The Hand in the Glove* (1937) the beauteous Theodolinda (Dol) Bonner, who dislikes all men, loathes being touched, and had to toss a coin in order to decide whether to be a detective or a landscape designer. At the opposite extreme is Elizabeth Dean's charming and lively Emma Marsh, who thinks nothing of a night on the town with three or four attentive escorts and who is distracted from her social life only by murder. More of a fringe manifestation was the "girl sleuth," who had begun to appear in the late twenties, with Nancy Drew as, if not the first, the figurehead of this legion.

The thirties also saw the rise of the sleuthing couple, a staple pair of characters that achieved immense popularity after the publication of Dashiell Hammett's 1934 novel *The Thin Man* and the subsequent film. In these often lighthearted tales, the female half alternates in the roles of Watson and Holmes and can toss off sophisticated repartee while wielding either a cocktail shaker or a pistol. In addition to married duos like Nick and Nora Charles and the Lockridges' Pam and Jerry North, there are other combinations: partners in detection (Bertha Cool and Donald Lam), employer and secretary (Perry Mason and Della Street), and damsel-in-distress and perpetual rescuer (Grace Latham and Colonel John Primrose). An almost endless number of changes can be rung on this theme, and though it is true that a large percentage of the female sleuths have detected in tandem or with some form of masculine assistance, there are instances where the woman is the dominant personality. Bertha Cool, Grace Latham, and Hildegarde Withers are good examples of this, as is Dwight V. Babcock's Hannah "the Gorgeous Ghoul" Van Doren, whose zest for homicide is accompanied by her boyfriend's solutions to the crime. And of course, there are the many patient and helpful wives of detectivedom's greats who play minor roles: Joan Fortune, Amanda Campion, Troy Alleyn, Judith Appleby, et al., not to mention Madame Maigret, who was given her "own case" (1959).

During the mid-forties, the younger women were edged out and replaced by wry, sexless, ageless female sleuths such as H. H. Holmes's Sister Ursula and Matthew Head's medical missionary Dr. Mary Finney.[10] Except for the well-worn and omnipresent Grace Latham, no major heroine was battling fifth-columnists, although wartime provided the setting for innumerable detective novels. Towards the end of the decade, however, two books appeared featuring Gale Gallagher.[11] An extremely attractive, casehardened "skip-tracer" (specialist in missing persons), she seems to be the first woman to make a clear-cut attempt to stride manfully down Raymond Chandler's "mean streets." "I could be any of the women who work through the night in a big city—waitress, telephone operator, nurse, small-time entertainer, or . . . even a call girl," she says of herself. Despite her fondness for coordinated outfits and spike heels, she is a businesslike professional who carries a gun and doesn't scare easily, refusing to quit a case even after she has been roughed up.

The years 1950 to 1960 provide scant material for examining the woman detective, a dearth that has been more than rectified in the period following this decade. In Edward Grierson's much-acclaimed novel *The Second Man* (1956), young lawyer Marion Kerrison argues a murder case to an unexpectedly triumphant conclusion, overcoming her colleagues' distrust and demonstrating admirable skills of reasoning and detection. The narrator, a member of Marion's firm who becomes her husband, judiciously observes that "in the law the ghost of the belief still

[10] "H. H. Holmes," like "Anthony Boucher," is a pseudonym for William Anthony Parker White. "Matthew Head" is the nom de plume of John Canaday.

[11] As in the Ellery Queen titles, the author and the main character bear the same name. The writer "Gale Gallagher" of *I Found Him Dead* (1947) and *Chord in Crimson* (1949) is novelist Will Oursler.

survived that women barristers were temperamentally unsuited to their work"—a theme not unique to any particular era. And in G. G. Fickling's series featuring the shapely private eye Honey West, another familiar motif is repeated, for Honey— like Leslie Maughan, Hannah Van Doren, and Gale Gallagher— is the daughter of a now-dead detective. During the course of her detecting career, she manages to survive a phenomenal amount of physical abuse and to solve a large number of intricate cases, and still to be coyly flirtatious with a handsome police lieutenant.

Two interesting trends and one truly unusual heroine have appeared since 1961. One of the trends, the female parody of superagent James Bond as manifested in Modesty Blaise and Emma Peel, is now as passé as the male prototype, though recently there has been a spate of paperback originals featuring similar heroines, notably "the Baroness." With their use of the martial arts and futuristic technology, these two crimefighters bear a marginal relation to the woman detective but have historical relevance as an adaptation of a popular fad. The other movement is one that comes full circle, for, with a good deal more credibility than Mrs. Paschal, policewomen have been taking to the streets and solving important crimes. Jennie Melville's Charmian Daniels and Dorothy Uhnak's Christie Opara are two of this modern breed of urban sleuth, while Lillian O'Donnell's admirable Detective Norah Mulcahaney of the New York Police Department has made a special practice of tracking down perverts and rapists and other felons who prey upon women.

Cordelia Gray, a "slight but tough" young woman who assumes the management of a seedy detective agency after the suicide of her partner, is the unique creation. An orphan, she is alone in the world, and author P. D. James adds no emotional entanglements to alleviate her austerity. Cordelia is stubborn and she is fallible, and she holds to a purity of view which demands the truth. It is fitting that this best of the recent innovative portrayals of the woman detective refutes its title, *An Unsuitable Job for a Woman*.

As in any specialized field, there are querulous critics and diplomatic apologists in the realm of detective fiction. Most are unable to agree even on a simple definition of *detection*, let alone on more general canons or on which characters can be gracefully accepted into what hierarchy. My views tend to coincide with those of W. H. Auden, in that he considered detective stories to be escape literature which provides a "magical satisfaction." Within such a designation, it seems to me there is ample room for amateurs and professionals, snooping spinsters, alluring private eyes, nosy-parker nurses, and crime-busting police-women.

The stories I have selected are intended to acquaint readers with heroines whose adventures offer period charm along with a glimpse into the development of the woman detective. To borrow the words of "Anonyma," all of these female sleuths have been "much dreaded but little known" for too long.

M.B.S.

New York City, 1974

Crime On Her Mind

CATHERINE LOUISA PIRKIS (?–1910) was a granddaughter of the Reverend Richard Lyne, who wrote both a Latin grammar and a primer. She herself was married to a naval officer and wrote a total of fourteen novels, of which *The Experiences of Loveday Brooke, Lady Detective* (1894) was the last. With the end of her writing career, she began to devote herself to good works; along with her husband she founded the National Canine Defence League, which is still active in Great Britain.

With poverty staring her in the face and not a recognizably marketable skill to her name, Loveday Brooke "had forthwith defied conventions, and had chosen for herself a career that had cut her off sharply from her former associates and position in society." It took her about six years to work up from a lowly position in the Fleet Street agency that employed her. At this stage of her career, she was "a little over thirty years of age, and could be best described in a series of negations. She was not tall, she was not short; she was not dark, she was not fair; she was neither handsome nor ugly. Her features were altogether nondescript; her one noticeable trait was a habit she had, when absorbed in thought, of dropping her eyelids over her eyes till only a line of eyeball showed, and she appeared to be looking at the world through a slit. . . ." Loveday usually dressed in black and was "almost Quaker-like" in her prim attire. Her employer said of her that she was "the most sensible and practical woman" he had ever met.

The Murder at Troyte's Hill

by C. L. Pirkis

"Griffiths, of the Newcastle Constabulary, has the case in hand," said Mr. Dyer. "Those Newcastle men are keen-witted, shrewd fellows, and very jealous of outside interference. They only sent to me under protest, as it were, because they wanted your sharp wits at work inside the house."

"I suppose throughout I am to work with Griffiths, not with you?" said Miss Brooke.

"Yes; when I have given you in outline the facts of the case, I simply have nothing more to do with it, and you must depend on Griffiths for assistance of any sort that you may require."

Here, with a swing, Mr. Dyer opened his big ledger and turned rapidly over its leaves till he came to the heading "Troyte's Hill" and the date "September 6th."

"I am all attention," said Loveday, leaning back in her chair in the attitude of a listener.

"The murdered man," resumed Mr. Dyer, "is a certain Alexander Henderson—usually known as old Sandy—lodge-keeper to Mr. Craven, of Troyte's Hill, Cumberland. The lodge consists merely of two rooms on the ground floor, a bedroom and a sitting room; these Sandy occupied alone, having neither kith nor kin of any degree. On the morning of September sixth, some children, going up to the house with milk from the farm, noticed that Sandy's bedroom window stood wide open. Curiosity prompted them to peep in; and then, to their horror, they saw old Sandy, in his nightshirt, lying dead on the floor, as if he had fallen backwards from the window. They raised an alarm; and on examination it was found that death had ensued from a heavy blow on the temple, given either by a strong fist or some blunt instrument. The room, on being entered, presented a curious appearance. It was as if a herd of monkeys had been turned into it and allowed to work their impish will. Not an article of furniture remained in its place: the bedclothes had been rolled into a bundle and stuffed into the chimney; the bedstead—a small iron one—lay on its side; the one chair in the room stood on the top of the table; fender and fire irons lay across the washstand, whose basin was to be found in a farther corner, holding bolster and pillow. The clock stood on its head in the middle of the mantelpiece; and the small vases and ornaments, which flanked it on either side, were walking, as it were, in a straight line towards the door. The old man's clothes had been rolled into a ball and thrown on the top of a high cupboard in which he kept his savings and whatever valuables he had. This cupboard, however, had not been meddled with, and its contents remained intact, so it was evident that robbery was not the motive for the crime. At the inquest, subsequently held, a verdict of 'wilful murder' against some person or persons unknown was returned. The local police are diligently investigating the affair, but, as yet, no arrests have been made. The opinion that at present prevails in the neighbourhood is that the crime has been perpetrated by some lunatic, escaped or otherwise, and inquiries are being made at the local asylums as to missing or lately released inmates.

Griffiths, however, tells me that his suspicions set in in another direction."

"Did anything of importance transpire at the inquest?"

"Nothing specially important. Mr. Craven broke down in giving his evidence when he alluded to the confidential relations that had always subsisted between Sandy and himself, and spoke of the last time that he had seen him alive. The evidence of the butler, and one or two of the female servants, seems clear enough, and they let fall something of a hint that Sandy was not altogether a favourite among them, on account of the overbearing manner in which he used his influence with his master. Young Mr. Craven, a youth of about twenty, home from Oxford for the long vacation, was not present at the inquest; a doctor's certificate was put in stating that he was suffering from typhoid fever, and could not leave his bed without risk to his life. Now this young man is a thoroughly bad sort, and as much a gentleman-blackleg as it is possible for such a young fellow to be. It seems to Griffiths that there is something suspicious about this illness of his. He came back from Oxford on the verge of delirium tremens, pulled round from that, and then suddenly, on the day after the murder, Mrs. Craven rings the bell, announces that he has developed typhoid fever, and orders a doctor to be sent for."

"What sort of man is Mr. Craven senior?"

"He seems to be a quiet old fellow, a scholar and learned philologist. Neither his neighbours nor his family see much of him; he almost lives in his study, writing a treatise, in seven or eight volumes, on comparative philology. He is not a rich man. Troyte's Hill, though it carries position in the county, is not a paying property, and Mr. Craven is unable to keep it up properly. I am told he has had to cut down expenses in all directions in order to send his son to college, and his daughter, from first to last, has been entirely educated by her mother. Mr. Craven was originally intended for the Church, but for some reason or other, when his college career came to an end, he did not present himself for ordination—went out to Natal instead, where he obtained some civil appointment, and where he remained for about fifteen years. Henderson was his servant during the latter portion of his Oxford career, and must have been greatly respected by him, for although the remuneration derived from his appointment at Natal was small, he paid Sandy a regular yearly allowance out of it. When, about ten years ago, he succeeded to Troyte's Hill, on the death of his elder brother, and returned home with his family, Sandy was immediately installed as lodge-keeper, and at so high a rate of pay that the butler's wages were cut down to meet it."

"Ah, that wouldn't improve the butler's feelings towards him," ejaculated Loveday.

Mr. Dyer went on: "But, in spite of his high wages, he doesn't appear to have troubled much about his duties as lodge-keeper, for they were performed, as a rule, by the gardener's boy, while he took his meals and passed his time at the house, and, speaking generally, put his finger into every pie. You know the old adage respecting the servant of twenty-one years' standing: 'Seven years my servant, seven years my equal, seven years my master.' Well, it appears to have held good in the case of Mr. Craven and Sandy. The old gentleman, absorbed in his philological studies, evidently let the reins slip through his fingers, and Sandy seems to have taken easy possession of them. The servants frequently had to go to him for orders, and he carried things, as a rule, with a high hand."

"Did Mrs. Craven never have a word to say on the matter?"

"I've not heard much about her. She seems to be a quiet sort of person. She is a Scotch missionary's daughter; perhaps she spends her time working for the Cape mission and that sort of thing."

"And young Mr. Craven: did he knock under to Sandy's rule?"

"Ah, now you're hitting the bull's-eye and we come to Griffiths' theory. The young man and Sandy appear to have been at loggerheads ever since the Cravens took possession of Troyte's Hill. As a schoolboy Master Harry defied Sandy and threatened him with his hunting crop; and subsequently, as a young man, has used strenuous endeavours to put the old servant in his place. On the day before the murder, Griffiths says, there was a terrible scene between the two, in which the young gentleman, in the presence of several witnesses, made use of strong language and threatened the old man's life. Now, Miss Brooke, I have told you all the circumstances of the case so far as I know them. For fuller particulars I must refer you to Griffiths. He, no doubt, will meet you at Grenfell—the nearest station to Troyte's Hill—and tell you in what capacity he has procured for you an entrance into the house. By the way, he has wired to me this morning that he hopes you will be able to save the Scotch express tonight."

Loveday expressed her readiness to comply with Mr. Griffiths' wishes.

"I shall be glad," said Mr. Dyer, as he shook hands with her at the office door, "to see you immediately on your return—that, however, I suppose, will not be yet awhile. This promises, I fancy, to be a longish affair?" This was said interrogatively.

"I haven't the least idea on the matter," answered Loveday. "I start on my work without theory of any sort—in fact, I may say, with my mind a perfect blank."

And any one who had caught a glimpse of her blank, expressionless features, as she said this, would have taken her at her word.

Grenfell, the nearest post town to Troyte's Hill, is a fairly busy, populous little town—looking south towards

the Black Country, and northwards to low, barren hills.
Pre-eminent among these stands Troyte's Hill, famed in
the old days as a border keep, and possibly at a still earlier
date as a Druid stronghold.

At a small inn at Grenfell, dignified by the title of
"The Station Hotel," Mr. Griffiths, of the Newcastle
Constabulary, met Loveday, and still further initiated her
into the mysteries of the Troyte's Hill murder.

"A little of the first excitement has subsided," he said,
after preliminary greetings had been exchanged; "but still
the wildest rumours are flying about and repeated as
solemnly as if they were Gospel truths. My chief here and
my colleagues generally adhere to their first conviction,
that the criminal is some suddenly crazed tramp or else an
escaped lunatic, and they are confident that sooner or
later we shall come upon his traces. Their theory is that
Sandy, hearing some strange noise at the park gates, put
his head out of the window to ascertain the cause, and
immediately had his death-blow dealt him; then they
suppose that the lunatic scrambled into the room through
the window and exhausted his frenzy by turning things
generally upside down. They refuse altogether to share my
suspicions respecting young Mr. Craven."

Mr. Griffiths was a tall, thin-featured man, with
iron-grey hair, cut so close to his head that it refused to do
anything but stand on end. This gave a somewhat comic
expression to the upper portion of his face, and clashed
oddly with the melancholy look that his mouth habitually
wore.

"I have made all smooth for you at Troyte's Hill," he
presently went on. "Mr. Craven is not wealthy enough to
allow himself the luxury of a family lawyer, so he
occasionally employs Messrs. Wells and Sugden, lawyers in
this place, and who, as it happens, have, off and on, done a
good deal of business for me. It was through them I heard
that Mr. Craven was anxious to secure the assistance of an

amanuensis. I immediately offered your services, stating that you were a friend of mine, a lady of impoverished means, who would gladly undertake the duties for the munificent sum of a guinea a month, with board and lodging. The old gentleman at once jumped at the offer, and is anxious for you to be at Troyte's Hill as soon as possible."

Loveday expressed her satisfaction with the programme that Mr. Griffiths had sketched for her; then she had a few questions to ask.

"Tell me," she said, "what led you, in the first instance, to suspect young Mr. Craven of the crime?"

"The footing on which he and Sandy stood towards each other, and the terrible scene that occurred between them only the day before the murder," answered Griffiths promptly. "Nothing of this, however, was elicited at the inquest, where a very fair face was put on Sandy's relations with the whole of the Craven family. I have subsequently unearthed a good deal respecting the private life of Mr. Harry Craven, and, among other things, I have found out that on the night of the murder he left the house shortly after ten o'clock, and no one, so far as I have been able to ascertain, knows at what hour he returned. Now I must draw your attention, Miss Brooke, to the fact that at the inquest the medical evidence went to prove that the murder had been committed between ten and eleven at night."

"Do you surmise, then, that the murder was a planned thing on the part of this young man?"

"I do. I believe that he wandered about the grounds until Sandy shut himself in for the night, then aroused him by some outside noise, and, when the old man looked out to ascertain the cause, dealt him a blow with a bludgeon or loaded stick that caused his death."

"A cold-blooded crime that, for a young fellow of twenty!"

"Yes. He's a good-looking, gentlemanly youngster, too, with manners as mild as milk, but from all accounts is as full of wickedness as an egg is full of meat. Now, to come to another point—if, in connection with these ugly facts, you take into consideration the suddenness of his illness, I think you'll admit that it bears a suspicious appearance, and might reasonably give rise to the surmise that it was a plant on his part in order to keep out of the inquest."

"Who is the doctor attending him?"

"A man called Waters; not much of a practitioner, from all accounts, and no doubt he feels himself highly honoured in being summoned to Troyte's Hill. The Cravens, it seems, have no family doctor. Mrs. Craven, with her missionary experience, is half a doctor herself, and never calls in one except in a serious emergency."

"The certificate was in order, I suppose?"

"Undoubtedly. And, as if to give colour to the gravity of the case, Mrs. Craven sent a message down to the servants, that if any of them were afraid of the infection they could at once go to their homes. Several of the maids, I believe, took advantage of her permission, and packed their boxes. Miss Craven, who is a delicate girl, was sent away with her maid to stay with friends at Newcastle, and Mrs. Craven isolated herself with her patient in one of the disused wings of the house."

"Has any one ascertained whether Miss Craven arrived at her destination at Newcastle?"

Griffiths drew his brows together in thought.

"I did not see any necessity for such a thing," he answered. "I don't quite follow you. What do you mean to imply?"

"Oh, nothing. I don't suppose it matters much: it might have been interesting as a side-issue." She broke off for a moment, then added:

"Now tell me a little about the butler, the man whose wages were cut down to increase Sandy's pay."

"Old John Hales? He's a thoroughly worthy, respectable man; he was butler for five or six years to Mr.
Craven's brother, when he was master of Troyte's Hill, and
then took duty under this Mr. Craven. There's no ground
for suspicion in that quarter. Hales's exclamation when he
heard of the murder is quite enough to stamp him as an
innocent man: 'Serve the old idiot right!' he cried: 'I
couldn't pump up a tear for him if I tried for a month of
Sundays!' Now I take it, Miss Brooke, a guilty man
wouldn't dare make such a speech as that!"

"You think not?"

Griffiths stared at her. "I'm a little disappointed in
her," he thought. "I'm afraid her powers have been slightly
exaggerated if she can't see such a straightforward thing as
that."

Aloud he said, a little sharply, "Well, I don't stand
alone in my thinking. No one yet has breathed a word
against Hales, and if they did I've no doubt he could prove
an alibi without any trouble, for he lives in the house, and
every one has a good word for him."

"I suppose Sandy's lodge has been put into order by
this time?"

"Yes; after the inquest, and when all possible evidence
had been taken, everything was put straight."

"At the inquest it was stated that no marks of footsteps
could be traced in any direction?"

"The long drought we've had would render such a
thing impossible, let alone the fact that Sandy's lodge
stands right on the gravelled drive, without flowerbeds or
grass borders of any sort around it. But look here, Miss
Brooke, don't you be wasting your time over the lodge and
its surroundings. Every iota of fact on that matter has
been gone through over and over again by me and my
chief. What we want you to do is to go straight into the
house and concentrate attention on Master Harry's sickroom, and find out what's going on there. What he did

outside the house on the night of the sixth, I've no doubt I shall be able to find out for myself. Now, Miss Brooke, you've asked me no end of questions, to which I have replied as fully as it was in my power to do; will you be good enough to answer one question that I wish to put, as straightforwardly as I have answered yours? You have had fullest particulars given you of the condition of Sandy's room when the police entered it on the morning after the murder. No doubt, at the present moment, you can see it all in your mind's eye—the bedstead on its side, the clock on its head, the bedclothes halfway up the chimney, the little vases and ornaments walking in a straight line towards the door?"

Loveday inclined her head.

"Very well. Now will you be good enough to tell me what this scene of confusion recalls to your mind before anything else?"

"The room of an unpopular Oxford freshman after a raid upon it by undergrads," answered Loveday promptly.

Mr. Griffiths rubbed his hands.

"Quite so!" he ejaculated. "I see, after all, we are one at heart in this matter, in spite of a little surface disagreement of ideas. Depend upon it, by and by, like the engineers tunneling from different quarters under the Alps, we shall meet at the same point and shake hands. By the way, I have arranged for daily communication between us through the postboy who takes the letters to Troyte's Hill. He is trustworthy, and any letter you give him for me will find its way into my hands within the hour."

It was about three o'clock in the afternoon when Loveday drove in through the park gates of Troyte's Hill, past the lodge where old Sandy had met with his death. It was a pretty little cottage, covered with Virginia creeper and wild honeysuckle, and showed no outward sign of the tragedy that had been enacted within.

The park and pleasure grounds of Troyte's Hill were

extensive, and the house itself was a somewhat imposing red brick structure, built, possibly, at the time when Dutch William's taste had grown popular in the country. Its frontage presented a somewhat forlorn appearance, its centre windows—a square of eight—alone seeming to show signs of occupation. With the exception of two windows at the extreme end of the bedroom floor of the north wing, where, possibly, the invalid and his mother were located, and two windows at the extreme end of the ground floor of the south wing, which Loveday ascertained subsequently were those of Mr. Craven's study, not a single window in either wing owned blind or curtain. The wings were extensive, and it was easy to understand that at the extreme end of the one the fever patient would be isolated from the rest of the household, and that at the extreme end of the other Mr. Craven could secure the quiet and freedom from interruption which, no doubt, were essential to the due prosecution of his philological studies.

, Alike on the house and on the ill-kept grounds were present the stamp of the smallness of the income of the master and owner of the place. The terrace, which ran the length of the house in front, and on to which every window on the ground floor opened, was miserably out of repair: not a lintel or doorpost, window ledge or balcony, but what seemed to cry aloud for the touch of the painter. "Pity me! I have seen better days," Loveday could fancy written as a legend across the red brick porch that gave entrance to the old house.

The butler, John Hales, admitted Loveday, shouldered her portmanteau, and told her he would show her to her room. He was a tall, powerfully built man, with a ruddy face and dogged expression of countenance. It was easy to understand that, off and on, there must have been many a sharp encounter between him and old Sandy. He treated Loveday in an easy, familiar fashion, evidently considering that an amanuensis took much the same rank as a nursery governess—that is to say, a little below a lady's maid and a little above a housemaid.

"We're short of hands, just now," he said, in broad Cumberland dialect, as he led the way up the wide staircase. "Some of the lasses downstairs took fright at the fever and went home. Cook and I are singlehanded, for Moggie, the only maid left, has been told off to wait on Madam and Master Harry. I hope you're not afeared of fever?"

Loveday answered that she was not, and asked if the room at the extreme end of the north wing was the one assigned to "Madam and Master Harry."

"Yes," said the man; "it's convenient for sick nursing; there's a flight of stairs runs straight down from it to the kitchen quarters. We put all Madam wants at the foot of those stairs and Moggie comes down and fetches it. Moggie herself never enters the sickroom. I take it you'll not be seeing Madam for many a day, yet awhile."

"When shall I see Mr. Craven? At dinner tonight?"

"That's what naebody could say," answered Hales. "He may not come out of his study till past midnight; sometimes he sits there till two or three in the morning. Shouldn't advise you to wait till he wants his dinner—better have a cup of tea and a chop sent up to you. Madam never waits for him at any meal."

As he finished speaking he deposited the portmanteau outside one of the many doors opening into the gallery.

"This is Miss Craven's room," he went on; "cook and me thought you'd better have it, as it would want less getting ready than the other rooms, and work is work when there are so few hands to do it. Oh, my stars! I do declare there is cook putting it straight for you now."

The last sentence was added as the opened door laid bare to view the cook, with duster in her hand, polishing a mirror; the bed had been made, it is true, but otherwise the room must have been much as Miss Craven had left it, after a hurried packing up.

To the surprise of the two servants Loveday took the matter very lightly.

"I have a special talent for arranging rooms, and would prefer getting this one straight for myself," she said. "Now, if you will go and get ready that chop and cup of tea we were talking about just now, I shall think it much kinder than if you stayed here doing what I can so easily do for myself."

When, however, the cook and butler had departed in company, Loveday showed no disposition to exercise the "special talent" of which she had boasted.

She first carefully turned the key in the lock, and then proceeded to make a thorough and minute investigation of every corner of the room. Not an article of furniture, not an ornament or toilet accessory, but what was lifted from its place and carefully scrutinized. Even the ashes in the grate, the debris of the last fire made there, were raked over and well looked through.

This careful investigation of Miss Craven's late surroundings occupied in all about three-quarters of an hour, and Loveday, with her hat in her hand, descended the stairs to see Hales crossing the hall to the dining room with the promised cup of tea and chop.

In silence and solitude she partook of the simple repast in a dining hall that could with ease have banqueted a hundred and fifty guests.

"Now for the grounds before it gets dark," she said to herself, as she noted that already the outside shadows were beginning to slant.

The dining hall was at the back of the house; and here, as in the front, the windows, reaching to the ground, presented easy means of egress. The flower garden was on this side of the house, and sloped downhill to a pretty stretch of well-wooded country.

Loveday did not linger here even to admire, but passed at once round the south corner of the house to the windows which she had ascertained, by a careless question to the butler, were those of Mr. Craven's study.

Very cautiously she drew near them, for the blinds were up, the curtains drawn back. A side glance, however, relieved her apprehensions, for it showed her the occupant of the room, seated in an easy-chair, with his back to the windows. From the length of his outstretched limbs he was evidently a tall man. His hair was silvery and curly, the lower part of his face was hidden from her view by the chair, but she could see that one hand was pressed tightly across his eyes and brows. The whole attitude was that of a man absorbed in deep thought. The room was comfortably furnished, but presented an appearance of disorder from the books and manuscripts scattered in all directions. A whole pile of torn fragments of foolscap sheets, overflowing from a waste-paper basket beside the writing table, seemed to proclaim the fact that the scholar had of late grown weary of or else dissatisfied with his work, and had condemned it freely.

Although Loveday stood looking in at this window for over five minutes, not the faintest sign of life did that tall, reclining figure give, and it would have been as easy to believe him locked in sleep as in thought.

From here she turned her steps in the direction of Sandy's lodge. As Griffiths had said, it was gravelled up to its doorstep. The blinds were closely drawn, and it presented the ordinary appearance of a disused cottage.

A narrow path beneath overarching boughs of cherry-laurel and arbutus, immediately facing the lodge, caught her eye, and down this she at once turned her footsteps.

This path led, with many a wind and turn, through a belt of shrubbery that skirted the frontage of Mr. Craven's grounds, and eventually, after much zigzagging, ended in close proximity to the stables. As Loveday entered it, she seemed literally to leave daylight behind her.

"I feel as if I were following the course of a circuitous mind," she said to herself as the shadows closed around her. "I could fancy the great Machiavelli himself delighting in such a wind-about alley as this!"

The path showed greyly in front of her out of the dimness. On and on she followed it; here and there the roots of the old laurels, struggling out of the ground, threatened to trip her up. Her eyes, however, had now grown accustomed to the half-gloom, and not a detail of her surroundings escaped her as she went along.

A bird flew from out the thicket on her right hand with a startled cry. A dainty little frog leaped out of her way into the shrivelled leaves lying below the laurels. Following the movements of this frog, her eye was caught by something black and solid among those leaves. What was it? A bundle—a shiny black coat? Loveday knelt down, and using her hands to assist her eyes, found that they came into contact with the dead, stiffened body of a beautiful black retriever. She parted, as well as she was able, the lower boughs of the evergreens, and minutely examined the poor animal. Its eyes were still open, though glazed and bleared, and its death had, undoubtedly, been caused by the blow of some blunt, heavy instrument, for on one side its skull was almost battered in.

"Exactly the death that was dealt to Sandy," she thought, as she groped hither and thither beneath the trees in hopes of lighting upon the weapon of destruction.

She searched until increasing darkness warned her that search was useless. Then, still following the zigzagging path, she made her way out by the stables and thence back to the house.

She went to bed that night without having spoken to a soul beyond the cook and butler. The next morning, however, Mr. Craven introduced himself to her across the breakfast table. He was a man of really handsome personal appearance, with a fine carriage of the head and shoulders, and eyes that had a forlorn, appealing look in them. He entered the room with an air of great energy, apologised to Loveday for the absence of his wife, and for his own remissness in not being in the way to receive her on the previous day. Then he bade her make herself at home at the breakfast table, and expressed his delight in having found a coadjutor in his work.

"I hope you understand what a great—a stupendous work it is?" he added, as he sank into a chair. "It is a work that will leave its impress upon thought in all the ages to come. Only a man who has studied comparative philology as I have for the past thirty years could gauge the magnitude of the task I have set myself."

With the last remark, his energy seemed spent, and he sank back in his chair, covering his eyes with his hand in precisely the same attitude as that in which Loveday had seen him overnight, and utterly oblivious of the fact that breakfast was before him and a stranger-guest seated at table. The butler entered with another dish. "Better go on with your breakfast," he whispered to Loveday; "he may sit like that for another hour."

He placed his dish in front of his master.

"Captain hasn't come back yet, sir," he said, making an effort to arouse him from his reverie.

"Eh, what?" said Mr. Craven, for a moment lifting his hand from his eyes.

"Captain, sir—the black retriever," repeated the man.

The pathetic look in Mr. Craven's eyes deepened.

"Ah, poor Captain!" he murmured; "the best dog I ever had."

Then he again sank back in his chair, putting his hand to his forehead.

The butler made one more effort to arouse him.

"Madam sent you down a newspaper, sir, that she

thought you would like to see," he shouted almost into his master's ear, and at the same time laid the morning's paper on the table beside his plate.

"Confound you! leave it there," said Mr. Craven irritably. "Fools! dolts that you all are! With your trivialities and interruptions you are sending me out of the world with my work undone!"

And again he sank back in his chair, closed his eyes, and became lost to his surroundings.

Loveday went on with her breakfast. She changed her place at table to one on Mr. Craven's right hand, so that the newspaper sent down for his perusal lay between his plate and hers. It was folded into an oblong shape, as if it were wished to direct attention to a certain portion of a certain column.

A clock in a corner of the room struck the hour with a loud, resonant stroke. Mr. Craven gave a start and rubbed his eyes.

"Eh, what's this?" he said. "What meal are we at?" He looked around with a bewildered air. "Eh!—who are you?" he went on, staring hard at Loveday. "What are you doing here? Where's Nina?—Where's Harry?"

Loveday began to explain, and gradually recollection seemed to come back to him.

"Ah, yes, yes," he said. "I remember; you've come to assist me with my great work. You promised, you know, to help me out of the hole I've got into. Very enthusiastic, I remember they said you were, on certain abstruse points in comparative philology. Now, Miss—Miss—I've forgotten your name—tell me a little of what you know about the elemental sounds of speech that are common to all languages. Now, to how many would you reduce those elemental sounds—to six, eight, nine? No, we won't discuss the matter here, the cups and saucers distract me. Come into my den at the other end of the house; we'll have perfect quiet there."

And, utterly ignoring the fact that he had not as yet broken his fast, he rose from the table, seized Loveday by the wrist, and led her out of the room and down the long corridor that led through the south wing to his study.

But seated in that study his energy once more speedily exhausted itself.

He placed Loveday in a comfortable chair at his writing table, consulted her taste as to pens, and spread a sheet of foolscap before her. Then he settled himself in his easy-chair, with his back to the light, as if he were about to dictate folios to her.

In a loud, distinct voice he repeated the title of his learned work, then its subdivision, then the number and heading of the chapter that was at present engaging his attention. Then he put his hand to his head. "It's the elemental sounds that are my stumbling-block," he said. "Now, how on earth is it possible to get a notion of a sound of agony that is not in part a sound of terror? or a sound of surprise that is not in part a sound of either joy or sorrow?"

With this his energies were spent, and although Loveday remained seated in that study from early morning till daylight began to fade, she had not ten sentences to show for her day's work as amanuensis.

Loveday in all spent only two clear days at Troyte's Hill.

On the evening of the first of those days Detective Griffiths received, through the trustworthy postboy, the following brief note from her:

> I have found out that Hales owed Sandy close upon a hundred pounds, which he had borrowed at various times. I don't know whether you will think this fact of any importance.—L. B.

Mr. Griffiths repeated the last sentence blankly. "If Harry Craven were put upon his defence, his counsel, I take it, would consider the fact of first importance," he muttered. And for the remainder of that day Mr. Griffiths went about his work in a perturbed state of mind, doubtful whether to hold or to let go his theory concerning Harry Craven's guilt.

The next morning there came another brief note from Loveday, which ran thus:

> As a matter of collateral interest, find out if a person, calling himself Harold Cousins, sailed two days ago from London Docks for Natal in the *Bonnie Dundee*.

To this missive Loveday received in reply the following somewhat lengthy despatch:

> I do not quite see the drift of your last note, but have wired to our agents in London to carry out its suggestion. On my part, I have important news to communicate. I have found out what Harry Craven's business out of doors was on the night of the murder, and at my instance a warrant has been issued for his arrest. This warrant it will be my duty to serve on him in the course of today. Things are beginning to look very black against him, and I am convinced his illness is all a sham. I have seen Waters, the man who is supposed to be attending him, and have driven him into a corner and made him admit that he has only seen young Craven once—on the first day of his illness— and that he gave his certificate entirely on the strength of what Mrs. Craven told him of her son's condition. On the occasion of this, his first and only visit, the lady, it seems, also told him that it would not be necessary for him to continue his attendance, as she felt herself quite competent to treat the case, having had so much experience in fever cases among the blacks at Natal.
>
> As I left Waters's house, after eliciting this important information, I was accosted by a man who keeps a low-class inn in the place, McQueen by name. He said that he wished to speak to me on a matter of importance. To make a long story short, this McQueen stated that on the

night of the sixth, shortly after eleven o'clock, Harry Craven came to his house, bringing with him a valuable piece of plate—a handsome epergne—and requested him to lend him a hundred pounds on it, as he hadn't a penny in his pocket. McQueen complied with his request to the extent of ten sovereigns, and now, in a fit of nervous terror, comes to me to confess himself a receiver of stolen goods and play the honest man! He says he noticed that the young gentleman was very much agitated as he made the request, and he also begged him to mention his visit to no one. Now, I am curious to learn how Master Harry will get over the fact that he passed the lodge at the hour at which the murder was most probably committed; or how he will get out of the dilemma of having repassed the lodge on his way back to the house, and not noticed the wide-open window with the full moon shining down on it?

Another word! Keep out of the way when I arrive at the house, somewhere between two and three in the afternoon, to serve the warrant. I do not wish your professional capacity to get wind, for you will most likely yet be of some use to us in the house.—S. G.

Loveday read this note, seated at Mr. Craven's writing table, with the old gentleman himself reclining motionless beside her in his easy-chair. A little smile played about the corners of her mouth as she read over again the words— "for you will most likely yet be of some use to us in the house."

Loveday's second day in Mr. Craven's study promised to be as unfruitful as the first. For fully an hour after she had received Griffiths' note, she sat at the writing table with her pen in her hand, ready to transcribe Mr. Craven's inspirations. Beyond, however, the phrase, muttered with closed eyes—"It's all here, in my brain, but I can't put it into words"—not a half-syllable escaped his lips.

At the end of that hour the sound of footsteps on the outside gravel made her turn her head towards the window. It was Griffiths approaching with two constables.

She heard the hall door opened to admit them, but beyond that not a sound reached her ear, and she realised how fully she was cut off from communication with the rest of the household at the farther end of this unoccupied wing.

Mr. Craven, still reclining in his semi-trance, evidently had not the faintest suspicion that so important an event as the arrest of his only son on a charge of murder was about to be enacted in the house.

Meantime, Griffiths and his constables had mounted the stairs leading to the north wing, and were being guided through the corridors to the sickroom by the flying figure of Moggie, the maid.

"Hoot, mistress!" cried the girl, "here are three men coming up the stairs—policemen, every one of them—will ye come and ask them what they be wanting?"

Outside the door of the sickroom stood Mrs. Craven— a tall, sharp-featured woman with sandy hair going rapidly to grey.

"What is the meaning of this? What is your business here?" she said haughtily, addressing Griffiths, who headed the party.

Griffiths respectfully explained what his business was, and requested her to stand on one side that he might enter her son's room.

"This is my daughter's room; satisfy yourself of the fact," said the lady, throwing back the door as she spoke.

And Griffiths and his confreres entered, to find pretty Miss Craven, looking very white and scared, seated beside a fire in a long, flowing *robe-de-chambre*.

Griffiths departed in haste and confusion, without the chance of a professional talk with Loveday. That afternoon saw him telegraphing wildly in all directions, and despatching messengers in all quarters. Finally, he spent over an hour drawing up an elaborate report to his chief at Newcastle, assuring him of the identity of one Harold

Cousins, who had sailed in the *Bonnie Dundee* for Natal, with Harry Craven, of Troyte's Hill, and advising that the police authorities in that faraway district should be immediately communicated with.

The ink had not dried on the pen with which this report was written before a note, in Loveday's writing, was put into his hand.

Loveday evidently had had some difficulty in finding a messenger for this note, for it was brought by a gardener's boy, who informed Griffiths that the lady had said he would receive a gold sovereign if he delivered the letter all right.

Griffiths paid the boy and dismissed him, and then proceeded to read Loveday's communication.

It was written hurriedly in pencil, and ran as follows:

> Things are getting critical here. Directly you receive this, come up to the house with two of your men, and post yourselves anywhere in the grounds where you can see and not be seen. There will be no difficulty in this, for it will be dark by the time you are able to get there. I am not sure whether I shall want your aid tonight, but you had better keep in the grounds until morning, in case of need; and, above all, never once lose sight of the study windows. [This was underscored.] If I put a lamp with a green shade in one of those windows, do not lose a moment in entering by that window, which I will contrive to keep unlocked.

Griffiths rubbed his forehead—rubbed his eyes, as he finished reading this.

"Well, I daresay it's all right," he said, "but I'm bothered, that's all, and for the life of me I can't see one step of the way she is going."

He looked at his watch; the hands pointed to a quarter past six. The short September day was drawing rapidly to a close. A good five miles lay between him and Troyte's Hill—there was evidently not a moment to lose.

At the very moment that Griffiths, with his two constables, were once more starting along the Grenfell High Road behind the best horse they could procure, Mr. Craven was rousing himself from his long slumber, and beginning to look around him. That slumber, however, though long, had not been a peaceful one, and it was sundry of the old gentleman's muttered exclamations, as he had started uneasily in his sleep, that had caused Loveday to pen, and then to creep out of the room to despatch, her hurried note.

What effect the occurrence of the morning had had upon the household generally, Loveday, in her isolated corner of the house, had no means of ascertaining. She only noted that when Hales brought in her tea, as he did precisely at five o'clock, he wore a particularly ill-tempered expression of countenance, and she heard him mutter, as he set down the tea-tray with a clatter, something about being a respectable man, and not used to such "goings-on."

It was not until nearly an hour and a half after this that Mr. Craven had awakened with a sudden start, and, looking wildly around him, had questioned Loveday as to who had entered the room.

Loveday explained that the butler had brought in lunch at one, and tea at five, but that since then no one had come in.

"Now that's false," said Mr. Craven, in a sharp, unnatural sort of voice; "I saw him sneaking round the room, the whining, canting hypocrite, and you must have seen him, too. Didn't you hear him say, in his squeaky old voice, 'Master, I knows your secret—'" He broke off abruptly, looking wildly round. "Eh, what's this?" he cried. "No, no, I'm all wrong—Sandy is dead and buried—they held an inquest on him, and we all praised him up as if he were a saint."

"He must have been a bad man, that old Sandy," said Loveday sympathetically.

"You're right! you're right!" cried Mr. Craven, springing up excitedly from his chair and seizing her by the hand. "If ever a man deserved his death, he did. For thirty years he held that rod over my head, and then—ah, where was I?"

He put his hand to his head, and again sank, as if exhausted, into his chair.

"I suppose it was some early indiscretion of yours at college that he knew of?" said Loveday, eager to get at as much of the truth as possible while the mood for confidence held sway in the feeble brain.

"That was it! I was fool enough to marry a disreputable girl—a barmaid in the town—and Sandy was present at the wedding, and then—" Here his eyes closed again and his mutterings became incoherent.

For ten minutes he lay back in his chair, muttering thus. "A yelp—a groan," were the only words Loveday could distinguish among those mutterings, then, suddenly, slowly and distinctly, he said, as if answering some plainly put question: "A good blow with the hammer and the thing was done."

"I should like amazingly to see that hammer," said Loveday; "do you keep it anywhere at hand?"

His eyes opened with a wild, cunning look in them.

"Who's talking about a hammer? I did not say I had one. If any one says I did it with a hammer, they're telling a lie."

"Oh, you've spoken to me about the hammer, two or three times," said Loveday calmly; "the one that killed your dog, Captain, and I should like to see it, that's all."

The look of cunning died out of the old man's eye. "Ah, poor Captain! splendid dog that! Well, now, where were we? Where did we leave off? Ah, I remember, it was the elemental sounds of speech that bothered me so that night. Were you here then? Ah, no! I remember. I had been trying all day to assimilate a dog's yelp of pain to a human groan, and I couldn't do it. The idea haunted me—followed me about wherever I went. If they were both elemental sounds, they must have something in common, but the link between them I could not find; then it occurred to me, would a well-bred, well-trained dog like my Captain in the stables, there, at the moment of death give an unmitigated currish yelp; would there not be something of a human note in his death-cry? The thing was worth putting to the test. If I could hand down in my treatise a fragment of fact on the matter, it would be worth a dozen dogs' lives. So I went out into the moonlight—ah! but you know all about it—now, don't you?"

"Yes. Poor Captain! did he yelp or groan?"

"Why, he gave one loud, long, hideous yelp, just as if he had been a common cur. I might just as well have let him alone; it only set that other brute opening his window and spying out on me, and saying in his cracked old voice, 'Master, what are you doing out here at this time of night?' "

Again he sank back in his chair, muttering incoherently with half-closed eyes.

Loveday let him alone for a minute or so; then she had another question to ask.

"And that other brute—did he yelp or groan when you dealt him his blow?"

"What, old Sandy—the brute? he fell back. Ah, I remember, you said you would like to see the hammer that stopped his babbling old tongue—now, didn't you?"

He rose a little unsteadily from his chair, and seemed to drag his long limbs with an effort across the room to a cabinet at the farther end. Opening a drawer in this cabinet, he produced, from amidst some specimens of strata and fossils, a large-sized geological hammer.

He brandished it for a moment over his head, then paused with his finger on his lip.

"Hush!" he said, "we shall have the fools creeping in to peep at us if we don't take care." And to Loveday's horror he suddenly made for the door, turned the key in the lock, withdrew it, and put it into his pocket.

She looked at the clock; the hands pointed to half-past seven. Had Griffiths received her note at the proper time, and were the men now in the grounds? She could only pray that they were.

"The light is too strong for my eyes," she said, and, rising from her chair, she lifted the green-shaded lamp and placed it on a table that stood at the window.

"No, no, that won't do," said Mr. Craven; "that would show every one outside what we're doing in here." He crossed to the window as he spoke and removed the lamp thence to the mantelpiece.

Loveday could only hope that in the few seconds it had remained in the window it had caught the eye of the outside watchers.

The old man beckoned to Loveday to come near and examine his deadly weapon. "Give it a good swing round," he said, suiting the action to the word, "and down it comes with a splendid crash." He brought the hammer round within an inch of Loveday's forehead.

She started back.

"Ha, ha!" he laughed harshly and unnaturally, with the light of madness dancing in his eyes now; "did I frighten you? I wonder what sort of sound you would make if I were to give you a little tap just there." Here he lightly touched her forehead with the hammer. "Elemental, of course, it would be, and—"

Loveday steadied her nerves with difficulty. Locked in

with this lunatic, her only chance lay in gaining time for the detectives to reach the house and enter through the window.

"Wait a minute," she said, striving to divert his attention; "you have not yet told me what sort of an elemental sound old Sandy made when he fell. If you'll give me pen and ink, I'll write down a full account of it all, and you can incorporate it afterwards in your treatise."

For a moment a look of real pleasure flitted across the old man's face, then it faded. "The brute fell back dead without a sound," he answered; "it was all for nothing, that night's work; yet not altogether for nothing. No, I don't mind owning I would do it all over again to get the wild thrill of joy at my heart that I had when I looked down into that old man's dead face and felt myself free at last! Free at last!" his voice rang out excitedly—once more he brought his hammer round with an ugly swing.

"For a moment I was a young man again; I leaped into his room—the moon was shining full in through the window—I thought of my old college days and the fun we used to have at Pembroke—topsy-turvy I turned every-thing—" He broke off abruptly, and drew a step nearer to Loveday. "The pity of it all was," he said, suddenly dropping from his high, excited tone to a low, pathetic one, "that he fell without a sound of any sort." Here he drew another step nearer. "I wonder—" he said, then broke off again, and came close to Loveday's side. "It has only this moment occurred to me," he said, now with his lips close to Loveday's ear, "that a woman, in her death agony, would be much more likely to give utterance to an elemental sound than a man."

He raised his hammer, and Loveday fled to the window, which was at that moment opened from the outside by three pairs of strong arms.

"I thought I was conducting my very last case—I never

had such a narrow escape before!" said Loveday, as she stood talking with Mr. Griffiths on the Grenfell platform, awaiting the train to carry her back to London. "It seems strange that no one before suspected the old gentleman's sanity—I suppose, however, people were so used to his eccentricities that they did not notice how they had deepened into positive lunacy. His cunning evidently stood him in good stead at the inquest."

"It is possible," said Griffiths thoughtfully, "that he did not absolutely cross the very slender line that divides eccentricity from madness until after the murder. The excitement consequent upon the discovery of the crime may just have pushed him over the border. Now, Miss Brooke, we have exactly ten minutes before your train comes in. I should feel greatly obliged to you if you would explain one or two things that have a professional interest for me."

"With pleasure," said Loveday. "Put your questions in categorical order and I will answer them."

"Well, then, in the first place, what suggested to your mind the old man's guilt?"

"The relations that subsisted between him and Sandy seemed to me to savor too much of fear on the one side and power on the other. Also the income paid to Sandy during Mr. Craven's absence in Natal bore, to my mind, an unpleasant resemblance to hush-money."

"Poor wretched being! And I hear that, after all, the woman he married in his wild young days died soon afterwards of drink. I have no doubt, however, that Sandy sedulously kept up the fiction of her existence, even after his master's second marriage. Now for another question: How was it you knew that Miss Craven had taken her brother's place in the sickroom?"

"On the evening of my arrival I discovered a rather long lock of fair hair in the unswept fireplace of my room, which, as it happened, was usually occupied by Miss

Craven. It at once occurred to me that the young lady had been cutting off her hair, and that there must be some powerful motive to induce such a sacrifice. The suspicious circumstances attending her brother's illness soon supplied me with such a motive."

"Ah! that typhoid fever business was very cleverly done. Not a servant in the house, I verily believe, but who thought Master Harry was upstairs, ill in bed, and Miss Craven away at her friends' in Newcastle. The young fellow must have got a clear start off within an hour of the murder. His sister, sent away the next day to Newcastle, dismissed her maid there, I hear, on the plea of no accommodation at her friends' house—sent the girl to her own home for a holiday, and herself returned to Troyte's Hill in the middle of the night, having walked the five miles from Grenfell. No doubt her mother admitted her through one of those easily opened front windows, cut her hair, and put her to bed to personate her brother without delay. With Miss Craven's strong likeness to Master Harry, and in a darkened room, it is easy to understand that the eyes of a doctor, personally unacquainted with the family, might easily be deceived. Now, Miss Brooke, you must admit that with all this elaborate chicanery and double-dealing going on, it was only natural that my suspicions should set in strongly in that quarter."

"I read it all in another light, you see," said Loveday. "It seemed to me that the mother, knowing her son's evil proclivities, believed in his guilt in spite, possibly, of his assertions of innocence. The son, most likely, on his way back to the house after pledging the family plate, had met old Mr. Craven with the hammer in his hand. Seeing, no doubt, how impossible it would be for him to clear himself without incriminating his father, he preferred flight to Natal to giving evidence at the inquest."

"Now about his alias?" said Mr. Griffiths briskly, for the train was at that moment steaming into the station.

"How did you know that Harold Cousins was identical with Harry Craven, and had sailed in the *Bonnie Dundee?*"

"Oh, that was easy enough," said Loveday, as she stepped into the train; "a newspaper sent down to Mr. Craven by his wife was folded so as to direct his attention to the shipping list. In it I saw that the *Bonnie Dundee* had sailed two days previously for Natal. Now it was only natural to connect Natal with Mrs. Craven, who had passed the greater part of her life there; and it was easy to understand her wish to get her scapegrace son among her early friends. The alias under which he sailed came readily enough to light. I found it scribbled all over one of Mr. Craven's writing pads in his study; evidently it had been drummed into his ears by his wife as his son's alias, and the old gentleman had taken this method of fixing it in his memory. We'll hope that the young fellow, under his new name, will make a new reputation for himself—at any rate, he'll have a better chance of doing so with the ocean between him and his evil companions. Now it's goodbye, I think."

"No," said Mr. Griffiths; "it's *au revoir*, for you'll have to come back again for the assizes, and give the evidence that will shut old Mr. Craven in an asylum for the rest of his life."

GEORGE ROBERT SIMS (1847–1922) was educated in England and in Germany. He tried his hand at almost every form of literary endeavor: journalism, fiction and nonfiction, plays, and poetry. Primarily, however, he is remembered for *The Dagonet Ballads*, a collection of verses from a column he wrote. In addition to the two casebooks of Dorcas Dene's investigations, Sims produced apparently only one other pair of detective volumes, *The Case of George Candlemas* (1899) and *The Death Gamble* (1909), plus a series of Scotland Yard detective tales published in *The Sketch* (1911). He also published several books about London life, with titles like *Mysteries of Modern London* (1905) and *London by Night* (1906). In 1905 Sims was honored by a Norwegian order of distinction and made a Knight of St. Olaf.

The cases of Dorcas Dene are narrated by a Mr. Saxon, a dramatist who had been acquainted with her in the days when she was Dorcas Lester, an aspiring actress. He sometimes assists her, maintaining an avuncular interest in her household, which her activities as a detective support. The Dene home contains Paul, Dorcas' husband, a painter who has been denied his art by the onset of blindness; Mrs. Lester, Dorcas' mother; and a large brindle bulldog named Toddlekins. Dorcas is a mistress of disguise, and "has been mixed up in some of the most remarkable cases of the day—cases that sometimes come into court, but which are more frequently settled in a solicitor's office."

The Man with the Wild Eyes

by George R. Sims

I had become a constant visitor at Oak Tree Road. I had conceived a great admiration for the brave and yet womanly woman who, when her artist husband was stricken with blindness, and the future looked dark for both of them, had gallantly made the best of her special gifts and opportunities and nobly undertaken a profession which was not only a harassing and exhausting one for a woman, but by no means free from grave personal risks.

Dorcas Dene was always glad to welcome me for her husband's sake. "Paul has taken to you immensely," she said to me one afternoon, "and I hope you will call in and spend an hour or two with him whenever you can. My cases take me away from home so much—he cannot read, and my mother, with the best intentions in the world, can never converse with him for more than five minutes without irritating him. Her terribly matter-of-fact views of life are, to use his own expression, absolutely 'rasping' to his dreamy, artistic temperament."

I had plenty of spare time on my hands, and so it became my custom to drop in two or three times a week, and smoke a pipe and chat with Paul Dene. His conversation was always interesting, and the gentle resignation with which he bore his terrible affliction quickly won my heart. But I am not ashamed to confess that my frequent journeys to Oak Tree Road were also largely influenced by my desire to see Dorcas Dene, and hear more of her strange adventures and experiences as a lady detective.

From the moment she knew that her husband valued my companionship she treated me as one of the family, and when I was fortunate enough to find her at home, she discussed her professional affairs openly before me. I was grateful for this confidence, and frequently I was able to assist her by going about with her in cases where the presence of a male companion was a material advantage to her. I had upon one occasion laughingly dubbed myself her "assistant," and by that name I was afterwards generally known. There was only one drawback to the pleasure I felt at being associated with Dorcas Dene in her detective work. I saw that it would be quite impossible for me to avoid reproducing my experiences in some form or other. One day I broached the subject to her cautiously.

"Are you not afraid of the assistant one day revealing the professional secrets of his chief?" I said.

"Not at all," replied Dorcas (everybody called her Dorcas, and I fell into the habit when I found that she and her husband preferred it to the formal "Mrs. Dene"); "I am quite sure that you will not be able to resist the temptation."

"And you don't object?"

"Oh, no, but with this stipulation, that you will use the material in such a way as not to identify any of the cases with the real parties concerned."

That lifted a great responsibility from my shoulders, and made me more eager than ever to prove myself a valuable "assistant" to the charming lady who honored me with her confidence.

•   •   •

We were sitting in the dining room one evening after dinner. Mrs. Lester was looking contemptuously over the last number of the *Queen*, and wondering out loud what on earth young women were coming to with their tailor-mades and their bicycle costumes. Paul was smoking the old briar-root pipe which had been his constant companion in the studio when he was able to paint, poor fellow, and Dorcas was lying down on the sofa. Toddlekins, nestled up close to her, was snoring gently after the manner of his kind.

Dorcas had had a hard and exciting week, and had not been ashamed to confess that she felt a little played out. She had just succeeded in rescuing a young lady of fortune from the toils of an unprincipled Russian adventurer, and stopping the marriage almost at the altar rails by the timely production of the record of the would-be bridegroom, which she obtained with the assistance of M. Goron, the head of the French detective police. It was a return compliment. Dorcas had only a short time previously undertaken for M. Goron a delicate investigation, in which the son of one of the noblest houses in France was involved, and had nipped in the bud a scandal which would have kept the Boulevards chattering for a month.

Paul and I were conversing below our voices, for Dorcas's measured breathing showed us that she had fallen into a doze.

Suddenly Toddlekins opened his eyes and uttered an angry bark. He had heard the front-gate bell.

A minute later the servant entered and handed a card to her mistress, who, with her eyes still half closed, was sitting up on the sofa.

"The gentleman says he must see you at once, ma'am, on business of the greatest importance."

Dorcas looked at the card. "Show the gentleman into the dining room," she said to the servant, "and say that I will be with him directly."

Then she went to the mantel-glass and smoothed away the evidence of her recent forty winks. "Do you know him at all?" she said, handing me the card.

"Colonel Hargreaves, Orley Park, near Godalming." I shook my head, and Dorcas, with a little tired sigh, went to see her visitor.

A few minutes later the dining-room bell rang, and presently the servant came into the drawing room. "Please, sir," she said, addressing me, "mistress says will you kindly come to her at once?"

When I entered the dining room I was astonished to see an elderly, soldierly-looking man lying back unconscious in the easy chair, and Dorcas Dene bending over him.

"I don't think it's anything but a faint," she said. "He's very excited and overwrought, but if you'll stay here I'll go and get some brandy. You had better loosen his collar—or shall we send for a doctor?"

"No, I don't think it is anything serious," I said, after a hasty glance at the invalid.

As soon as Dorcas had gone I began to loosen the Colonel's cravat, but I had hardly commenced before, with a deep sigh, he opened his eyes and came to himself.

"You're better now," I said. "Come—that's all right."

The Colonel stared about him for a moment, and then said, "I—I—where is the lady?"

"She'll be here in a moment. She's gone to get some brandy."

"Oh, I'm all right now, thank you. I suppose it was the excitement, and I've been travelling, had nothing to eat, and I'm so terribly upset. I don't often do this sort of thing, I assure you."

Dorcas returned with the brandy. The Colonel brightened up directly she came into the room. He took the glass she offered him and drained the contents.

"I'm all right now," he said. "Pray let me get on with

my story. I hope you will be able to take the case up at once. Let me see—where was I?"

He gave a little uneasy glance at me. "You can speak without reserve before this gentleman," said Dorcas. "It is possible he may be able to assist us if you wish me to come to Orley Park at once. So far you have told me that your only daughter, who is five-and-twenty and lives with you, was found last night on the edge of the lake in your grounds, half in the water and half out. She was quite insensible, and was carried into the house and put to bed. You were in London at the time, and returned to Orley Park this morning in consequence of a telegram you received. That is as far as you had got when you became ill."

"Yes—yes!" exclaimed the Colonel, "but I am quite well again now. When I arrived at home this morning shortly before noon I was relieved to find that Maud— that is my poor girl's name—was quite conscious, and the doctor had left a message that I was not to be alarmed, and that he would return and see me early in the afternoon.

"I went at once to my daughter's room and found her naturally in a very low, distressed state. I asked her how it had happened, as I could not understand it, and she told me that she had gone out in the grounds after dinner and must have turned giddy when by the edge of the lake and fallen in."

"Is it a deep lake?" asked Dorcas.

"Yes, in the middle, but shallow near the edge. It is a largish lake, with a small fowl island in the centre, and we have a boat upon it."

"Probably it was a sudden fainting fit—such as you yourself have had just now. Your daughter may be subject to them."

"No, she is a thoroughly strong, healthy girl."

"I am sorry to have interrupted you," said Dorcas;

"pray go on, for I presume there is something behind this accident besides a fainting fit, or you would not have come to engage my services in the matter."

"There is a great deal more behind it," replied Colonel Hargreaves, pulling nervously at his grey moustache. "I left my daughter's bedside devoutly thankful that Providence had preserved her from such a dreadful death, but when the doctor arrived he gave me a piece of information which caused me the greatest uneasiness and alarm."

"He didn't believe in the fainting fit?" said Dorcas, who had been closely watching the Colonel's features.

The Colonel looked at Dorcas Dene in astonishment. "I don't know how you have divined that," he said, "but your surmise is correct. The doctor told me that he had questioned Maud himself, and she had told him the same story—sudden giddiness and a fall into the water. But he had observed that on her throat there were certain marks, and that her wrists were bruised.

"When he told me this I did not at first grasp his meaning. 'It must have been the violence of the fall,' I said.

"The doctor shook his head and assured me that no accident would account for the marks his experienced eye had detected. The marks round the throat must have been caused by the clutch of an assailant. The wrists could only have been bruised in the manner they were by being held in a violent and brutal grip."

Dorcas Dene, who had been listening apparently without much interest, bent eagerly forward as the Colonel made this extraordinary statement. "I see," she said. "Your daughter told you that she had fallen into the lake, and the doctor assures you that she must have told you an untruth. She had been pushed or flung in by someone else after a severe struggle."

"Yes!"

"And the young lady, when you questioned her further, with this information in your possession, what did she say?"

"She appeared very much excited, and burst into tears. When I referred to the marks on her throat, which were now beginning to show discoloration more distinctly, she declared that she had invented the story of the faint in order not to alarm me—that she had been attacked by a tramp who must have got into the grounds, and that he had tried to rob her, and that in the struggle, which took place near the edge of the lake, he had thrown her down at the water's edge and then made his escape."

"And that explanation you *do* accept?" said Dorcas, looking at the Colonel keenly.

"How can I? Why should my daughter try to screen a tramp? Why did she tell the doctor an untruth? Surely the first impulse of a terrified woman rescued from a terrible death would have been to have described her assailant in order that he might have been searched for and brought to justice."

"And the police, have they made any inquiries? Have they learned if any suspicious persons were seen about that evening?"

"I have not been to the police. I talked the matter over with the doctor. He says that the police inquiries would make the whole thing public property, and it would be known everywhere that my daughter's story, which has now gone all over the neighbourhood, was untrue. But the whole affair is so mysterious, and to me so alarming, that I could not leave it where it is. It was the doctor who advised me to come to you and let the inquiry be a private one."

"You need employ no one if your daughter can be persuaded to tell the truth. Have you tried?"

"Yes. But she insists that it was a tramp, and declares

that until the bruises betrayed her she kept to the fainting-fit story in order to make the affair as little alarming to me as possible."

Dorcas Dene rose. "What time does the last train leave for Godalming?"

"In an hour," said the Colonel, looking at his watch. "At the station my carriage will be waiting to take us to Orley Court. I want you to stay beneath my roof until you have discovered the key to the mystery."

"No," said Dorcas, after a minute's thought. "I could do no good tonight, and my arrival with you would cause talk among the servants. Go back by yourself. Call on the doctor. Tell him to say his patient requires constant care during the next few days, and that he has sent for a trained nurse from London. The trained nurse will arrive about noon tomorrow."

"And you?" exclaimed the Colonel, "won't you come?"

Dorcas smiled. "Oh, yes; I shall be the trained nurse."

The Colonel rose. "If you can discover the truth and let me know what it is my daughter is concealing from me I shall be eternally grateful," he said. "I shall expect you tomorrow at noon."

"Tomorrow at noon you will expect the trained nurse for whom the doctor has telegraphed. Good evening."

I went to the door with Colonel Hargreaves, and saw him down the garden to the front gate.

When I went back to the house Dorcas Dene was waiting for me in the hall. "Are you busy for the next few days?" she said.

"No—I have practically nothing to do."

"Then come to Godalming with me tomorrow. You are an artist, and I must get you permission to sketch that lake while I am nursing my patient indoors."

It was past noon when the fly, hired from the station,

stopped at the lodge gates of Orley Park, and the lodge-keeper's wife opened them to let us in.

"You are the nurse for Miss Maud, I suppose, miss?" she said, glancing at Dorcas's neat hospital nurse's costume.

"Yes."

"The Colonel and the doctor are both at the house expecting you, miss—I hope it isn't serious with the poor young lady."

"I hope not," said Dorcas, with a pleasant smile.

A minute or two later the fly pulled up at the door of a picturesque old Elizabethan mansion. The Colonel, who had seen the fly from the window, was on the steps waiting for us, and at once conducted us into the library. Dorcas explained my presence in a few words. I was her assistant, and through me she would be able to make all the necessary inquiries in the neighbourhood.

"To your people Mr. Saxon will be an artist to whom you have given permission to sketch the house and the grounds—I think that will be best."

The Colonel promised that I should have free access at all hours to the grounds, and it was arranged that I should stay at a pretty little inn which was about half a mile from the park. Having received full instructions on the way down from Dorcas, I knew exactly what to do, and bade her goodbye until the evening, when I was to call at the house to see her.

The doctor came into the room to conduct the new nurse to the patient's bedside, and I left to fulfil my instructions.

At "The Chequers," which was the name of the inn, it was no sooner known that I was an artist, and had permission to sketch in the grounds of Orley Park, than the landlady commenced to entertain me with accounts of the accident which had nearly cost Miss Hargreaves her life.

The fainting-fit story, which was the only one that had got about, had been accepted in perfect faith.

"It's a lonely place, that lake, and there's nobody about the grounds, you see, at night, sir—it was a wonder the poor young lady was found so soon."

"Who found her?" I asked.

"One of the gardeners who lives in a cottage in the park. He'd been to Godalming for the evening, and was going home past the lake."

"What time was it?"

"Nearly ten o'clock. It was lucky he saw her, for it had been dark nearly an hour then, and there was no moon."

"What did he think when he found her?"

"Well, sir, to tell you the truth, he thought at first it was suicide, and that the young lady hadn't gone far enough in and had lost her senses."

"Of course, he couldn't have thought it was murder or anything of that sort," I said, "because nobody could get in at night—without coming through the lodge gates."

"Oh! yes, they could at one place, but it 'ud have to be somebody who knew the dogs or was with someone who did. There's a couple of big mastiffs have got a good run there, and no stranger 'ud try to clamber over—it's a side gate used by the family, sir—after they'd started barking."

"Did they bark that night at all, do you know?"

"Well, yes," said the landlady. "Now I come to think of it, Mr. Peters—that's the lodge-keeper—heard 'em, but they was quiet in a minute, so he took no more notice."

That afternoon the first place I made up my mind to sketch was the lodge. I found Mr. Peters at home, and my pass from the Colonel secured his good graces at once. His wife had told him of the strange gentleman who had arrived with the nurse, and I explained that there being only one fly at the station and our destination the same, the nurse had kindly allowed me to share the vehicle with her.

I made elaborate pencil marks and notes in my new sketching book, telling Mr. Peters I was only doing something preliminary and rough, in order to conceal the amateurish nature of my efforts and keep the worthy man gossiping about the "accident" to his young mistress.

I referred to the landlady's statement that he had heard dogs bark that night.

"Oh, yes, but they were quiet directly."

"Probably some stranger passing down by the side gate, eh?"

"Most likely, sir. I was a bit uneasy at first, but when they quieted down I thought it was all right."

"Why were you uneasy?"

"Well, there'd been a queer sort of a looking man hanging about that evening. My missus saw him peering in at the lodge gates about seven o'clock."

"A tramp?"

"No, a gentlemanly sort of man, but he gave my missus a turn, he had such wild, staring eyes. But he spoke all right. My missus asked him what he wanted, and he asked her what was the name of the big house he could see, and who lived there. She told him it was Orley Park, and Colonel Hargreaves lived there, and he thanked her and went away. A tourist, maybe, sir, or perhaps an artist gentleman, like yourself."

"Staying in the neighbourhood and examining its beauties, perhaps."

"No; when I spoke about it the next day in the town I heard as he'd come by the train that afternoon; the porters had noticed him, he seemed so odd."

I finished my rough sketch and then asked Mr. Peters to take me to the scene of the accident. It was a large lake and answered the description given by the Colonel.

"That there's the place where Miss Maud was found," said Mr. Peters. "You see it's shallow there, and her head was just on the bank here out of the water."

"Thank you. That's a delightful little island in the middle. I'll smoke a pipe here and sketch. Don't let me detain you."

The lodge-keeper retired, and obeying the instructions received from Dorcas Dene, I examined the spot carefully.

The marks of hobnailed boots were distinctly visible in the mud at the side, near the place where the struggle, admitted by Miss Hargreaves, had taken place. They might be the tramp's—they might be the gardener's; I was not skilled enough in the art of footprints to determine. But I had obtained a certain amount of information, and with that, at seven o'clock, I went to the house and asked for the Colonel.

I had, of course, nothing to say to him, except to ask him to let Dorcas Dene know that I was there. In a few minutes Dorcas came to me with her bonnet and cloak on.

"I'm going to get a walk while it is light," she said; "come with me."

Directly we were outside I gave her my information, and she at once decided to visit the lake.

She examined the scene of the accident carefully, and I pointed out the hobnailed boot marks.

"Yes," she said, "those are the gardener's, probably— I'm looking for someone else's."

"Whose?"

"These," she said, suddenly stopping and pointing to a series of impressions in the soil at the edge. "Look—here are a woman's footprints, and here are larger ones beside them—now close to—now a little way apart—now crossing each other. Do you see anything particular in these footprints?"

"No—except that there are no nails in them."

"Exactly—the footprints are small, but larger than Miss Hargreaves'—the shape is an elegant one, you see the toes are pointed, and the sole is a narrow one. No tramp would have boots like those. Where did you say Mrs. Peters saw that strange-looking gentleman?"

"Peering through the lodge gates."

"Let us go there at once."

Mrs. Peters came out and opened the gates for us.

"What a lovely evening," said Dorcas. "Is the town very far?"

"Two miles, miss."

"Oh, that's too far for me tonight."

She took out her purse and selected some silver.

"Will you please send down the first thing in the morning and buy me a bottle of Wood Violet scent at the chemist's. I always use it, and I've come away without any."

She was just going to hand some silver to Mrs. Peters, when she dropped her purse in the roadway, and the money rolled in every direction.

We picked most of it up, but Dorcas declared there was another half-sovereign. For fully a quarter of an hour she peered about in every direction outside the lodge gates for that missing half-sovereign, and I assisted her. She searched for quite ten minutes in one particular spot, a piece of sodden, loose roadway close against the right-hand gate.

Suddenly she exclaimed that she had found it, and, slipping her hand into her pocket, rose, and, handing Mrs. Peters a five-shilling piece for the scent, beckoned me to follow her, and strolled down the road.

"How came you to drop your purse? Are you nervous tonight?" I said.

"Not at all," replied Dorcas, with a smile. "I dropped my purse that the money might roll and give me an opportunity of closely examining the ground outside the gates."

"Did you really find your half-sovereign?"

"I never lost one; but I found what I wanted."

"And that was?"

"The footprints of the man who stood outside the gates that night. They are exactly the same shape as those by the side of the lake. The person Maud Hargreaves struggled with that night, the person who flung her into the lake and whose guilt she endeavoured to conceal by declaring she had met with an accident, was the man who wanted to know the name of the place, and asked who lived there—*the man with the wild eyes.*"

"You are absolutely certain that the footprints of the man with the wild eyes, who frightened Mrs. Peters at the gate, and the footprints which are mixed up with those of Miss Hargreaves by the side of the lake, are the same?" I said to Dorcas Dene.

"Absolutely certain."

"Then perhaps, if you describe him, the Colonel may be able to recognise him."

"No," said Dorcas Dene, "I have already asked him if he knew anyone who could possibly bear his daughter a grudge, and he declares that there is no one to his knowledge. Miss Hargreaves has scarcely any acquaintances."

"And has had no love affair?" I asked.

"None, her father says, but of course he can only answer for the last three years. Previously to that he was in India, and Maud—who was sent home at the age of fourteen, when her mother died—had lived with an aunt at Norwood."

"Who do you think this man was who managed to get into the grounds and meet or surprise Miss Hargreaves by the lake—a stranger to her?"

"No; had he been a stranger, she would not have shielded him by inventing the fainting-fit story."

We had walked some distance from the house, when

an empty station fly passed us. We got in, Dorcas telling the man to drive us to the station.

When we got there, she told me to go and interview the porters and try and find out if a man of the description of our suspect had left on the night of the "accident."

I found the man who had told Mr. Peters that he had seen such a person arrive, and had noticed the peculiar expression of his eyes. This man assured me that no such person had left from that station. He had told his mates about him, and some of them would be sure to have seen him. The stranger brought no luggage, and gave up a single ticket from Waterloo.

Dorcas was waiting for me outside, and I gave her my information.

"No luggage," she said; "then he wasn't going to an hotel or to stay at a private house."

"But he might be living somewhere about."

"No; the porters would have recognised him if he had been in the habit of coming here."

"But he must have gone away after flinging Miss Hargreaves into the water. He might have got out of the grounds again and walked to another station, and caught a train back to London."

"Yes, he might," said Dorcas, "but I don't think he did. Come, we'll take the fly back to Orley Park."

Just before we reached the park Dorcas stopped the driver, and we got out and dismissed the man.

"Whereabouts are those dogs—near the private wooden door in the wall used by the family, aren't they?" she said to me.

"Yes, Peters pointed the spot out to me this afternoon."

"Very well, I'm going in. Meet me by the lake tomorrow morning about nine. But watch me now as far as the gates. I'll wait outside five minutes before ringing. When you see I'm there, go to that portion of the wall near the private door. Clamber up and peer over. When the dogs begin to bark, and come at you, notice if you could possibly drop over and escape them without someone they knew called them off. Then jump down again and go back to the inn."

I obeyed Dorcas's instructions; and when I had succeeded in climbing to the top of the wall, the dogs flew out of their kennel and commenced to bark furiously. Had I dropped I must have fallen straight into their grip. Suddenly I heard a shout, and I recognised the voice—it was the lodge-keeper. I dropped back into the road and crept along in the shadow of the wall. In the distance I could hear Peters talking to someone, and I knew what had happened. In the act of letting Dorcas in, he had heard the dogs, and had hurried off to see what was the matter. Dorcas had followed him.

At nine o'clock next morning I found Dorcas waiting for me.

"You did your work admirably last night," she said. "Peters was in a terrible state of alarm. He was very glad for me to come with him. He quieted the dogs, and we searched about everywhere in the shrubbery to see if anyone was in hiding. That man wasn't let in at the door that night by Miss Hargreaves; he dropped over. I found the impression of two deep footprints close together, exactly as they would be made by a drop or jump down from a height."

"Did he go back that way—*were there return footprints?*"

I thought I had made a clever suggestion, but Dorcas smiled and shook her head. "I didn't look. How could he return past the dogs when Miss Hargreaves was lying in the lake? They'd have torn him to pieces."

"And you still think this man with the wild eyes is guilty? Who can he have been?"

"His name was Victor."

"You have discovered that!" I exclaimed. "Has Miss Hargreaves been talking to you?"

"Last night I tried a little experiment. When she was asleep, and evidently dreaming, I went quietly in the dark and stood just behind the bed, and in the gruffest voice I could assume, I said, bending down to her ear, 'Maud!'

"She started up, and cried out, 'Victor!'

"In a moment I was by her side, and found her trembling violently. 'What's the matter, dear?' I said, 'have you been dreaming?'

" 'Yes—yes,' she said. 'I—I was dreaming.'

"I soothed her, and talked to her a little while, and finally she lay down again and fell asleep."

"That's something," I said, "to have got the man's Christian name."

"Yes, it's a little, but I think we shall have the surname today. You must go up to town and do a little commission for me presently. In the meantime, pull that boat in and row me across to the fowl island. I want to search it."

"You don't imagine the man's hiding there," I said. "It's too small."

"Pull me over," said Dorcas, getting into the boat.

I obeyed, and presently we were on the little island.

Dorcas carefully surveyed the lake in every direction. Then she walked round and examined the foliage and the reeds that were at the edge and drooping into the water.

Suddenly pushing a mass of close, overhanging growth aside, she thrust her hand deep down under it into the water and drew up a black, saturated felt hat.

"I thought if anything drifted that night, this is where it would get caught and entangled," said Dorcas.

"If it is that man's hat, he must have gone away bareheaded."

"Quite so," replied Dorcas, "but first let us ascertain if it is his. Row ashore at once."

She wrung the water from the hat, squeezed it together and wrapped it up in her pocket handkerchief, and put it under her cloak.

When we were ashore, I went to the lodge and got Mrs. Peters onto the subject of the man with the wild eyes. Then I asked what sort of a hat he had on, and Mrs. Peters said it was a felt hat with a dent in the middle, and I knew that our find was a good one.

When I told Dorcas she gave a little smile of satisfaction.

"We've got his Christian name and his hat," she said; "now we want the rest of him. You can catch the eleven-twenty easily."

"Yes."

She drew an envelope from her pocket and took a *carte de visite* from it.

"That's the portrait of a handsome young fellow," she said. "By the style and size I should think it was taken four or five years ago. The photographers are the London Stereoscopic Company—the number of the negative is 111,492. If you go to Regent Street, they will search their books and give you the name and address of the original. Get it, and come back here."

"Is that the man?" I said.

"I think so."

"How on earth did you get it?"

"I amused myself while Miss Hargreaves was asleep by looking over the album in her boudoir. It was an old album, and filled with portraits of relatives and friends. I should say there were over fifty, some of them being probably her schoolfellows. I thought I *might* find something, you know. People have portraits given them, put them in an album, and almost forget they are there. I fancied Miss Hargreaves might have forgotten."

"But how did you select this from fifty? There were other male portraits, I suppose?"

"Oh, yes, but I took out every portrait and examined the back and the margin."

I took the photo from Dorcas and looked at it. I noticed that a portion of the back had been rubbed away and was rough.

"That's been done with an ink eraser," said Dorcas. "That made me concentrate on this particular photo. There has been a name written there or some word the recipient didn't want other eyes to see."

"That is only surmise."

"Quite so—but there's a certainty in the photo itself. Look closely at that little diamond scarf-pin in the necktie. What shape is it?"

"It looks like a small V."

"Exactly. It was fashionable a few years ago for gentlemen to wear a small initial pin. V stands for Victor—take that and the erasure together, and I think it's worth a return fare to town to find out what name and address are opposite the negative number in the books of the London Stereoscopic Company."

Before two o'clock I was interviewing the manager of the Stereoscopic Company, and he readily referred to the books. The photograph had been taken six years previously, and the name and address of the sitter were "Mr. Victor Dubois, Anerley Road, Norwood."

Following Dorcas Dene's instructions, I proceeded at once to the address given, and made enquiries for a Mr. Victor Dubois. No one of that name resided there. The present tenants had been in possession for three years.

As I was walking back along the road I met an old postman. I thought I would ask him if he knew the name anywhere in the neighbourhood. He thought a minute, then said, "Yes—now I come to think of it there was a Dubois here at Number ——, but that was five years ago or more. He was an oldish, white-haired gentleman."

"An old gentleman—Victor Dubois!"

"Ah, no—the old gentleman's name was Mounseer Dubois, but there was a Victor. I suppose that must have been his son as lived with him. I know the name. There used to be letters addressed there for Mr. Victor most every day—sometimes twice a day—always in the same handwriting, a lady's—that's what made me notice it."

"And you don't know where Monsieur Dubois and his son went to?"

"No, I did hear as the old gentleman went off his head, and was put in a lunatic asylum; but they went out o' my round."

"You don't know what he was, I suppose?"

"Oh, it said on the brass plate, 'Professor of Languages.' "

I went back to town and took the first train to Godalming, and hastened to Orley Court to report the result of my enquiries to Dorcas.

She was evidently pleased, for she complimented me. Then she rang the bell—we were in the dining room—and the servant entered.

"Will you let the Colonel know that I should like to see him?" said Dorcas, and the servant went to deliver the message.

"Are you going to tell him everything?" I said.

"I am going to tell him nothing yet," replied Dorcas. "I want him to tell me something."

The Colonel entered. His face was worn, and he was evidently worrying himself a great deal.

"Have you anything to tell me?" he said eagerly. "Have you found out what my poor girl is hiding from me?"

"I'm afraid I cannot tell you yet. But I want to ask you a few questions."

"I have given you all the information I can already," replied the Colonel a little bitterly.

"All you recollect, but now try and think. Your

daughter, before you came back from India, was with her aunt at Norwood. Where was she educated from the time she left India?"

"She went to school at Brighton at first, but from the time she was sixteen she had private instruction at home."

"She had professors, I suppose, for music, French, et cetera?"

"Yes, I believe so. I paid bills for that sort of thing. My sister sent them out to me to India."

"Can you remember the name of Dubois?"

The Colonel thought a little while.

"Dubois? Dubois? Dubois?" he said. "I have an idea there was such a name among the accounts my sister sent to me, but whether it was a dressmaker or a French master I really can't say."

"Then I think we will take it that your daughter had lessons at Norwood from a French professor named Dubois. Now, in any letters that your late sister wrote you to India, did she ever mention anything that had caused her uneasiness on Maud's account?"

"Only once," replied the Colonel, "and everything was satisfactorily explained afterwards. She left home one day at nine o'clock in the morning, and did not return until four in the afternoon. Her aunt was exceedingly angry, and Maud explained that she had met some friends at the Crystal Palace—she attended the drawing class there—had gone to see one of her fellow students off at the station, and sitting in the carriage, the train had started before she could get out and she had had to go on to London. I expect my sister told me that to show me how thoroughly I might rely upon her as my daughter's guardian."

"Went on to London?" said Dorcas to me under her voice, "and she could have got out in three minutes at the next station to Norwood!" Then turning to the Colonel, she said, "Now, Colonel, when your wife died, what did you do with her wedding ring?"

"Good heavens, madam!" exclaimed the Colonel, rising and pacing the room, "what can my poor wife's wedding ring have to do with my daughter's being flung into the lake yonder?"

"I am sorry if my question appears absurd," replied Dorcas quietly, "but will you kindly answer it?"

"My wife's wedding ring is on my dead wife's finger in her coffin in the graveyard at Simla," exclaimed the Colonel, "and now perhaps you'll tell me what all this means!"

"Tomorrow," said Dorcas. "Now, if you'll excuse me, I'll take a walk with Mr. Saxon. Miss Hargreaves' maid is with her, and she will be all right until I return."

"Very well, very well!" exclaimed the Colonel, "but I beg—I pray of you to tell me what you know as soon as you can. I am setting spies upon my own child, and to me it is monstrous—and yet—and yet—what can I do? She won't tell me, and for her sake I must know—I must know."

"You shall, Colonel Hargreaves," said Dorcas, going up to him and holding out her hand. "Believe me, you have my sincerest sympathy."

The old Colonel grasped the proffered hand of Dorcas Dene.

"Thank you," he said, his lips quivering.

Directly we were in the grounds Dorcas Dene turned eagerly to me.

"I'm treating you very badly," she said, "but our task is nearly over. You must go back to town tonight. The first thing tomorrow morning go to Somerset House. You will find an old fellow named Daddy Green, a searcher in the inquiry room. Tell him you come from me, and give him this paper. When he has searched, telegraph the result to me, and come back by the next train."

I looked at the paper, and found written on it in Dorcas's hand:

Search wanted.
Marriage—Victor Dubois and Maud Eleanor Hargreaves —probably between the years 1890 and 1893—London.

I looked up from the paper at Dorcas Dene.

"Whatever makes you think she is a married woman?" I said.

"This," exclaimed Dorcas, drawing an unworn wedding ring from her purse. "I found it among a lot of trinkets at the bottom of a box her maid told me was her jewel case. I took the liberty of trying all her keys till I opened it. A jewel box tells many secrets to those who know how to read them."

"And you concluded from that—?"

"That she wouldn't keep a wedding ring without it had belonged to someone dear to her or had been placed on her own finger. It is quite unworn, you see, so it was taken off immediately after the ceremony. It was only to make doubly sure that I asked the Colonel where his wife's was."

I duly repaired to Somerset House, and soon after midday, Daddy Green, the searcher, brought a paper and handed it to me. It was a copy of the certificate of the marriage of Victor Dubois, bachelor, aged twenty-six, and Maud Eleanor Hargreaves, aged twenty-one, in London, in the year 1891. I telegraphed the news, wording the message simply "Yes" and the date, and I followed my wire by the first train.

When I arrived at Orley Park I rang several times before anyone came. Presently Mrs. Peters, looking very white and excited, came from the grounds and apologised for keeping me waiting.

"Oh, sir—such a dreadful thing!" she said—"a body in the lake!"

"A body!"

"Yes, sir—a man. The nurse as came with you here that day, she was rowing herself on the lake, and she must have stirred it. pushing with her oar, for it come up all tangled with weeds. It's a man, sir, and I do believe it's the man I saw at the gate that night."

"The man with the wild eyes!" I exclaimed.

"Yes, sir! Oh, it is dreadful—Miss Maud first, and then this. Oh, what can it mean!"

I found Dorcas standing at the edge of the lake, and Peters and two of the gardeners lifting the drowned body of a man into the boat which was alongside.

Dorcas was giving instructions. "Lay it in the boat, and cover it with a tarpaulin," she said. "Mind, nothing is to be touched till the police come. I will go and find the Colonel."

As she turned away I met her.

"What a terrible thing! Is it Dubois?"

"Yes," replied Dorcas. "I suspected he was there yesterday, but I wanted to find him myself instead of having the lake dragged."

"Why?"

"Well, I didn't want anyone else to search the pockets. There might have been papers or letters, you know, which would have been read at the inquest, and might have compromised Miss Hargreaves. But there was nothing—"

"What—you searched!"

"Yes, after I'd brought the poor fellow to the surface with the oars."

"But how do you think he got in?"

"Suicide—insanity. The father was taken to a lunatic asylum—you learned that at Norwood yesterday. Son doubtless inherited tendency. Looks like a case of homicidal mania—he attacked Miss Hargreaves, whom he had probably tracked after years of separation, and after he had as he thought killed her, he drowned himself. At any rate, Miss Hargreaves is a free woman. She was evidently terrified of her husband when he was alive, and so—"

I guessed what Dorcas was thinking as we went together to the house. At the door she held out her hand. "You had better go to the inn and return to town tonight," she said. "You can do no more good, and had better keep out of it. I shall be home tomorrow. Come to Oak Tree Road in the evening."

The next evening Dorcas told me all that had happened after I left. Paul had already heard it, and when I arrived was profuse in his thanks for the assistance I had rendered his wife. Mrs. Lester, however, felt compelled to remark that she never thought a daughter of hers would go gadding about the country fishing up corpses for a living.

Dorcas had gone to the Colonel and told him everything. The Colonel was in a terrible state, but Dorcas told him that the only way in which to ascertain the truth was for them to go to the unhappy girl together, and attempt, with the facts in their possession, to persuade her to divulge the rest.

When the Colonel told his daughter that the man she had married had flung her into the lake that night, she was dumbfounded and became hysterical, but when she learned that Dubois had been found in the lake she became alarmed and instantly told all she knew.

She had been in the habit of meeting Victor Dubois constantly when she was at Norwood, at first with his father—her French master—and afterwards alone. He was handsome, young, romantic, and they fell madly in love. He was going away for some time to an appointment abroad, and he urged her to marry him secretly. She foolishly consented, and they parted at the church, she returning to her home and he going abroad the same evening.

She received letters from him clandestinely from time

to time. Then he wrote that his father had become insane and had to be removed to a lunatic asylum, and he was returning. He had only time to see to his father's removal and return to his appointment. She did not hear from him for a long time, and then through a friend at Norwood who knew the Dubois and their relatives she made enquiries. Victor had returned to England, and met with an accident which had injured his head severely. He became insane and was taken to a lunatic asylum.

The poor girl resolved to keep her marriage a secret forever then, especially as her father had returned from India, and she knew how bitterly it would distress him to learn that his daughter was the wife of a madman.

On the night of the affair Maud was in the grounds by herself. She was strolling by the lake after dinner, when she heard a sound, and the dogs began to bark. Looking up, she saw Victor Dubois scaling the wall. Fearful that the dogs would bring Peters or someone on the scene, she ran to them and silenced them, and her husband leapt down and stood by her.

"Come away!" she said, fearing the dogs might attack him or begin to bark again, and she led him round by the lake which was out of sight of the house and the lodge.

She forgot for the moment in her excitement that he had been mad. At first he was gentle and kind. He told her he had been ill and in an asylum, but had recently been discharged cured. Directly he regained his liberty he set out in search of his wife, and ascertained from an old Norwood acquaintance that Miss Hargreaves was now living with her father at Orley Park, near Godalming.

Maud begged him to go away quietly, and she would write to him. He tried to take her in his arms and kiss her, but instinctively she shrank from him. Instantly he became furious. Seized with a sudden mania, he grasped her by the throat. She struggled and freed herself.

They were at the edge of the lake. Suddenly the

maniac got her by the throat again, and hurled her down into the water. She fell in up to her waist, but managed to drag herself towards the edge; but before she emerged she fell senseless—fortunately with her head on the shore just out of the water.

The murderer, probably thinking that she was dead, must have waded out into the deep water and drowned himself.

Before she left Orley Park, Dorcas advised the Colonel to let the inquest be held without any light being thrown on the affair by him. Only he was to take care that the police received information that a man answering the description of the suicide had recently been discharged from a lunatic asylum.

We heard later that at the inquest an official from the asylum attended, and the local jury found that Victor Dubois, a lunatic, got into the grounds in some way, and drowned himself in the lake while temporarily insane. It was suggested by the coroner that probably Miss Hargreaves, who was too unwell to attend, had not seen the man, but might have been alarmed by the sound of his footsteps, and that this would account for her fainting away near the water's edge. At any rate, the inquest ended in a satisfactory verdict, and the Colonel shortly afterwards took his daughter abroad with him on a Continental tour for the benefit of her health.

But of this of course we knew nothing on the evening after the eventful discovery, when I met Dorcas once more beneath her own roof-tree.

Paul was delighted to have his wife back again, and she devoted herself to him, and that evening had eyes and ears for no one else—not even for her faithful "assistant."

BIOGRAPHICAL INFORMATION on Clarence Rook (?–1915) seems to be practically nonexistent. In *Hooligan Nights* (1899), he describes himself as an American tourist in London and goes on to relate how, through the auspices of the English publisher Grant Richards, he met Alf, "a young and unrepentant criminal," who told him about his life and habits and offered him an intimate glance into the seamier reaches of London's underworld. Other book titles credited to Rook are *A Lesson for Life* (1901), *London Side-Lights* (1908), and *Switzerland: The Country and Its People* (1907).

According to the *Oxford English Dictionary*, the verb "to snoop" comes from the Dutch *snoepen*, which means "to enjoy stealthily." The following is the only known story about Miss Van Snoop.

The Stir Outside
the Café Royal

A Story of Miss Van Snoop, Detective

by Clarence Rook

Colonel Mathurin was one of the aristocrats of crime; at least Mathurin was the name under which he had accomplished a daring bank robbery in Detroit which had involved the violent death of the manager, though it was generally believed by the police that the Rossiter who was at the bottom of some long firm frauds in Melbourne was none other than Mathurin under another name, and that the designer and chief gainer in a sensational murder case in the Midlands was the same mysterious and ubiquitous personage.

But Mathurin had for some years successfully eluded pursuit; indeed, it was generally known that he was the most desperate among criminals, and was determined never to be taken alive. Moreover, as he invariably worked through subordinates who knew nothing of his whereabouts and were scarcely acquainted with his appearance, the police had but a slender clue to his identity.

As a matter of fact, only two people beyond his immediate associates in crime could have sworn to Mathurin if they had met him face to face. One of them was the Detroit bank manager whom he had shot with his own hand before the eyes of his fiancée. It was through the other that Mathurin was arrested, extradited to the States, and finally made to atone for his life of crime. It all happened in a distressingly commonplace way, so far as the average spectator was concerned. But the story, which I have pieced together from the details supplied—firstly, by a certain detective sergeant whom I met in a tavern hard by Westminster, and secondly, by a certain young woman named Miss Van Snoop—has an element of romance, if you look below the surface.

It was about half-past one o'clock, on a bright and pleasant day, that a young lady was driving down Regent Street in a hansom which she had picked up outside her boardinghouse near Portland Road Station. She had told the cabman to drive slowly, as she was nervous behind a horse; and so she had leisure to scan, with the curiosity of a stranger, the strolling crowd that at nearly all hours of the day throngs Regent Street. It was a sunny morning, and everybody looked cheerful. Ladies were shopping, or looking in at the shop windows. Men about town were collecting an appetite for lunch; flower girls were selling "nice vi'lets, sweet vi'lets, penny a bunch"; and the girl in the cab leaned one arm on the apron and regarded the scene with alert attention. She was not exactly pretty, for the symmetry of her features was discounted by a certain hardness in the set of the mouth. But her hair, so dark as to be almost black, and her eyes of greyish blue set her beyond comparison with the commonplace.

Just outside the Café Royal there was a slight stir, and a temporary block in the foot traffic. A brougham was setting down, behind it was a victoria, and behind that a hansom; and as the girl glanced round the heads of the pair in the brougham, she saw several men standing on the steps. Leaning back suddenly, she opened the trapdoor in the roof.

"Stop here," she said, "I've changed my mind."

The driver drew up by the curb, and the girl skipped out.

"You shan't lose by the change," she said, handing him half-a-crown.

There was a tinge of American accent in the voice; and the cabman, pocketing the half-crown with thanks, smiled.

"They may talk about that McKinley tariff," he soliloquised as he crawled along the curb towards Picca-dilly Circus, "but it's better 'n free trade—lumps!"

Meanwhile the girl walked slowly back towards the Café Royal, and, with a quick glance at the men who were standing there, entered. One or two of the men raised their eyebrows; but the girl was quite unconscious, and went on her way to the luncheon room.

"American, you bet," said one of the loungers. "They'll go anywhere and do anything."

Just in front of her as she entered was a tall, clean-shaven man, faultlessly dressed in glossy silk hat and frock coat, with a flower in his buttonhole. He looked around for a moment in search of a convenient table. As he hesitated, the girl hesitated; but when the waiter waved him to a small table laid for two, the girl immediately sat down behind him at the next table.

"Excuse me, madam," said the waiter, "this table is set for four; would you mind—"

"I guess," said the girl, "I'll stay where I am." And the look in her eyes, as well as a certain sensation in the waiter's palm, ensured her against further disturbance.

The restaurant was full of people lunching, singly or in twos, in threes, and even larger parties; and many curious glances were directed to the girl who sat at a table alone and pursued her way calmly through the menu. But the girl appeared to notice no one. When her eyes were off her plate they were fixed straight ahead—on the back of the man who had entered in front of her. The man, who had drunk a half-bottle of champagne with his lunch, ordered a liqueur to accompany his coffee. The girl, who had drunk an aerated water, leaned back in her chair and wrinkled her brows. They were very straight brows, that seemed to meet over her nose when she wrinkled them in perplexity. Then she called a waiter.

"Bring me a sheet of notepaper, please," she said, "and my bill."

The waiter laid the sheet of paper before her, and the girl proceeded, after a few moments' thought, to write a few lines in pencil upon it. When this was done, she folded the sheet carefully and laid it in her purse. Then, having paid her bill, she returned her purse to her dress pocket, and waited patiently.

In a few minutes the clean-shaven man at the next table settled his bill and made preparations for departure. The girl at the same time drew on her gloves, keeping her eyes immovably upon her neighbour's back. As the man rose to depart and passed the table at which the girl had been sitting, the girl was looking into the mirror upon the wall and patting her hair. Then she turned and followed the man out of the restaurant, while a pair at an adjacent table remarked to one another that it was a rather curious coincidence for a man and woman to enter and leave at the same moment when they had no apparent connection.

But what happened outside was even more curious.

The man halted for a moment upon the steps at the entrance. The porter, who was in conversation with a policeman, turned, whistle in hand.

"Hansom, sir?" he asked.

"Yes," said the clean-shaven man.

The porter was raising his whistle to his lips when he noticed the girl behind.

"Do you wish for a cab, madam?" he asked, and blew upon his whistle.

As he turned again for an answer, he plainly saw the girl, who was standing close behind the clean-shaven man, slip her hand under his coat, and snatch from his hip pocket something which she quickly transferred to her own.

"Well, I'm—" began the clean-shaven man, swinging round and feeling in his pocket.

"Have you missed anything, sir?" said the porter, standing full in front of the girl to bar her exit.

"My cigarette case is gone," said the man, looking from one side to another.

"What's this?" said the policeman, stepping forward.

"I saw the woman's hand in the gentleman's pocket, plain as a pikestaff," said the porter.

"Oh, that's it, is it?" said the policeman, coming close to the girl. "I thought as much."

"Come now," said the clean-shaven man, "I don't want to make a fuss. Just hand back that cigarette case, and we'll say no more about it."

"I haven't got it," said the girl. "How dare you? I never touched your pocket."

The man's face darkened.

"Oh, come now!" said the porter.

"Look here, that won't do," said the policeman, "you'll have to come along of me. Better take a four-wheeler, eh, sir?"

For a knot of loafers, seeing something interesting in the wind, had collected round the entrance.

A four-wheeler was called, and the girl entered, closely followed by the policeman and the clean-shaven man.

"I was never so insulted in my life," said the girl.

Nevertheless, she sat back quite calmly in the cab, as though she was perfectly ready to face this or any other situation, while the policeman watched her closely to make sure that she did not dispose in any surreptitious way of the stolen article.

At the police station hard by, the usual formalities were gone through, and the clean-shaven man was constituted prosecutor. But the girl stoutly denied having been guilty of any offence.

The inspector in charge looked doubtful.

"Better search her," he said.

And the girl was led off to a room for an interview with the female searcher.

The moment the door closed the girl put her hand into her pocket, pulled out the cigarette case, and laid it upon the table.

"There you are," she said. "That will fix matters so far."

The woman looked rather surprised.

"Now," said the girl, holding out her arms, "feel in this other pocket, and find my purse."

The woman picked out the purse.

"Open it and read the note on the bit of paper inside."

On the sheet of paper which the waiter had given her, the girl had written these words, which the searcher read in a muttered undertone:

> I am going to pick this man's pocket as the best way of getting him into a police station without violence. He is Colonel Mathurin, alias Rossiter, alias Connell, and he is wanted in Detroit, New York, Melbourne, Colombo, and London. Get four men to pin him unawares, for he is armed and desperate. I am a member of the New York detective force—Nora Van Snoop.

"It's all right," said Miss Van Snoop, quickly, as the searcher looked up at her after reading the note. "Show that to the boss—right away."

The searcher opened the door. After whispered consultation the inspector appeared, holding the note in his hand.

"Now then, be spry," said Miss Van Snoop. "Oh, you needn't worry! I've got my credentials right here," and she dived into another pocket.

"But do you know—can you be sure," said the inspector, "that this is the man who shot the Detroit bank manager?"

"Great heavens! Didn't I see him shoot Will Stevens with my own eyes! And didn't I take service with the police to hunt him out?"

The girl stamped her foot, and the inspector left. For two, three, four minutes, she stood listening intently. Then a muffled shout reached her ears. Two minutes later the inspector returned.

"I think you're right," he said. "We have found enough evidence on him to identify him. But why didn't you give him in charge before to the police?"

"I wanted to arrest him myself," said Miss Van Snoop, "and I have. Oh, Will! Will!"

Miss Van Snoop sank into a cane-bottomed chair, laid her head upon the table, and cried. She had earned the luxury of hysterics. In half an hour she left the station, and, proceeding to a post office, cabled her resignation to the head of the detective force in New York.

$\mathfrak{T}$HERE HAS BEEN much speculation about the identity of the Robert Eustace who served as medical/scientific collaborator to a varied group of authors spanning several periods of detective fiction. He is presumed to be one Dr. Eustace Robert Barton (1854–?), who also used the pseudonym Eustace Rawlins. His best-known efforts include aiding L. T. Meade in the creation of *The Sorceress of the Strand* (1903), whose title character is a female master criminal; partnering Edgar Jepson in writing "The Tea Leaf" (1925), whose heroine who does scientific detection; and helping Dorothy Sayers with the toxicological details of *The Documents in the Case* (1930).

Lillie Thomasina Meade—the nom de plume of Elizabeth Thomasina (Meade) Smith (1854–1914)—was of Irish parentage. Her short stories were so numerous as to be fixtures in turn-of-the-century periodicals, and she also wrote novels for young girls. Among the collections of stories she wrote with Robert Eustace are *A Master of Mysteries* (1898) and *The Sanctuary Club* (1900).

During 1899 and 1900 there appeared in *The Harmsworth Magazine* four tales of the young woman sleuth Florence Cusack. In "The Arrest of Captain Vandaleur" she discovered that gentlemen's scents had been used as the basis for a code, and in "The Outside Ledge, a Cablegram Mystery," that cats manipulated by catnip were carrying messages. In "A Terrible Railway Ride," the reader was told that Miss Cusack had "one of the most acute detective brains in the whole of London."

Mr. Bovey's Unexpected Will

by L. T. Meade and Robert Eustace

Amongst all my patients there were none who excited my sense of curiosity like Miss Florence Cusack. I never thought of her without a sense of baffled inquiry taking possession of me, and I never visited her without the hope that someday I should get to the bottom of the mystery which surrounded her.

Miss Cusack was a young and handsome woman. She possessed to all appearance superabundant health, her energies were extraordinary, and her life completely out of the common. She lived alone in a large house in Kensington Court Gardens, kept a good staff of servants, and went much into society. Her beauty, her sprightliness, her wealth, and, above all, her extraordinary life caused her to be much talked about. As one glanced at this handsome girl with her slender figure, her eyes of the darkest blue, her raven-black hair and clear complexion, it was almost impossible to believe that she was a power in the police courts, and highly respected by every detective in Scotland Yard.

I shall never forget my first visit to Miss Cusack. I had been asked by a brother doctor to see her in his absence.

Strong as she was, she was subject to periodical and very acute nervous attacks. When I entered her house she came up to me eagerly.

"Pray do not ask me too many questions or look too curious, Dr. Lonsdale," she said. "I know well that my whole condition is abnormal; but, believe me, I am forced to do what I do."

"What is that?" I inquired.

"You see before you," she continued, with emphasis, "the most acute and, I believe, successful lady detective in the whole of London."

"Why do you lead such an extraordinary life?" I asked.

"To me the life is fraught with the very deepest interest," she answered. "In any case," and now the colour faded from her cheeks, and her eyes grew full of emotion, "I have no choice; I am under a promise, which I must fulfil. There are times, however, when I need help—such help as you, for instance, can give me. I have never seen you before, but I like your face. If the time should ever come, will you give me your assistance?"

I asked her a few more questions, and finally agreed to do what she wished.

From that hour Miss Cusack and I became the staunchest friends. She constantly invited me to her house, introduced me to her friends, and gave me her confidence to a marvellous extent.

On my first visit I noticed in her study two enormous brazen bulldogs. They were splendidly cast, and made a striking feature in the arrangements of the room; but I did not pay them any special attention until she happened to mention that there was a story, and a strange one, in connection with them.

"But for these dogs," she said, "and the mystery attached to them, I should not be the woman I am, nor would my life be set apart for the performance of duties at once herculean and ghastly."

When she said these words her face once more turned pale, and her eyes flashed with an ominous fire.

On a certain afternoon in November 1894, I received a telegram from Miss Cusack, asking me to put aside all other work and go to her at once. Handing my patients over to the care of my partner, I started for her house. I found her in her study and alone. She came up to me holding a newspaper in her hand.

"Do you see this?" she asked. As she spoke she pointed to the agony column. The following words met my eyes:

Send more sand and charcoal dust. Core and mould ready for casting.—JOSHUA LINKLATER.

I read these curious words twice, then glanced at the eager face of the young girl.

"I have been waiting for this," she said, in a tone of triumph.

"But what can it mean?" I said. " *'Core and mould ready for casting'?*"

She folded up the paper, and laid it deliberately on the table.

"I thought that Joshua Linklater would say something of the kind," she continued. "I have been watching for a similar advertisement in all the dailies for the last three weeks. This may be of the utmost importance."

"Will you explain?" I said.

"I may never have to explain, or, on the other hand, I may," she answered. "I have not really sent for you to point out this advertisement, but in connection with another matter. Now, pray, come into the next room with me."

She led me into a prettily and luxuriously furnished boudoir on the same floor. Standing by the hearth was a slender fair-haired girl, looking very little more than a child.

"May I introduce you to my cousin, Letitia Ransom?"

said Miss Cusack eagerly. "Pray sit down, Letty," she
continued, addressing the girl with a certain asperity, "Dr.
Lonsdale is the man of all others we want. Now, doctor,
will you give me your very best attention, for I have an
extraordinary story to relate."

At Miss Cusack's words Miss Ransom immediately
seated herself. Miss Cusack favoured her with a quick
glance, and then once more turned to me.

"You are much interested in queer mental phases, are
you not?" she said.

"I certainly am," I replied.

"Well, I should like to ask your opinion with regard to
such a will as this."

Once again she unfolded a newspaper, and, pointing to
a paragraph, handed it to me. I read as follows:

EXTRAORDINARY TERMS OF
A MISER'S WILL

Mr. Henry Bovey, who died last week at a small house at
Kew, has left one of the most extraordinary wills on record.
During his life his eccentricities and miserly habits were
well known, but this eclipses them all, by the surprising
method in which he has disposed of his property.

Mr. Bovey was unmarried, and, as far as can be proved,
has no near relations in the world. The small balance at his
banker's is to be used for defraying fees, duties, and sundry
charges, also any existing debts, but the main bulk of
his securities were recently realised, and the money in
sovereigns is locked in a safe in his house.

A clause in the will states that there are three claimants
to this property, and that the one whose net bodily weight
is nearest to the weight of these sovereigns is to become
the legatee. The safe containing the property is not to be
opened till the three claimants are present; the competition is then to take place, and the winner is at once to
remove his fortune.

Considerable excitement has been manifested over the affair, the amount of the fortune being unknown. The date of the competition is also kept a close secret for obvious reasons.

"Well," I said, laying the paper down, "whoever this Mr. Bovey was, there is little doubt that he must have been out of his mind. I never heard of a more crazy idea."

"Nevertheless it is to be carried out," replied Miss Cusack. "Now listen, please, Dr. Lonsdale. This paper is a fortnight old. It is now three weeks since the death of Mr. Bovey, his will has been proved, and the time has come for the carrying out of the competition. I happen to know two of the claimants well, and intend to be present at the ceremony."

I did not make any answer, and after a pause she continued:

"One of the gentlemen who is to be weighed against his own fortune is Edgar Wimburne. He is engaged to my cousin Letitia. If he turns out to be the successful claimant, there is nothing to prevent their marrying at once; if otherwise—" here she turned and looked full at Miss Ransom, who stood up, the colour coming and going in her cheeks—"if otherwise, Mr. Campbell Graham has to be dealt with."

"Who is he?" I asked.

"Another claimant, a much older man than Edgar. Nay, I must tell you everything. He is a claimant in a double sense, being also a lover, and a very ardent one, of Letitia's.

"Letty must be saved," she said, looking at me, "and I believe I know how to do it."

"You spoke of three claimants," I interrupted; "who is the third?"

"Oh, he scarcely counts, unless indeed he carries off the prize. He is William Tyndall, Mr. Bovey's servant and retainer."

"And when, may I ask, is this momentous competition to take place?" I continued.

"Tomorrow morning at half-past nine, at Mr. Bovey's house. Will you come with us tomorrow, Dr. Lonsdale, and be present at the weighing?"

"I certainly will," I answered; "it will be a novel experience."

"Very well; can you be at this house a little before half-past eight, and we will drive straight to Kew?"

I promised to do so, and soon after took my leave. The next day I was at Miss Cusack's house in good time. I found waiting for me Miss Cusack herself, Miss Ransom, and Edgar Wimburne.

A moment or two later we all found ourselves seated in a large landau, and in less than an hour had reached our destination. We drew up at a small dilapidated-looking house, standing in a row of prim suburban villas, and found that Mr. Graham, the lawyer, and the executors had already arrived.

The room into which we had been ushered was fitted up as a sort of study. The furniture was very poor and scanty, the carpet was old, and the only ornaments on the walls were a few tattered prints yellow with age.

As soon as ever we came in, Mr. Southby, the lawyer, came forward and spoke.

"We are met here today," he said, "as you are all of course aware, to carry out the clause of Mr. Bovey's last will and testament. What reasons prompted him to make these extraordinary conditions we do not know; we only know that we are bound to carry them out. In a safe in his bedroom there is, according to his own statement, a large sum of money in gold, which is to be the property of the one of these three gentlemen whose weight shall nearest approach to the weight of the gold. Messrs. Hutchinson and Company have been kind enough to supply one of their latest weighing machines, which has been carefully checked, and now if you three gentlemen will kindly come with me into the next room we will begin the business at once. Perhaps you, Dr. Lonsdale, as a medical man, will be kind enough to accompany us."

Leaving Miss Cusack and Miss Ransom we then went into the old man's bedroom, where the three claimants undressed and were carefully weighed. I append their respective weights, which I noted down:

Graham	13 stone	9 lbs. 6 oz.
Tyndall	11 stone	6 lbs. 3 oz.
Wimburne	12 stone	11 lbs.

The three candidates having resumed their attire, Miss Cusack and Miss Ransom were summoned, and the lawyer, drawing out a bunch of keys, went across to a large iron safe which had been built into the wall.

We all pressed round him, every one anxious to get the first glimpse of the old man's hoard. The lawyer turned the key, shot back the lock, and flung open the heavy doors. We found that the safe was literally packed with small canvas bags—indeed, so full was it that as the doors swung open two of the bags fell to the floor with a heavy crunching noise. Mr. Southby lifted them up, and then cutting the strings of one, opened it. It was full of bright sovereigns.

An exclamation burst from us all. If all those bags contained gold there was a fine fortune awaiting the successful candidate! The business was now begun in earnest. The lawyer rapidly extracted bag after bag, untied the string, and shot the contents with a crash into the great copper scale pan, while the attendant kept adding weights to the other side to balance it, calling out the amounts as he did so. No one spoke, but our eyes were fixed as if by some strange fascination on the pile of yellow metal that rose higher and higher each moment.

As the weight reached one hundred and fifty pounds, I

heard the old servant behind me utter a smothered oath. I turned and glanced at him; he was staring at the gold with a fierce expression of disappointment and avarice. He at any rate was out of the reckoning, as at eleven stone six, or one hundred and sixty pounds, he could be nowhere near the weight of the sovereigns, there being still eight more bags to untie.

The competition, therefore, now lay between Wimburne and Graham. The latter's face bore strong marks of the agitation which consumed him: the veins stood out like cords on his forehead, and his lips trembled. It would evidently be a near thing, and the suspense was almost intolerable. The lawyer continued to deliberately add to the pile. As the last bag was shot into the scale, the attendant put four ten-pound weights into the other side. It was too much. The gold rose at once. He took one off, and then the two great pans swayed slowly up and down, finally coming to a dead stop.

"Exactly one hundred and eighty pounds, gentlemen," he cried, and a shout went up from us all. Wimburne at twelve stone eleven, or one hundred and seventy-nine pounds, had won.

I turned and shook him by the hand.

"I congratulate you most heartily," I cried. "Now let us calculate the amount of your fortune."

I took a piece of paper from my pocket and made a rough calculation. Taking £56 to the pound avoirdupois, there were at least ten thousand and eighty sovereigns in the scale before us.

"I can hardly believe it," cried Miss Ransom.

I saw her gazing down at the gold, then she looked up into her lover's face.

"Is it true?" she said, panting as she spoke.

"Yes, it is true," he answered. Then he dropped his voice. "It removes all difficulties," I heard him whisper to her.

Her eyes filled with tears, and she turned aside to conceal her emotion.

"There is no doubt whatever as to your ownership of this money, Mr. Wimburne," said the lawyer, "and now the next thing is to ensure its safe transport to the bank."

As soon as the amount of the gold had been made known, Graham, without bidding goodbye to anyone, abruptly left the room, and I assisted the rest of the men in shovelling the sovereigns into a stout canvas bag, which we then lifted and placed in a four-wheeled cab which had arrived for the purpose of conveying the gold to the city.

"Surely someone is going to accompany Mr. Wimburne?" said Miss Cusack at this juncture. "My dear Edgar," she continued, "you are not going to be so mad as to go alone?"

To my surprise, Wimburne coloured, and then gave a laugh of annoyance.

"What could possibly happen to me?" he said. "Nobody knows that I am carrying practically my own weight in gold into the city."

"If Mr. Wimburne wishes I will go with him," said Tyndall, now coming forward. The old man had to all appearance got over his disappointment, and spoke eagerly.

"The thing is fair and square," he added. "I am sorry I did not win, but I'd rather you had it, sir, than Mr. Graham. Yes, that I would, and I congratulate you, sir."

"Thank you, Tyndall," replied Wimburne, "and if you like to come with me I shall be very glad of your company."

The bag of sovereigns being placed in the cab, Wimburne bade us all a hasty goodbye, told Miss Ransom that he would call to see her at Miss Cusack's house that evening, and, accompanied by Tyndall, started off. As we watched the cab turn the corner I heard Miss Ransom utter a sigh.

"I do hope it will be all right," she said, looking at me. "Don't you think it is a risky thing to drive with so much gold through London?"

I laughed in order to reassure her.

"Oh, no, it is perfectly safe," I answered, "safer perhaps than if the gold were conveyed in a more pretentious vehicle. There is nothing to announce the fact that it is bearing ten thousand and eighty sovereigns to the bank."

A moment or two later I left the two ladies and returned to my interrupted duties. The affair of the weighing, the strange clause in the will, Miss Ransom's eager pathetic face, Wimburne's manifest anxiety, had all impressed me considerably, and I could scarcely get the affair off my mind. I hoped that the young couple would now be married quickly, and I could not help being heartily glad that Graham had lost, for I had by no means taken to his appearance.

My work occupied me during the greater part of the afternoon, and I did not get back again to my own house until about six o'clock. When I did so I was told to my utter amazement that Miss Cusack had arrived and was waiting to see me with great impatience. I went at once into my consulting room, where I found her pacing restlessly up and down.

"What is the matter?" I asked.

"Matter!" she cried; "have you not heard? Why, it has been cried in the streets already—the money is gone, was stolen on the way to London. There was a regular highway robbery in the Richmond Road, in broad daylight too. The facts are simply these: Two men in a dogcart met the cab, shot the driver, and after a desperate struggle, in which Edgar Wimburne was badly hurt, seized the gold and drove off. The thing was planned, of course—planned to a moment."

"But what about Tyndall?" I asked.

"He was probably in the plot. All we know is that he has escaped and has not been heard of since."

"But what a daring thing!" I cried. "They will be caught, of course; they cannot have gone far with the money."

"You do not understand their tricks, Dr. Lonsdale; but I do," was her quick answer, "and I venture to guarantee that if we do not get that money back before the morning, Edgar Wimburne has seen the last of his fortune. Now, I mean to follow up this business, all night if necessary."

I did not reply. Her dark, bright eyes were blazing with excitement, and she began to pace up and down.

"You must come with me," she continued; "you promised to help me if the necessity should arise."

"And I will keep my word," I answered.

"That is an immense relief." She gave a deep sigh as she spoke.

"What about Miss Ransom?" I asked.

"Oh, I have left Letty at home. She is too excited to be of the slightest use."

"One other question," I interrupted, "and then I am completely at your service. You mentioned that Wimburne was hurt."

"Yes, but I believe not seriously. He has been taken to the hospital. He has already given evidence, but it amounts to very little. The robbery took place in a lonely part of the road, and just for the moment there was no one in sight."

"Well," I said, as she paused, "you have some scheme in your head, have you not?"

"I have," she answered. "The fact is this: from the very first I feared some such catastrophe as has really taken place. I have known Mr. Graham for a long time, and—distrusted him. He has passed for a man of position and means, but I believe him to be a mere adventurer.

There is little doubt that all his future depended on his getting this fortune. I saw his face when the scales declared in Edgar Wimburne's favour—but there! I must ask you to accompany me to Hammersmith immediately. On the way I will tell you more."

"We will go in my carriage," I said. "It happens to be at the door."

We started directly. As we had left the more noisy streets Miss Cusack continued:

"You remember the advertisement I showed you yesterday morning?"

I nodded.

"You naturally could make no sense of it, but to me it was fraught with much meaning. This is by no means the first advertisement which has appeared under the name of Joshua Linklater. I have observed similar advertisements, and all, strange to say, in connection with founder's work, appearing at intervals in the big dailies for the last four or five months, but my attention was never specially directed to them until a circumstance occurred of which I am about to tell you."

"What is that?" I asked.

"Three weeks ago a certain investigation took me to Hammersmith in order to trace a stolen necklace. It was necessary that I should go to a small pawnbroker's shop—the man's name was Higgins. In my queer work, Dr. Lonsdale, I employ many disguises. That night, dressed quietly as a domestic servant on her evening out, I entered the pawnbroker's. I wore a thick veil and a plainly trimmed hat. I entered one of the little boxes where one stands to pawn goods, and waited for the man to appear.

"For the moment he was engaged, and looking through a small window in the door I saw to my astonishment that the pawnbroker was in earnest conversation with no less a person than Mr. Campbell Graham. This was the last place I should have expected to see Mr.

Graham in, and I immediately used both my eyes and ears. I heard the pawnbroker address him as Linklater.

"Immediately the memory of the advertisements under that name flashed through my brain. From the attitude of the two men there was little doubt that they were discussing a matter of the utmost importance, and as Mr. Graham, alias Linklater, was leaving the shop, I distinctly overheard the following words: 'In all probability Bovey will die tonight. I may or may not be successful, but in order to insure against loss we must be prepared. It is not safe for me to come here often—look out for advertisement—it will be in the agony column.'

"I naturally thought such words very strange, and when I heard of Mr. Bovey's death and read an account of the queer will, it seemed to me that I began to see daylight. It was also my business to look out for the advertisement, and when I saw it yesterday morning you may well imagine that my keenest suspicions were aroused. I immediately suspected foul play, but could do nothing except watch and await events. Directly I heard the details of the robbery I wired to the inspector at Hammersmith to have Higgins's house watched. You remember that Mr. Wimburne left Kew in the cab at ten o'clock; the robbery must therefore have taken place some time about ten-twenty. The news reached me shortly after eleven, and my wire was sent off about eleven-fifteen. I mention these hours, as much may turn upon them. Just before I came to you I received a wire from the police station containing startling news. This was sent off about five-thirty. Here, you had better read it."

As she spoke she took a telegram from her pocket and handed it to me. I glanced over the words it contained.

Just heard that cart was seen at Higgins's this morning. Man and assistant arrested on suspicion. House searched. No gold there. Please come down at once.

"So they have bolted with it?" I said.

"That we shall see," was her reply.

Shortly afterwards we arrived at the police station. The inspector was waiting for us, and took us at once into a private room.

"I am glad you were able to come, Miss Cusack," he said, bowing with great respect to the handsome girl.

"Pray tell me what you have done," she answered; "there is not a moment to spare."

"When I received your wire," he said, "I immediately placed a man on duty to watch Higgins's shop, but evidently before I did this the cart must have arrived and gone—the news with regard to the cart being seen outside Higgins's shop did not reach me till four-thirty. On receiving it I immediately arrested both Higgins and his assistant, and we searched the house from attic to cellar, but have found no gold whatever. There is little doubt that the pawnbroker received the gold, and has already removed it to another quarter."

"Did you find a furnace in the basement?" suddenly asked Miss Cusack.

"We did," he replied, in some astonishment; "but why do you ask?"

To my surprise Miss Cusack took out of her pocket the advertisement which she had shown me that morning and handed it to the inspector. The man read the queer words aloud in a slow and wondering voice:

Send more sand and charcoal dust. Core and mould ready for casting—JOSHUA LINKLATER.

"I can make nothing of it, miss," he said, glancing at Miss Cusack. "These words seem to me to have something to do with founder's work."

"I believe they have," was her eager reply. "It is also highly probable that they have something to do with the furnace in the basement of Higgins's shop."

"I do not know what you are talking about, miss, but you have something at the back of your head which does not appear."

"I have," she answered, "and in order to confirm certain suspicions I wish to search the house."

"But the place has just been searched by us," was the man's almost testy answer. "It is impossible that a mass of gold should be there and be overlooked: every square inch of space has been accounted for."

"Who is in the house now?"

"No one; the place is locked up, and one of our men is on duty."

"What size is the furnace?"

"Unusually large," was the inspector's answer.

Miss Cusack gave a smile which almost immediately vanished.

"We are wasting time," she said; "let us go there immediately."

"I must do so, of course, if nothing else will satisfy you, miss; but I assure you—"

"Oh, don't let us waste any more time in arguing," said Miss Cusak, her impatience now getting the better of her. "I have a reason for what I do, and must visit the pawnbroker's immediately."

The man hesitated no longer, but took a bunch of keys down from the wall. A blaze of light from a public-house guided us to the pawnbroker's, which bore the well-known sign, the three golden balls. These were just visible through the fog above us. The inspector nodded to the man on duty, and unlocking the door we entered a narrow passage into which the swing doors of several smaller compartments opened. The inspector struck a match, and, lighting the lantern, looked at Miss Cusack, as much as to say, "What do you propose to do now?"

"Take me to the room where the furnace is," said the lady.

"Come this way," he replied.

We turned at once in the direction of the stairs which led to the basement, and entered a room on the right. At the further end was an open range which had evidently been enlarged in order to allow the consumption of a great quantity of fuel, and upon it now stood an iron vessel, shaped as a chemist's crucible. Considerable heat still radiated from it. Miss Cusack peered inside, then she slowly commenced raking out the ashes with an iron rod, examining them closely and turning them over and over. Two or three white fragments she examined with peculiar care.

"One thing at least is abundantly clear," she said at last; "gold has been melted here, and within a very short time; whether it was the sovereigns or not we have yet to discover."

"But surely, Miss Cusack," said the inspector, "no one would be rash enough to destroy sovereigns."

"I am thinking of Joshua Linklater's advertisement," she said. " '*Send more sand and charcoal dust.*' This," she continued, once more examining the white fragments, "is undoubtedly sand."

She said nothing further, but went back to the ground floor and now commenced a systematic search on her own account.

At last we reached the top floor, where the pawnbroker and his assistant had evidently slept. Here Miss Cusack walked at once to the window and flung it open. She gazed out for a minute, and then turned to face us. Her eyes looked brighter than ever, and a certain smile played about her face.

"Well, miss," said the police inspector, "we have now searched the whole house, and I hope you are satisfied."

"I am," she replied.

"The gold is not here, miss."

"We will see," she said. As she spoke she turned once

more and bent slightly out, as if to look down through the murky air at the street below.

The inspector gave an impatient exclamation.

"If you have quite finished, miss, we must return to the station," he said. "I am expecting some men from Scotland Yard to go into this affair."

"I do not think they will have much to do," she answered, "except, indeed, to arrest the criminal." As she spoke she leant a little further out of the window, and then withdrawing her head said quietly, "Yes, we may as well go back now; I have quite finished. Things are exactly as I expected to find them; we can take the gold away with us."

Both the inspector and I stared at her in utter amazement.

"What do you mean, Miss Cusack?" I cried.

"What I say," she answered, and now she gave a light laugh; "the gold is here, close to us; we have only to take it away. Come," she added, "look out, both of you. Why, you are both gazing at it."

I glanced round in utter astonishment. My expression of face was reproduced in that of the inspector's.

"Look," she said, "what do you call that?" As she spoke she pointed to the sign that hung outside—the sign of the three balls.

"Lean out and feel that lower ball," she said to the inspector.

He stretched out his arm, and as his fingers touched it he started back.

"Why, it is hot," he said; "what in the world does it mean?"

"It means the lost gold," replied Miss Cusack; "it has been cast as that ball. I said that the advertisement would give me the necessary clue, and it has done so. Yes, the lost fortune is hanging outside the house. The gold was melted in the crucible downstairs and cast as this ball between twelve o'clock and four-thirty today. Remember it was after four-thirty that you arrested the pawnbroker and his assistant."

To verify her extraordinary words was the work of a few moments. Owing to its great weight, the inspector and I had some difficulty in detaching the ball from its hook. At the same time we noticed that a very strong stay, in the shape of an iron-wire rope, had been attached to the iron frame from which the three balls hung.

"You will find, I am sure," said Miss Cusack, "that this ball is not of solid gold; if it were, it would not be the size of the other two balls. It has probably been cast round a centre of plaster of Paris to give it the same size as the others. This explains the advertisement with regard to the charcoal and sand. A ball of that size in pure gold would weigh nearly three hundred pounds, or twenty stone."

"Well," said the inspector, "of all the curious devices that I have ever seen or heard of, this beats the lot. But what did they do with the real ball? They must have put it somewhere."

"They burnt it in the furnace, of course," she answered; "these balls, as you know, are only wood covered with gold paint. Yes, it was a clever idea, worthy of the brain of Mr. Graham; and it might have hung there for weeks and been seen by thousands passing daily, till Mr. Higgins was released from imprisonment, as nothing whatever could be proved against him."

Owing to Miss Cusack's testimony, Graham was arrested that night, and, finding that circumstances were dead against him, he confessed the whole. For long years he was one of a gang of coiners, but managed to pass as a gentleman of position. He knew old Bovey well, and had heard him speak of the curious will he had made. Knowing of this, he determined, at any risk, to secure the fortune, intending, when he had obtained it, to immediately leave the country. He had discovered the exact amount of the money which he would leave behind him, and had gone carefully into the weight which such a number of sovereigns would make. He knew at once that Tyndall would be out of the reckoning, and that the competition would really be between himself and Wimburne. To provide against the contingency of Wimburne's being the lucky man, he had planned the robbery; the gold was to be melted, and made into a real golden ball, which was to hang over the pawnshop until suspicion had died away.

EMMUSKA, BARONESS ORCZY (1864–1947), was of noble Hungarian descent. Forced to flee her native country, she arrived with her family to live in England when she was eight years old. Her earliest career was as an artist, a profession that she shared with her husband, Montagu Barstow. It was he who aided and encouraged her in the creation of her most famous character—Sir Percy Blakeney, "the demn'd elusive" Scarlet Pimpernel—and who urged her to make the attempt at writing detective stories. Her other sleuths include the string-knotting, sedentary Old Man in the Corner and the unscrupulous lawyer Patrick Mulligan, nicknamed "Skin O' My Tooth."

Lady Molly is attached to the Female Department of Scotland Yard, where, as her adoring companion Mary relates, "she has worked her way upwards, analyzing and studying, exercising her powers of intuition and of deduction, until . . . she is considered, by chiefs and men alike, the greatest authority among them on criminal investigation." Her origins are shrouded in mystery, and her private life is marred by the tragic incarceration of the man to whom she is secretly married, Captain Hubert de Mazereen—sentenced to twenty years penal servitude for a crime he did not commit. Having joined the police in order to achieve her obsessive goal of proving him innocent, she eventually accomplishes this, in the last chapters of the single book relating her adventures, *Lady Molly of Scotland Yard* (1910).

The Fordwych Castle Mystery

by Emmuska, Baroness Orczy

Can you wonder that, when some of the ablest of our fellows at the Yard were at their wits' ends to know what to do, the chief instinctively turned to Lady Molly?

Surely the Fordwych Castle Mystery, as it was universally called, was a case which more than any other required feminine tact, intuition, and all those qualities of which my dear lady possessed more than her usual share.

With the exception of Mr. McKinley, the lawyer, and young Jack d'Alboukirk, there were only women connected with the case.

If you have studied Debrett at all, you know as well as I do that the peerage is one of those old English ones which date back some six hundred years, and that the present Lady d'Alboukirk is a baroness in her own right, the title and estates descending to heirs-general. If you have perused that same interesting volume carefully, you will also have discovered that the late Lord d'Alboukirk had two daughters, the eldest, Clementina Cecilia—the present Baroness, who succeeded him—the other, Margaret Florence, who married in 1884 Jean Laurent Duplessis, a Frenchman whom Debrett vaguely describes as "of Pondicherry, India," and of whom she had issue two daughters, Henriette Marie, heir now to the ancient barony of d'Alboukirk of Fordwych, and Joan, born two years later.

There seems to have been some mystery or romance attached to this marriage of the Honourable Margaret Florence d'Alboukirk to the dashing young officer of the Foreign Legion. Old Lord d'Alboukirk at the time was British Ambassador in Paris, and he seems to have had grave objections to the union, but Miss Margaret, openly flouting her father's displeasure, and throwing prudence to the winds, ran away from home one fine day with Captain Duplessis, and from Pondicherry wrote a curt letter to her relatives telling them of her marriage with the man she loved best in all the world. Old Lord d'Alboukirk never got over his daughter's wilfulness. She had been his favourite, it appears, and her secret marriage and deceit practically broke his heart. He was kind to her, however, to the end, and when the first baby girl was born and the young pair seemed to be in straitened circumstances, he made them an allowance until the day of his daughter's death, which occurred three years after her elopement, on the birth of her second child.

When, on the death of her father, the Honourable Clementina Cecilia came into the title and fortune, she seemed to have thought it her duty to take some interest in her late sister's eldest child, who, failing her own marriage, and issue, was heir to the barony of d'Alboukirk. Thus it was that Miss Henriette Marie Duplessis came, with her father's consent, to live with her aunt at Fordwych Castle. Debrett will tell you, moreover, that in 1901 she assumed the name of d'Alboukirk, in lieu of her own, by royal licence. Failing her, the title and estate would devolve firstly on her sister Joan, and subsequently on a fairly distant cousin, Captain John d'Alboukirk, at present a young officer in the Guards.

According to her servants, the present Baroness D'Alboukirk is very self-willed, but otherwise neither more nor less eccentric than any north-country old maid would be who had such an exceptional position to keep up in the social world. The one soft trait in her otherwise not very lovable character is her great affection for her late sister's child. Miss Henriette Duplessis d'Alboukirk has inherited from her French father dark eyes and hair and a somewhat swarthy complexion, but no doubt it is from her English ancestry that she has derived a somewhat masculine frame and a very great fondness for all outdoor pursuits. She is very athletic, knows how to fence and to box, rides to hounds, and is a remarkably good shot.

From all accounts, the first hint of trouble in that gorgeous home was coincident with the arrival at Fordwych of a young, very pretty girl visitor, who was attended by her maid, a half-caste woman, dark-complexioned and surly of temper, but obviously of doglike devotion towards her young mistress. This visit seems to have come as a surprise to the entire household at Fordwych Castle, her ladyship having said nothing about it until the very morning that the guests were expected. She then briefly ordered one of the housemaids to get a bedroom ready for a young lady, and to put up a small camp bedstead in an adjoining dressing room. Even Miss Henriette seems to have been taken by surprise at the announcement of this visit, for, according to Jane Taylor, the housemaid in question, there was a violent word-passage between the old lady and her niece, the latter winding up an excited speech with the words:

"At any rate, aunt, there won't be room for both of us in this house!" After which she flounced out of the room, banging the door behind her.

Very soon the household was made to understand that the newcomer was none other than Miss Joan Duplessis, Miss Henriette's younger sister. It appears that Captain

Duplessis had recently died in Pondicherry, and that the young girl then wrote to her aunt, Lady d'Alboukirk, claiming her help and protection, which the old lady naturally considered it her duty to extend to her.

It appears that Miss Joan was very unlike her sister, as she was petite and fair, more English-looking than foreign, and had pretty, dainty ways which soon endeared her to the household. The devotion existing between her and the half-caste woman she had brought from India was, moreover, unique.

It seems, however, that from the moment these newcomers came into the house, dissensions, often degenerating into violent quarrels, became the order of the day. Henriette seemed to have taken a strong dislike to her younger sister, and most particularly to the latter's dark attendant, who was vaguely known in the house as Roonah.

That some events of serious import were looming ahead, the servants at Fordwych were pretty sure. The butler and footmen at dinner heard scraps of conversation which sounded very ominous. There was talk of "lawyers," of "proofs," of "marriage and birth certificates," quickly suppressed when the servants happened to be about. Her ladyship looked terribly anxious and worried, and she and Miss Henriette spent long hours closeted together in a small boudoir, whence proceeded ominous sounds of heart-rending weeping on her ladyship's part, and angry and violent words from Miss Henriette.

Mr. McKinley, the eminent lawyer from London, came down two or three times to Fordwych, and held long conversations with her ladyship, after which the latter's eyes were very swollen and red. The household thought it more than strange that Roonah, the Indian servant, was almost invariably present at these interviews between Mr. McKinley, her ladyship, and Miss Joan. Otherwise the woman kept herself very much aloof; she spoke very little, hardly took any notice of anyone save of her ladyship and of her young mistress, and the outbursts of Miss Henriette's temper seemed to leave her quite unmoved. A strange fact was that she had taken a sudden and great fancy for frequenting a small Roman Catholic convent chapel which was distant about half a mile from the Castle, and presently it was understood that Roonah, who had been a Parsee, had been converted by the attendant priest to the Roman Catholic faith.

All this happened, mind you, within the last two or three months; in fact, Miss Joan had been in the Castle exactly twelve weeks when Captain Jack d'Alboukirk came to pay his cousin one of his periodical visits. From the first he seems to have taken a great fancy to his cousin Joan, and soon everyone noticed that this fancy was rapidly ripening into love. It was equally certain that from that moment dissensions between the two sisters became more frequent and more violent; the generally accepted opinion being that Miss Henriette was jealous of Joan, whilst Lady d'Alboukirk herself, for some unexplainable reason, seems to have regarded this love-making with marked disfavour.

Then came the tragedy.

One morning Joan ran downstairs, pale, and trembling from head to foot, moaning and sobbing as she ran:

"Roonah!—my poor old Roonah!—I knew it—I knew it!"

Captain Jack happened to meet her at the foot of the stairs. He pressed her with questions, but the girl was unable to speak. She merely pointed mutely to the floor above. The young man, genuinely alarmed, ran quickly upstairs; he threw open the door leading to Roonah's room, and there, to his horror, he saw the unfortunate woman lying across the small camp bedstead, with a handkerchief over her nose and mouth, and her throat cut.

The sight was horrible.

Poor Roonah was obviously dead.

Without losing his presence of mind, Captain Jack quietly shut the door again, after urgently begging Joan to compose herself, and to try to keep up, at any rate until the local doctor could be sent for and the terrible news gently broken to Lady d'Alboukirk.

The doctor, hastily summoned, arrived some twenty minutes later. He could but confirm Joan's and Captain Jack's fears. Roonah was indeed dead—in fact, she had been dead some hours.

From the very first, mind you, the public took a more than usually keen interest in this mysterious occurrence. The evening papers on the very day of the murder were ablaze with flaming headlines such as:

THE TRAGEDY AT FORDWYCH CASTLE

Mysterious Murder of an Important Witness
Grave Charges Against Persons in High Life

and so forth.

As time went on, the mystery deepened more and more, and I suppose Lady Molly must have had an inkling that sooner or later the chief would have to rely on her help and advice, for she sent me down to attend the inquest, and gave me strict orders to keep eyes and ears open for every detail in connection with the crime—however trivial it might seem. She herself remained in town, awaiting a summons from the chief.

The inquest was held in the dining room of Fordwych Castle, and the noble hall was crowded to its utmost when the coroner and jury finally took their seats, after having viewed the body of the poor murdered woman upstairs.

The scene was dramatic enough to please any novelist, and an awed hush descended over the crowd when, just before the proceedings began, a door was thrown open, and in walked—stiff and erect—the Baroness d'Alboukirk, escorted by her niece, Miss Henriette, and closely followed by her cousin, Captain Jack, of the Guards.

The old lady's face was as indifferent and haughty as usual, and so was that of her athletic niece. Captain Jack, on the other hand, looked troubled and flushed. Everyone noted that, directly he entered the room, his eyes sought a small, dark figure that sat silent and immovable beside the portly figure of the great lawyer, Mr. Hubert McKinley. This was Miss Joan Duplessis, in a plain black stuff gown, her young face pale and tear-stained.

Dr. Walker, the local practitioner, was, of course, the first witness called. His evidence was purely medical. He deposed to having made an examination of the body, and stated that he found that a handkerchief saturated with chloroform had been pressed to the woman's nostrils, probably while she was asleep, her throat having subsequently been cut with a sharp knife; death must have been instantaneous, as the poor thing did not appear to have struggled at all.

In answer to a question from the coroner, the doctor said that no great force or violence would be required for the gruesome deed, since the victim was undeniably unconscious when it was done. At the same time it argued unusual coolness and determination.

The handkerchief was produced, also the knife. The former was a bright-coloured one, stated to be the property of the deceased. The latter was a foreign, old-fashioned hunting knife, one of a panoply of small arms and other weapons which adorned a corner of the hall. It had been found by Detective Elliott in a clump of gorse on the adjoining golf links. There could be no question that it had been used by the murderer for his fell purpose, since at the time it was found it still bore traces of blood.

Captain Jack was the next witness called. He had very little to say, as he merely saw the body from across the room, and immediately closed the door again and, having begged his cousin to compose herself, called his own valet and sent him off for the doctor.

Some of the staff of Fordwych Castle were called, all of whom testified to the Indian woman's curious taciturnity, which left her quite isolated among her fellow servants. Miss Henriette's maid, however, Jane Partlett, had one or two more interesting facts to record. She seems to have been more intimate with the deceased woman than anyone else, and on one occasion, at least, had quite a confidential talk with her.

"She talked chiefly about her mistress," said Jane, in answer to a question from the coroner, "to whom she was most devoted. She told me that she loved her so, she would readily die for her. Of course, I thought that silly-like, and just mad, foreign talk, but Roonah was very angry when I laughed at her, and then she undid her dress in front, and showed me some papers which were sewn in the lining of her dress. 'All these papers my little missee's fortune,' she said to me. 'Roonah guard these with her life. Someone must kill Roonah before taking them from her!'

"This was about six weeks ago," continued Jane, whilst a strange feeling of awe seemed to descend upon all those present whilst the girl spoke. "Lately she became much more silent, and, on my once referring to the papers, she turned on me savage-like and told me to hold my tongue."

Asked if she had mentioned the incident of the papers to anyone, Jane replied in the negative.

"Except to Miss Henriette, of course," she added, after a slight moment of hesitation.

Throughout all these preliminary examinations Lady d'Alboukirk, sitting between her cousin Captain Jack and her niece Henriette, had remained quite silent in an erect attitude expressive of haughty indifference. Henriette, on the other hand, looked distinctly bored. Once or twice she had yawned audibly, which caused quite a feeling of anger against her among the spectators. Such callousness in the midst of so mysterious a tragedy, and when her own sister was obviously in such deep sorrow, impressed everyone very unfavourably. It was well known that the young lady had had a fencing lesson just before the inquest in the room immediately below that where Roonah lay dead, and that within an hour of the discovery of the tragedy she was calmly playing golf.

Then Miss Joan Duplessis was called.

When the young girl stepped forward there was that awed hush in the room which usually falls upon an attentive audience when the curtain is about to rise on the crucial act of a dramatic play. But she was calm and self-possessed, and wonderfully pathetic-looking in her deep black and with the obvious lines of sorrow which the sad death of a faithful friend had traced on her young face.

In answer to the coroner, she gave her name as Joan Clarissa Duplessis, and briefly stated that until the day of her servant's death she had been a resident at Fordwych Castle, but that since then she had left that temporary home, and had taken up her abode at the d'Alboukirk Arms, a quiet little hostelry on the outskirts of the town.

There was a distinct feeling of astonishment on the part of those who were not aware of this fact, and then the coroner said kindly:

"You were born, I think, in Pondicherry, in India, and are the younger daughter of Captain and Mrs. Duplessis, who was own sister to her ladyship?"

"I was born in Pondicherry," replied the young girl, quietly, "and I am the only legitimate child of the late Captain and Mrs. Duplessis, own sister to her ladyship."

A wave of sensation, quickly suppressed by the coroner, went through the crowd at these words. The emphasis which the witness had put on the word "legitimate" could not be mistaken, and everyone felt that here must lie the clue to the so far impenetrable mystery of the Indian woman's death.

All eyes were now turned on old Lady d'Alboukirk and on her niece Henriette, but the two ladies were carrying on a whispered conversation together, and had apparently ceased to take any further interest in the proceedings.

"The deceased was your confidential maid, was she not?" asked the coroner, after a slight pause.

"Yes."

"She came over to England with you recently?"

"Yes; she had to accompany me in order to help me to make good my claim to being my late mother's only legitimate child, and therefore the heir to the barony of d'Alboukirk."

Her voice had trembled a little as she said this, but now, as breathless silence reigned in the room, she seemed to make a visible effort to control herself, and, replying to the coroner's question, she gave a clear and satisfactory account of her terrible discovery of her faithful servant's death. Her evidence had lasted about a quarter of an hour or so, when suddenly the coroner put the momentous question to her:

"Do you know anything about the papers which the deceased woman carried about her person, and reference to which has already been made?"

"Yes," she replied quietly; "they were the proofs relating to my claim. My father, Captain Duplessis, had in early youth, and before he met my mother, contracted a secret union with a half-caste woman, who was Roonah's own sister. Being tired of her, he chose to repudiate her—she had no children—but the legality of the marriage was never for a moment in question. After that, he married my mother, and his first wife subsequently died, chiefly of a broken heart; but her death only occurred two months *after* the birth of my sister Henriette. My father, I think, had been led to believe that his first wife had died some two years previously, and he was no doubt very much shocked when he realised what a grievous wrong he had done our mother. In order to mend matters somewhat, he and she went through a new form of marriage—a legal one this time—and my father paid a lot of money to Roonah's relatives to have the matter hushed up. Less than a year after this second—and only legal—marriage, I was born and my mother died."

"Then these papers of which so much has been said—what did they consist of?"

"There were the marriage certificates of my father's first wife—and two sworn statements as to her death, two months *after* the birth of my sister Henriette; one by Dr. Rénaud, who was at the time a well-known medical man in Pondicherry, and the other by Roonah herself, who had held her dying sister in her arms. Dr. Rénaud is dead, and now Roonah has been murdered, and all the proofs have gone with her—"

Her voice broke in a passion of sobs, which, with manifest self-control, she quickly suppressed. In that crowded court you could have heard a pin drop, so great was the tension of intense excitement and attention.

"Then those papers remained in your maid's possession? Why was that?" asked the coroner.

"I did not dare to carry the papers about with me," said the witness, while a curious look of terror crept into her young face as she looked across at her aunt and sister. "Roonah would not part with them. She carried them in the lining of her dress, and at night they were all under her pillow. After her—her death, and when Dr. Walker had left, I thought it my duty to take possession of the papers which meant my whole future to me, and which I desired then to place in Mr. McKinley's charge. But, though I carefully searched the bed and all the clothing by my poor Roonah's side, I did not find the papers. They were gone."

I won't attempt to describe to you the sensation caused by the deposition of this witness. All eyes wandered from her pale young face to that of her sister, who sat almost opposite to her, shrugging her athletic shoulders and gazing at the pathetic young figure before her with callous and haughty indifference.

"Now, putting aside the question of the papers for the moment," said the coroner, after a pause, "do you happen to know anything of your late servant's private life? Had she an enemy, or perhaps a lover?"

"No," replied the girl; "Roonah's whole life was centred in me and in my claim. I had often begged her to place our papers in Mr. McKinley's charge, but she would trust no one. I wish she had obeyed me," here moaned the poor girl involuntarily, "and I should not have lost what means my whole future to me, and the being who loved me best in all the world would not have been so foully murdered."

Of course, it was terrible to see this young girl thus instinctively, and surely unintentionally, proffering so awful an accusation against those who stood so near to her. That the whole case had become hopelessly involved and mysterious, nobody could deny. Can you imagine the mental picture formed in the mind of all present by the story, so pathetically told, of this girl who had come over to England in order to make good her claim which she felt to be just, and who, in one fell swoop, saw that claim rendered very difficult to prove through the dastardly murder of her principal witness?

That the claim was seriously jeopardised by the death of Roonah and the disappearance of the papers, was made very clear, mind you, through the statements of Mr. McKinley, the lawyer. He could not say very much, of course, and his statements could never have been taken as actual proof, because Roonah and Joan had never fully trusted him and had never actually placed the proofs of the claim in his hands. He certainly had seen the marriage certificate of Captain Duplessis's first wife, and a copy of this, as he very properly stated, could easily be obtained. The woman seems to have died during the great cholera epidemic of 1881, when, owing to the great number of deaths which occurred, the deceit and concealment practised by the natives at Pondicherry, and the supineness of the French Government, death certificates were very casually and often incorrectly made out.

Roonah had come over to England ready to swear that her sister had died in her arms two months after the birth of Captain Duplessis's eldest child, and there was the sworn testimony of Dr. Rénaud, since dead. These affidavits Mr. McKinley had seen and read.

Against that, the only proof which now remained of the justice of Joan Duplessis's claim was the fact that her mother and father went through a second form of marriage sometime *after* the birth of their first child, Henriette. This fact was not denied, and, of course, it could be easily proved, if necessary, but even then it would in no way be conclusive. It implied the presence of a doubt in Captain Duplessis's mind, a doubt which the second marriage ceremony may have served to set at rest; but it in no way established the illegitimacy of his eldest daughter.

In fact, the more Mr. McKinley spoke, the more convinced did everyone become that the theft of the papers had everything to do with the murder of the unfortunate Roonah. She would not part with the proofs which meant her mistress's fortune, and she paid for her devotion with her life.

Several more witnesses were called after that. The servants were closely questioned, the doctor was recalled, but, in spite of long and arduous efforts, the coroner and jury could not bring a single real fact to light beyond those already stated.

The Indian woman had been murdered!

The papers which she always carried about her body had disappeared.

Beyond that, nothing! An impenetrable wall of silence and mystery!

The butler at Fordwych Castle had certainly missed the knife with which Roonah had been killed from its accustomed place on the morning after the murder had been committed, but not before, and the mystery further gained in intensity from the fact that the only purchase of chloroform in the district had been traced to the murdered woman herself.

She had gone down to the local chemist one day some two or three weeks previously, and shown him a prescription for cleansing the hair which required some chloroform in it. He gave her a very small quantity in a tiny bottle, which was subsequently found empty on her own dressing table. No one at Fordwych Castle could swear to having heard any unaccustomed noise during that memorable night. Even Joan, who slept in the room adjoining that where the unfortunate Roonah lay, said she had heard nothing unusual. But then, the door of communication between the two rooms was shut, and the murderer had been quick and silent.

Thus this extraordinary inquest drew to a close, leaving in its train an air of dark suspicion and of unexplainable horror.

The jury returned a verdict of "Wilful murder against some person or persons unknown," and the next moment Lady d'Alboukirk rose, and, leaning on her niece's arm, quietly walked out of the room.

Two of our best men from the Yard, Pegram and Elliott, were left in charge of the case. They remained at Fordwych (the little town close by), as did Miss Joan, who had taken up her permanent abode at the d'Alboukirk

Arms, whilst I returned to town immediately after the inquest. Captain Jack had rejoined his regiment, and apparently the ladies of the Castle had resumed their quiet, luxurious life just the same as heretofore. The old lady led her own somewhat isolated, semi-regal life; Miss Henriette fenced and boxed, played hockey and golf, and over the fine Castle and its haughty inmates there hovered like an ugly bird of prey the threatening presence of a nameless suspicion.

The two ladies might choose to flout public opinion, but public opinion was dead against them. No one dared formulate a charge, but everyone remembered that Miss Henriette had, on the very morning of the murder, been playing golf in the field where the knife was discovered, and that if Miss Joan Duplessis ever failed to make good her claim to the barony of d'Alboukirk, Miss Henriette would remain in undisputed possession. So now, when the ladies drove past in the village street, no one doffed a cap to salute them, and when at church the parson read out the Sixth Commandment, "Thou shalt do no murder," all eyes gazed with fearsome awe at the old Baroness and her niece.

Splendid isolation reigned at Fordwych Castle. The daily papers grew more and more sarcastic at the expense of the Scotland Yard authorities, and the public more and more impatient.

Then it was that the chief grew desperate and sent for Lady Molly, the result of the interview being that I once more made the journey down to Fordwych, but this time in the company of my dear lady, who had received carte blanche from headquarters to do whatever she thought right in the investigation of the mysterious crime.

She and I arrived at Fordwych at 8:00 P.M., after the usual long wait at Newcastle. We put up at the d'Alboukirk Arms, and, over a hasty and very bad supper, Lady Molly allowed me a brief insight into her plans.

"I can see every detail of that murder, Mary," she said earnestly, "just as if I had lived at the Castle all the time. I know exactly where our fellows are wrong, and why they cannot get on. But, although the chief has given me a free hand, what I am going to do is so irregular that if I fail I shall probably get my immediate *congé*, whilst some of the disgrace is bound to stick to you. It is not too late—you may yet draw back, and leave me to act alone."

I looked her straight in the face. Her dark eyes were gleaming; there was the power of second sight in them, or of marvellous intuition of "men and things."

"I'll follow your lead, my Lady Molly," I said quietly.

"Then go to bed now," she replied, with that strange transition of manner which to me was so attractive and to everyone else so unaccountable.

In spite of my protest, she refused to listen to any more talk or to answer any more questions, and, perforce, I had to go to my room. The next morning I saw her graceful figure, immaculately dressed in a perfect tailor-made gown, standing beside my bed at a very early hour.

"Why, what is the time?" I ejaculated, suddenly wide awake.

"Too early for you to get up," she replied quietly. "I am going to early Mass at the Roman Catholic convent close by."

"To Mass at the Roman Catholic convent?"

"Yes. Don't repeat all my words, Mary; it is silly, and wastes time. I have introduced myself in the neighbourhood as the American, Mrs. Silas A. Ogden, whose motor has broken down and is being repaired at Newcastle, while I, its owner, amuse myself by viewing the beauties of the neighbourhood. Being a Roman Catholic, I go to Mass first, and, having met Lady d'Alboukirk once in London, I go to pay her a respectful visit afterwards. When I come back we will have breakfast together. You might try in the meantime to scrape up an acquaintance with Miss Joan Duplessis, who is still staying here, and ask her to join us at breakfast."

She was gone before I could make another remark, and I could but obey her instantly to the letter.

An hour later I saw Miss Joan Duplessis strolling in the hotel garden. It was not difficult to pass the time of day with the young girl, who seemed quite to brighten up at having someone to talk to. We spoke of the weather and so forth, and I steadily avoided the topic of the Fordwych Castle tragedy until the return of Lady Molly at about ten o'clock. She came back looking just as smart, just as self-possessed, as when she had started three hours earlier. Only I, who knew her so well, noted the glitter of triumph in her eyes, and knew that she had not failed. She was accompanied by Pegram, who, however, immediately left her side and went straight into the hotel, whilst she joined us in the garden and, after a few graceful words, introduced herself to Miss Joan Duplessis and asked her to join us in the coffee room upstairs.

The room was empty and we sat down to table, I quivering with excitement and awaiting events. Through the open window I saw Elliott walking rapidly down the village street. Presently the waitress went off, and I being too excited to eat or to speak, Lady Molly carried on a running conversation with Miss Joan, asking her about her life in India and her father, Captain Duplessis. Joan admitted that she had always been her father's favourite.

"He never liked Henriette, somehow," she explained.

Lady Molly asked her when she had first known Roonah.

"She came to the house when my mother died," replied Joan, "and she had charge of me as a baby." At Pondicherry no one had thought it strange that she came as a servant into an officer's house where her own sister had reigned as mistress. Pondicherry is a French settlement, and manners and customs there are often very peculiar.

I ventured to ask her what were her future plans.

"Well," she said, with a great touch of sadness, "I can, of course, do nothing whilst my aunt is alive. I cannot force her to let me live at Fordwych or to acknowledge me as her heir. After her death, if my sister does assume the title and fortune of d'Albourkirk," she added, whilst suddenly a strange look of vengefulness—almost of hatred and cruelty—marred the childlike expression of her face, "then I shall revive the story of the tragedy of Roonah's death, and I hope that public opinion—"

She paused here in her speech, and I, who had been gazing out of the window, turned my eyes on her. She was ashy-pale, staring straight before her; her hands dropped the knife and fork which she had held. Then I saw that Pegram had come into the room, that he had come up to the table and placed a packet of papers in Lady Molly's hand.

I saw it all as in a flash!

There was a loud cry of despair like an animal at bay, a shrill cry, followed by a deep one from Pegram of "No, you don't," and before anyone could prevent her, Joan's graceful young figure stood outlined for a short moment at the open window.

The next moment she had disappeared into the depth below, and we heard a dull thud which nearly froze the blood in my veins.

Pegram ran out of the room, but Lady Molly sat quite still.

"I have succeeded in clearing the innocent," she said quietly; "but the guilty has meted out to herself her own punishment."

"Then it was she?" I murmured, horror-struck.

"Yes. I suspected it from the first," replied Lady Molly

calmly. "It was this conversion of Roonah to Roman Catholicism and her consequent change of manner which gave me the first clue."

"But why—why?" I muttered.

"A simple reason, Mary," she rejoined, tapping the packet of papers with her delicate hand; and, breaking open the string that held the letters, she laid them out upon the table. "The whole thing was a fraud from beginning to end. The woman's marriage certificate was all right, of course, but I mistrusted the genuineness of the other papers from the moment that I heard that Roonah would not part with them and would not allow Mr. McKinley to have charge of them. I am sure that the idea at first was merely one of blackmail. The papers were only to be the means of extorting money from the old lady, and there was no thought of taking them into court.

"Roonah's part was, of course, the important thing in the whole case, since she was here prepared to swear to the actual date of the first Madame Duplessis's death. The initiative, of course, may have come either from Joan or from Captain Duplessis himself, out of hatred for the family who would have nothing to do with him and his favourite younger daughter. That, of course, we shall never know. At first Roonah was a Parsee, with a doglike devotion to the girl whom she had nursed as a baby, and who no doubt had drilled her well into the part she was to play. But presently she became a Roman Catholic—an ardent convert, remember, with all a Roman Catholic's fear of hell-fire. I went to the convent this morning. I heard the priest's sermon there, and I realised what an influence his eloquence must have had over poor, ignorant, superstitious Roonah. She was still ready to die for her young mistress, but she was no longer prepared to swear to a lie for her sake. After Mass I called at Fordwych Castle. I explained my position to old Lady d'Alboukirk, who took me into the room where Roonah had slept and died. There I found two things," continued Lady Molly, as she opened the elegant reticule which still hung upon her arm, and placed a big key and a prayer book before me.

"The key I found in a drawer of an old cupboard in the dressing room where Roonah slept, with all sorts of odds and ends belonging to the unfortunate woman, and going to the door which led into what had been Joan's bedroom, I found that it was locked, and that this key fitted into the lock. Roonah had locked that door herself on her own side—*she was afraid of her mistress.* I knew now that I was right in my surmise. The prayer book is a Roman Catholic one. It is heavily thumbmarked there, where false oaths and lying are denounced as being deadly sins for which hell-fire would be the punishment. Roonah, terrorised by fear of the supernatural, a new convert to the faith, was afraid of committing a deadly sin.

"Who knows what passed between the two women, both of whom have come to so violent and terrible an end? Who can tell what prayers, tears, persuasions Joan Duplessis employed from the time she realised that Roonah did not mean to swear to the lie which would have brought her mistress wealth and glamour until the awful day when she finally understood that Roonah would no longer even hold her tongue, and devised a terrible means of silencing her for ever?

"With this certainty before me, I ventured on my big coup. I was so sure, you see. I kept Joan talking in here whilst I sent Pegram to her room with orders to break open the locks of her handbag and dressing case. There!— I told you that if I was wrong I would probably be dismissed the force for irregularity, as of course I had no right to do that; but if Pegram found the papers there where I felt sure they would be, we could bring the murderer to justice. I know my own sex pretty well, don't I, Mary? I knew that Joan Duplessis had not destroyed— never would destroy—those papers."

Even as Lady Molly spoke we could hear heavy tramping outside the passage. I ran to the door, and there was met by Pegram.

"She is quite dead, miss," he said. "It was a drop of forty feet, and a stone pavement down below."

The guilty had indeed meted out her own punishment to herself!

Lady d'Alboukirk sent Lady Molly a cheque for £5,000 the day the whole affair was made known to the public.

I think you will say that it had been well earned. With her own dainty hands my dear lady had lifted the veil which hung over the tragedy of Fordwych Castle, and with the finding of the papers in Joan Duplessis's dressing bag, and the unfortunate girl's suicide, the murder of the Indian woman was no longer a mystery.

HUGH C. WEIR (1884–1934) was a native Virginian who became a newspaperman and magazine editor in New York City. He wrote over three hundred movie scenarios and made official films for the Polish government during the First World War. With a partner, he founded an advertising agency, and, both alone and in collaboration, he wrote a number of books. *Miss Madelyn Mack, Detective* (1914) is apparently his only work of detective fiction; among the other books he published are two pieces of nonfiction dealing with the building of the Panama Canal.

Weir dedicates *Miss Madelyn Mack* to one Mary Holland, saying:

> This is your book. It is you, woman detective of real life, who suggested Madelyn. It was the stories told me from your own notebook of men's knavery that suggested these exploits of Miss Mack. None should know better than you that the riddles of fiction fall ever short of the riddles of truth. What plot of the novelist could equal the grotesqueness of your affair of the Mystic Circle, or the subtleness of your Chicago University exploit of the Egyptian bar? I pray you, however, in the fullness of your generosity to give Madelyn welcome—not as a rival but as a student.

The Man with Nine Lives

by Hugh C. Weir

Now that I seek a point of beginning in the curious comradeship between Madelyn Mack and myself, the weird problems of men's knavery that we have confronted together come back to me with almost a shock.

Perhaps the events which crowd into my memory followed each other too swiftly for thoughtful digest at the time of their occurrence. Perhaps only a sober retrospect can supply a properly appreciative angle of view.

Madelyn Mack! What newspaper reader does not know the name? Who, even among the most casual followers of public events, does not recall the young woman who found the missing heiress, Virginia Denton, after a three months' disappearance; who convicted "Archie" Irwin, chief of the "firebug trust"; who located the absconder, Wolcott, after a pursuit from Chicago to Khartoum; who solved the riddle of the double Peterson murder; who—

But why continue the enumeration of Miss Mack's achievements? They are of almost household knowledge, at least that portion which, from one cause or another, have found their way into the newspaper columns. Doubtless those admirers of Miss Mack, whose opinions have been formed through the press chronicles of her exploits, would be startled to know that not one in ten of her cases has ever been recorded outside of her own file cases. And many of them—the most sensational from a newspaper viewpoint—will never be!

It is the woman, herself, however, who has seemed to me always a greater mystery than any of the problems to whose unraveling she has brought her wonderful genius. In spite of the deluge of printer's ink that she has inspired, I question if it has been given to more than a dozen persons to know the true Madelyn Mack.

I do not refer, of course, to her professional career. The salient points of that portion of her life, I presume, are more or less generally known—the college girl confronted suddenly with the necessity of earning her own living; the epidemic of mysterious "shoplifting" cases chronicled in the newspaper she was studying for employment advertisements; her application to the New York department stores, that had been victimized, for a place on their detective staffs, and their curt refusal; her sudden determination to undertake the case as a free-lance, and her remarkable success, which resulted in the conviction of the notorious Madame Bousard, and which secured for Miss Mack her first position as assistant house detective with the famous Niegel dry-goods firm. I sometimes think that this first case, and the realization which it brought her of her peculiar talent, is Madelyn's favorite—that its place in her memory is not even shared by the recovery of Mrs. Niegel's fifty-thousand-dollar pearl necklace, stolen a few months after the employment of the college girl detective at the store, and the reward for which, incidentally, enabled the ambitious Miss Mack to open her own office.

Next followed the Bergner kidnapping case, which gave Madelyn her first big advertising broadside, and which brought the beginning of the steady stream of business that resulted, after three years, in her Fifth Avenue suite in the Maddox Building, where I found her on that—to me—memorable afternoon when a sapient Sunday editor dispatched me for an interview with the woman who had made so conspicuous a success in a man's profession.

I can see Madelyn now, as I saw her then—my first close-range view of her. She had just returned from Omaha that morning, and was planning to leave for Boston on the midnight express. A suitcase and a fat portfolio of papers lay on a chair in a corner. A young woman stenographer was taking a number of letters at an almost incredible rate of dictation. Miss Mack finished the last paragraph as she rose from a flat-top desk to greet me.

I had vaguely imagined a masculine-appearing woman, curt of voice, sharp of feature, perhaps dressed in a severe, tailor-made gown. I saw a young woman of maybe twenty-five, with red and white cheeks, crowned by a softly waved mass of dull gold hair, and a pair of vivacious, grey-blue eyes that at once made one forget every other detail of her appearance. There was a quality in the eyes which for a long time I could not define. Gradually I came to know that it was the spirit of optimism, of joy in herself, and in her life, and in her work, the exhilaration of doing things. And there was something contagious in it. Almost unconsciously you found yourself *believing* in her and in her sincerity.

Nor was there a suggestion foreign to her sex in my appraisal. She was dressed in a simply embroidered white shirtwaist and white broadcloth skirt. One of Madelyn's few peculiarities is that she always dresses either in complete white or complete black. On her desk was a jar of white chrysanthemums.

"How do I do it?" she repeated, in answer to my question, in a tone that was almost a laugh. "Why—just by hard work, I suppose. Oh, there isn't anything wonderful about it! You can do almost anything, you know, if you make yourself really *think* you can! I am not at all unusual or abnormal. I work out my problems just as I would work out a problem in mathematics, only instead of figures I deal with human motives. A detective is always given certain known factors, and I keep building them up, or subtracting them, as the case may be, until I know that the answer *must* be correct.

"There are only two real rules for a successful detective, hard work and common sense—not uncommon sense such as we associate with our old friend Sherlock Holmes, but common, *business* sense. And, of course, imagination! That may be one reason why I have made what you call a success. A woman, I think, always has a more acute imagination than a man!"

"Do you then prefer women operatives on your staff?" I asked.

She glanced up with something like a twinkle from the jade paper-knife in her hands.

"Shall I let you into a secret? All of my staff, with the exception of my stenographer, are men. But I do most of my work in person. The factor of imagination can't very well be used second, or third, or fourth handed. And then, if I fail, I can only blame Madelyn Mack! Someday"—the gleam in her grey-blue eyes deepened—"someday I hope to reach a point where I can afford to do only consulting work or personal investigation. The business details of an office staff, I am afraid, are a bit too much of routine for me!"

The telephone jingled. She spoke a few crisp sentences into the receiver, and turned. The interview was over.

When I next saw her, three months later, we met across the body of Morris Anthony, the murdered bibliophile. It was a chance discovery of mine which Madelyn was good enough to say suggested to her the solution of the affair, and which brought us together in the final melodramatic climax in the grim mansion on Washington Square, when I presume my hysterical warning saved her from the fangs of Dr. Lester Randolph's hidden cobra. In any event, our acquaintanceship crystallized gradually into a comradeship, which revolutionized two angles of my life.

Not only did it bring to me the stimulus of Madelyn Mack's personality, but it gave me exclusive access to a fund of newspaper "copy" that took me from scant-paid Sunday "features" to a "space" arrangement in the city room, with an income double that which I had been earning. I have always maintained that in our relationship Madelyn gave all, and I contributed nothing. Although she invariably made instant disclaimer, and generally ended by carrying me up to the "Rosary," her chalet on the Hudson, as a cure for what she termed my attack of the "blues," she was never able to convince me that my protest was not justified!

It was at the "Rosary" where Miss Mack found haven from the stress of business. She had copied its design from an ivy-tangled Swiss chalet that had attracted her fancy during a summer vacation ramble through the Alps, and had built it on a jagged bluff of the river at a point near enough to the city to permit of fairly convenient motoring, although, during the first years of our friendship, when she was held close to the commercial grindstone, weeks often passed without her being able to snatch a day there. In the end, it was the gratitude of Chalmers Walker for her remarkable work which cleared his chorus-girl wife from the seemingly unbreakable coil of circumstantial evidence in the murder of Dempster, the theatrical broker, that enabled Madelyn to realize her long-cherished dream of setting up as a consulting expert. Although she still maintained an office in town, it was confined to one room and a small reception hall, and she limited her attendance there to two days of the week. During the remainder of the time, when not engaged directly on a case, she seldom appeared in the city at all. Her flowers and her music—she was passionately devoted to both—appeared to content her effectually.

I charged her with growing old, to which she replied with a shrug. I upbraided her as a cynic, and she smiled inscrutably. But the manner of her life was not changed. In a way I envied her. It was almost like looking down on the world and watching tolerantly its mad scramble for the rainbow's end. The days I snatched at the "Rosary," particularly in the summer, when Madelyn's garden looked like nothing so much as a Turner picture, left me with almost a repulsion for the grind of Park Row. But a workaday newspaper woman cannot indulge the dreams of a genius whom fortune has blessed. Perhaps this was why Madelyn's invitations came with a frequency and a subtleness that could not be resisted. Somehow they always reached me when I was in just the right receptive mood.

It was late on a Thursday afternoon of June, the climax of a racking five days for me under the blistering Broadway sun, that Madelyn's motor caught me at the *Bugle* office, and Madelyn insisted on bundling me into the tonneau without even a suitcase.

"We'll reach the Rosary in time for a fried chicken supper," she promised. "What you need is four or five days' rest where you can't smell the asphalt."

"You fairy godmother!" I breathed as I snuggled down on the cushions.

Neither of us knew that already the crimson trail of crime was twisting toward us—that within twelve hours we were to be pitchforked from a quiet weekend's rest into the vortex of tragedy.

We had breakfasted late and leisurely. When at length we had finished, Madelyn had insisted on having her phonograph brought to the rose garden, and we were listening to

Sturveysant's matchless rendering of "The Jewel Song"—
one of the three records for which Miss Mack had sent the
harpist her check for two hundred dollars the day before. I
had taken the occasion to read her a lazy lesson on
extravagance. The beggar had probably done the work in
less than two hours!

As the plaintive notes quivered to a pause, Susan,
Madelyn's housekeeper, crossed the garden, and laid a
little stack of letters and the morning papers on a rustic
table by our bench. Madelyn turned to her correspondence with a shrug.

"From the divine to the prosaic!"

Susan sniffed with the freedom of seven years of
service.

"I heard one of them Eyetalian fiddling chaps at
Hammerstein's last week who could beat that music with
his eyes closed!"

Madelyn stared at her sorrowfully.

"At your age—Hammerstein's!"

Susan tossed her prim rows of curls, glanced contemptuously at the phonograph by way of retaliation, and made
a dignified retreat. In the doorway she turned.

"Oh, Miss Madelyn, I am baking one of your old-
fashioned strawberry shortcakes for lunch!"

"Really?" Madelyn raised a pair of sparkling eyes.
"Susan, you're a dear!"

A contented smile wreathed Susan's face even to the
tips of her precise curls. Madelyn's gaze crossed to me.

"What are you chuckling over, Nora?"

"From a psychological standpoint, the pair of you have
given me two interesting studies," I laughed. "A single
sentence compensates Susan for a week of your glumness!"

Madelyn extended a hand toward her mail.

"And what is the other feature that appeals to your
dissecting mind?"

"Fancy a world-known detective rising to the point of enthusiasm at the mention of strawberry shortcake!"

"Why not? Even a detective has to be human once in a while!" Her eyes twinkled. "Another point for my memoirs, Miss Noraker!"

As her gaze fell to the half-opened letter in her hand, my eyes traveled across the garden to the outlines of the chalet, and I breathed a sigh of utter content. Broadway and Park Row seemed very, very far away. In a momentary swerving of my gaze, I saw that a line as clear-cut as a pencil stroke had traced itself across Miss Mack's forehead.

The suggestion of lounging indifference in her attitude had vanished like a wind-blown veil. Her glance met mine suddenly. The twinkle I had last glimpsed in her eyes had disappeared. Silently she pushed a square sheet of close, cramped writing across the table to me.

My Dear Madam:

When you read this, it is quite possible that it will be a letter from a dead man.

I have been told by no less an authority than my friend, Cosmo Hamilton, that you are a remarkable woman. While I will say at the outset that I have little faith in the analytical powers of the feminine brain, I am prepared to accept Hamilton's judgment.

I cannot, of course, discuss the details of my problem in correspondence.

As a spur to quick action, I may say, however, that, during the past five months, my life has been attempted no fewer than eight different times, and I am convinced that the ninth attempt, if made, will be successful. The curious part of it lies in the fact that I am absolutely unable to guess the reason for the persistent vendetta. So far as I know, there is no person in the world who should desire my removal. And yet I have been shot at from ambush on four occasions, thugs have rushed me once, a speeding automobile has grazed me twice, and this evening I found a cunning little dose of cyanide of potassium in my favorite cherry pie!

All of this, too, in the shadow of a New Jersey skunk farm! It is high time, I fancy, that I secure expert advice. Should the progress of the mysterious vendetta, by any chance, render me unable to receive you personally, my niece, Miss Muriel Jansen, I am sure, will endeavor to act as a substitute.

Respectfully Yours,
Wendell Marsh

Three Forks Junction, N. J.
June 16

At the bottom of the page a lead pencil had scrawled the single line in the same cramped writing:

"For God's sake, hurry!"

Madelyn retained her curled-up position on the bench, staring across at a bush of deep crimson roses.

"Wendell Marsh?" She shifted her glance to me musingly. "Haven't I seen that name somewhere lately?" (Madelyn pays me the compliment of saying that I have a card-index brain for newspaper history!)

"If you have read the Sunday supplements," I returned drily, with a vivid remembrance of Wendell Marsh as I had last seen him, six months before, when he crossed the gangplank of his steamer, fresh from England, his face browned from the Atlantic winds. It was a face to draw a second glance—almost gaunt, self-willed, with more than a hint of cynicism. (Particularly when his eyes met the waiting press group!) Someone had once likened him to the pictures of Oliver Cromwell.

"Wendell Marsh is one of the greatest newspaper copy-makers that ever dodged an interviewer," I explained. "He hates reporters like an upstate farmer hates an automobile, and yet has a flock of them on his trail constantly. His latest exploit to catch the spotlight was the purchase of the Bainford relics in London. Just before that he published a three-volume history on 'The World's Great Cynics.' Paid for the publication himself."

Then came a silence between us, prolonging itself. I was trying, rather unsuccessfully, to associate Wendell Marsh's half-hysterical letter with my mental picture of the austere millionaire . . .

"For God's sake, hurry!"

What wrenching terror had reduced the ultra-reserved Mr. Marsh to an appeal like this? As I look back now I know that my wildest fancy could not have pictured the ghastliness of the truth!

Madelyn straightened abruptly.

"Susan, will you kindly tell Andrew to bring around the car at once? If you will find the New Jersey automobile map, Nora, we'll locate Three Forks Junction."

"You are going down?" I asked mechanically.

She slipped from the bench.

"I am beginning to fear," she said irrelevantly, "that we'll have to defer our strawberry shortcake!"

The sound eye of Daniel Peddicord, liveryman by avocation, and sheriff of Merino County by election, drooped over his florid left cheek. Mr. Peddicord took himself and his duties to the taxpayers of Merino County seriously.

Having lowered his sound eye with befitting official dubiousness, while his glass eye stared guilelessly ahead, as though it took absolutely no notice of the procedure, Mr. Peddicord jerked a fat red thumb toward the winding stairway at the rear of the Marsh hall.

"I reckon as how Mr. Marsh is still up there, Miss Mack. You see, I told 'em not to disturb the body until—"

Our stares brought the sentence to an abrupt end. Mr. Peddicord's sound eye underwent a violent agitation.

"You don't mean that you haven't—heard?"

The silence of the great house seemed suddenly oppressive. For the first time I realized the oddity of our having been received by an ill-at-ease policeman instead of by a member of the family. I was abruptly conscious of the incongruity between Mr. Peddicord's awkward figure and the dim, luxurious background.

Madelyn gripped the chief's arm, bringing his sound eye circling around to her face.

"Tell me what has happened!"

Mr. Peddicord drew a huge red handkerchief over his forehead.

"Wendell Marsh was found dead in his library at eight o'clock this morning! He had been dead for hours."

Tick-tock! Tick-tock! Through my daze beat the rhythm of a tall, gaunt clock in the corner. I stared at it dully. Madelyn's hands had caught themselves behind her back, her veins swollen into sharp blue ridges. Mr. Peddicord still gripped his red handkerchief.

"It sure is queer you hadn't heard! I reckoned as how that was what had brought you down. It—it looks like murder!"

In Madelyn's eyes had appeared a greyish glint like cold steel.

"Where is the body?"

"Upstairs in the library. Mr. Marsh had worked—"

"Will you kindly show me the room?"

I do not think we noted at the time the crispness in her tones, certainly not with any resentment. Madelyn had taken command of the situation quite as a matter of course.

"Also, will you have my card sent to the family?"

Mr. Peddicord stuffed his handkerchief back into a rear trousers' pocket. A red corner protruded in jaunty abandon from under his blue coat.

"Why, there ain't no family—at least none but Muriel Jansen." His head cocked itself cautiously up the stairs. "She's his niece, and I reckon now everything here is hers. Her maid says as how she is clear bowled over. Only left her room once since—since it happened. And that was to tell me as how nothing was to be disturbed." Mr. Peddicord drew himself up with the suspicion of a frown. "Just as though an experienced officer wouldn't know *that* much!"

Madelyn glanced over her shoulder to the end of the hall. A hatchet-faced man in russet livery stood staring at us with wooden eyes.

Mr. Peddicord shrugged.

"That's Peters, the butler. He's the chap what found Mr. Marsh."

I could feel the wooden eyes following us until a turn in the stairs blocked their range.

A red-glowing room—oppressively red. Scarlet-frescoed walls, deep red draperies, cherry-upholstered furniture, Turkish-red rugs, rows on rows of red-bound books. Above, a great, flat glass roof, open to the sky from corner to corner, through which the splash of the sun on the rich colors gave the weird semblance of a crimson pool almost in the room's exact center. Such was Wendell Marsh's library—as eccentrically designed as its master.

It was the wreck of a room that we found. Shattered vases littered the floor—books were ripped savagely apart —curtains were hanging in ribbons—a heavy leather rocker was splintered.

The wreckage might have marked the death-struggle of giants. In the midst of the destruction, Wendell Marsh was twisted on his back. His face was shriveled, his eyes were staring. There was no hint of a wound or even a bruise. In his right hand was gripped an object partially turned from me.

I found myself stepping nearer, as though drawn by a magnet. There is something hypnotic in such horrible scenes! And then I barely checked a cry.

Wendell Marsh's dead fingers held a pipe—a strangely carved red sandstone bowl, and a long, glistening stem.

Sheriff Peddicord noted the direction of my glance.

"Mr. Marsh got that there pipe in London, along with those other relics he brought home. They do say as how it was the first pipe ever smoked by a white man. The Indians of Virginia gave it to a chap named Sir Walter Raleigh. Mr. Marsh had a new stem put to it, and his butler says he smoked it every day. Queer, ain't it, how some folks' tastes do run?"

The sheriff moistened his lips under his scraggly yellow moustache.

"Must have been some fight what done this!" His head included the wrecked room in a vague sweep.

Madelyn strolled over to a pair of the ribboned curtains, and fingered them musingly.

"But that isn't the queerest part." The chief glanced at Madelyn expectantly. "There was no way for any one else to get out—or in!"

Madelyn stooped lower over the curtains. They seemed to fascinate her. "The door?" she hazarded absently. "It was locked?"

"From the inside. Peters and the footman saw the key when they broke in this morning . . . Peters swears he heard Mr. Marsh turn it when he left him writing at ten o'clock last night."

"The windows?"

"Fastened as tight as a drum—and, if they wasn't, it's a matter of a good thirty foot to the ground."

"The roof, perhaps?"

"A cat *might* get through it—if every part wasn't clamped as tight as the windows."

Mr. Peddicord spoke with a distinct inflection of triumph. Madelyn was still staring at the curtains.

"Isn't it rather odd," I ventured, "that the sounds of

the struggle, or whatever it was, didn't alarm the house?"

Sheriff Peddicord plainly regarded me as an outsider. He answered my question with obvious shortness.

"You could fire a blunderbuss up here and no one would be the wiser. They say as how Mr. Marsh had the room made sound-proof. And, besides, the servants have a building to themselves, all except Miss Jansen's maid, who sleeps in a room next to her at the other end of the house."

My eyes circled back to Wendell Marsh's knotted figure—his shriveled face—horror-frozen eyes—the hand gripped about the fantastic pipe. I think it was the pipe that held my glance. Of all incongruities, a pipe in the hand of a dead man!

Maybe it was something of the same thought that brought Madelyn of a sudden across the room. She stooped, straightened the cold fingers, and rose with the pipe in her hand.

A new stem had obviously been added to it, of a substance which I judged to be jessamine. At its end, teeth-marks had bitten nearly through. The stone bowl was filled with the cold ashes of half-consumed tobacco. Madelyn balanced it musingly.

"Curious, isn't it, Sheriff, that a man engaged in a life-or-death struggle should cling to a heavy pipe?"

"Why—I suppose so. But the question, Miss Mack, is what became of that there other man? It isn't natural as how Mr. Marsh could have fought with himself."

"The other man?" Madelyn repeated mechanically. She was stirring the rim of the dead ashes.

"And how in tarnation was Mr. Marsh killed?"

Madelyn contemplated a dust-covered finger.

"Will you do me a favor, Sheriff?"

"Why, er—of course."

"Kindly find out from the butler if Mr. Marsh had cherry pie for dinner last night!"

The sheriff gulped.

"Che-cherry pie?"

Madelyn glanced up impatiently.

"I believe he was very fond of it."

The sheriff shuffled across to the door uncertainly. Madelyn's eyes flashed to me.

"You might go, too, Nora."

For a moment I was tempted to flat rebellion. But Madelyn affected not to notice the fact. She is always so aggravatingly sure of her own way!—With what I tried to make a mood of aggrieved silence, I followed the sheriff's blue-coated figure. As the door closed, I saw that Madelyn was still balancing Raleigh's pipe.

From the top of the stairs, Sheriff Peddicord glanced across at me suspiciously.

"I say, what I would like to know is what became of that there other man!"

A wisp of a black-gowned figure, peering through a dormer window at the end of the second-floor hall, turned suddenly as we reached the landing. A white, drawn face, suggesting a tired child, stared at us from under a frame of dull-gold hair, drawn low from a careless part. I knew at once it was Muriel Jansen, for the time, at least, mistress of the house of death.

"Has the coroner come yet, Sheriff?"

She spoke with one of the most liquid voices I have ever heard. Had it not been for her bronze hair, I would have fancied her at once of Latin descent. The fact of my presence she seemed scarcely to notice, not with any suggestion of aloofness, but rather as though she had been drained even of the emotion of curiosity.

"Not yet, Miss Jansen. He should be here now."

She stepped closer to the window, and then turned slightly.

"I told Peters to telegraph to New York for Dr. Dench

when he summoned you. He was one of Uncle's oldest friends. I—I would like him to be here when—when the coroner makes his examination."

The sheriff bowed awkwardly.

"Miss Mack is upstairs now."

The pale face was staring at us again with raised eyebrows.

"Miss Mack? I don't understand." Her eyes shifted to me.

"She had a letter from Mr. Marsh by this morning's early post," I explained. "I am Miss Noraker. Mr. Marsh wanted her to come down at once. She didn't know, of course—couldn't know—that—that he was—dead!"

"A letter from—Uncle?" A puzzled line gathered in her face.

I nodded.

"A distinctly curious letter. But—Miss Mack would perhaps prefer to give you the details."

The puzzled line deepened. I could feel her eyes searching mine intently.

"I presume Miss Mack will be down soon," I volunteered. "If you wish, however, I will tell her—"

"That will hardly be necessary. But—you are quite sure—a letter?"

"Quite sure," I returned, somewhat impatiently.

And then, without warning, her hands darted to her head, and she swayed forward. I caught her in my arms with a side-view of Sheriff Peddicord staring, open-mouthed.

"Get her maid!" I gasped.

The sheriff roused into belated action. As he took a cumbersome step toward the nearest door, it opened suddenly. A gaunt, middle-aged woman, in a crisp white apron, digested the situation with cold grey eyes. Without a word, she caught Muriel Jansen in her arms.

"She has fainted," I said rather vaguely. "Can I help you?"

The other paused with her burden.

"When I need you, I'll ask you!" she snapped, and banged the door in our faces.

In the wake of Sheriff Peddicord, I descended the stairs. A dozen question-marks were spinning through my brain. Why had Muriel Jansen fainted? Why had the mention of Wendell Marsh's letter left such an atmosphere of bewildered doubt? Why had the dragonlike maid—for such I divined her to be—faced us with such hostility? The undercurrent of hidden secrets in the dim, silent house seemed suddenly intensified.

With a vague wish for fresh air and the sun on the grass, I sought the front veranda, leaving the sheriff in the hall, mopping his face with his red handkerchief.

A carefully tended yard of generous distances stretched an inviting expanse of graded lawn before me. Evidently Wendell Marsh had provided a discreet distance between himself and his neighbors. The advance guard of a morbid crowd was already shuffling about the gate. I knew that it would not be long, too, before the press siege would begin.

I could picture frantic city editors pitchforking their star men New Jerseyward. I smiled at the thought. The *Bugle*—the slave driver that presided over my own financial destinies—was assured of a generous "beat" in advance. The next train from New York was not due until late afternoon.

From the staring line about the gate, the figure of a well-set-up young man in blue serge detached itself with swinging step.

"A reporter?" I breathed, incredulous.

With a glance at me, he ascended the steps and paused at the door, awaiting an answer to his bell. My stealthy glances failed to place him among the "stars" of New York newspaperdom. Perhaps he was a local correspondent. With smug expectancy, I awaited his discomfiture when Peters received his card. And then I rubbed my eyes. Peters was stepping back from the door, and the other was following him with every suggestion of assurance.

I was still gasping when a maid, broom in hand, zigzagged toward my end of the veranda. She smiled at me with a pair of friendly black eyes.

"Are you a detective?"

"Why?" I parried.

She drew her broom idly across the floor.

"I—I always thought detectives different from other people."

She sent a rivulet of dust through the railing, with a side-glance still in my direction.

"Oh, you will find them human enough," I laughed, "outside of detective stories!"

She pondered my reply doubtfully.

"I thought it about time Mr. Truxton was appearing!" she ventured suddenly.

"Mr. Truxton?"

"He's the man that just came—Mr. Homer Truxton. Miss Jansen is going to marry him!"

A light broke through my fog.

"Then he is not a reporter?"

"Mr. Truxton? He's a lawyer." The broom continued its dilatory course. "Mr. Marsh didn't like him—so they *say!*"

I stepped back, smoothing my skirts. I have learned the cardinal rule of Madelyn never to pretend too great an interest in the gossip of a servant.

The maid was mechanically shaking out a rug.

"For my part, I always thought Mr. Truxton far and away the pick of Miss Jansen's two steadies. I never could understand what she could see in Dr. Dench! Why, he's old enough to be her—"

In the doorway, Sheriff Peddicord's bulky figure beckoned.

"Don't you reckon as how it's about time we were going back to Miss Mack?" he whispered.

"Perhaps," I assented rather reluctantly.

From the shadows of the hall, the sheriff's sound eye fixed itself on me belligerently.

"I say, what I would like to know is what became of that there other man!"

As we paused on the second landing the well-set-up figure of Mr. Homer Truxton was bending toward a partially opened door. Beyond his shoulder, I caught a fleeting glimpse of a pale face under a border of rumpled dull-gold hair. Evidently Muriel Jansen had recovered from her faint.

The door closed abruptly, but not before I had seen that her eyes were red with weeping.

Madelyn was sunk into a red-backed chair before a huge flat-top desk in the corner of the library, a stack of Wendell Marsh's red-bound books, from a wheel-cabinet at her side, bulked before her. She finished the page she was reading—a page marked with a broad blue pencil—without a hint that she had heard us enter.

Sheriff Peddicord stared across at her with a disappointment that was almost ludicrous. Evidently Madelyn was falling short of his conception of the approved attitudes for a celebrated detective!

"Are you a student of Elizabethan literature, Sheriff?" she asked suddenly.

The sheriff gurgled weakly.

"If you are, I am quite sure you will be interested in Mr. Marsh's collection. It is the most thorough on the subject that I have ever seen. For instance, here is a volume on the inner court life of Elizabeth—perhaps you would like me to read you this random passage?"

The sheriff drew himself up with more dignity than I thought he possessed.

"We are investigating a crime, Miss Mack!"

Madelyn closed the book with a sigh.

"So we are! May I ask what is your report from the butler?"

"Mr. Marsh did *not* have cherry pie for dinner last night!" the sheriff snapped.

"You are quite confident?"

And then abruptly the purport of the question flashed to me.

"Why, Mr. Marsh, himself, mentioned the fact in his letter!" I burst out.

Madelyn's eyes turned to me reprovingly.

"You must be mistaken, Nora."

With a lingering glance at the books on the desk, she rose. Sheriff Peddicord moved toward the door, opened it, and faced about with an abrupt clearing of his throat.

"Begging your pardon, Miss Mack, have—have you found any *clues* in the case?"

Madelyn had paused again at the ribboned curtains.

"Clues? The man who made Mr. Marsh's death possible, Sheriff, was an expert chemist, of Italian origin, living for some time in London—and he died three hundred years ago!"

From the hall we had a fleeting view of Sheriff Peddicord's face, flushed as red as his handkerchief, and then it and the handkerchief disappeared.

I whirled on Madelyn sternly.

"You are carrying your absurd joke, Miss Mack, altogether too—"

I paused, gulping in my turn. It was as though I had stumbled from the shadows into an electric glare.

Madelyn had crossed to the desk, and was gently shifting the dead ashes of Raleigh's pipe into an envelope.

A moment she sniffed at its bowl, peering down at the crumpled body at her feet.

"The pipe!" I gasped. "Wendell Marsh was poisoned with the pipe!"

Madelyn sealed the envelope slowly.

"Is that fact just dawning on you, Nora?"

"But the rest of it—what you told the—"

Madelyn thrummed on the bulky volume of Elizabethan history.

"Someday, Nora, if you will remind me, I will give you the material for what you call a Sunday 'feature' on the historic side of murder as a fine art!"

In a curtain-shadowed nook of the side veranda Muriel Jansen was awaiting us, pillowed back against a bronze-draped chair, whose colors almost startlingly matched the gold of her hair. Her resemblance to a tired child was even more pronounced than when I had last seen her.

I found myself glancing furtively for signs of Homer Truxton, but he had disappeared.

Miss Jansen took the initiative in our interview with a nervous abruptness, contrasting oddly with her hesitancy at our last meeting.

"I understand, Miss Mack, that you received a letter from my uncle asking your presence here. May I see it?"

The eagerness of her tones could not be mistaken.

From her wrist-bag Madelyn extended the square envelope of the morning post, with its remarkable message. Twice Muriel Jansen's eyes swept slowly through its contents. Madelyn watched her with a little frown. A sudden tenseness had crept into the air, as though we were all keying ourselves for an unexpected climax. And then, like a thunderclap, it came.

"A curious communication," Madelyn suggested. "I had hoped you might be able to add to it?"

The tired face in the bronze-draped chair stared across the lawn.

"I can. The most curious fact of your communication, Miss Mack, is that *Wendell Marsh did not write it!*"

Never have I admired more keenly Madelyn's remarkable poise. Save for an almost imperceptible indrawing of her breath, she gave no hint of the shock which must have stunned her as it did me. I was staring with mouth agape. But, then, I presume you have discovered by this time that I was not designed for a detective!

Strangely enough, Muriel Jansen gave no trace of wonder in her announcement. Her attitude suggested a sense of detachment from the subject as though suddenly it had lost its interest. And yet, less than an hour ago, it had prostrated her in a swoon.

"You mean the letter is a forgery?" asked Madelyn quietly.

"Quite obviously."

"And the attempts on Mr. Marsh's life to which it refers?"

"There have been none. I have been with my uncle continuously for six months. I can speak definitely."

Miss Jansen fumbled in a white crocheted bag.

"Here are several specimens of Mr. Marsh's writing. I think they should be sufficient to convince you of what I say. If you desire others—"

I was gulping like a truant schoolgirl as Madelyn spread on her lap the three notes extended to her. Casual business and personal references they were, none of more than half a dozen lines. Quite enough, however, to complete the sudden chasm at our feet—quite enough to emphasize a bold, aggressive penmanship, almost perpendicular, without the slightest resemblance to the cramped, shadowy writing of the morning's astonishing communication.

Madelyn rose from her chair, smoothing her skirts

thoughtfully. For a moment she stood at the railing, gazing down upon a trellis of yellow roses, her face turned from us. For the first time in our curious friendship, I was actually conscious of a feeling of pity for her! The blank wall which she faced seemed so abrupt—so final!

Muriel Jansen shifted her position slightly.

"Are you satisfied, Miss Mack?"

"Quite." Madelyn turned, and handed back the three notes. "I presume this means that you do not care for me to continue the case?"

I whirled in dismay. I had never thought of this possibility.

"On the contrary, Miss Mack, it seems to me an additional reason why you should continue!"

I breathed freely again. At least we were not to be dismissed with the abruptness that Miss Jansen's maid had shown! Madelyn bowed rather absently.

"Then if you will give me another interview, perhaps this afternoon—"

Miss Jansen fumbled with the lock of her bag. For the first time her voice lost something of its directness.

"Have—have you any explanation of this astonishing —forgery?"

Madelyn was staring out toward the increasing crowd at the gate. A sudden ripple had swept through it.

"Have you ever heard of a man by the name of Orlando Julio, Miss Jansen?"

My own eyes, following the direction of Madelyn's gaze, were brought back sharply to the veranda. For the second time, Muriel Jansen had crumpled back in a faint.

As I darted toward the servants' bell Madelyn checked me. Striding up the walk were two men with the unmistakable air of physicians. At Madelyn's motioning hand they turned toward us.

The foremost of the two quickened his pace as he caught sight of the figure in the chair. Instinctively I knew that he was Dr. Dench—and it needed no profound analysis to place his companion as the local coroner.

With a deft hand on Miss Jansen's heartbeats, Dr. Dench raised a ruddy, brown-whiskered face inquiringly toward us.

"Shock!" Madelyn explained. "Is it serious?"

The hand on the wavering breast darted toward a medicine case and selected a vial of brownish liquid. The gaze above it continued its scrutiny of Madelyn's slender figure.

Dr. Dench was of the rugged, German type, steel-eyed, confidently sure of movement, with the physique of a splendidly muscled animal. If the servant's tattle was to be credited, Muriel Jansen could not have attracted more opposite extremes in her suitors.

The coroner—a rusty-suited man of middle age, in quite obvious professional awe of his companion—extended a glass of water. Miss Jansen wearily opened her eyes before it reached her lips.

Dr. Dench restrained her sudden effort to rise.

"Drink this, please!" There was nothing but professional command in his voice. If he loved the gray-pallored girl in the chair, his emotions were under superb control.

Madelyn stepped to the background, motioning me quietly.

"I fancy I can leave now safely. I am going back to town."

"Town?" I echoed.

"I should be back the latter part of the afternoon. Would it inconvenience you to wait here?"

"But, why on earth—" I began.

"Will you tell the butler to send around the car? Thanks!"

When Madelyn doesn't choose to answer questions she ignores them. I subsided as gracefully as possible. As her machine whirled under the porte cochere, however, my curiosity again overflowed my restraint.

"At least, who is Orlando Julio?" I demanded.

Madelyn carefully adjusted her veil.

"The man who provided the means for the death of Wendell Marsh!" And she was gone.

I swept another glance at the trio on the side veranda, and with what I tried to convince myself was a philosophical shrug, although I knew perfectly well it was merely a pettish fling, sought a retired corner of the rear drawing room, with my pad and pencil.

After all, I was a newspaper woman, and it needed no elastic imagination to picture the scene in the city room of the *Bugle*, if I failed to send a proper accounting of myself.

A few minutes later a tread of feet, advancing to the stairs, told me that the coroner and Dr. Dench were ascending for the belated examination of Wendell Marsh's body. Miss Jansen had evidently recovered, or been assigned to the ministrations of her maid. Once Peters, the wooden-faced butler, entered ghostily to inform me that luncheon would be served at one, but effaced himself almost before my glance returned to my writing.

I partook of the meal in the distinguished company of Sheriff Peddicord. Apparently Dr. Dench was still busied in his gruesome task upstairs, and it was not surprising that Miss Jansen preferred her own apartments.

However much the sheriff's professional poise might have been jarred by the events of the morning, his appetite had not been affected. His attention was too absorbed in the effort to do justice to the Marsh hospitality to waste time in table talk.

He finished his last spoonful of strawberry ice cream with a heavy sigh of contentment, removed the napkin, which he had tucked under his collar, and, as though mindful of the family's laundry bills, folded it carefully and wiped his lips with his red handkerchief. It was not until then that our silence was interrupted.

Glancing cautiously about the room, and observing that the butler had been called kitchenward, to my amazement he essayed a confidential wink.

"I say," he ventured enticingly, leaning his elbow on the table, "what I would like to know is what became of that there other man!"

"Are you familiar with the Fourth Dimension, Sheriff?" I returned solemnly. I rose from my chair, and stepped toward him confidentially in my turn. "I believe that a thorough study of that subject would answer your question."

It was three o'clock when I stretched myself in my corner of the drawing-room, and stuffed the last sheets of my copy paper into a special-delivery-stamped envelope.

My story was done. And Madelyn was not there to blue-pencil the Park Row adjectives! I smiled rather gleefully as I patted my hair and leisurely addressed the envelope. The city editor would be satisfied, if Madelyn wasn't!

As I stepped into the hall, Dr. Dench, the coroner, and Sheriff Peddicord were descending the stairs. Evidently the medical examination had been completed. Under other circumstances the three expressions before me would have afforded an interesting study in contrasts—Dr. Dench trimming his nails with professional stoicism, the coroner endeavoring desperately to copy the other's *sang-froid*, and the sheriff buried in an owllike solemnity.

Dr. Dench restored his knife to his pocket.

"You are Miss Mack's assistant, I understand?"

I bowed.

"Miss Mack has been called away. She should be back, however, shortly."

I could feel the doctor's appraising glance dissecting me with much the deliberateness of a surgical operation. I raised my eyes suddenly, and returned his stare. It was a virile, masterful face—and, I had to admit, coldly handsome!

Dr. Dench snapped open his watch.

"Very well then, Miss, Miss—"

"Noraker!" I supplied crisply.

The blond beard inclined the fraction of an inch.

"We will wait."

"The autopsy?" I ventured. "Has it—"

"The result of the autopsy I will explain to—Miss Mack!"

I bit my lip, felt my face flush as I saw that Sheriff Peddicord was trying to smother a grin, and turned with a rather unsuccessful shrug.

Now, if I had been of a vindictive nature, I would have opened my envelope and inserted a retaliating paragraph that would have returned the snub of Dr. Dench with interest. I flatter myself that I consigned the envelope to the Three Forks post office, in the rear of the Elite Dry Goods Emporium, with its contents unchanged.

As a part recompense, I paused at a corner drugstore and permitted a young man with a gorgeous pink shirt to make me a chocolate ice-cream soda. I was bent over an asthmatic straw when, through the window, I saw Madelyn's car skirt the curb.

I rushed out to the sidewalk, while the young man stared dazedly after me. The chauffeur swerved the machine as I tossed a dime to the Adonis of the fountain.

Madelyn shifted to the end of the seat as I clambered to her side. One glance was quite enough to show that her town mission, whatever it was, had ended in failure. Perhaps it was the consciousness of this fact that brought my eyes next to her blue turquoise locket. It was open. I glared accusingly.

"So you have fallen back on the cola stimulant again, Miss Mack?"

She nodded glumly, and perversely slipped into her mouth another of the dark brown berries, on which I have known her to keep up for forty-eight hours without sleep and almost without food.

For a moment I forgot even my curiosity as to her errand.

"I wish the duty would be raised so high you couldn't get those things into the country!"

She closed her locket, without deigning a response. The more volcanic my outburst, the more glacial Madelyn's coldness—particularly on the cola topic. I shrugged in resignation. I might as well have done so in the first place!

I straightened my hat, drew my handkerchief over my flushed face, and coughed questioningly. Continued silence. I turned in desperation.

"Well?" I surrendered.

"Don't you know enough, Nora Noraker, to hold your tongue?"

My pent-up emotions snapped.

"Look here, Miss Mack, I have been snubbed by Dr. Dench and the coroner, grinned at by Sheriff Peddicord, and I am not going to be crushed by you! What is your report—good, bad, or indifferent?"

Madelyn turned from her stare into the dust-yellow road.

"I have been a fool, Nora—a blind, bigoted, self-important fool!"

I drew a deep breath.

"Which means—"

From her bag Madelyn drew the envelope of dead tobacco ashes from the Marsh library, and tossed it over the side of the car. I sank back against the cushions.

"Then the tobacco after all—"

"Is nothing but tobacco—harmless tobacco!"

"But the pipe—I thought the pipe—"

"That's just it! The pipe, my dear girl, killed Wendell Marsh! But I don't know how! *I don't know how!*"

"Madelyn," I said severely, "you are a woman, even if you are making your living at a man's profession! What you need is a good cry!"

Dr. Dench, pacing back and forth across the veranda, knocked the ashes from an amber-stemmed meerschaum and advanced to meet us as we alighted. The coroner and Sheriff Peddicord were craning their necks from wicker chairs in the background. It was easy enough to surmise that Dr. Dench had parted from them abruptly in the desire for a quiet smoke to marshal his thoughts.

"Fill your pipe again if you wish," said Madelyn. "I don't mind."

Dr. Dench inclined his head, and dug the mouth of his meerschaum into a fat leather pouch. A spiral of blue smoke soon curled around his face. He was one of that type of men to whom a pipe lends a distinction of studious thoughtfulness.

With a slight gesture he beckoned in the direction of the coroner.

"It is proper, perhaps, that Dr. Williams in his official capacity should be heard first."

Through the smoke of his meerschaum, his eyes were searching Madelyn's face. It struck me that he was rather puzzled as to just how seriously to take her.

The coroner shuffled nervously. At his elbow, Sheriff Peddicord fumbled for his red handkerchief.

"We have made a thorough examination of Mr. Marsh's body, Miss Mack, a most thorough examination—"

"Of course he was not shot, nor stabbed, nor strangled, nor sandbagged?" interrupted Madelyn crisply.

The coroner glanced at Dr. Dench uncertainly. The latter was smoking with inscrutable face.

"Nor poisoned!" finished the coroner with a quick breath.

A blue smoke curl from Dr. Dench's meerschaum vanished against the sun. The coroner jingled a handful of coins in his pocket. The sound jarred on my nerves oddly. Not poisoned! Then Madelyn's theory of the pipe—

My glance swerved in her direction. Another blank wall—the blankest in this riddle of blank walls!

But the bewilderment I had expected in her face I did not find. The black dejection I had noticed in the car had dropped like a whisked-off cloak. The tired lines had been erased as by a sponge. Her eyes shone with that tense glint which I knew came only when she saw a befogged way swept clear before her.

"You mean that you *found* no trace of poison?" she corrected.

The coroner drew himself up.

"Under the supervision of Dr. Dench, we have made a most complete probe of the various organs—lungs, stomach, heart—"

"And brain, I presume?"

"Brain? Certainly not!"

"And you?" Madelyn turned toward Dr. Dench. "You subscribe to Dr. Williams' opinion?"

Dr. Dench removed his meerschaum.

"From our examination of Mr. Marsh's body, I am prepared to state emphatically that there is no trace of toxic condition of any kind!"

"Am I to infer then that you will return a verdict of—natural death?"

Dr. Dench stirred his pipe-ashes.

"I was always under the impression, Miss Mack, that the verdict in a case of this kind must come from the coroner's jury."

Madelyn pinned back her veil, and removed her gloves. "There is no objection to my seeing the body again?" The coroner stared.

"Why, er—the undertaker has it now. I don't see why he should object, if you wish—"

Madelyn stepped to the door. Behind her, Sheriff Peddicord stirred suddenly.

"I say, what I would like to know, gents, is what became of that there other man!"

It was not until six o'clock that I saw Madelyn again, and then I found her in Wendell Marsh's red library. She was seated at its late tenant's huge desk. Before her were a vial of whitish-grey powder, a small rubber inked roller, a half a dozen sheets of paper, covered with what looked like smudges of black ink, and Raleigh's pipe. I stopped short, staring.

She rose with a shrug.

"Fingerprints," she explained laconically. "This sheet belongs to Miss Jansen; the next to her maid; the third to the butler, Peters; the fourth to Dr. Dench; the fifth to Wendell Marsh, himself. It was my first experiment in taking the 'prints' of a dead man. It was—interesting."

"But what has that to do with a case of this kind?" I demanded.

Madelyn picked up the sixth sheet of smudged paper.

"We have here the fingerprints of Wendell Marsh's murderer!"

I did not even cry my amazement. I suppose the kaleidoscope of the day had dulled my normal emotions. I remember that I readjusted a loose pin in my waist before I spoke.

"The murderer of Wendell Marsh!" I repeated mechanically. "Then he *was* poisoned?"

Madelyn's eyes opened and closed without answer.

I reached over to the desk, and picked up Mr. Marsh's letter of the morning post at Madelyn's elbow.

"You have found the man who forged this?"

"It was *not* forged!"

In my daze I dropped the letter to the floor.

"You have discovered then the other man in the death-struggle that wrecked the library?"

"There was no other man!"

Madelyn gathered up her possessions from the desk. From the edge of the row of books she lifted a small, red-bound volume, perhaps four inches in width, and then with a second thought laid it back.

"By the way, Nora, I wish you would come back here at eight o'clock. If this book is still where I am leaving it, please bring it to me! I think that will be all for the present."

"All?" I gasped. "Do you realize that—"

Madelyn moved toward the door.

"I think eight o'clock will be late enough for your errand," she said without turning.

The late June twilight had deepened into a somber darkness when, my watch showing ten minutes past the hour of my instructions, I entered the room on the second floor that had been assigned to Miss Mack and myself. Madelyn at the window was staring into the shadow-blanketed yard.

"Well?" she demanded.

"Your book is no longer in the library!" I said crossly.

Madelyn whirled with a smile.

"Good! And now if you will be so obliging as to tell Peters to ask Miss Jansen to meet me in the rear drawing room, with any of the friends of the family she desires to be present, I think we can clear up our little puzzle."

It was a curious group that the graceful Swiss clock in the bronze drawing room of the Marsh house stared down upon as it ticked its way past the half hour after eight. With a grave, rather insistent bow, Miss Mack had seated the other occupants of the room as they answered her summons. She was the only one of us that remained standing.

Before her were Sheriff Peddicord, Homer Truxton, Dr. Dench, and Muriel Jansen. Madelyn's eyes swept our faces for a moment in silence, and then she crossed the room and closed the door.

"I have called you here," she began, "to explain the mystery of Mr. Marsh's death." Again her glance swept our faces. "In many respects it has provided us with a peculiar, almost an unique problem.

"We find a man, in apparently normal health, dead. The observer argues at once foul play; and yet on his body is no hint of wound or bruise. The medical examination discovers no trace of poison. The autopsy shows no evidence of crime. Apparently we have eliminated all forms of unnatural death.

"I have called you here because the finding of the autopsy is incorrect, or rather incomplete. We are not confronted by natural death—but by a crime. And I may say at the outset that I am not the only person to know this fact. My knowledge is shared by one other in this room."

Sheriff Peddicord rose to his feet and rather ostentatiously stepped to the door and stood with his back against it. Madelyn smiled faintly at the movement.

"I scarcely think there will be an effort at escape, Sheriff," she said quietly.

Muriel Jansen was crumpled back into her chair, staring. Dr. Dench was studying Miss Mack with the professional frown he might have directed at an abnormality on the operating table. It was Truxton who spoke first in the fashion of the impulsive boy.

"If we are not dealing with natural death, how on earth then was Mr. Marsh killed?"

Madelyn whisked aside a light covering from a stand at her side, and raised to view Raleigh's red sandstone pipe. For a moment she balanced it musingly.

"The three-hundred-year-old death tool of Orlando Julio," she explained. "It was this that killed Wendell Marsh!"

She pressed the bowl of the pipe into the palm of her hand. "As an instrument of death, it is *almost* beyond detection. We examined the ashes, and found nothing but harmless tobacco. The organs of the victim showed no trace of foul play."

She tapped the long stem gravely.

"But the examination of the organs did *not* include the brain. And it is through the brain that the pipe strikes, killing first the mind in a nightmare of insanity, and then the body. That accounts for the wreckage that we found—the evidences apparently of *two* men engaged in a desperate struggle. The wreckage was the work of only one man—a maniac in the moment before death. The drug with which we are dealing drives its victim into an insane fury before his body succumbs. I believe such cases are fairly common in India."

"Then Mr. Marsh was poisoned after all?" cried Truxton. He was the only one of Miss Mack's auditors to speak.

"No, not poisoned! You will understand as I proceed. The pipe, you will find, contains apparently but one bowl and one channel, and at a superficial glance is filled only with tobacco. In reality, there is a lower chamber concealed beneath the upper bowl, to which extends a second channel. This secret chamber is charged with a certain compound of Indian hemp and dhatura leaves, one of the most powerful brain stimulants known to science—and one of the most dangerous if used above a certain strength. From the lower chamber it would leave no trace, of course, in the ashes above.

"Between the two compartments of the pipe is a slight connecting opening, sufficient to allow the hemp beneath to be ignited gradually by the burning tobacco. When a small quantity of the compound is used, the smoker is stimulated as by no other drug, not even opium. Increase the quantity above the danger point, and mark the result. The victim is not poisoned in the strict sense of the word, but literally *smothered to death by the fumes!*"

In Miss Mack's voice was the throb of the student before the creation of the master.

"I should like this pipe, Miss Jansen, if you ever care to dispose of it!"

The girl was still staring woodenly.

"It was Orlando Julio, the medieval poisoner," she gasped, "that Uncle described—"

"In his seventeenth chapter of 'The World's Great Cynics,' " finished Madelyn. "I have taken the liberty of reading the chapter in manuscript form. Julio, however, was not the discoverer of the drug. He merely introduced it to the English public. As a matter of fact, it is one of the oldest stimulants of the East. It is easy to assume that it was not as a stimulant that Julio used it, but as a baffling instrument of murder. The mechanism of the pipe was his own invention, of course. The smoker, if not in the secret, would be completely oblivious to his danger. He might even use the pipe in perfect safety—until its lower chamber was loaded!"

Sheriff Peddicord, against the door, mopped his face with his red handkerchief, like a man in a daze. Dr. Dench was still studying Miss Mack with his intent frown. Madelyn swerved her angle abruptly.

"Last night was not the first time the hemp-chamber of Wendell Marsh's pipe had been charged. We can trace the effect of the drug on his brain for several months—

hallucinations, imaginative enemies seeking his life, incipi-
ent insanity. That explains his astonishing letter to me.
Wendell Marsh was not a man of nine lives, but only one.
The perils which he described were merely fantastic
figments of the drug. For instance, the episode of the
poisoned cherry pie. There was no pie at all served at the
table yesterday.

"The letter to me was not a forgery, Miss Jansen,
although you were sincere enough when you pronounced
it such. The complete change in your uncle's handwriting
was only another effect of the drug. It was this fact, in the
end, which led me to the truth. You did not perceive that
the dates of your notes and mine were *six months apart!* I
knew that some terrific mental shock *must* have occurred
in the meantime.

"And then, too, the ravages of a drug-crazed victim
were at once suggested by the curtains of the library. They
were not simply torn, but fairly *chewed* to pieces!"

A sudden tension fell over the room. We shifted
nervously, rather avoiding one another's eyes. Madelyn
laid the pipe back on the stand. She was quite evidently in
no hurry to continue. It was Truxton again who put the
leading question of the moment.

"If Mr. Marsh was killed as you describe, Miss Mack,
who killed him?"

Madelyn glanced across at Dr. Dench.

"Will you kindly let me have the red leather book that
you took from Mr. Marsh's desk this evening, Doctor?"

The physician met her glance steadily.

"You think it—necessary?"

"I am afraid I must insist."

For an instant Dr. Dench hesitated. Then, with a
shrug, he reached into a coat pocket and extended the
red-bound volume, for which Miss Mack had dispatched
me on the fruitless errand to the library. As Madelyn
opened it we saw that it was not a printed volume, but

filled with several hundred pages of close, cramped writing. Dr. Dench's gaze swerved to Muriel Jansen as Miss Mack spoke.

"I have here the diary of Wendell Marsh, which shows us that he had been in the habit of seeking the stimulant of Indian hemp, or 'hasheesh' for some time, possibly as a result of his retired, sedentary life and his close application to his books. Until his purchase of the Bainford relics, however, he had taken the stimulant in the comparatively harmless form of powdered leaves or 'bhang,' as it is termed in the Orient. His acquisition of Julio's drug-pipe, and an accidental discovery of its mechanism, led him to adopt the compound of hemp and dhatura, prepared for smoking—in India called 'charas.' No less an authority than Captain E. N. Windsor, bacteriologist of the Burmese government, states that it is directly responsible for a large percentage of the lunacy of the Orient. Wendell Marsh, however, did not realize his danger, nor how much stronger the latter compound is than the form of the drug to which he had been accustomed.

"Dr. Dench endeavored desperately to warn him of his peril and free him from the bondage of the habit as the diary records, but the victim was too thoroughly enslaved. In fact, the situation had reached a point just before the final climax when it could no longer be concealed. The truth was already being suspected by the older servants. I assume this was why you feared my investigations in the case, Miss Jansen."

Muriel Jansen was staring at Madelyn in a sort of dumb appeal.

"I can understand and admire Dr. Dench's efforts to conceal the fact from the public—first, in his supervision of the inquest, which might have stumbled on the truth, and then in his removal of the betraying diary, which I left purposely exposed in the hope that it might inspire such an action. Had it *not* been removed, I might have suspected another explanation of the case—in spite of certain evidence to the contrary!"

Dr. Dench's face had gone white.

"God! Miss Mack, do you mean that after all it was not suicide?"

"It was not suicide," said Madelyn quietly. She stepped across toward the opposite door.

"When I stated that my knowledge that we are not dealing with natural death was shared by another person in this room, I might have added that it was shared by still a third person—*not in the room!*"

With a sudden movement she threw open the door before her. From the adjoining anteroom lurched the figure of Peters, the butler. He stared at us with a face grey with terror, and then crumpled to his knees. Madelyn drew away sharply as he tried to catch her skirts.

"You may arrest the murderer of Wendell Marsh, Sheriff!" she said gravely. "And I think perhaps you had better take him outside."

She faced our bewildered stares as the drawing-room door closed behind Mr. Peddicord and his prisoner. From her stand she again took Raleigh's sandstone pipe, and with it two sheets of paper, smudged with the prints of a human thumb and fingers.

"It was the pipe in the end which led me to the truth, not only as to the method but the identity of the assassin," she explained. "The hand, which placed the fatal charge in the concealed chamber, left its imprint on the surface of the bowl. The fingers, grimed with the dust of the drug, made an impression which I would have at once detected had I not been so occupied with what I might find *inside* that I forgot what I might find *outside!* I am very much afraid that I permitted myself the great blunder of the modern detective—lack of thoroughness.

"Comparison with the fingerpints of the various agents in the case, of course, made the next step a mere detail of mathematical comparison. To make my identity sure, I found that my suspect possessed not only the opportunity and the knowledge for the crime, but the motive.

"In his younger days Peters was a chemist's apprentice; a fact which he utilized in his master's behalf in obtaining the drugs which had become so necessary a part of Mr. Marsh's life. Had Wendell Marsh appeared in person for so continuous a supply, his identity would soon have made the fact a matter of common gossip. He relied on his servant for his agent, a detail which he mentions several times in his diary, promising Peters a generous bequest in his will as a reward. I fancy that it was the dream of this bequest, which would have meant a small fortune to a man in his position, that set the butler's brain to work on his treacherous plan of murder."

Miss Mack's dull gold hair covered the shoulders of her white peignoir in a great, thick braid. She was propped in a nest of pillows, with her favorite romance, *The Three Musketeers,* open at the historic siege of Porthos in the wine cellar. We had elected to spend the night at the Marsh house.

Madelyn glanced up as I appeared in the doorway of our room.

"Allow me to present a problem to your analytical skill, Miss Mack," I said humbly. "Which man does your knowledge of feminine psychology say Muriel Jansen will reward—the gravely protecting physician, or the boyishly admiring Truxton?"

"If she were thirty," retorted Madelyn, yawning, "she would be wise enough to choose Dr. Dench. But, as she is only twenty-two, it will be Truxton."

With a sigh, she turned again to the swashbuckling exploits of the gallant Porthos.

ANNA KATHARINE GREEN (Mrs. Charles Rohlfs, 1846–1935) published her first book, *The Leavenworth Case*, in 1878, nine years before Conan Doyle's "A Study in Scarlet," and its immediate success had an immeasurable effect on the respectable reading public's acceptance of the detective genre. Her total output was prodigious, explained partly by the fact that she lived to be eighty-nine, surviving such later writers as Gaston Leroux and Edgar Wallace. Three years old when Poe died, she had by the time of her own death witnessed the appearance of most of Dorothy Sayers' Peter Wimsey novels. At seventy-seven, she published *The Step on the Stair*, three years after Agatha Christie's mystery-writing debut in 1920 with *The Mysterious Affair at Styles*. The daughter of an eminent Brooklyn attorney, she married a furniture designer and manufacturer and lived most of her life in Buffalo, New York.

Like the same author's Amelia Butterworth, Violet Strange is an aristocratic New Yorker, albeit a much younger one, who aids the police in getting an insider's view of crime in privileged places. Unlike Miss Butterworth, she refuses to betray the principles instilled by her breeding and disdains anything so vulgar as spying or eavesdropping unless the matter is dire. At the end of her collected cases, *The Golden Slipper and Other Problems for Violet Strange* (1915), she reveals she has been sleuthing in order to pay for the musical training of a dishonored and disinherited sister.

The Golden Slipper

by Anna Katharine Green

"She's here! I thought she would be. She's one of the three young ladies you see in the right-hand box near the proscenium."

The gentleman thus addressed—a man of middle age and a member of the most exclusive clubs—turned his opera glass toward the spot designated, and in some astonishment retorted:

"She? Why those are the Misses Pratt and—"

"Miss Violet Strange; no other."

"And do you mean to say—"

"I do—"

"That yon silly little chit, whose father I know, whose fortune I know, who is seen everywhere, and who is called one of the season's belles is an agent of yours; a—a—"

"No names here, please. You want a mystery solved. It is not a matter for the police—that is, as yet—and so you come to me, and when I ask for the facts, I find that women and only women are involved, and that these women are not only young but one and all of the highest society. Is it a man's work to go to the bottom of a combination like this? No. Sex against sex, and, if possible, youth against youth. Happily, I know such a person—a girl of gifts and extraordinarily well placed for the purpose. Why she uses her talents in this direction—why, with means enough to play the part natural to her as a successful debutante, she consents to occupy herself with social and other mysteries, you must ask her, not me. Enough that I promise you her aid if you want it. That is, if you can interest her. She will not work otherwise."

Mr. Driscoll again raised his opera glass.

"But it's a comedy face," he commented. "It's hard to associate intellectuality with such quaintness of expression. Are you sure of her discretion?"

"Whom is she with?"

"Abner Pratt, his wife, and daughters."

"Is he a man to entrust his affairs unadvisedly?"

"Abner Pratt! Do you mean to say that she is anything more to him than his daughters' guest?"

"Judge. You see how merry they are. They were in deep trouble yesterday. You are witness to a celebration."

"And she?"

"Don't you observe how they are loading her with attentions? She's too young to rouse such interest in a family of notably unsympathetic temperament for any other reason than that of gratitude."

"It's hard to believe. But if what you hint is true, secure me an opportunity at once of talking to this youthful marvel. My affair is serious. The dinner I have mentioned comes off in three days and—"

"I know. I recognize your need; but I think you had better enter Mr. Pratt's box without my intervention. Miss Strange's value to us will be impaired the moment her connection with us is discovered."

"Ah, there's Ruthven! He will take me to Mr. Pratt's box," remarked Driscoll as the curtain fell on the second act. "Any suggestions before I go?"

"Yes, and an important one. When you make your

bow, touch your left shoulder with your right hand. It is a signal. She may respond to it; but if she does not, do not be discouraged. One of her idiosyncrasies is a theoretical dislike of her work. But once she gets interested, nothing will hold her back. That's all, except this. In no event give away her secret. That's part of the compact, you remember."

Driscoll nodded and left his seat for Ruthven's box. When the curtain rose for the third time he could be seen sitting with the Misses Pratt and their vivacious young friend. A widower and still on the right side of fifty, his presence there did not pass unnoted, and curiosity was rife among certain onlookers as to which of the twin belles was responsible for this change in his well-known habits. Unfortunately, no opportunity was given him for showing. Other and younger men had followed his lead into the box, and they saw him forced upon the good graces of the fascinating but inconsequent Miss Strange, whose rapid fire of talk he was hardly of a temperament to appreciate.

Did he appear dissatisfied? Yes; but only one person in the opera house knew why. Miss Strange had shown no comprehension of or sympathy with his errand. Though she chatted amiably enough between duets and trios, she gave him no opportunity to express his wishes though she knew them well enough, owing to the signal he had given her.

This might be in character but it hardly suited his views; and, being a man of resolution, he took advantage of an absorbing minute on the stage to lean forward and whisper in her ear:

"It's my daughter for whom I request your services; as fine a girl as any in this house. Give me a hearing. You certainly can manage it."

She was a small, slight woman whose naturally quaint appearance was accentuated by the extreme simplicity of her attire. In the tier upon tier of boxes rising before his eyes, no other personality could vie with hers in strangeness, or in the illusive quality of her ever-changing expression. She was vivacity incarnate and, to the ordinary observer, light as thistledown in fibre and in feeling. But not to all. To those who watched her long, there came moments—say, when the music rose to heights of greatness—when the mouth so given over to laughter took on curves of the rarest sensibility, and a woman's lofty soul shone through her odd, bewildering features.

Driscoll had noted this, and consequently awaited her reply in secret hope.

It came in the form of a question and only after an instant's display of displeasure or possibly of pure nervous irritability.

"What has she done?"

"Nothing. But slander is in the air, and any day it may ripen into public accusation."

"Accusation of what?" Her tone was almost pettish.

"Of—of *theft*," he murmured. "On a great scale," he emphasized, as the music rose to a crash.

"Jewels?"

"Inestimable ones. They are always returned by somebody. People say, by me."

"Ah!" The little lady's hands grew steady—they had been fluttering all over her lap. "I will see you tomorrow morning at my father's house," she presently observed, and turned her full attention to the stage.

Some three days after this Mr. Driscoll opened his house on the Hudson to notable guests. He had not desired the publicity of such an event, nor the opportunity it gave for an increase of the scandal secretly in circulation against his daughter. But the Ambassador and his wife were foreign and any evasion of the promised hospitality would be sure to be misunderstood; so the scheme was carried forward, though with less *éclat* than possibly was expected.

Among the lesser guests, who were mostly young and well acquainted with the house and its hospitality, there was one unique figure—that of the lively Miss Strange, who, if personally unknown to Miss Driscoll, was so gifted with the qualities which tell on an occasion of this kind, that the stately young hostess hailed her presence with very obvious gratitude.

The manner of their first meeting was singular, and of great interest to one of them at least. Miss Strange had come in an automobile and had been shown her room; but there was nobody to accompany her downstairs afterward, and, finding herself alone in the great hall, she naturally moved toward the library, the door of which stood ajar. She had pushed this door half-open before she noticed that the room was already occupied. As a consequence, she was made the unexpected observer of a beautiful picture of youth and love.

A young man and a young woman were standing together in the glow of a blazing wood-fire. No word was to be heard, but in their faces, eloquent with passion, there shone something so deep and true that the chance intruder hesitated on the threshold, eager to lay this picture away in her mind with the other lovely and tragic memories now fast accumulating there. Then she drew back, and readvancing with a less noiseless foot, came into the full presence of Captain Holliday drawn up in all the pride of his military rank beside Alicia, the accomplished daughter of the house, who, if under a shadow as many whispered, wore that shadow as some women wear a crown.

Miss Strange was struck with admiration, and turned upon them the brightest facet of her vivacious nature, all the time she was saying to herself: "Does she know why I am here? Or does she look upon me only as an additional guest foisted upon her by a thoughtless parent?"

There was nothing in the manner of her cordial but

composed young hostess to show, and Miss Strange, with but one thought in mind since she had caught the light of feeling on the two faces confronting her, took the first opportunity that offered of running over the facts given her by Mr. Driscoll, to see if any reconcilement were possible between them and an innocence in which she must henceforth believe.

They were certainly of a most damaging nature.

Miss Driscoll and four other young ladies of her own station in life had formed themselves, some two years before, into a coterie of five, called The Inseparables. They lunched together, rode together, visited together. So close was the bond and their mutual dependence so evident, that it came to be the custom to invite the whole five whenever the size of the function warranted it. In fact, it was far from an uncommon occurrence to see them grouped at receptions or following one another down the aisles of churches or through the mazes of the dance at balls or assemblies. And no one demurred at this, for they were all handsome and attractive girls, till it began to be noticed that, coincident with their presence, some article of value was found missing from the dressing room or from the tables where wedding gifts were displayed. Nothing was safe where they went, and though, in the course of time, each article found its way back to its owner in a manner as mysterious as its previous abstraction, the scandal grew and, whether with good reason or bad, finally settled about the person of Miss Driscoll, who was the showiest, least pecuniarily tempted, and most dignified in manner and speech of them all.

Some instances had been given by way of further enlightenment. This is one: A theatre party was in progress. There were twelve in the party, five of whom were Inseparables. In the course of the last act, another lady—in fact, their chaperon—missed her handkerchief, an almost priceless bit of lace. Positive that she had brought it with her into the box, she caused a careful search, but without the least success. Recalling certain whispers she had heard, she noted which of the five girls were with her in the box. They were Miss Driscoll, Miss Hughson, Miss Yates, and Miss Benedict. Miss West sat in the box adjoining.

A fortnight later this handkerchief reappeared—and where? Among the cushions of a yellow satin couch in her own drawing room. The Inseparables had just made their call, and the three who had sat on the couch were Miss Driscoll, Miss Hughson, and Miss Benedict.

The next instance seemed to point still more insistently toward the lady already named. Miss Yates had an expensive present to buy, and the whole five Inseparables went in an imposing group to Tiffany's. A tray of rings was set before them. All examined and eagerly fingered the stock out of which Miss Yates presently chose a finely set emerald. She was leading her friends away when the clerk suddenly whispered in her ear, "I miss one of the rings." Dismayed beyond speech, she turned and consulted the faces of her four companions who stared back at her with immovable serenity. But one of them was paler than usual, and this lady (it was Miss Driscoll) held her hands in her muff and did not offer to take them out. Miss Yates, whose father had completed a big "deal" the week before, wheeled round upon the clerk. "Charge it! charge it at its full value," said she. "I buy both the rings."

And in three weeks the purloined ring came back to her, in a box of violets with no name attached.

The third instance was a recent one, and had come to Mr. Driscoll's ears directly from the lady suffering the loss. She was a woman of uncompromising integrity, who felt it her duty to make known to this gentleman the following facts: She had just left a studio reception, and was standing at the curb waiting for a taxicab to draw up, when a small boy—a street arab—darted toward her from the other side of the street, and thrusting into her hand something small and hard, cried breathlessly as he slipped away, "It's yours, ma'am; you dropped it." Astonished, for she had not been conscious of any loss, she looked down at her treasure trove and found it to be a small medallion which she sometimes wore on a chain at her belt. But she had not worn it that day, nor any day for weeks. Then she remembered. She had worn it a month before to a similar reception at this same studio. A number of young girls had stood about her admiring it—she remembered well who they were; the Inseparables, of course; and to please them she had slipped it from its chain. Then something had happened—something which diverted her attention entirely—and she had gone home without the medallion; had, in fact, forgotten it, only to recall its loss now. Placing it in her bag, she looked hastily about her. A crowd was at her back; nothing to be distinguished there. But in front, on the opposite side of the street, stood a clubhouse, and in one of its windows she perceived a solitary figure looking out. It was that of Miss Driscoll's father. He could imagine her conclusion.

In vain he denied all knowledge of the matter. She told him other stories which had come to her ears of thefts as mysterious, followed by restorations as peculiar as this one, finishing with, "It is your daughter, and people are beginning to say so."

And Miss Strange, brooding over these instances, would have said the same, but for Miss Driscoll's absolute serenity of demeanour and complete abandonment to love. These seemed incompatible with guilt; these, whatever the appearances, proclaimed innocence—an innocence she was here to prove if fortune favoured and the really guilty person's madness should again break forth.

For madness it would be and nothing less, for any hand, even the most experienced, to draw attention to itself by a repetition of old tricks on an occasion so marked. Yet because it would take madness, and madness knows no law, she prepared herself for the contingency under a mask of girlish smiles which made her at once the delight and astonishment of her watchful and uneasy host.

With the exception of the diamonds worn by the Ambassadress, there was but one jewel of consequence to be seen at the dinner that night; but how great was that consequence and with what splendour it invested the snowy neck it adorned!

Miss Strange, in compliment to the noble foreigners, had put on one of her family heirlooms—a filigree pendant of extraordinary sapphires which had once belonged to Marie Antoinette. As its beauty flashed upon the women, and its value struck the host, the latter could not restrain himself from casting an anxious eye about the board in search of some token of the cupidity with which one person there must welcome this unexpected sight.

Naturally his first glance fell upon Alicia, seated opposite to him at the other end of the table. But her eyes were elsewhere, and her smile for Captain Holliday, and the father's gaze travelled on, taking up each young girl's face in turn. All were contemplating Miss Strange and her jewels, and the cheeks of one were flushed and those of the others pale, but whether with dread or longing who could tell? Struck with foreboding, but alive to his duty as host, he forced his glances away, and did not even allow himself to question the motive or the wisdom of the temptation thus offered.

Two hours later and the girls were all in one room. It was a custom of the Inseparables to meet for a chat before retiring, but always alone and in the room of one of their number. But this was a night of innovations; Violet was not only included, but the meeting was held in her room. Her way with girls was even more fruitful of result than her way with men. They might laugh at her, criticize her, or even call her names significant of disdain, but they never left her long to herself or missed an opportunity to make the most of her irrepressible chatter.

Her satisfaction at entering this charmed circle did not take from her piquancy, and story after story fell from her lips as she fluttered about, now here now there, in her endless preparations for retirement. She had taken off her historic pendant after it had been duly admired and handled by all present, and, with the careless confidence of an assured ownership, thrown it down upon the end of her dresser, which, by the way, projected very close to the open window.

"Are you going to leave your jewel *there?*" whispered a voice in her ear as a burst of laughter rang out in response to one of her sallies.

Turning, with a simulation of round-eyed wonder, she met Miss Hughson's earnest gaze with the careless rejoinder, "What's the harm?" and went on with her story with all the reckless ease of a perfectly thoughtless nature.

Miss Hughson abandoned her protest. How could she explain her reasons for it to one apparently uninitiated in the scandal associated with their especial clique.

Yes, she left the jewel there; but she locked her door and quickly, so that they must all have heard her before reaching their rooms. Then she crossed to the window, which, like all on this side, opened on a balcony running the length of the house. She was aware of this balcony, also of the fact that only young ladies slept in the corridor communicating with it. But she was not quite sure that this one corridor accommodated them all. If one of them should room elsewhere! (Miss Driscoll, for instance.) But no! the anxiety displayed for the safety of her jewel precluded that supposition. Their hostess, if none of the others, was within access of this room and its open window. But how about the rest? Perhaps the lights would tell. Eagerly the little schemer looked forth, and let her glances travel down the full length of the balcony. Two separate beams of light shot across it as she looked, and presently another, and, after some waiting, a fourth. But the fifth failed to appear. This troubled her, but not seriously. Two of the girls might be sleeping in one bed.

Drawing her shade, she finished her preparations for the night; then with her kimono on, lifted the pendant and thrust it into a small box she had taken from her trunk. A curious smile, very unlike any she had shown to man or woman that day, gave a sarcastic lift to her lips, as with a slow and thoughtful manipulation of her dainty fingers she moved the jewel about in this small receptacle and then returned it, after one quick examining glance, to the very spot on the dresser from which she had taken it. "If only the madness is great enough!" that smile seemed to say. Truly, it was much to hope for, but a chance is a chance; and comforting herself with the thought, Miss Strange put out her light, and, with a hasty raising of the shade she had previously pulled down, took a final look at the prospect.

Its aspect made her shudder. A low fog was rising from the meadows in the far distance, and its ghostliness under the moon woke all sorts of uncanny images in her excited mind. To escape them she crept into bed, where she lay with her eyes on the end of her dresser. She had closed that half of the French window over which she had drawn the shade; but she had left ajar the one giving free access to the jewels; and when she was not watching the scintillation of her sapphires in the moonlight, she was dwelling in fixed attention on this narrow opening.

But nothing happened, and two o'clock, then three o'clock struck, without a dimming of the blue scintillations on the end of her dresser. Then she suddenly sat up. Not that she heard anything new, but that a thought had come to her. "If an attempt is made," so she murmured softly to herself, "it will be by—" She did not finish. Something—she could not call it sound—set her heart beating tumultuously, and listening—listening—watching —watching—she followed in her imagination the approach down the balcony of an almost inaudible step, not daring to move herself, it seemed so near, but waiting with eyes fixed, for the shadow which must fall across the shade she had failed to raise over that half of the swinging window she had so carefully left shut.

At length she saw it projecting slowly across the slightly illuminated surface. Formless, save for the outreaching hand, it passed the casement's edge, nearing with pauses and hesitations the open gap beyond through which the neglected sapphires beamed with steady lustre. Would she ever see the hand itself appear between the dresser and the window frame? Yes, there it comes—small, delicate, and startlingly white, threading that gap—darting with the suddenness of a serpent's tongue toward the dresser and disappearing again with the pendant in its clutch.

As she realized this—she was but young, you know—as she saw her bait taken and the hardly expected event fulfilled, her pent-up breath sped forth in a sigh which sent the intruder flying, and so startled herself that she sank back in terror on her pillow.

The breakfast call had sounded its musical chimes through the halls. The Ambassador and his wife had responded, so had most of the young gentlemen and ladies, but the daughter of the house was not amongst them, nor Miss Strange, whom one would naturally expect to see down first of all.

These two absences puzzled Mr. Driscoll. What might they not portend? But his suspense, at least in one regard, was short. Before his guests were well seated, Miss Driscoll entered from the terrace in company with Captain Holliday. In her arms she carried a huge bunch of roses and was looking very beautiful. Her father's heart warmed at the sight. No shadow from the night rested upon her.

But Miss Strange!—where was she? He could not feel quite easy till he knew.

"Have any of you seen Miss Strange?" he asked, as they sat down at table. And his eyes sought the Inseparables.

Five lovely heads were shaken, some carelessly, some wonderingly, and one with a quick, forced smile. But he was in no mood to discriminate, and he had beckoned one of the servants to him, when a step was heard at the door and the delinquent slid in and took her place, in a shamefaced manner suggestive of a cause deeper than mere tardiness. In fact, she had what might be called a frightened air, and stared into her plate, avoiding every eye, which was certainly not natural to her. What did it mean? and why, as she made a poor attempt at eating, did four of the Inseparables exchange glances of doubt and dismay and then concentrate their looks upon his daughter? That Alicia failed to notice this, but sat abloom above her roses now fastened in a great bunch upon her breast, offered him some comfort; yet, for all the volubility of his chief guests, the meal was a great trial to his patience, as well as a poor preparation for the hour when, the noble pair gone, he stepped into the library to find Miss Strange awaiting him with one hand behind her back and a piteous look on her infantile features.

"Oh, Mr. Driscoll," she began—and then he saw that a group of anxious girls hovered in her rear—"my pendant! my beautiful pendant! It is gone! Somebody reached in from the balcony and took it from my dresser in the night. Of course, it was to frighten me; all of the girls told me not to leave it there. But I—I cannot make them give it back, and papa is so particular about this jewel that I'm afraid to go home. Won't you tell them it's no joke, and see that I get it again. I won't be so careless another time."

Hardly believing his eyes, hardly believing his ears—she

was so perfectly the spoiled child detected in a fault—he looked sternly about upon the girls and bade them end the jest and produce the gems at once.

But not one of them spoke, and not one of them moved; only his daughter grew pale until the roses seemed a mockery, and the steady stare of her large eyes was almost too much for him to bear.

The anguish of this gave asperity to his manner, and in a strange, hoarse tone he loudly cried:

"One of you did this. Which? If it was you, Alicia, speak. I am in no mood for nonsense. I want to know whose foot traversed the balcony and whose hand abstracted these jewels."

A continued silence, deepening into painful embarrassment for all. Mr. Driscoll eyed them in ill-concealed anguish, then turning to Miss Strange was still further thrown off his balance by seeing her pretty head droop and her gaze fall in confusion.

"Oh! it's easy enough to tell whose foot traversed the balcony," she murmured. "It left *this* behind." And drawing forward her hand, she held out to view a small gold-coloured slipper. "I found it outside my window," she explained. "I hoped I should not have to show it."

A gasp of uncontrollable feeling from the surrounding group of girls, then absolute stillness.

"I fail to recognize it," observed Mr. Driscoll, taking it in his hand. "Whose slipper is this?" he asked in a manner not to be gainsaid.

Still no reply, then as he continued to eye the girls one after another a voice—the last he expected to hear—spoke and his daughter cried:

"It is mine. But it was not I who walked in it down the balcony."

"Alicia!"

A month's apprehension was in that cry. The silence,

the pent-up emotion brooding in the air was intolerable. A
fresh young laugh broke it.

"Oh," exclaimed a roguish voice, "I knew that you
were all in it! But the especial one who wore the slipper
and grabbed the pendant cannot hope to hide herself. Her
fingertips will give her away."

Amazement on every face and a convulsive movement
in one half-hidden hand.

"You see," the airy little being went on, in her light
way, "I have some awfully funny tricks. I am always being
scolded for them, but somehow I don't improve. One is to
keep my jewelry bright with a strange foreign paste an old
Frenchwoman once gave me in Paris. It's of a vivid red,
and stains the fingers dreadfully if you don't take care. Not
even water will take it off, see mine. I used that paste on
my pendant last night just after you left me, and being
awfully sleepy I didn't stop to rub it off. If your fingertips
are not red, you never touched the pendant, Miss Driscoll.
Oh, see! They are as white as milk.

"But someone took the sapphires, and I owe that
person a scolding, as well as myself. Was it you, Miss
Hughson? You, Miss Yates? or—" and here she paused
before Miss West: "Oh, you have your gloves on! You are
the guilty one!" and her laugh rang out like a peal of bells,
robbing her next sentence of even a suggestion of sarcasm.
"Oh, what a sly-boots!" she cried. "How you have deceived
me! Whoever would have thought you to be the one to
play the mischief!"

Who indeed! Of all the five, she was the one who was
considered absolutely immune from suspicion ever since
the night Mrs. Barnum's handkerchief had been taken,
and she not in the box. Eyes which had surveyed Miss
Driscoll askance now rose in wonder toward hers, and
failed to fall again because of the stoniness into which her
delicately carved features had settled.

"Miss West, I know you will be glad to remove your gloves; Miss Strange certainly has a right to know her special tormentor," spoke up her host in as natural a voice as his great relief would allow.

But the cold, half-frozen woman remained without a movement. She was not deceived by the banter of the moment. She knew that to all of the others, if not to Peter Strange's odd little daughter, it was the thief who was being spotted and brought thus hilariously to light. And her eyes grew hard, and her lips grey, and she failed to unglove the hands upon which all glances were concentrated.

"You do not need to see my hands; I confess to taking the pendant."

"Caroline!"

A heart overcome by shock had thrown up this cry. Miss West eyed her bosom-friend disdainfully.

"Miss Strange has called it a jest," she coldly commented. "Why should you suggest anything of a graver character?"

Alicia brought thus to bay, and by one she had trusted most, stepped quickly forward, and quivering with vague doubts, aghast before unheard-of possibilities, she tremulously remarked:

"We did not sleep together last night. You had to come into my room to get my slippers. Why did you do this? What was in your mind, Caroline?"

A steady look, a low laugh choked with many emotions answered her.

"Do you want me to reply, Alicia? Or shall we let it pass?"

"Answer!"

It was Mr. Driscoll who spoke. Alicia had shrunk back, almost to where a little figure was cowering with wide eyes fixed in something like terror on the aroused father's face.

"Then hear me," murmured the girl, entrapped and

suddenly desperate. "I wore Alicia's slippers and I took the jewels, because it was time that an end should come to your mutual dissimulation. The love I once felt for her she has herself deliberately killed. I had a lover—she took him. I had faith in life, in honour, and in friendship. She destroyed all. A thief—she has dared to aspire to *him!* And *you* condoned her fault. You, with your craven restoration of her booty, thought the matter cleared and her a fit mate for a man of highest honour."

"Miss West"—no one had ever heard that tone in Mr. Driscoll's voice before, "before you say another word calculated to mislead these ladies, let me say that this hand never returned anyone's booty or had anything to do with the restoration of any abstracted article. You have been caught in a net, Miss West, from which you cannot escape by slandering my innocent daughter."

"Innocent!" All the tragedy latent in this peculiar girl's nature blazed forth in the word. "Alicia, face me. Are you innocent? Who took the Dempsey corals, and that diamond from the Tiffany tray?"

"It is not necessary for Alicia to answer," the father interposed with not unnatural heat. "Miss West stands self-convicted."

"How about Lady Paget's scarf? I was not there that night."

"You are a woman of wiles. That could be managed by one bent on an elaborate scheme of revenge."

"And so could the abstraction of Mrs. Barnum's five-hundred-dollar handkerchief by one who sat in the next box," chimed in Miss Hughson, edging away from the friend to whose honour she would have pinned her faith an hour before. "I remember now seeing her lean over the railing to adjust the old lady's shawl."

With a start, Caroline West turned a tragic gaze upon the speaker.

"You think me guilty of all because of what I did last night?"

"Why shouldn't I."

"And you, Anna?"

"Alicia has my sympathy," murmured Miss Benedict. Yet the wild girl persisted.

"But I have told you my provocation. You cannot believe that I am guilty of her sin; not if you look at her as I am looking now."

But their glances hardly followed her pointing finger. Her friends—the comrades of her youth, the Inseparables with their secret oath—one and all held themselves aloof, struck by the perfidy they were only just beginning to take in. Smitten with despair, for these girls were her life, she gave one wild leap and sank on her knees before Alicia.

"Oh speak!" she began. "Forgive me, and—"

A tremble seized her throat; she ceased to speak and let fall her partially uplifted hands. The cheery sound of men's voices had drifted in from the terrace, and the figure of Captain Holliday could be seen passing by. The shudder which shook Caroline West communicated itself to Alicia Driscoll, and the former rising quickly, the two women surveyed each other, possibly for the first time, with open soul and a complete understanding.

"Caroline!" murmured the one.

"Alicia!" pleaded the other.

"Caroline, trust me," said Alicia Driscoll in that moving voice of hers, which more than her beauty caught and retained all hearts. "You have served me ill, but it was not all undeserved. Girls," she went on, eyeing both them and her father with the wistfulness of a breaking heart, "neither Caroline nor myself are worthy of Captain Holliday's love. Caroline has told you her fault, but mine is perhaps a worse one. The ring—the scarf—the diamond pins—I took them all—took them if I did not retain them. A curse has been over my life—the curse of a longing I could not combat. But love was working a change in me. Since I have known Captain Holliday—but that's all over. I was mad to think I could be happy with such memories in my life. I shall never marry now—or touch jewels again—my own or another's. Father, father, you won't go back on your girl! I couldn't see Caroline suffer for what I have done. You will pardon me and help—help—"

Her voice choked. She flung herself into her father's arms; his head bent over hers, and for an instant not a soul in the room moved. Then Miss Hughson gave a spring and caught her by the hand.

"We are inseparable," said she, and kissed the hand, murmuring, "Now is our time to show it."

Then other lips fell upon those cold and trembling fingers, which seemed to warm under these embraces. And then a tear. It came from the hard eye of Caroline, and remained a sacred secret between the two.

"You have your pendant?"

Mr. Driscoll's suffering eye shone down on Violet Strange's uplifted face as she advanced to say goodbye prepatory to departure.

"Yes," she acknowledged, "but hardly, I fear, your gratitude."

And the answer astonished her.

"I am not sure that the real Alicia will not make her father happier than the unreal one has ever done."

"And Captain Holliday?"

"He may come to feel the same."

"Then I do not quit in disgrace?"

"You depart with my thanks."

When a certain personage was told of the success of Miss Strange's latest manoeuvre, he remarked:

"The little one progresses. We shall have to give her a case of prime importance next."

STRANGE TO SAY, the detective novels of Arthur Benjamin Reeve (1880–1936) were once almost as popular as Conan Doyle's. His most famous character, Craig Kennedy—billed as a "scientific detective"—solved cases by using Reeve's overimaginative adaptations of what were then wondrous "modern" inventions—moving pictures, the lie detector (called a "crimeometer"), X-rays, the dictograph. Chemical bombs, blood tests, and a primitive form of psychoanalysis also provided subjects for Craig Kennedy's pseudo-didactic lectures on his methods. A native of Long Island, Reeve was trained as a lawyer though he never practiced, choosing instead to be a journalist. As public taste became more sophisticated, he gave up fictional detection and turned his efforts to being a lay specialist in real-life crime prevention. He also wrote serials for the early silent movies.

Constance Dunlap, featured in *Constance Dunlap: Woman Detective* (1916), is a criminal-turned-sleuth, more or less in the tradition of T. W. Hanshew's Cleek, Maurice Leblanc's Arsène Lupin, and Louis Joseph Vance's Lone Wolf. With her first husband, and after his suicide, with another man, she is an accomplice to forgery and embezzlement, for which crimes she is shadowed throughout her problem-solving career by the evil detective Drummond. Like Craig Kennedy, she detects with the aid of technological inventions the rather weird descriptions of which are apt to confuse the modern reader, to whom many of these former marvels are commonplace.

The Dope Fiends

by Arthur B. Reeve

"I have a terrible headache," remarked Constance Dunlap to her friend, Adele Gordon, the petite cabaret singer and dancer of the Mayfair, who had dropped in to see her one afternoon.

"You poor, dear creature," soothed Adele. "Why don't you go to see Dr. Price? He has cured me. He's splendid—splendid."

Constance hesitated. Dr. Morcland Price was a well-known physician. All day and even at night, she knew, automobiles and cabs rolled up to his door and their occupants were, for the most part, stylishly gowned women.

"Oh, come on," urged Adele. "He doesn't charge as highly as people seem to think. Besides, I'll go with you and introduce you, and he'll charge only as he does the rest of us in the profession."

Constance's head throbbed frantically. She felt that she must have some relief soon. "All right," she agreed, "I'll go with you, and thank you, Adele."

Dr. Price's office was on the first floor of the fashionable Recherché Apartments, and, as she expected, Constance noted a line of motor cars before it.

They entered and were admitted to a richly furnished room, in mahogany and expensive Persian rugs, where a number of patients waited. One after another an attendant summoned them noiselessly and politely to see the doctor, until at last the turn of Constance and Adele came.

Dr. Price was a youngish middle-aged man, tall, with a sallow countenance and a self-confident, polished manner which went a long way in reassuring the patients, most of whom were ladies.

As they entered the doctor's sanctum behind the folding doors, Adele seemed to be on very good terms indeed with him.

They seated themselves in the deep leather chairs beside Dr. Price's desk, and he inclined his head to listen to the story of their ailments.

"Doctor," began Constance's introducer, "I've brought my friend, Mrs. Dunlap, who is suffering from one of those awful headaches. I thought perhaps you could give her some of that medicine that has done me so much good."

The doctor bowed without saying anything and shifted his eyes from Adele to Constance. "Just what seems to be the difficulty?" he inquired.

Constance told him how she felt, of her general lassitude and the big, throbbing veins in her temples.

"Ah—a woman's headaches!" he smiled, adding, "Nothing serious, however, in this case, as far as I can see. We can fix this one all right, I think."

He wrote out a prescription quickly and handed it to Constance.

"Of course," he added, as he pocketed his fee, "it makes no difference to me personally, but I would advise that you have it filled at Muller's—Miss Gordon knows the place. I think Muller's drugs are perhaps fresher than those of most druggists, and that makes a great deal of difference."

He had risen and was politely and suavely bowing them out of another door, at the same time, by pressing a button, signifying to his attendant to admit the next patient.

Constance had preceded Adele, and, as she passed through the other door, she overheard the doctor whisper to her friend, "I'm going to stop for you tonight to take a ride. I have something important I want to say to you."

She did not catch Adele's answer, but as they left the marble and onyx, brass-grilled entrance, Adele remarked, "That's his car—over there. Oh, but he is a reckless driver—dashes along pell-mell—but always seems to have his eye out for everything—never seems to be arrested, never in an accident."

Constance turned in the direction of the car and was startled to see the familiar face of Drummond across the street dodging behind it. What was it now, she wondered —a divorce case, a scandal—what?

The medicine was made up into little powders, to be taken until they gave relief, and Constance folded the paper of one, poured it on the back of her tongue, and swallowed a glass of water afterward.

Her head continued to throb, but she felt a sense of well-being that she had not before. Adele urged her to take another, and Constance did so.

The second powder increased the effect of the first marvelously. But Constance noticed that she now began to feel queer. She was not used to taking medicine. For a moment she felt that she was above, beyond the reach of ordinary rules and laws. She could have done any sort of physical task, she felt, no matter how difficult. She was amazed at herself, as compared to what she had been only a few moments before.

"Another one?" asked Adele finally.

Constance was by this time genuinely alarmed at the sudden unwonted effect on herself. "N-no," she replied dubiously, "I don't think I want to take any more, just yet."

"Not another?" asked Adele in surprise. "I wish they would affect me that way. Sometimes I have to take the whole dozen before they have any effect."

They chatted for a few minutes, and finally Adele rose.

"Well," she remarked with a nervous twitching of her body, as if she were eager to be doing something, "I really must be going. I can't say I feel any too well myself."

"I think I'll take a walk with you," answered Constance, who did not like the continued effect of the two powders. "I feel the need of exercise—and air."

Adele hesitated, but Constance already had her hat on. She had seen Drummond watching Dr. Price's door, and it interested her to know whether he could possibly have been following Adele or someone else.

As they walked along Adele quickened her pace, until they came again to the drug store.

"I believe I'll go in and get something," she remarked, pausing.

For the first time in several minutes Constance looked at the face of her friend. She was amazed to discover that Adele looked as if she had had a spell of sickness. Her eyes were large and glassy, her skin cold and sweaty, and she looked positively pallid and thin.

As they entered the store Muller, the druggist, bowed again and looked at Adele a moment as she leaned over the counter and whispered something to him. Without a word he went into the arcana behind the partition that cuts off the mysteries of the prescription room in every drug store from the front of the store.

When Muller returned he handed her a packet, for

which she paid and which she dropped quickly into her pocketbook, hugging the pocketbook close to herself.

Adele turned and was about to hurry from the store with Constance. "Oh, excuse me," she said suddenly as if she had just recollected something, "I promised a friend of mine I'd telephone this afternoon, and I have forgotten to do it. I see a pay station here." Constance waited.

Adele returned much quicker than one would have expected she could call up a number, but Constance thought nothing of it at the time. She did notice, however, that as her friend emerged from the booth a most marvelous change had taken place in her. Her step was firm, her eye clear, her hand steady. Whatever it was, reasoned Constance, it could not have been serious to have disappeared so quickly.

It was with some curiosity as to just what she might expect that Constance went around to the famous cabaret that night. The Mayfair occupied two floors of what had been a wide brownstone house before business and pleasure had crowded the residence district further and further uptown. It was a very well-known bohemian rendezvous, where under-, demi-, and upper-world rubbed elbows without friction and seemed to enjoy the novelty and be willing to pay for it.

Adele, who was one of the performers, had not arrived yet, but Constance, who had come with her mind still full of the two unexpected encounters with Drummond, was startled to see him here again. Fortunately he did not see her, and she slipped unobserved into an angle near the window overlooking the street.

Drummond had been engrossed in watching someone already there, and Constance made the best use she could of her eyes to determine who it was. The outdoor walk and a good dinner had checked her headache, and now the excitement of the chase of something, she knew not what, completed the cure.

It was not long before she discovered that Drummond was watching intently, without seeming to do so, a nervous-looking fellow whose general washed-out appearance of face was especially unattractive for some reason or other. He was very thin, very pale, and very stary about the eyes. Then, too, it seemed as if the bone in his nose was going, due perhaps to the shrinkage of the blood vessels from some cause.

Constance noticed a couple of girls whom she had seen Adele speak to on several other occasions approaching the young man.

There came an opportune lull in the music, and from around the corner of her protecting angle Constance could just catch the greeting of one of the girls: "Hello, Sleighbells! Got any snow?"

It was a remark that seemed particularly malapropos to the sultry weather, and Constance half expected a burst of laughter at the unexpected sally.

Instead, she was surprised to hear the young man reply in a very serious and matter-of-fact manner, "Sure. Got any money, May?"

She craned her neck, carefully avoiding coming into Drummond's line of vision, and as she did so she saw two silver quarters gleam momentarily from hand to hand, and the young man passed each girl stealthily a small white paper packet.

Others came to him, both men and women. It seemed to be an established thing, and Constance noted that Drummond watched it all covertly.

"Who is that?" asked Constance of the waiter who had served her sometimes when she had been with Adele, and knew her.

"Why, they call him Sleighbells Charley," he replied, "a coke fiend."

"Which means a cocaine fiend, I suppose?" she queried.

"Yes. He's a lobbygow* for the grapevine system they have now of selling the dope in spite of this new law."

"Where does he get the stuff?" she asked.

The waiter shrugged his shoulders. "Nobody knows, I guess. I don't. But he gets it in spite of the law and peddles it. Oh, it's all adulterated—with some white stuff, I don't know what, and the price they charge is outrageous. They must make an ounce retail at five or six times the cost. Oh, you can bet that someone who is at the top is making a pile of money out of that graft, all right."

He said it not with any air of righteous indignation, but with a certain envy.

Constance was thinking the thing over in her mind. Where did the "coke" come from? The "grapevine" system interested her.

"Sleighbells" seemed to have disposed of all the "coke" he had brought with him. As the last packet went, he rose slowly and shuffled out. Constance, who knew that Adele would not come for some time, determined to follow him. She rose quietly and, under cover of a party going out, managed to disappear without, as far as she knew, letting Drummond catch a glimpse of her. This would not only employ her time, but it was better to avoid Drummond as far as possible at present, too, she felt.

At a distance of about half a block she followed the curiously shuffling figure. He crossed the avenue, turned and went uptown, turned again, and, before she knew it, disappeared in a drug store. She had been so engrossed in following the lobbygow that it was with a start that she realized that he had entered Muller's.

What did it all mean? Was the druggist, Muller, the

* In underworld slang, *lobbygow* means a hanger-on, go-between, or message runner, particularly one involved in the drug traffic—the speculation being that such persons usually hang about in lobbies.

man higher up? She recalled suddenly her own experience of the afternoon. Had Muller tried to palm off something on her? The more she thought of it the more sure she was that the powders she had taken had been doped.

Slowly, turning the matter over in her mind, she returned to the Mayfair. As she peered in cautiously before entering she saw that Drummond had gone. Adele had not come in yet, and she went in and sat down again in her old place.

Perhaps half an hour later, outside, she heard a car drive up with a furious rattle of gears. She looked out of the window and, as far as she could determine in the shadows, it was Dr. Price. A woman got out—Adele. For a moment she stopped to talk, then Dr. Price waved a gay goodbye and was off. All she could catch was a hasty, "No; I don't think I'd better come in tonight," from him.

As Adele entered the Mayfair she glanced about, caught sight of Constance, and came and sat down by her.

It would have been impossible for her to enter unobserved, so popular was she. It was not long before the two girls whom Constance had seen dealing with "Sleighbells" sauntered over.

"Your friend was here tonight," remarked one to Adele.

"Which one?" laughed Adele.

"The one who admired your dancing the other night and wanted to take lessons."

"You mean the young fellow who was selling something?" asked Constance pointedly.

"Oh, no," returned the girl quite casually. "That was Sleighbells," and they all laughed.

Constance thought immediately of Drummond. "The other one, then," she said, "the thickset man who was all alone?"

"Yes; he went away afterward. Do you know him?"

"I've seen him somewhere," evaded Constance; "but I just can't quite place him."

She had not noticed Adele particularly until now. Under the light she had a peculiar worn look, the same as she had had before.

The waiter came up to them. "Your turn is next," he hinted to Adele.

"Excuse me a minute," she apologized to the rest of the party. "I must fix up a bit. No," she added to Constance, "don't come with me."

She returned from the dressing room a different person, and plunged into the wild dance for which the limited orchestra was already tuning up. It was a veritable riot of whirl and rhythm. Never before had Constance seen Adele dance with such abandon. As she executed the wild mazes of a newly imported dance, she held even the jaded Mayfair spellbound. And when she concluded with one daring figure and sat down, flushed and excited, the diners applauded and even shouted approval. It was an event for even the dance-mad Mayfair.

Constance did not share in the applause. At last she understood. Adele was a dope fiend, too. She felt it with a sense of pain. Always, she knew, the fiends tried to get away alone somewhere for a few minutes to snuff some of their favorite nepenthe. She had heard before of the cocaine "snuffers" who took a little of the deadly powder, placed it on the back of the hand, and inhaled it up the nose with a quick intake of breath. Adele was one. It was not Adele who danced. It was the dope.

Constance was determined to speak.

"You remember that man the girls spoke of?" she began.

"Yes. What of him?" asked Adele with almost a note of defiance.

"Well, I really *do* know him," confessed Constance. "He is a detective."

Constance watched her companion curiously, for at the mere word she had stopped short and faced her. "He is?" she asked quickly. "Then that was why Dr. Price—"

She managed to suppress the remark and continued her walk home without another word.

In Adele's little apartment Constance was quick to note that the same haggard look had returned to her friend's face.

Adele had reached for her pocketbook with a sort of clutching eagerness and was about to leave the room.

Constance rose. "Why don't you give up the stuff?" she asked earnestly. "Don't you want to?"

For a moment Adele faced her angrily. Then her real nature seemed slowly to come to the surface. "Yes," she murmured frankly.

"Then why don't you?" pleaded Constance.

"I haven't the power. There is an indescribable excitement to do something great, to make a mark. It's soon gone, but while it lasts, I can sing, dance, do anything— and then—every part of my body begins crying for more of the stuff again."

There was no longer any necessity of concealment from Constance. She took a pinch of the stuff, placed it on the back of her wrist, and quickly sniffed it. The change in her was magical. From a quivering, wretched girl she became a self-confident neurasthenic.

"I don't care," she laughed hollowly now. "Yes, I know what you are going to tell me. Soon I'll be 'hunting the cocaine bug,' as they call it, imagining that in my skin, under the flesh, are worms crawling, perhaps see them, see the little animals running around and biting me."

She said it with a half-reckless cynicism. "Oh, you don't know. There are two souls in the cocainist—one tortured by the pain of not having the stuff, the other laughing and mocking at the dangers of it. It stimulates. It makes your mind work—without effort, by itself. And it gives such visions of success, makes you feel able to do so much, and to forget. All the girls use it."

"Where do they get it?" asked Constance. "I thought the new law prohibited it."

"Get it?" repeated Adele. "Why, they get it from that fellow they call 'Sleighbells.' They call it 'snow,' you know, and the girls who use it 'snowbirds.' The law does prohibit its sale, but—"

She paused significantly.

"Yes," agreed Constance; "but Sleighbells is only a part of the system after all. Who is the man at the top?"

Adele shrugged her shoulders and was silent. Still, Constance did not fail to note a sudden look of suspicion which Adele shot at her. Was Adele shielding someone?

Constance knew that someone must be getting rich from the traffic, probably selling hundreds of ounces a week and making thousands of dollars. Somehow she felt a sort of indignation at the whole thing. Who was it? Who was the man higher up?

In the morning as she was working about her little kitchenette an idea came to her. Why not hire the vacant apartment cross the hall from Adele? An optician, who was a friend of hers, in the course of a recent conversation had mentioned an invention, a model of which he had made for the inventor. She would try it.

Since, with Constance, the outlining of a plan was tantamount to the execution, it was not many hours later before she had both the apartment and the model of the invention.

Her wall separated her from the drug store, and by careful calculation she determined about where came the little prescription department. Carefully, so as to arouse no suspicion, she began to bore away at the wall with various tools, until finally she had a small, almost imperceptible opening. It was tedious work, and toward the end needed great care so as not to excite suspicion. But finally she was rewarded. Through it she could see just a trace of daylight, and by squinting could see a row of bottles on a shelf opposite.

Then, through the hole, she pushed a long, narrow tube, like a putty blower. When at last she placed her eye at it, she gave a low exclamation of satisfaction. She could now see the whole of the little room.

It was a detectascope, invented by Gaillard Smith, adapter of the detectaphone, an instrument built up on the principle of the cytoscope which physicians use to explore internally down the throat. Only, in the end of the tube, instead of an ordinary lens, was placed what is known as a "fish-eye" lens, which had a range something like nature has given the eyes of fishes, hence the name. Ordinarily cameras, because of the flatness of their lenses, have a range of only a few degrees, the greatest being scarcely more than ninety. But this lens was globular, and, like a drop of water, refracted light from all directions. When placed so that half of it caught the light it "saw" through an angle of 180 degrees, "saw" everything in the room instead of just that little row of bottles on the shelf opposite.

Constance set herself to watch, and it was not long before her suspicions were confirmed, and she was sure that this was nothing more than a "coke" joint. Still she wondered whether Muller was the real source of the traffic of which Sleighbells was the messenger. She was determined to find out.

All day she watched through her detectascope. Once she saw Adele come in and buy more dope. It was with difficulty that she kept from interfering. But, she reflected, the time was not ripe. She had thought the thing out. There was no use in trying to get at it through Adele. The only way was to stop the whole curse at its source, to dam the stream. People came and went. She soon found that he was selling them packets from a box hidden in the woodwork. That much she had learned, anyhow.

Constance watched faithfully all day with only time enough taken out for dinner. It was after her return from this brief interval that she felt her heart give a leap of apprehension, as she looked again through the detectascope. There was Drummond in the back of the store talking to Muller and a woman who looked as if she might be Mrs. Muller, for both seemed nervous and anxious.

As nearly as she could make out, Drummond was alternately threatening and arguing with Muller. Finally the three seemed to agree, for Drummond walked over to a typewriter on a table, took a fresh sheet of carbon paper from a drawer, placed it between two sheets of paper, and hastily wrote something.

Drummond read over what he had written. It seemed to be short, and the three apparently agreed on it. Then, in a trembling hand, Muller signed the two copies which Drummond had made, one of which Drummond himself kept and the other he sealed in an envelope and sent away by a boy. Drummond reached into his pocket and pulled out a huge roll of bills of large denomination. He counted out what seemed to be approximately half, handed it to the woman, and replaced the rest in his pocket. What it was all about Constance could only vaguely guess. She longed to know what was in the letter and why the money had been paid to the woman.

Perhaps a quarter of an hour after Drummond left Adele appeared again, pleading for more dope. Muller went back of the partition and made up a fresh paper of it from a bottle also concealed.

Constance was torn by conflicting impulses. She did not want to miss anything in the perplexing drama that was being enacted before her, yet she wished to interfere with the deadly course of Adele. Still, perhaps the girl would resent interference if she found out that Constance was spying on her. She determined to wait a little while before seeing Adele. It was only after a decided effort that she tore herself away from the detectascope and knocked on Adele's door as if she had just come in for a visit. Again she knocked, but still there was no answer. Every minute something might be happening next door. She hurried back to her post of observation.

One of the worst aspects of the use of cocaine, she knew, was the desire of the user to share his experience with someone else. The passing on of the habit, which seemed to be one of the strongest desires of the drug fiend, made him even more dangerous to society than he would otherwise have been. That thought gave Constance an idea.

She recalled also now having heard somewhere that it was a common characteristic of these poor creatures to have a passion for fast automobiling, to go on long rides, perhaps even without having the money to pay for them. That, too, confirmed the idea which she had.

As the night advanced she determined to stick to her post. What could it have been that Drummond was doing? It was no good, she felt positive.

Suddenly before her eye, glued to its eavesdropping aperture, she saw a strange sight. There was a violent commotion in the store. Blue-coated policemen seemed to swarm in from nowhere. And in the rear, directing them, appeared Drummond, holding by the arm the unfortunate Sleighbells, quaking with fear, evidently having been picked up already elsewhere by the wily detective.

Muller put up a stout resistance, but the officers easily seized him and, after a hasty but thorough search, unearthed his cache of the contraband drug.

As the scene unfolded, Constance was more and more bewildered after having witnessed that which preceded it, the signing of the letter and the passing of the money.

Muller evidently had nothing to say about that. What did it mean?

The police were still holding Muller, and Constance had not noted that Drummond had disappeared.

"It's on the first floor—left, men," sounded a familiar voice outside her own door. "I know she's there. My shadow saw her buy the dope and take it home."

Her heart was thumping wildly. It was Drummond leading his squad of raiders, and they were about to enter the apartment of Adele. They knocked, but there was no answer.

A few moments before Constance would have felt perfectly safe in saying that Adele was out. But if Drummond's man had seen her enter, might she not have been there all the time, be there still, in a stupor? She dreaded to think of what might happen if the poor girl once fell into their hands. It would be the final impulse that would complete her ruin.

Constance did not stop to reason it out. Her woman's intuition told her that now was the time to act—that there was no retreat.

She opened her own door just as the raiders had forced in the flimsy affair that guarded the apartment of Adele.

"So!" sneered Drummond, catching sight of her in the dim light of the hallway. "You are mixed up in these violations of the new drug law, too!"

Constance said nothing. She had determined first to make Drummond display his hand.

"Well," he ground out, "I'm going to get these people this time. I represent the Medical Society and the Board of Health. These men have been assigned to me by the Commissioner as a dope squad. We want this girl. We have others who will give evidence; but we want this one, too."

He said it with a bluster that even exaggerated the theatrical character of the raid itself. Constance did not stop to weigh the value of his words, but through the door she brushed quickly. Adele might need her if she was indeed there.

As she entered the little living room she saw a sight which almost transfixed her. Adele was there—lying across a divan, motionless.

Constance bent over. Adele was cold. As far as she could determine there was not a breath or a heartbeat!

What did it mean? She did not stop to think. Instantly there flashed over her the recollection of an instrument she had read about at one of the city hospitals. It might save Adele. Before any one knew what she was doing she had darted to the telephone in the lower hall of the apartment and had called up the hospital frantically, imploring them to hurry. Adele must be saved.

Constance had no very clear idea of what happened next in the hurly-burly of events, until the ambulance pulled up at the door and the white-coated surgeon burst in carrying a heavy suitcase.

With one look at the unfortunate girl he muttered, "Paralysis of the respiratory organs—too large a dose of the drug. You did perfectly right," and began unpacking the case.

Constance, calm now in the crisis, stood by him and helped as deftly as could any nurse.

It was a curious arrangement of tubes and valves, with a large rubber bag, and a little pump that the doctor had brought. Quickly he placed a cap, attached to it, over the nose and mouth of the poor girl, and started the machine.

"Wh-what is it?" gasped Drummond as he saw Adele's hitherto motionless breast now rise and fall.

"A pulmotor," replied the doctor, working quickly and carefully, "an artificial lung. Sometimes it can revive even the medically dead. It is our last chance with this girl."

Constance had picked up the packet which had fallen beside Adele and was looking at the white powder.

"Almost pure cocaine," remarked the young surgeon, testing it. "The hydrochloride, large crystals, highest quality. Usually it is adulterated. Was she in the habit of taking it this way?"

Constance said nothing. She had seen Muller make up the packet—specially now, she recalled. Instead of the adulterated dope he had given Adele the purest kind. Why? Was there some secret he wished to lock in her breast forever?

Mechanically the pulmotor pumped. Would it save her?

Constance was living over what she had already seen through the detectascope. Suddenly she thought of the strange letter and of the money.

She hurried into the drug store. Muller had already been taken away, but before the officer left in charge could interfere she picked up the carbon sheet on which the letter had been copied, turned it over, and held it eagerly to the light.

She read in amazement. It was a confession. In it Muller admitted to Dr. Moreland Price that he was the head of a sort of dope trust, that he had messengers out, like Sleighbells, that he had often put dope in the prescriptions sent him by the doctor, and had repeatedly violated the law and refilled such prescriptions. On its face it was complete and convincing.

Yet it did not satisfy Constance. She could not believe that Adele had committed suicide. Adele must possess some secret. What was it?

"Is—is there any change?" she asked anxiously of the young surgeon now engrossed in his work.

For answer he merely nodded to the apparently motionless form on the bed, and for a moment stopped the pulmotor.

The mechanical movement of the body ceased. But in its place was a slight tremor about the lips and mouth.

Adele moved—was faintly gasping for breath!

"Adele!" cried Constance softly in her ear. "Adele!"

Something, perhaps a faraway answer of recognition, seemed to flicker over her face. The doctor redoubled his efforts.

"Adele—do you know me?" whispered Constance again.

"Yes," came back faintly at last. "There—there's something—wrong with it—They—they—"

"How? What do you mean?" urged Constance. "Tell me, Adele."

The girl moved uneasily. The doctor administered a stimulant and she vaguely opened her eyes, began to talk hazily, dreamily. Constance bent over to catch the faint words which would have been lost to the others.

"They—are going to—double-cross the Health Department," she murmured as if to herself, then gathering strength she went on, "Muller and Sleighbells will be arrested and take the penalty. They have been caught with the goods, anyhow. It has all been arranged so that the detective will get his case. Money—will be paid to both of them, to Muller and the detective, to swing the case and protect him. He made me do it. I saw the detective, even danced with him, and he agreed to do it. Oh, I would do anything—I am his willing tool when I have the stuff. But—this time—it was—" She rambled off incoherently.

"Who made you do it? Who told you?" prompted Constance. "For whom would you do anything?"

Adele moaned and clutched Constance's hand convulsively. Constance did not pause to consider the ethics of questioning a half-unconscious girl. Her only idea was to get at the truth.

"Who was it?" she reiterated.

Adele turned weakly.

"Dr. Price," she murmured as Constance bent her ear to catch even the faintest sound. "He told me—all about it—last night—in the car."

Instantly Constance understood. Adele was the only one outside who held the secret, who could upset the carefully planned frame-up that was to protect the real head of the dope trust who had paid liberally to save his own wretched skin.

She rose quickly and wheeled about suddenly on Drummond.

"You will convict Dr. Price also," she said in a low tone. "This girl must not be dragged down, too. You will leave her alone, and both you and Mr. Muller will hand over that money to her for her cure of the habit."

Drummond started forward angrily, but fell back as Constance added in a lower but firmer tone, "Or I'll have you all up on a charge of attempting murder."

Drummond turned surlily to those of his "dope squad," who remained.

"You can go, boys," he said brusquely. "There's been some mistake here."

As AN OFFICE BOY, a reporter, a playwright, an actor, an employee of a crooked investment house, and as an author, William Hulbert Footner (1879–1944) enjoyed a varied career. By birth a Canadian, he spent the later part of his life residing in a historic seventeenth-century house in Maryland. In addition to Madame Storey, he created two other sleuths: B. Enderby and Amos Lee Mappin. He also wrote novels of the criminal underworld and tales of backwoods adventure, the latter based on his experiences during a solitary 1,200-mile northern trek he took as a young man.

Rosika Storey chose to be called "Madame" because, as she states ruefully, "no one would believe that a woman as beautiful as I could be still unmarried—and respectable," adding "but I am both, worse luck!" Actually, in the many stories and novels detailing her cases, she maintains a stern aloofness towards would-be suitors (most of them turn out to be villains, anyway), and, for the public at large, she cultivates an aura of mystery and goddesslike superiority. Describing herself as "a practical psychologist—specializing in the feminine," she admits that there is both more publicity and more money in solving criminal cases, money being necessary to keep her in exquisite Fortuny gowns and to support her Gramercy Park menage, which includes her devoted secretary, Bella Brickley, and a pampered pet monkey.

The Murder at Fernhurst

by Hulbert Footner

In order to rest and to escape from the strain of the tremendous publicity that followed upon her success in the famous case of the Smoke Bandit, Madame Storey retired for a few days to the house of her friends, the Andrew Lipscombs, who lived in the Connecticut hills remote from any neighbor. I accompanied my employer, since she insisted that I needed a holiday as well as herself. We simply locked up our offices and went away, leaving the telephone to ring, the mail to accumulate, and the hordes of curiosity-seekers to mill around the door as they would.

We supposed that we had kept the place of our retreat a secret from all, but that fond hope was soon dissipated. Late on the night of our arrival as we were playing bridge with our friends in the blessed quiet of their house, Madame Storey was called to the telephone. She returned to the card table with the grave, remote look that I knew so well, her *working* look, and my heart sank.

"Well, Bella, we have another case," she said.

I laid down my cards. It was useless to protest, of course.

"There's been a terrible affair down at Frémont-on-the-Sound," she went on; "a gentleman has been found in his study, shot dead, and a young girl has been arrested. The man who called me up, evidently the girl's lover, begged me to come and try to get her off. His voice, coming through the receiver, had an extraordinary quality; young and manly; shaken with grief and agitation; yet proud and confident in his girl; it won me completely. I said I would drive right down."

"Murder?" said Mr. Lipscomb, startled; "and so close to us? Who's been murdered?"

"Cornelius Suydam."

"No!" cried our host, springing up. "Why, he's the great man of the neighborhood. His house, Fernhurst, is one of the showplaces! . . . Who is said to have killed him?"

"The girl's name is Laila Darnall."

Both Mr. and Mrs. Lipscomb stared at my employer in stupefied amazement. The former was the first to find his voice. "Merciful Heaven!" he gasped. "She's his ward! Said to be richer than he is. An exquisite young creature; a sort of golden princess; we see her being whisked about in automobiles from one great country house to another. Oh, this will create a terrible sensation! . . . Who called you up?"

"He called himself Alvan Wayger."

"I never heard of him."

"A sort of princess!" Mrs. Lipscomb echoed, aghast; "with everything in the world a girl could wish for! Why on earth should she want to kill her guardian?"

"I don't know," said Madame Storey. "We must go and find out . . . I suppose you will lend me a car and a chauffeur, Andrew."

"Certainly. I'll go with you for a bit of extra protection. I suppose you'll be out the rest of the night. It's near midnight now."

The distance was about twenty miles, and we made it in better than thirty minutes. Fernhurst proved to be an immense country house built of stone in the elaborate style of twenty-five years ago, and standing in its own private park. The house was all lighted up, but we found it perfectly deserted except for a solitary constable on guard, and the young man who had telephoned to Madame Storey. He was a striking-looking fellow with a shock of shining black hair and fiery dark eyes. Somewhat rough in dress and abrupt in manner, but with a glance full of resolution and capacity. It was that kind of terribly direct glance which is disconcerting to ordinary persons, but it is always a sure passport to Madame Storey's favor.

In spite of his grinding anxiety his whole face softened at the sight of my employer's beauty. It was a fine tribute. "I never thought you would be like this," he murmured.

They wasted no time in exchanging amenities. The young man explained that everybody in the house had just gone down to the magistrate's in the village, where a sort of preliminary hearing was about to be held.

"We mustn't miss anything that takes place at that hearing," Madame Storey said crisply. "Drive on down, Bella, and take notes of the proceedings. I will follow as soon as I have looked over the ground here."

I was directed to a large old-fashioned double house standing at the head of one of the village streets. This was the residence of "Judge" Waynham, the magistrate. Already there were half a dozen cars standing in the road, and a knot of people whispering at the gate. A strange sight at midnight in the quiet village! Mr. Lipscomb, who did not wish to intrude himself in any way, waited in the car. Inside, there were people all over the house. No one questioned my presence. The magistrate had not yet come downstairs and everybody was standing about with frozen, horrified faces. A maidservant was threading her way back and forth between them like a distracted person.

The judge's office was in the back parlor on the left-hand side, and everybody tried to push in there. A quaint room which suggested the era of 1885. I saw the accused girl sitting on a little sofa with her face hidden on the shoulder of a youngish woman in black. Picture a slender, silken girl wearing a flowerlike evening dress of printed chiffon and a white fur cloak which had slipped back. I could not see her face, but the short fair curls that showed against her slender neck were somehow most piteous. She was making no sound, but her delicate, girlish shoulders were shaken with sobs. It was too dreadful to think of anything so fresh and young and fair in connection with murder.

As more and more people crowded in, they opened the folding doors into the front parlor. The distracted maid-servant was bringing in chairs. I maneuvered myself alongside a comfortable village matron who looked promising as a source of information. She whispered to me that the lady in black was Mr. Suydam's housekeeper, Miss Beckington. A good-looking woman of thirty-five, I should have said, who appeared younger; very modish, very efficient, one guessed, though at present the tears were rolling down her pale cheeks as she held the girl close. Miss Beckington was something more than a mere housekeeper, my informant said, since she was a person of good family herself, and perfectly capable of acting as hostess to Mr. Suydam's guests. She was wearing a plain black morning dress, a close-fitting hat, and a raccoon coat.

Near these two sat a portly, nervous-looking elderly gentleman, fingering his watch chain. This I learned was "Judge" Gray, the girl's lawyer.

The magistrate entered the room. He had forgotten to brush his hair and it stood straight up all over his head in a very odd fashion. A rosy, kindly old gentleman, he was so nervous and distressed he scarcely knew what he was saying. "Who are all these people?" he demanded. "After all, this is my private house!"

Nobody answered him, and he was obliged to accept the crowd. He had the constable shepherd everybody but the principals into the front room. I got myself a chair in the second row where I could use my notebook without being conspicuous. Judge Waynham sat at his desk facing the rest of us, and a scared village stenographer took a place beside him with *her* notebook.

"Lavell," said the magistrate sharply, "you made the arrest, I assume. It is your place to lay a charge."

This was the chief constable, a tall lanky man with a good-humored, heavily seamed face. Like everybody else connected with the case he seemed completely overcome. He stood beside the magistrate's desk, hanging his head as if he were the guilty one, and mumbled in a scarcely audible voice:

"I charge Miss Laila Darnall with the murder of her guardian, Cornelius Suydam."

One could feel a shiver go through the room.

Suddenly the girl sprang to her feet, showing us all a white and agonizing face, the face of a terrified and uncomprehending child. Her slender frame was racked with sobs, but her eyes were dry. I shall never forget that desperate face. Though the other woman and the lawyer tried to silence her, she cried out: "How could I . . . how could I have done such a thing? Don't you believe me? Have I not a friend here? Why has everybody turned against me? I am the same girl!" Perceiving three handsomely dressed ladies sitting in the front room (these I learned were her cousins) she ran to them crying: "Helen! Isabel! You believe me, don't you? You know I could not have done such a thing. Tell them all that you believe me!"

"Hush, Laila, hush!" said one of them in cold, correct

tones. "Of course we believe you. But let the proceedings go on."

Laila turned from her in despair. "Haven't I a friend here?" she cried.

Miss Beckington held out her arms. "Come, dear," she said tenderly, while the tears rolled down her cheeks. "I am your friend. I know you could not have done it!"

The girl flung herself into her arms. "Oh, thank you! thank you!" she murmured, weeping freely at last. "Forgive me because I have not always been friendly towards you. Once I thought you were cold and unfeeling."

They sank down on the sofa together. It was very affecting, the more so because one could see that Miss Beckington was ordinarily a somewhat hard and self-controlled young woman.

"Do you wish to answer to this charge, my child?" asked Judge Waynham.

"I didn't do it! I didn't do it!" she cried without raising her face from Miss Beckington's shoulder.

"The prisoner pleads not guilty," murmured the magistrate to his stenographer. "Who is your complaining witness?" he asked the constable.

"Mr. Lumley, your honor, Mr. Suydam's butler."

This man stepped forward to testify. A large, soft-looking man with a dead-white skin, he was obviously educated and intelligent, and made a very good impression. He kept glancing at his young mistress commiseratingly. His obvious unwillingness to testify against her gave his evidence all the more deadly effect.

While he was speaking, Madame Storey and Alvan Wayger entered the front parlor from the hall and took seats in the darkest corner. I had a great curiosity concerning this interesting-looking young man who was said to be the heiress's lover. The village matron was still beside me. Calling her attention to him, I asked who he was.

"Oh, that's Alvan Wayger," she said indifferently. "He's nobody in particular. New people here. Haven't made friends much. They say he's a clever inventor, but I never heard of his inventions. Lives with his mother in a little house across the railway tracks. That's his mother against the wall across the room."

I saw a plain, middle-aged woman glancing at her son and his unknown companion with that peculiar jealousy that one sometimes sees in the faces of mothers with an only son. It is a sad thing to see.

Madame Storey had draped a light veil around the brim of her hat so that she could see all without being recognized.

Lumley the butler testified as follows:

"My name is Alfred Lumley. I have been employed by Mr. Cornelius Suydam as butler for the past four years. At the present time the household consists of Mr. Suydam, his ward Miss Darnall, his housekeeper Miss Beckington, myself butler, Mrs. Finucane cook, and five maids. There is also Dugan the engineer, who has a room in the basement; Leavitt the gardener, who lives with his family in the cottage at the park gates; and Pressley and Gordon, chauffeurs, unmarried men who board with the gardener's wife.

"I retired tonight shortly before eleven. There were no guests in the house, and I believed at the time that everybody was in bed except my master, whom I left reading in his study, as was his custom. The study occupies a separate wing of the house, somewhat cut off from the other rooms. I was in bed, but had not fallen asleep when I heard the sound of a muffled shot. Had I been asleep I should probably not have heard it. But I thought it came from inside the house. I sprang out of bed and flung on my clothes. I heard the clock of St. Agnes' strike eleven. My room is on the third floor of the house. I didn't attempt to waken any of the womenfolks. I ran down the two flights of stairs. I knocked on the library door. No answer. I tried the door. It was locked."

"One moment," interrupted Judge Waynham, "was it your master's custom to lock the door when he was in his library?"

"No, sir. No indeed, sir."

"Well, go on."

"I called loudly. There was no answer. My first thought was of robbers. The safe was in the library. I could not tell how many there might be, and I was afraid to venture outside the house alone. So I ran down to the basement and wakened Dugan. He was provided with a gun and electric torches. He threw on his clothes and came with me. We went out the front door and around the house to the library windows. There is a big bay with French windows opening directly on the terrace. The windows were open . . ."

"Cool as it was?" interrupted the magistrate.

"It was my master's custom, sir . . . The room was brightly lighted. We saw . . ." Lumley hesitated, and a shudder went through his stout frame.

"Go on," prompted Judge Waynham.

"My master was seated at his desk in the center of the room. His head had fallen forward on the desk blotter. There was a bullet hole just back of the left temple. His blood had spread over the desk and was already dripping to the floor. He was dead. The door of the safe stood wide open. Beside it lying open and face down on the rug was a little memorandum book. I recognized it as a book my master always carried on his person. On the open page was written down the combination of the safe. The safe was full of papers, none of which appeared to have been disturbed, but there was a little drawer which had been pulled out and emptied. An empty jewel box lay beside it."

"Do you mean to say," interrupted Judge Waynham,

"that Mr. Suydam sat in that brightly lighted room late at night with the windows open and unshuttered?"

"Such was his custom, sir," said Lumley, deprecatively. "I had ventured to remonstrate with him about it, but he only laughed at the idea of personal danger. The windows were protected by copper screens, of course. The murderer had fired through the screen, and had then raised it to enter."

"Well, go on."

"Dugan and I searched outside with the electric torches. Bordering the terrace is a flowerbed, and in the loose earth of the bed we immediately found the tracks of the murderer where he had come and where he had left again. Only one set of tracks. They appeared to be those of a large man wearing rubbers, but there was a peculiarity in the tracks . . ."

"Please explain yourself."

"Well, in the middle of the print of each foot there was a roughness which suggested to both of us that the rubbers had been tied to the wearer's feet by strips of rag or something of that sort."

The man's story was almost too painful to follow. A deathly silence filled the room which suggested that his hearers were actually holding their breaths.

"We followed the tracks to the edge of the flowerbed," he went on. "In the grass we lost them, but knowing that a person leaving a place in a hurry usually runs in a straight line, I kept on in the same direction. This took us across a rosebed in the center of the lawn, and here I found the tracks again. By taking a line with the library window and the rosebed we were enabled to find the tracks again where the murderer had struck into the woods. A little way in the woods we came to a place where the earth had lately been disturbed . . ."

"How do you mean?"

"Well, a hole had been dug, and hastily filled in again.

We dug there and found firstly a pair of old overshoes gray with dust and dried mud; secondly a thirty-two-caliber automatic pistol; thirdly several pieces of diamond jewelry tied up in a woman's handkerchief. Dugan immediately recognized the overshoes as an old pair that he used in the winter when he shoveled snow. He had last seen them lying beside the furnace pit where they had been dropped and forgotten." Lumley hesitated, with a piteous glance in the direction of his young mistress.

"Go on! Go on!" said Judge Waynham impatiently.

"The tracks that led away from that place had been made by a woman," said Lumley very reluctantly. "She was wearing what is called, I think, a commonsense shoe, that is a shoe with a moderately broad toe and a low heel. The tracks led us towards the main driveway, but we lost them in the grass before we got there, and of course the hard driveway revealed nothing. So we turned back towards the house meaning to call up the police." His voice sank. "As we approached the house we saw a figure standing in the driveway, its back towards us. The figure of a woman. We stepped into the grass to avoid giving warning of our approach. A moment later I recognized . . . Miss Darnall . . ."

A low murmur of horror escaped from the listeners.

"When I touched her she screamed," Lumley went on. "I thought she was about to faint . . ."

The girl suddenly cried out, "Was that strange? Was that strange? A man coming up on you in the dark without warning . . ."

Judge Gray and Miss Beckington quieted her.

"I led her into the house," Lumley went on unhappily. "As soon as we got in the light I saw—though she was dressed just as you see her now—that she was wearing shoes with broad toes and low heels. Moreover, the gun was quickly identified as one which had been given her by Mr. Suydam some months ago. It was his opinion that

everybody ought to be furnished with the means of
personal defense. One shot had been fired from it. The
handkerchief was also Miss Darnall's. It has her initials
embroidered in it."

There was a silence. The girl's shuddering sobs could
be heard. Miss Beckington patted her shoulder.

Judge Waynham wiped his agitated face on his handkerchief. "Well, is that all you have to say?" he asked.

"Not quite all, sir," said Lumley in an almost inaudible
voice, while we in the front room leaned forward to hear.
"I had Miss Beckington roused up, and I delivered Miss
Darnall into her care. I forced Miss Darnall to take off one
of her shoes—I thought it my duty to do so—and Dugan
and I returned to the woods with it. I had read somewhere
that the proper procedure was not to attempt to fit the
shoe into the suspected tracks, but to make a new
impression alongside. This I did. I am sorry to say that the
impressions correspond exactly . . . That is all I have to
say, sir. When I got back to the house I telephoned for the
police."

Lavell the constable laid the sport shoe on the desk.

"One question," said Judge Waynham. "How could
Miss Darnall ever have got hold of those overshoes? I
assume she was not in the habit of visiting the cellar."

"I asked that question of Dugan, sir," said Lumley.
"He told me that a week ago when he was confined to his
bed by an attack of tonsillitis, Miss Laila came down to his
room to visit him. To reach his room she had to pass the
furnace. She must have seen the overshoes then."

The girl tore herself out of the protecting arm of Miss
Beckington. Her soft young face worked piteously. "It's a
lie!" she cried. "I never saw the overshoes until tonight!
It's all lies! I . . . I . . ."

Judge Gray put an arm around her shoulders. "My
child," he said soothingly, "be silent! This is neither the
time nor the place. You must be guided by me . . ."

She sprang to her feet. "Let me be!" she cried hysterically. "I *will* speak! I won't have these people thinking I did this awful thing! I can explain everything. I have nothing to conceal . . . I had been out of the house ever since nine o'clock," she went on wildly and incoherently. "As for my shoes, I always put on sport shoes when I went out in the park at night. Would they have me wear slippers? . . . Since nine o'clock! I heard no shot. I didn't know anything was the matter. But when I got back to the house I found that the hall was lighted up and the front door standing open. So I was afraid to go in. That's why I was standing there looking at the house . . . My handkerchief . . . my handkerchief, I still have it with me. One wouldn't carry two. In the pocket of my cape . . ." Turning, she searched with frantic trembling hands in the folds of the cape. "It's here . . . I'll show you . . ." Then a despairing cry: "Oh, it's gone! . . . I swear I had it a while ago!" She dropped on the sofa shaken with fresh sobs. It was an unspeakably painful exhibition.

"What did you go out of the house for?" Judge Waynham asked gently. ". . . You don't need to answer unless you wish."

"Yes, yes, I will answer," she cried, striving hard for self-control. "I went out to meet my . . . to meet the man I am engaged to marry. He wasn't allowed to come to the house, I was forbidden to see him. That's why I had to meet him by stealth. I'm not ashamed of it. It's Alvan Wayger . . ."

A soft, long-drawn Oh! of astonishment escaped from the listeners. In a village where everybody prided themselves on knowing everything this was a startling disclosure. The heiress and the poor young inventor! Everybody looked at the handsome, dark young man who sat there with a perfectly blank mask upon his face. So far as I had observed the two had not once looked at each other during the proceedings.

Judge Waynham energetically polished his glasses. When he recovered from his surprise he looked relieved. I think we all had the same thought. Perhaps after all, here was a perfectly natural explanation of the girl's movements. "Will you answer a few questions, Mr. Wayger?" asked the judge.

"Certainly, sir," said the young man, marching up to his desk.

"Miss Darnall met you in the park at Fernhurst tonight?"

"Yes, sir. We had an appointment to meet at nine o'clock at a certain stone bench under an elm tree near the entrance gates."

"How long did she remain with you?"

"About two hours, sir."

"Can't you tell me exactly what time you left her?"

"No, sir, I didn't look."

"Did you then go straight home?"

"Yes, sir."

"How long does it take you to walk home?"

"Fifteen minutes, sir."

"At what time did you reach home?"

"I cannot tell you exactly, sir. I took no notice."

Here there was an interruption from the front room. "If you please, Judge, I can tell you," said a bitter voice. Mrs. Wayger, the young man's mother, had risen. She cast a look of dislike on the girl. "I was lying awake when my son came home," she said. "After he was in his room I heard the clock in St. Agnes' steeple strike eleven." She sat down again.

Young Wayger received this without a sign of emotion beyond lowering his head slightly. His face was not hard, but simply inscrutable. For my part I could not help but sympathize with his determination not to betray his private feelings before that gaping crowd.

Judge Waynham's face fell. "So," he said heavily,

"then it appears you must have left her at quarter to eleven or earlier."

Wayger made no answer.

"Miss Laila," said Judge Waynham, turning to the girl, "if Mr. Wayger left you at quarter to eleven, and Lumley found you at quarter past eleven, what had you been doing during that half-hour! You need not answer unless you wish."

We all held our breaths waiting for what she would say.

"I will answer . . . I will answer," she stammered. "I hadn't been doing anything . . . Just walking up and down the driveway. I was greatly troubled in my mind. I was trying to think . . . to think of some way out!"

It was a deplorably lame answer. In spite of his iron self-control I saw a spasm of pain pass across the young man's face. I think we all gave the girl up for lost then. Judge Waynham's kindly old face was heavy with distress. He tapped his glasses on his desk blotter while he considered. Suddenly a gleam of hope lighted up his eyes.

"The circumstances are unfortunate, most unfortunate," he said, "but no motive for such a terrible deed has been shown, or even suggested . . . Mr. Wayger, I would like to ask you a few more questions."

The young man signified his readiness to answer.

"What were the relations between Miss Darnall and her guardian?"

"I object!" said Judge Gray instantly.

Judge Waynham wagged a soothing hand in his direction. "This is only a magistrate's hearing," he said. "You will have your day before a jury later." He repeated his question of Wayger.

That young man's face hardened. "I don't know that I care to answer that," he said firmly. "It's not up to me to repeat what I learned from Miss Darnall in confidence."

At this juncture Madame Storey raised her clear,

distinct voice from the back of the room. If you had heard
that voice in the dark you would have known that it
belonged to a notability. "Mr. Wayger, I advise you to
answer," she said. "The whole truth must come out. By
your apparent reluctance you are only prejudicing Miss
Darnall's interest."

All the people goggled at the veiled woman, then
looked at each other. "Who is this?" you could see them
saying.

The young man instantly changed his attitude. "Very
well," he said, "the relations between Miss Darnall and her
guardian were bad. He was a very oppressive guardian. He
had peculiar notions. It is well known that Miss Darnall's
income runs into hundreds of thousands of dollars annu-
ally, but he would not allow her a cent of spending
money."

"What?" exclaimed Judge Waynham.

"It is quite true, sir. Of course, she was provided with
everything a fashionable young lady might be supposed to
require. She was encouraged to buy whatever she wanted
in the shops and have the bills sent in. But she had no
money to spend. She was not allowed to drive her own car.
In fact she was never allowed out unless accompanied by a
chauffeur or a chaperon. All this was very galling on a girl
of spirit.

"We wished to get married," he went on in his quiet
and self-respecting manner, "but that was quite out of the
question, of course. I have all I can do to make ends meet
as it is, and Mr. Suydam had absolute control over Miss
Darnall's money for two years longer, and partial control
for four years after that. He had no use for me at all. He
made no bones of calling me an impostor and a fortune
hunter. That didn't bother me at all—I have my work to
do—but it distressed Miss Darnall very much."

"But this has been going on for some time," suggested
Judge Waynham; "this would not account for Miss

Darnall's special trouble of mind tonight. Can you tell me what caused that?"

"Certainly, sir. It was what we had been talking about all evening. I have completed an invention. I need not go into detail about it. Properly applied, my invention would revolutionize a certain important industry. Well, I have received an offer from the corporation which controls that industry. Miss Darnall was strongly opposed to my accepting the offer. It was not a good offer, and what's more, there is reason to suppose that they mean to suppress my invention, as is sometimes done. Miss Darnall wanted to finance it, so that we could start manufacturing on our own account in competition with the trust. It was not the money she was thinking of so much as the publicity. She believed it would make me famous. But Mr. Suydam had positively refused to let her have the money."

"And the matter was at a critical stage?" asked Judge Waynham.

"Yes, sir. I am forced to accept this offer. Inventors must live."

"Hm!" said the judge unhappily. "What were the conditions of the late Mr. Darnall's will?"

"I see Mr. George Greenfield in the next room," Wayger said. "He is Mr. Suydam's attorney, and he can answer that question better than I can."

Mr. Greenfield was called upon. He was a handsome, middle-aged man with a youthful air and a good-tempered expression, the sort of man that children instinctively take to. As he came forward, he cast a deeply compassionate look on the unfortunate young girl. In answer to Judge Waynham's question, he carefully explained the provisions of her father's will. I need not repeat them beyond stating that Mr. Suydam was given absolute control of her affairs. In case of Mr. Suydam's death the will provided that Mr. Greenfield himself was to succeed him as Laila's guardian and trustee.

"Do you corroborate what this young man has told us respecting Mr. Suydam's attitude as guardian?" Judge Waynham asked him.

"I'm sorry that I must," he said regretfully, "for Mr. Suydam was one of my best friends. It was not mere harshness that made him behave in this manner. He was actuated by the best of motives. He looked about him and he saw how the young people of today were running wild, as he put it. It was to save Laila from that that he kept her under such strict control. I have often attempted to show him that he was mistaken in his method, but he was a very self-willed man."

"Had you heard anything about this invention of Mr. Wayger's?"

"Yes. Only today I lunched with Mr. Suydam at Fernhurst. Miss Darnall waylaid me as I arrived, and carried me to her sitting room where she told me all about it, and implored me to use my influence to persuade her guardian to advance the money necessary to finance Mr. Wayger's invention. But, knowing Mr. Suydam as well as I did, I told her it was useless. The poor girl was much upset. 'Can nothing be done?' she cried."

"And what did you reply?" asked Judge Waynham.

Mr. Greenfield started to answer, then, as a sudden realization came to him, caught himself up and changed color painfully. "I would rather not answer that," he said in a muffled voice.

"I must insist," said Judge Waynham.

"I answered jestingly," said Mr. Greenfield anxiously. "It had no significance whatever. I said, 'Nothing short of giving Cornelius a whiff of poison gas.' It was only in jest."

"Oh, quite, quite!" said Judge Waynham, and both men laughed in a strained fashion. But the incident created a very unfortunate impression.

Judge Waynham seemed to give up hope. His kindly face sagged with weary discouragement. He hesitated, tapping the blotter with his glasses. It was obvious that he could not bear to condemn the daintily reared girl to a cell. "I am reluctantly forced to order that Miss Darnall be . . ."

Madame Storey interrupted him. Rising and throwing back her veil, she said in that arresting voice of hers, "Mr. Magistrate, before you close the case, if I might be permitted to put a few questions in the light of what I have learned . . ."

Judge Waynham's jaw dropped in pure astonishment. "But, madam, who are you?" he asked.

Alvan Wayger answered for her. "Madame Rosika Storey," he announced.

A general exclamation escaped from all. Every head in the room turned towards my employer as if moved by a common lever. For the moment even the unfortunate Laila Darnall was forgotten. At this time Madame Storey was the most talked-of woman in the country, I suppose. "The cleverest woman in New York" the newspapers were calling her. Everybody present had the feeling that her entrance into the case would make their insignificant village famous.

The good little magistrate flushed and stammered in his gratification. "But of course . . . of course. . . . I am honored, Frémont is honored by your presence amongst us, Madame. Won't you be good enough to join me on the bench . . . I mean at my desk . . ." He relieved his feelings by suddenly shouting for the maid: "Nettie! Place a chair for Madame Storey."

Serenely oblivious to the goggling eyes, my employer seated herself beside him. "A prima facie case appears to have been made out," she drawled; "still, there are one or two little matters that might be gone into further."

Instantly everybody realized that the case, instead of closing, was only just starting.

"Miss Darnall required a large sum of money," Madame Storey continued; "therefore the few pieces of jewelry that were taken could have been of no use to her. The theory is, of course, that she opened the safe and took the jewelry merely to make it appear that robbers had done the deed . . . A very, very clever plot! Well, if she was such a clever plotter why didn't she plot a little further, and leave a way open to return to the house? She must have realized that someone would likely be awakened by the shot? There is a discrepancy here."

I saw a hope dawn in the magistrate's harassed face.

"I have made a hasty examination of Mr. Suydam's study," Madame Storey went on, "and . . . er . . . some other rooms in the house. Unfortunately for my purposes, the body had already been removed to Mr. Suydam's bedroom. I should therefore like to ask the butler a question or two concerning it, if I may."

Judge Waynham made haste to give an assent.

"Lumley," said Madame Storey, "you told us you left your master reading when you went to bed. But when you found his body he was sitting at his desk. This was not a position for reading, was it?"

"No, Madam. When I found him his fountain pen was still grasped in his right hand, and his left hand was spread on the blotter in such a way as to suggest that it was holding a paper. He was undoubtedly writing at the moment he was shot."

"But the paper itself was gone?"

"Yes, Madam."

"This suggests that he was writing something which was of interest to the murderer," remarked Madame Storey, "who therefore carried it away. That's all for the moment, thanks. . . . On Mr. Suydam's desk," she went on to Judge Waynham, "I found an ordinary calendar and memorandum pad on the top leaf of which he had written:

'Write G. G.,' then a dash and the word 'will.' Underneath was another memorandum: 'Write Eva Dinehart.' Now I take it 'G. G.' is Mr. Greenfield."

That gentleman spoke up for himself.

"Yes, Madam. Such was Mr. Suydam's nickname for me."

"Had you had any discussion with him today about his will?"

"No, Madam, it was not mentioned."

"Have you his will?"

"Yes, Madam, I drew it up. It is kept in my safe."

"Had you had any talk with him that would make it necessary for him to write to you?"

"No, Madam. Whatever it was, it must have come up after I had gone."

"What time did you leave him?"

"Three o'clock."

"Thank you. . . . Now, Lumley, what did your master do after Mr. Greenfield had gone?"

"He had Miss Beckington into the library, 'm," the butler answered with a wondering air. None of us could see which way this questioning was tending. "It was their day for going over the household bills."

"Can you tell me anything about what took place between them?"

"N . . . no, Madam."

"Why do you hesitate?"

"Well, there was an incident which was a little unusual."

"What was that?"

"Mr. Suydam called on the phone, and asked me to connect him with Central. Ordinarily he would let me get him what number he wanted."

"You listened?" suggested Madame Storey with a bland air.

"Well . . . yes, ma'am," said the butler in some

confusion. "Mr. Suydam asked for information. He read
the names of three New York business firms over the wire,
and asked to be given their telephone numbers. I remember the firms. They were: N. Hamill and Sons; Nicholas
Enslin; and Dobler and Levine. And information reported
to him that no such firms were listed."

"What did your master do after Miss Beckington left
him?"

"Went to the country club to play golf, Madam."

"And Miss Beckington?"

"She went into the city by train."

"Rather a hasty trip, wasn't it?"

"So it might seem, Madam."

"When did she get back?"

"Just before dinner."

"Carrying several parcels?"

"Why, yes, ma'am," said the butler with a look of
surprise, "now that you mention it."

"Wasn't that rather unusual?"

"Yes, ma'am. Ordinarily everything would be sent."

"That's all, thanks." Madame Storey turned to Judge
Waynham. Her beautiful face was as grave as that of some
antique head of Pallas. "I then asked to be shown Miss
Beckington's room," she went on. "The door was locked,
but the constable obligingly forced it for me. I am aware
that this was a high-handed proceeding on my part, but I
was sure that the owner of the room would forgive me if
her conscience was clear . . . In the room was a desk
which I likewise forced. In a drawer of the desk I found
these papers." From a sort of reticule of black velvet that
she carried, Madame Storey took a sheaf of papers and
spread them before the magistrate.

He blinked at them owlishly.

"They are, you see, blank bill heads for the three firms
whose names you have just heard mentioned; N. Hamill
and Sons; Nicholas Enslin; Dobler and Levine . . ."

"But what does it mean?"

Madame Storey held up her hand to bespeak a moment's patience. "I returned to the library. I found in a cabinet all the household bills for many months past. Upon consulting them I found every month a considerable bill from each of these mythical concerns . . ."

"You don't say, Madam . . . !"

"It means," said Madame Storey with her grave air, "that Miss Beckington has been systematically swindling her employer out of hundreds of dollars monthly."

Every eye in the room turned on the housekeeper. Laila Darnall jerked herself free of her arms, looking at her in astonishment and dismay. Miss Beckington, who had been pale before, now looked livid. There was an awful terror in her eyes. Her attempt to smile in a scornful and superior way was something you could not bear to look at. I mean, it seemed indecent to see a human creature expose herself like that.

"I take it that Mr. Suydam discovered the thefts today," said Madame Storey. "That brings us back to the will. Mr. Greenfield, is Miss Beckington mentioned in her employer's will?"

"Yes, Madam. A comfortable legacy."

"I thought so. Naturally, his first act upon discovering her treachery would be to write to you to cut that out. Now as to the second name on the memorandum pad: this Mrs. Eva Dinehart happens to be an acquaintance of mine. She conducts a special sort of employment agency. You go to her for help of a superior and confidential sort such as a social secretary or a lady housekeeper—need I say more?"

"But the murder, ma'am, the murder?" asked Judge Waynham excitedly.

"I am establishing the motive," said Madame Storey gravely. "Dishonor and disgrace faced this lady. At the very moment he was shot, her employer was writing the letters that would have ruined her."

"But have you any evidence?"

"I found none in her room—or next to none," said Madame Storey dryly.

Miss Beckington preened herself, bridled, smiled in that ghastly, would-be contemptuous manner.

". . . but I recommend that you have her searched," added Madame Storey quietly.

At these words, the woman sprang up electrified. "I won't submit to it!" she cried in a shrill, hysterical voice, and made as if to bolt for the door.

Lavell the constable seized her. She struggled like a wildcat. Everybody looked on dazed. It was inexpressibly shocking to see the elegant Miss Beckington suddenly reduced to such a state.

"Take her into the dining room," said Judge Waynham. "Lumley, will you please help him?"

Madame Storey added to me: "Miss Brickley, you search her while the men hold her."

It was not a job I relished, but I had no recourse other than to obey. To make a long story short, I found, firstly, in her stocking a handkerchief bearing Miss Darnall's initials; secondly, fastened inside the lining of the raccoon coat a pair of sport shoes; and thirdly, the strangest of all, wound around and around her body under the top part of her dress a ladder made of thin strong cord. Fastened to one end of it were two steel hooks. I returned across the hall, and laid these things on Judge Waynham's desk.

"I thought so," said Madame Storey offhand. "You see she had had no opportunity to dispose of them." She lifted up the objects one by one. "The handkerchief she stole from Miss Darnall as she sat beside her, hoping thereby to make the poor girl's story sound more incriminating. The shoes you see are replicas of Miss Darnall's from the same manufacturers. Miss Beckington bought them today, I have no doubt. She knew that Miss Darnall always wore such shoes in the park. The rope ladder she used to leave her room and to return to it. If you look for them you will find the marks made by the hooks on her windowsill."

At this sudden upset of the case, every vestige of order disappeared. All the people came pressing into the back room, crying out and attempting to congratulate the one or to abuse the other. Miss Beckington shrank from them. Judge Waynham's mild face crimsoned with anger, and above all the racket I heard his trembling voice.

"You miserable woman! You deliberately set out to fasten a horrible murder on this helpless child. In all my experience I have never known the like!"

Miss Beckington had collapsed now. All the fight had gone out of her. "I didn't! I didn't" she wailed. "I tried to make it appear that a robber had done it!"

"Your purchase of the shoes doesn't bear that out," said the judge sternly. "All through the proceedings you sat there with your arms around her whispering hypocritical comfort in her ear, while the evidence was produced against her. It is horrible!"

Miss Beckington's voice rose almost to a shriek. "I knew they wouldn't hurt her!" she cried. "Young and pretty as she is, and with all her money, no jury would convict her! She was safe!"

"Silence!" cried the magistrate. "Your excuses aren't helping you any! . . . Lock her up!" he said to the constable.

When Miss Beckington was removed, the crowd threatened completely to overwhelm Madame Storey and the young lovers in their well-meant efforts to congratulate them. Madame Storey regarded this demonstration with good-humored dismay. I opened the door into the hall to allow them to slip out, and held it until they had secured themselves in the dining room opposite. Over there, I presume, the lovers thanked Madame Storey in their own way for saving them. I was not present at the scene.

Presently the young couple escaped through a side door of the house, but were seen as they ran hand in hand for a car, and the crowd pursued them cheering.

EDWARD PHILLIPS OPPENHEIM (1866–1946), despite his origins as son of a Leicester leather merchant, found his spiritual home on the Côte d'Azur, where he supported his fondness for princely luxury on the earnings from his 150 novels and myriad short stories and articles. There is a curious emptiness to most of his work that seems to stem not from the vastness of his output but rather from his obsessive fascination with the rich and aristocratic, his boyishly romantic love of the trappings of the elite: titles, jewels, country estates, yachts, immense power. His tales of espionage and diplomatic intrigue also smack of the adolescent: sinister lady spies, secret treaties that govern the fate of the world, Teutonic villains with dueling scars, financial conspiracies. Yet his most famous book, *The Great Impersonation* (1920), was placed at the top of a list of spy novels as late as 1969 and is still quite readable today. Admitting his flaws, it can be said that his biography, published in 1957, is aptly titled *The Prince of Storytellers*, for his literary legacy has undeniable charm and his imagination makes his extravagant snobbishness seem a kind of forgivable naiveté.

The adventures of the glamorous Baroness Clara Linz are squarely in the Oppenheim mold; in her role as sole proprietor of ADVICE LIMITED, she is consulted by prime ministers, retired generals, and the Bank of England. She allows herself to be wooed by the Spanish nobleman Roderigo de Partegena de Cervera y Topete and, in the tenth and last of these tales, consents to become his wife.

Too Many Dukes

by E. Phillips Oppenheim

It was the spring sunshine and the tang of a southwesterly breeze through the open port window which induced Clara, Baroness Linz, to leave the privacy of *Cabine de Luxe* Number Fourteen and mount to the deck. It was perhaps chance which induced the officious seaman who brought her a chair to place it next to a solitary young man who was seated gazing gloomily over the rails towards the receding coastline. It was without a doubt sheer curiosity which induced Clara to remove for a moment the coloured glasses which she always wore in the sunshine to glance at the coronet upon the worn brown leather dressing case that reposed upon the deck by the side of her neighbour. She looked away again almost at once and there was no sign of interest in her face. Nevertheless, what she had seen provided her with matter for speculation at various periods during the remainder of the voyage.

"Madame desires a light, perhaps?" the young man asked a few minutes later, realising that she was in trouble with her cigarette.

Madame accepted the courtesy and leaned a trifle forward. One felt that nothing but his innate good breeding kept the admiration from the young man's eyes when he realised that he was seated next to a very beautiful woman.

"We shall have a pleasant crossing, I imagine," she remarked as she thanked him.

"If the fog which threatens does not approach," he agreed. "The sea is too calm for this time of the year. It is sometimes deceptive."

The conversation, never thoroughly launched, languished. The young man, however, appeared also to have developed some instinct of curiosity. Through his immovable eyeglass he stared at the label neatly attached to his companion's small jewel case. The printed letters were clearly visible.

"You will pardon me," he ventured, "but in glancing at your satchel I discover an address in Adam Street, London."

"That is where I live," Clara acknowledged.

"You will forgive my interest," he continued, "but I am not well acquainted with your city. To tell you the truth, I have been advised to call upon someone in Adam Street in connection with the purpose of my visit to London. Perhaps you would be kind enough to indicate in what direction this Adam Street is situated."

"You will find it without difficulty," she assured him. "It is a turning off the street which runs down to the Adelphi Terrace. Every taxicab driver knows it."

"I am exceedingly obliged," he acknowledged. "I am also," he added, "somewhat surprised to find that it is also a domiciliary neighbourhood. The address which I was given in Adam Street was the address of an enquiry office which I imagined might lie more in the direction of the City."

She smiled with sufficient indifference.

"The enquiry office you have in mind is doubtless the

one conducted under the name of ADVICE LIMITED," she observed.

"It is a famous firm, Madame?" he queried.

"They have an excellent reputation," she replied.

Her lack of curiosity seemed for the moment to intrigue him. He looked at her thoughtfully.

"One imagines, Madame," he remarked, with a slight hesitation, "that you yourself are not English?"

She shook her head.

"I am English by birth, Austrian by marriage, a cosmopolitan from habit," she told him. "As a place of residence, however, I prefer London to any other city. But for its climate I should probably be a permanent resident there."

He shivered as though the idea repelled him. Although the day was mild he was wearing a heavy, fashionably cut travelling coat with a band of crape upon the arm. The rest of his attire was also black—the meticulous mourning of the bereaved Frenchman. His cheeks were sallow and inclined to be puffy. There were lines under his eyes which were not altogether natural. He had, without doubt, a certain air of distinction but his appearance was not wholly agreeable.

"You surprise me very much, Madame," he said. "I should have imagined that Paris—"

"There is no Paris," she interrupted. "The circle has shrunk and shrunk until it has become too small. One cannot breathe in the atmosphere of the few French people who are left. It is a beautiful city but it is no part of France."

"There is, alas, truth in what Madame says," the young man lamented.

"We have, without a doubt, mutual acquaintances in the Faubourg," she remarked.

The young man took up a novel which had been lying

by his side and settled himself further back in his chair.

"Without a doubt, Madame," he assented courteously, but with his eyes already seeking the printed page.

Clara stared at him for a moment, permitted herself a faint unheard gasp, and took up her own paper. She had been treated like an inquisitive and intruding tourist. She had been "put in her place" by a young man whom she suspected to be one of the scapegraces of Europe. The humour of the situation, however, prevailed over its irritation. Presently she rose and strolled off. The young man read on undisturbed.

A stout dark woman with almost painfully brilliant eyes and the smudge of a moustache upon her upper lip leaned forward to her companion as Clara disappeared from sight. She was seated upon a bench a few yards away.

"Monseigneur does not trouble himself about the woman," she remarked. "That one, too, she was beautiful."

"She had also distinction," her companion, a man of the same type, agreed.

"She possesses an air of familiarity," the formidable-looking lady ruminated. "Somewhere she has been pointed out to me. She brings into my mind a sense of danger."

The man scrutinised his neighbour calmly. His face was almost as hard as hers, his deep-set eyes as bright. At first sight they seemed to be an ordinary bourgeois couple—probably tradespeople engaged in a voyage of commerce. Afterwards one might have been inclined to change one's impressions.

"It is not like you, Hortense," he observed, "to have ideas."

"If I had no ideas," she scoffed, "we might be living in another world by now! Henri, my lamb, we move slowly. It is not that I am nervous but we are surrounded by matters which need consideration. Walk slowly around the deck, come back to me and report. Amongst other things I

would like to know whether the beautiful lady has
descended."

He grumbled a little but he did her bidding. With his
hands thrust deep down in his overcoat pockets, so deep
that he could feel something hard in the inner recesses of
one of them, he made a complete revolution of the deck.
His walk was inclined to be a strut. His expression was
amiable but self-important. More than ever he looked the
prosperous shopkeeper. One could picture him bowing to
a patron from behind the counter of a jeweller's shop, or
standing in welcoming fashion upon the threshold of a
tailoring establishment. One could imagine him seated
behind a desk in an office of prosperous appearance
writing cheques—good fat cheques—or with the menu in
his hand at a popular restaurant ordering with care the
repast of a connoisseur with healthy appetite. He had
nothing of the air of a cocktail-bar lounger. One could
figure him peering at the rich dishes presented by a
respectful *maître d'hôtel* and criticising the flavour of a
stout bottle of wine.

"Madame," he reported to his companion, "remains at
the farther end of the deck. Monseigneur is apparently
engrossed in his book. Nothing changes."

"And the others—little Armand and the woman?"

"One believes that they have not mounted."

From far away ahead where the shores of England lay
under a glimmering haze there came the faint shriek of a
siren. The woman puckered her brows and turned around.
The man walked to the rail and came back.

"It is a trifle of mist," he announced. "Fortunately it
has not a serious appearance. We shall have landed before
it spreads."

The woman, notwithstanding her fur coat, shivered.

"*Grand Dieu!*" she exclaimed. "We spend all our time
travelling northwards. If we could but seek the sun!"

"*C'est les affaires,*" the man muttered.

．　　．　　．

Clara, Baroness Linz, saw ahead in the distance the grey mists thickening upon the water and heard behind them the sirens calling. The bells from the engine room rang and the race of the Channel steamer through the water was finished. Already they were going at half-speed. With a little grimace she turned round, passed through the open door, and descended the companionway. As she approached the door of her cabin a stout powerful-looking man, his hands thrust into his overcoat pockets, the remains of a cigar in his mouth, stepped aside to allow her to pass. Something about his appearance struck her as being familiar and she looked at him with some curiosity. His restless eyes appraised and admired her. He ogled her shamelessly. There were glimmerings of a smile upon her lips as she passed into the seclusion of *Cabine de Luxe* Number Fourteen. She rang the bell for the steward.

"Would a champagne cocktail be drinkable, Francis?" she asked him.

He smiled confidently. The Baroness was a well-known and valued client.

"I will see to it myself, your ladyship," he promised her. "The last time I left it to the barman. A dry biscuit too?"

She nodded and the man hurried away. She glanced out of the large square porthole at the thin vaporous fog, examined her face in the glass, and found nothing to correct.

"A dull voyage," she remarked to the man when he returned with her cocktail.

"Might have been worse, your ladyship," he told her cheerfully. "We have only just missed the fog. It is coming along now but a bit too late to do us any harm. I have arranged with your maid about the baggage."

She nodded, paid her bill, and tipped him, as usual, munificently. Faint little wisps of mist were stealing now and then through the window. She leaned over to close it but suddenly paused. She was always a curious woman and she listened. Someone was speaking in the next cabin.

"Port harbour light on the last train signal. Starboard on the Castle. *Le bon Dieu*, what an agony!"

The occupants of that next cabin, *Cabine de Luxe* Number Sixteen, appeared to have discovered a new form of amusement. All the time the woman, bareheaded but with her fur coat fastened tightly around her, stood at the porthole window muttering to herself.

"Port harbour light on the last train signal. Starboard on the Castle. If only Bouvard would hurry!"

The young man, her companion, who had risen from his chair and was looking over her shoulder, suddenly called out. His delicate white forefinger with its glittering ring—platinum with a green stone—flashed upwards.

"Bouvard must have failed!" he cried. "Something has happened! We do not move."

The woman, too, strained forward. It was true. The engines had either ceased or they had become inaudible. The sea was rippling gently by the side of the ship below but the curling wisps of mist had become stationary. The woman leaned farther forward, beautiful after a certain fashion, with her red hair, her delicately preserved cream-coloured skin, but with the lines of middle age already asserting themselves. Away in the distance, it was true, the faint outline of the shore was dimly visible but straight ahead the curtain had fallen. Barely a hundred yards distant was a dense wall of fog and behind it nothing but the screaming of sirens. The young man wiped his forehead. He was slim, typically Parisian with his elegantly controlled waist, his carefully draped tie, his closely cropped moustache, his modish linen and jewellery. He was not of the type, however, which had fought at Verdun. Even the sight of that bank of fog seemed to have reduced him to a state of terror.

"It is the evil one himself who mocks us," he babbled incoherently. "How shall we be able to see the land? And Bouvard—he must have failed us."

The woman threw a scornful glance at him.

"Bouvard does not fail," she said. "He told us to remember that it would be towards the end when people were gathering together their belongings. It is just as well that he has not hastened. They might have searched the cabins."

The young man was in bad shape. He wiped the glistening beads of perspiration from his forehead with a scented handkerchief.

"If one could only feel oneself safe on land," he muttered. "Safe anywhere in London."

"You forget," she reminded him. "We are not going to London."

He groaned.

"What misery!" he exclaimed. "A grim English hotel— the waiting around—the risk. The game is not worth the candle. Let us throw this thing overboard," he added, touching a large but flimsy paper parcel with his foot and upsetting ruthlessly what seemed to be a plant with stiff green leaves enclosed in a wicker-work cage. "Let us change cabins."

"And betray Bouvard!" the woman cried contemptuously. "Armand, you are not a man."

"It is my nerves," he moaned.

"I thought that they might fail you in a crisis," she said, and there was a hard light now in her brown eyes. "But listen. They shall not fail you now or if they do it will be the end. Drink some more of the brandy. Gain courage somehow. This is an affair already commenced. There is no drawing back. The fog will make not so much difference. Sooner or later we must move and when we do enough will be visible."

The young man drank from the tumbler which stood

upon the table. It contained neat brandy but he drank it greedily.

"You should have been a man, Lucie," he muttered.

"I should have made a better one than you," was the bitter retort.

He drew himself up but words died upon his lips. There was a knock at the door, a harsh peremptory summons. The woman crossed the room, her movements disclosing a curious feline grace. One might have divined that she was of that breed who love danger for its own sake.

"Who is there?" she enquired in a tone of unexpected sweetness. "I have already told the steward that monsieur is suffering and we do not wish to be disturbed."

"It is Bouvard. Open!" was the sharply spoken rejoinder.

She drew the bolt and opened the door without hesitation. The stout man who had been strutting about the upper deck stepped in. He was smoking a freshly lit cigar. His eyes seemed more brilliant than ever. He had the air of a man engaged in an enterprise every moment of which brought happiness. The young man—there was a duke's coronet upon his dressing case but the name on his passport was Armand de Boncourt—sank trembling into a chair. His presence to the other two became for the moment negligible.

"Success?" the woman asked swiftly.

"It is not Henri Bouvard who fails," he boasted. "Tell that little rabbit to close the window. It will be time enough to open it when we are going again. He can busy himself also with the parcel. The branch of the plant there must be attached in an upright position to the cork."

The young man was incapable of movement. The woman leaned over and closed the window.

"I changed my plans," the newcomer continued. "As usual, luck favoured me. The fog threatened and he and I were left alone. After that, it was easy. I confess, however, that I did not reckon upon complete stoppage. My fear is that Challes will find time now for action. If so and he has word with the Captain there may be a search before we proceed. I ask myself what is best."

The man's words were alarming enough in their suggestion. The woman, however, merely reflected.

"What have you done with—with it?" she asked.

"The dressing case I disposed of through the porthole in the lavatory," he replied. "It will not be easily found. The box is here."

It appeared that Monsieur Bouvard's corpulence was not altogether a substantial thing, for from underneath his two coats he produced a very sizable-looking though flat tin box. It was no sooner in the woman's hands than she commenced to wrap it up in a piece of matting which had lain upon the table.

"The immediate trouble might be," she said, listening to footsteps outside, "if anyone insists upon entering. What would two wealthy passengers in a *Cabine de Luxe* want with a thing like that?"

She pointed contemptuously to the untidy-looking bundle. The man stroked his chin thoughtfully. For a single moment his confidence seemed to waver.

"It was such a wonderful scheme too," he reflected.

"Imbecile!" she exclaimed furiously. "You men grow more *lache* every day. I am sorry that I spoke. There is poor little Armand shivering with what he calls nerves. What is that indeed but rank cowardice? Here are you, even you, deliberating—Zut! *Je me fiche de vous deux!* We take our risks. We stay as we are, Henri, until the engines beat again and we carry out our plans exactly as they were made. See here."

She picked up a tumbler and half filled it with brandy from the bottle which stood upon the table. Bouvard accepted it with a chuckle.

"I drink to you, my beautiful," he said. "It is not courage I need. I pause only to reflect upon what is best. Someday, mark you, I shall take you away from this little rabbit. You please me. Madame and I have squabbled for long enough."

He leaned towards her and put his arm around her shoulders. She gave him her lips without hesitation.

"So," he said with a deep sigh. "I shall take you like this when the time comes and the little rabbit there can do what he pleases. Once more—success!"

He drank from the tumbler. She followed his example with a laugh. This, after all, was the sort of man she understood.

The young man, ushered in by the saturnine-looking butler, entered Clara's charming little sitting room with a bow and stood with his hat in his hand. He was obviously very much shaken but a young man with precise manners.

"I wish," he confided, "an immediate interview with the principal of your firm. You have my card. I am the Duc de Challes."

Clara, who was wearing heavy spectacles and had established herself with her back to the light, waved him to a chair.

"To all effects and purposes, Duke," she told him, "you can look upon me as the head of the firm."

The young man frowned slightly.

"Mine is not a trivial affair," he warned her. "It is an affair which demands the immediate attention of the best brains in your organisation. It is of great importance, and it would surely save time if I were allowed to state my own case."

"We have our methods," Clara rejoined smiling, "and please forgive my assuring you that they cannot be changed. You must explain the business to me."

The young man recognised finality and took a chair.

"I was robbed yesterday afternoon," he announced, "of half a million pounds' worth of jewels on the steamboat between Calais and Dover."

Clara inclined her head sympathetically.

"There were rumours of a great theft in the papers this morning," she murmured. "I have heard no particulars."

"The particulars are simple," the Duke explained. "I inherited these jewels from my aunt, the late head of our house. They were handed over to me as my inheritance by the lawyers on Monday. I was to bring them to London at once to have them displayed at your great salesrooms—Messrs. Christie's. During the crossing from Calais to Dover they were stolen."

"In what fashion?"

"I was seated on deck," the Duke continued, "with my small articles of luggage—including a bag which contained the jewels—by my side. We ran into a mist and nearly all the other passengers descended to the saloon. I was suddenly attacked from behind and received a severe blow on the head. I try to put this in as few words as possible. The end was this. I did not see my assailant to recognise him. When I recovered my breath and my head ceased to swim the bag containing the jewels had gone and I was alone."

"Very simple so far," Clara observed. "Exactly what did you do when you discovered your loss?"

"We were in the middle of a bank of mist and they refused to permit me to speak to the Captain. The Purser, however, promised that no one should be allowed to leave the boat at Dover until they had passed through the customs and that a rigorous search should be made through everyone's hand baggage. I was obliged to be content with this. The search was made without result. There was no trace of the jewels."

"Did you enter into communication in any way with

the Dover Police?" she enquired. "They have the reputation of being a very clever force."

"Five minutes after the Purser had told me that the search had been in vain and that he could detain the passengers no longer I left my own luggage in the care of my servant and went to the Police Station," the Duke recounted. "I found the Chief of the Police most intelligent. He told me that there had been one or two cases in his time of thefts on board steamers and the—how is it you call it?—the booty thrown overboard in something which would float and returned for afterwards. Accordingly, I hired a motor boat and went out, as near as I could possibly guess, to the spot where I was attacked. It was still misty, but after about an hour's search we found my dressing case empty and the box which had contained the jewels attached to the wicker cage of a lobster pot—also empty."

"Indicating," Clara reflected, "the fact that the jewels had probably been thrown overboard attached in some fashion to this wicker basket, and the thieves, or their accomplices, had been lying in wait in a motor boat."

"It is possible," the Duke admitted. "Through the mist we could hear at times the hooting of a siren. The police are keeping a strict watch along the coast for any motor boat that might have been concerned."

Clara, who was deeply interested, leaned across towards her visitor.

"Was there anyone on board who to your knowledge was aware of the fact that you were taking the jewels across?"

The Duke hesitated.

"There was a relative of mine," he acknowledged, "a young man, very feeble in his head and anaemic, who probably knew. We do not converse. There was, however, some question of his having a claim to the succession.

French law is, as you may be aware, peculiar, and one of the reasons why my aunt transferred her property into jewels and insisted upon them being hastened into my possession on the day of her death was her fear that my cousin Armand might successfully contest my claim. She was a woman of spirit and she had a great contempt for Armand."

"He was on the boat, was he?" Clara meditated.

"He was on the boat, but it would be the height of absurdity to suggest that he could have come up and given me a blow on the head sufficient to make me half-unconscious. He would never have had the courage or the strength for such an exploit."

"He may have had an accomplice," she suggested.

The Duke shrugged his shoulders.

"Whoever it may have been who was responsible for the conspiracy, my cousin would have been quite capable of it if someone else did the work and ran the risk. How did they dispose of the jewels? That is what I want to know."

"I will study the facts," Clara promised, "and report to you tomorrow. You are staying in London?"

"At Claridge's Hotel," was the somewhat gloomy reply. "I hope you will bear in mind the fact that with every minute which passes the chances of escape on the part of the criminals become more favourable."

"I shall not waste time," she assured him.

"In this case," Clara reflected, as she mounted the gangway of the Channel steamer upon its return journey, "Scotland Yard has the facts, I have the ideas! I wonder!"

The first half-hour upon the boat was one of disappointment to Clara, Baroness Linz. There was no one amongst the passengers who resembled anyone she had ever seen before. She had better fortune, however, when she descended to the cabins. Walking up and down the corridor the picture of misery and despair was the elegant but dissipated young man who had occupied *Cabine de Luxe* Number Sixteen with the flamboyant-looking lady of the previous crossing! He appeared to be in the depths of depression and also in the throcs of a ncrvous attack. His china-blue eyes were bloodshot, the cigarette he was attempting to smoke hung limply from his twitching lips. Nevertheless, from sheer habitude, he watched with obvious admiration the approach of a very beautiful woman. Clara, as she entered her cabin, looked over her shoulder and smiled . . .

The voyage had commenced. Already they were passing out of the harbour. Clara threw off her furs and made herself comfortable upon the lounge. She had left the door ajar and she noticed with satisfaction that the footsteps outside had ceased. Presently there was a timid tapping. The door was pushed an inch or two wider open. The young man—a very timid *boulevardier*—peered in.

"Come in," she invited pleasantly. "You were in the next cabin yesterday, were you not? You have had as short a stay in England as I have."

She swung round and made room for him by her side. He bowed and accepted her invitation. Clara became aware of an overwhelming waft of perfume irresistibly reminiscent of the Rue de la Paix. The young man with delicate white fingers toyed with the pearl which held in its place a mauve tie of rich silk.

"I remember Madame, of course," he acknowledged. "No one who had seen her could fail to do so."

"Are you going to pay me compliments?" she laughed. "The voyage then will be so much the shorter."

"Alas," he sighed, "my heart is full of much that I would say but I am in terrible despair."

She looked at him with exquisitely simulated interest.

"You distress me," she said. "Despair? It is not possible," she added, as though the idea had suddenly occurred to her, "that you are connected in any way with the jewel robbery which took place yesterday?"

Once more he sighed deeply.

"Alas, Madame," he admitted, "I am the victim."

"You?" she exclaimed. "I thought that the jewels belonged to the Duc de Challes."

He coughed. He had perhaps been indiscreet.

"I am the Duc de Challes," he announced boldly.

"You surprise me," Clara confessed. "The Duc de Challes was pointed out to me upon the boat. He had not the appearance or presence of Monsieur, although he was taller. He was, too, of a different complexion."

"That was my cousin," the young man confided bitterly. "He calls himself the Duc de Challes although the title is by right mine. He helped himself to the jewels which were also mine. Through his carelessness they are lost. I am ruined. Madame, there has been treachery somewhere!"

"What you are telling me," she reflected, "seems very strange. Do I understand that you both call yourselves the Duc de Challes?"

He shook his head.

"During my aunt's lifetime," he said, "I humoured her whims. I called myself the Marquis de Boncourt, which is one of our minor titles."

"One understands, however," Clara continued, with an air of sympathetic interest, "that it was from your cousin that the jewels were stolen."

The young man coughed. It was perhaps borne upon him faintly that he was talking too much. The eyes of Madame, however, were so delightfully sympathetic!

"It is a complicated story," he explained. "I followed my cousin on to the boat. It was my intention to have taken him by the throat and to have demanded the return of my property. Before I could find an opportunity of doing so, however, the theft took place. The jewels have gone! Worse than that, I—the Marquis de Boncourt, to whom they justly belonged—am a pauper!"

"It is all very confusing," Clara acknowledged.

The young man sighed. He was gazing out of the porthole. Once more he was fingering his beautiful mauve tie.

"If one had the courage," he murmured. "If I dared, Madame, what happiness it would give me to tell you the story."

"I would love to hear it," she admitted.

"The details—no," he began after a moment's reflection. "Madame can imagine them for herself. I came on board yesterday with a friend—no, not a friend—a tradesman of the bourgeois class who has acted as my banker for years. We were firmly determined to possess ourselves of my property. I have been a soldier, Madame, and I knew how to deal with a crisis. We confronted my cousin with his treachery and we took from him the box containing the jewels."

"That was heroic!" Clara exclaimed.

"Then came the question," the Marquis went on, encouraged by the admiration in those beautiful hazel eyes, "how to conceal the property until we could prove our rights in the courts. My companion had arranged for that. It was a triumph of ingenuity. At a certain spot the case containing the jewels was thrown overboard in a wicker basket. We had men in a motor boat lying in wait. The thing was done—a magnificent exploit. We congratulated ourselves. Alas, we were too previous. My cousin had been too cunning. The case was discovered. The box opened. It contained a little sand and a few pebbles! My cousin was on his way to London with the jewels. He was safe from the law and from our pursuit."

"But, my dear Marquis," Clara argued, "there *was* a robbery. The Duc de Challes has sworn that the jewels were in the case which was taken from him."

The young man's lower jaw dropped, his face was almost pitiable in its vanity. He shook his head.

"That is my cousin's bluff," he declared. "He had the jewels with him when he left the Château. The case was empty when we took it from him. He disposed of them elsewhere."

"You poor man," Clara sighed. "Tell me—where is your friend now?"

The Marquis indulged in a silent but expressive gesture.

"That I must not say. He is afraid of the police. Our attempt was an illegal one. It was my own property we tried to regain but I too am in some danger."

"Nevertheless, where is he?" Clara persisted. "Somehow I have an idea he is not far away. Is he?"

The Marquis' expression was like that of a distressed and tortured child.

"I must not tell you about him. I have sworn that I will not open my lips. He was seen by more than one person with the case. They would never believe that he had not the jewels."

"I suppose," Clara reflected, "you have every confidence in your banker friend?"

"Why should I not have confidence? It is to his interest as well as mine to recover the jewels. With them in my possession my debts to him will be paid. Without them I am penniless."

She sighed once more.

"If only I could help you," she lamented. "And listen—come a little nearer to me—*I believe that I could.*"

He was under the spell of the light in her beautiful eyes, the slight quiver in her tone. Never in all his career of gallantry had such a thing happened to him with a woman so marvellous, so responsive.

"There is a way to help you," she confided. "You have courage, I know."

"Tell me," he begged.

"Tell me where your friend is," she whispered.

"He is in the next cabin," the Marquis replied. "Locked in. He would not even have me there with him. Furthermore—he is disguised."

She patted his hand.

"You will trust me?"

He drew a little nearer. She avoided what was after all only a timorous attempt at an embrace.

"Always, beloved," he murmured. "But first—"

Again she eluded him with a little laugh.

"They have told me that you are a dangerous person, Marquis," she said. "Even with a fortune at stake you show yourself a man of gallantry. But wait. The jewels first."

"The jewels first," he repeated in a mesmerised tone.

She rang the bell. Her friend the steward presently appeared. She drew him on one side. With a little nod and a gesture to the Marquis she stepped out into the corridor.

"Steward," she demanded, "who is in the next cabin?"

The man's face fell. He was evidently perturbed.

"Madame," he replied, "his name is Fontany but I know no more about him."

She shook her head gently but reproachfully.

"You are an honest man, Grayson," she said. "You do not wish to get into trouble? You do not wish to shield a thief?"

"Not for one moment, Madame," was the indignant answer.

"Then trust me," she insisted. "Fetch me the Purser as quickly as you can and tell him to bring two of the officers who have some courage. Tell him if he does this there may be a very pleasant surprise for him."

The steward's face was a study in expressions.

"I will tell you the truth, your ladyship," he confessed. "The man who is alone in the next stateroom has given me five pounds to see that he is not disturbed before we reach Calais. He has promised me another ten pounds when we arrive there."

She shook her head again, then leaned across to him and whispered in his ear. He sped away with a little gasp. Clara Linz returned to her seat upon the lounge. And here the young man welcomed her petulantly.

"You leave me alone," he complained, "and we have arranged nothing. You will travel to Paris with me—yes? I will arrange for a coupé."

"What about your friend in the next cabin?" she asked.

"He does not wish to be seen with me," the Marquis assured her. "He is afraid that we might be recognised. Although there was nothing in it we took the dressing case away from my cousin. There might be trouble."

"And the lady with the beautiful hair who was your companion?" Clara asked with a very creditable simulation of jealousy.

"She went to Folkestone to return by the other route to Boulogne," he explained. "Bouvard thought that it was better. For myself I am not afraid," the Marquis went on with a show of courage. "I try to recover from a relative my own property. It is a man's natural impulse. With Bouvard it is different."

"What do you suppose," she asked, "he is doing in there alone and with the door locked?"

"He is a very excitable person," the Marquis confided. "The anxiety has brought on an attack of seasickness."

There were steps in the corridor. The farce was coming to an end.

"Do you believe that?" she asked.

"Why not?" the Marquis demanded. "He is my good

friend. It is he who has financed me since the banks have been difficult."

There was a knock at the door. In response to Clara's invitation to enter the Purser and two of the ship's officers were disclosed upon the threshold. She rose to her feet.

"Mr. Brown," she said, addressing the Purser, "there is a man locked up in the next cabin who I believe stole the jewels belonging to the Duc de Challes. Furthermore, I believe that he has the jewels with him."

The Purser's eyes glittered.

"Baroness!" he exclaimed.

They all swung out on to the corridor. The Marquis had an attack of nerves. He was calling out feebly and trying to attach himself to Clara. The Purser knocked at the door of stateroom Number Sixteen. There was at first no reply. Then a very weak voice was heard.

"Who is that? Go away. I am ill. I have the *mal-de-mer*."

The Purser wasted no more time. He drew from his pocket a passkey and fitted it into the lock. He threw open the door. A man, who was lying upon the couch, sprang to his feet.

"What is the meaning of this intrusion?" he demanded, and his voice was suddenly strong.

The Purser looked round the room hurriedly.

"I see no trace of seasickness," he remarked.

"This is my reserved cabin for which I have paid," Bouvard exclaimed angrily. "I demand to be left alone."

"I should like to point out to you, Mr. Brown," Clara said with a sudden inspiration, "that this man crossed yesterday on the boat from which the jewels were stolen under the name of Bouvard. He has engaged this cabin under the name of Fontany! He was a stout man then with a black moustache. Look at him now! He has shaved off the moustache and got rid of his false front."

"But that is ridiculous!" Bouvard shouted.

"Take my advice," Clara begged. "Search the cabin."

The Purser, one of the officers and the steward set about their task. The other officer stood over the man upon the lounge. The latter, with a shrug of the shoulders, appeared to have resigned himself.

"For what you search I do not know," he said. "I have shaved my moustache because it pleased me. I do not break the law when I do that. You may look through my belongings. If you will you may search me. I do not know what it is you are looking for but I am not a thief . . ."

At the expiration of a quarter of an hour things began to look a little awkward. The carpet had been torn up and the boards tested. The lounge had been thoroughly examined and the two chairs dismantled. The Purser was distinctly uneasy. Clara herself was puzzled. Suddenly inspiration again befriended her. She pointed towards the lavatory basin.

"What is that lying by the side of the nailbrush?" she asked.

The Purser picked it up.

"It appears to be a screwdriver," he remarked. "Belong to you, Adams?" he asked the steward.

"Never saw it before, sir," the man replied. "I don't know how it got there."

"See if it fits the screws which hold the bowl in place," Clara suggested.

The steward went on his knees and made an effort. Clara smiled. She was spared the catastrophe of failure! They all stooped down. One by one the screws were withdrawn. The Purser pulled forward the lead pipe and bent it over. A little shower of jewels fell on to the floor!

"Don't you see what he has done?" he pointed out. "He has opened the pipe at the other end, put in some sort of an obstacle, rescrewed the pipe at the top, and there he has the most complete hiding place anyone could imagine."

"Purser, I suggest that you have the pipe carefully removed," Clara directed. "As for the jewels—I claim them on behalf of the Duc de Challes for whom I am acting."

Henri Bouvard's shouts filled the cabin. He tried to fight his way out but he was easily overpowered. He might, perhaps, have slipped away but he shrank back trembling before the revolver which the Marquis was pointing at him in unsteady fashion.

"The jewels were there after all, Bouvard!" the latter called out. "You have deceived me! It was you who secured the jewels!"

"For your sake, you puppy!" the other bellowed.

"*Je m'en doute*," the Marquis sneered.

"The whole affair," Clara pointed out, "is quite clear. This man Bouvard double-crossed his companion, who I daresay may be a cousin of the Duc de Challes, and who may think that the jewels are his. He reported failure having achieved success. You will take care of the jewels, Mr. Brown. So far as I am concerned the affair is over."

The Duc de Challes, who had already received the welcome news, presented himself at midday on the following morning in Adam Street. He was received as before by Clara, Baroness Linz.

"Madame," he said gratefully, "I extend to the firm of ADVICE LIMITED my sincere thanks and my hearty congratulations. I have here your fee of a thousand guineas."

He laid a cheque upon the table and looked more curiously than ever at his companion.

"I can scarcely be blamed now," he continued, "if I insist upon an introduction to your principal."

Clara pulled up the blind and removed her spectacles. That intriguing smile which had captivated him for a moment upon the boat had returned. He stared and took up his hat. Then he laughed. He was a man of the world and he understood very well how to mind his own business.

"I shall drink a toast to-night," he promised, "to the continued success of ADVICE LIMITED."

$\mathfrak{M}$IGNON GOOD EBERHART (1899–) was born in University Place, Nebraska, and attended Nebraska Wesleyan University. She began writing to keep herself occupied while traveling with her husband, a civil engineer. Starting with short stories, she soon progressed to novels; her first was *The Patient in Room 18* (1929), introducing Nurse Sarah Keate, who was to feature as a sleuth in quite a few other Eberhart titles. Her style and plotting are generally classified as HIBK, though much of the time her accomplishment transcends the trappings and she creates a superior puzzle. She has almost sixty novels to her credit and new ones keep appearing, the most recent being *Danger Money* (1975). Moreover, her many earlier titles, with translations into at least sixteen languages, are continually being reissued.

Susan Dare writes murder mysteries for her living: "lovely, grisly ones, with sensible solutions." She also finds herself called upon occasionally to provide solutions to real-life murders, leading the Chicago police force to regard her as a valuable consultant. Personal details are not easily extracted from the stories, although it appears that Susan is fair-haired, sometimes wears horn-rimmed spectacles, and has a pet dog. Her relationship with reporter Jim Byrne begins with her first adventure, "Introducing Susan Dare." "The Calico Dog" is her sixth and last case.

The Calico Dog

by Mignon G. Eberhart

It was nothing short of an invitation to murder.

"You don't mean to say," Susan Dare said in a small voice, "that both of them—*both* of them are living here?"

Idabelle Lasher—Mrs. Jeremiah Lasher, that is, widow of the patent-medicine emperor who died last year (resisting, it is said, his own medicine to the end with the strangest vehemence)—Idabelle Lasher turned large pale blue eyes upon Susan and sighed and said:

"Why, yes. There was nothing else to do. I can't turn my own boy out into the world."

Susan took a long breath. "Always assuming," she said, "that one of them is your own boy."

"Oh, there's no doubt about that, Miss Dare," said Idabelle Lasher simply.

"Let me see," Susan said, "if I have this straight. Your son Derek was lost twenty years ago. Recently he has returned. Rather, two of him has returned."

Mrs. Lasher was leaning forward, tears in her large pale eyes. "Miss Dare," she said, "one of them must be my son. I need him so much."

Her large blandness, her artificiality, the padded ease

and softness of her life dropped away before the earnestness and honesty of that brief statement. She was all at once pathetic—no, it was on a larger scale; she was tragic in her need for her child.

"And besides," she said suddenly and with an odd naïveté, "besides, there's all that money. Thirty millions."

"*Thirty*—" began Susan and stopped. It was simply not comprehensible. Half a million, yes; even a million. But thirty millions!

"But if you can't tell yourself which of the two young men is your son, how can I? And with so much money involved—"

"That's just it," said Mrs. Lasher, leaning forward earnestly again. "I'm sure that Papa would have wanted me to be perfectly sure. The last thing he said to me was to warn me. 'Watch out for yourself, Idabelle,' he said. 'People will be after your money. Impostors.' "

"But I don't see how I can help you," Susan repeated firmly.

"You *must* help me," said Mrs. Lasher. "Christabel Frame told me about you. She said you wrote mystery stories and were the only woman who could help me, and that you were right here in Chicago."

Her handkerchief poised, she waited with childlike anxiety to see if the name of Christabel Frame had its expected weight with Susan. But it was not altogether the name of one of her most loved friends that influenced Susan. It was the childlike appeal on the part of this woman.

"How do you feel about the two claimants?" she said. "Do you feel more strongly attracted to one than to the other?"

"That's just the trouble," said Idabelle Lasher. "I like them both."

"Let me have the whole story again, won't you? Try to tell it quite definitely, just as things occurred."

Mrs. Lasher put the handkerchief away and sat up briskly.

"Well," she began. "It was like this . . ." Two months ago a young man called Dixon March had called on her; he had not gone to her lawyer, he had come to see her. And he had told her a very straight story.

"You must remember something of the story—oh, but, of course, you couldn't. You're far too young. And then, too, we weren't as rich as we are now, when little Derek disappeared. He was four at the time. And his nursemaid disappeared at the same time, and I always thought, Miss Dare, that it was the nursemaid who stole him."

"Ransom?" asked Susan.

"No. That was the queer part of it. There never was any attempt to demand ransom. I always felt the nursemaid simply wanted him for herself—she was a very peculiar woman."

Susan brought her gently back to the present.

"So Dixon March is this claimant's name?"

"Yes. That's another thing. It seemed so likely to me that he could remember his name—Derek—and perhaps in saying Derek in his baby way, the people at the orphanage thought it was Dixon he was trying to say, so they called him Dixon. The only trouble is—"

"Yes," said Susan, as Idabelle Lasher's blue eyes wavered and became troubled.

"Well, you see, the other young man, the other Derek—well, his name is Duane. You see?"

Susan felt a little dizzy. "Just what is Dixon's story?"

"He said that he was taken in at an orphanage at the age of six. That he vaguely remembers a woman, dark, with a mole on her chin, which is an exact description of the nursemaid. Of course, we've had the orphanage records examined, but there's nothing conclusive and no way to identify the woman; she died—under the name of Sarah Gant, which wasn't the nursemaid's name—and she was very poor. A social worker simply arranged for the child's entrance into the orphanage."

"What makes him think he is your son, then?"

"Well, it's this way. He grew up and made as much as he could of the education they gave him and actually was making a nice thing with a construction company when he got to looking into his—his origins, he said—and an account of the description of our Derek, the dates, the fact that he could discover nothing of the woman, Sarah Gant, previous to her life in Ottawa—"

"Ottawa?"

"Yes. That was where he came from. The other one, Duane, from New Orleans. And the fact that, as Dixon remembered her, she looked very much like the newspaper pictures of the nursemaid, suggested the possibility that he was our lost child."

"So, on the evidence of corresponding dates and the likeness of the woman who was caring for him before he was taken to the orphanage, he comes to you, claiming to be your son. A year after your husband died."

"Yes, and—well—" Mrs. Lasher flushed pinkly. "There are some things he can remember."

"Things—such as what?"

"The—the green curtains in the nursery. There *were* green curtains in the nursery. And a—a calico dog. And—and a few other things. The lawyers say that isn't conclusive. But I think it's very important that he remembers the calico dog."

"You've had lawyers looking into his claims."

"Oh, dear, yes," said Mrs. Lasher. "Exhaustively."

"But can't they trace Sarah Gant?"

"Nothing conclusive, Miss Dare."

"His physical appearance?" suggested Susan.

"Miss Dare," said Mrs. Lasher. "My Derek was blond with gray eyes. He had no marks of any kind. His teeth were still his baby teeth. Any fair young man with gray eyes might be my son. And both these men—either of these men might be Derek. I've looked long and wearily, searching every feature and every expression for a likeness to my boy. It is equally there—and not there. I feel sure that one of them is my son. I am absolutely sure that he has—has come home."

"But you don't know which one?" said Susan softly.

"I don't know which one," said Idabelle Lasher. "But one of them *is Derek.*"

She turned suddenly and walked heavily to a window. Her pale green gown of soft crepe trailed behind her, its hem touching a priceless thin rug that ought to have been in a museum. Behind her, against the gray wall, hung a small Mauve, exquisite. Twenty-one stories below, traffic flowed unceasingly along Lake Shore Drive.

"One of them must be an impostor," Idabelle Lasher was saying presently in a choked voice.

"Is Dixon certain he is your son?"

"He says only that he thinks so. But since Duane has come, too, he is more—more positive—"

"Duane, of course." The rivalry of the two young men must be rather terrible. Susan had a fleeting glimpse again of what it might mean: one of them certainly an impostor, both impostors, perhaps, struggling over Idabelle Lasher's affections and her fortune. The thought opened, really, quite appalling and horrid vistas.

"What is Duane's story?" asked Susan.

"That's what makes it so queer, Miss Dare. Duane's story—is—well, it is exactly the same."

Susan stared at her wide green back, cushiony and bulgy in spite of the finest corseting that money could obtain.

"You don't mean *exactly* the same!" she cried.

"Exactly," the woman turned and faced her. "Exactly the same, Miss Dare, except for the names and places. The name of the woman in Duane's case was Mary Miller, the orphanage was in New Orleans, he was going to art school here in Chicago when—when, he says, just as Dixon said—he began to be more and more interested in his parentage and began investigating. And he, too, remembers things, little things from his babyhood and our house that only Derek could remember."

"Wait, Mrs. Lasher," said Susan, grasping at something firm. "Any servant, any of your friends, would know these details also."

Mrs. Lasher's pale, big eyes became more prominent.

"You mean, of course, a conspiracy. The lawyers have talked nothing else. But, Miss Dare, they authenticated everything possible to authenticate in both statements. I know what has happened to the few servants we had—all, that is, except the nursemaid. And we don't have many close friends, Miss Dare. Not since there was so much money. And none of them—none of them would do this."

"But both young men can't be Derek," said Susan desperately. She clutched at common sense again and said: "How soon after your husband's death did Dixon arrive?"

"Ten months."

"And Duane?"

"Three months after Dixon."

"And they are both living here with you now?"

"Yes." She nodded toward the end of the long room. "They are in the library now."

"Together?" said Susan irresistibly.

"Yes, of course," said Mrs. Lasher. "Playing cribbage."

"I suppose you and your lawyers have tried every possible test?"

"Everything, Miss Dare."

"You have no fingerprints of the baby?"

"No. That was before fingerprints were so important. We tried blood tests, of course. But they are of the same type."

"Resemblances to you or your husband?"

"You'll see for yourself at dinner tonight, Miss Dare. You will help me?"

Susan sighed. "Yes," she said.

The bedroom to which Mrs. Lasher herself took Susan was done in the French manner with much taffeta, inlaid satinwood, and lace cushions. It was very large and overwhelmingly magnificent, and gilt mirrors reflected Susan's small brown figure in unending vistas.

Susan dismissed the maid, thanked fate that the only dinner gown she had brought was a new and handsome one, and felt very awed and faintly dissolute in a great, sunken, black marble pool that she wouldn't have dared call a tub. After all, reflected Susan, finding that she could actually swim a stroke or two, thirty millions was thirty millions.

She got into a white chiffon dress with silver and green at the waist, and was stooping in a froth of white flounces to secure the straps of her flat-heeled silver sandals when Mrs. Lasher knocked.

"It's Derek's baby things," she said in a whisper and with a glance over her fat white shoulder. "Let's move a little farther from the door."

They sat down on a cushioned chaise-longue and between them, incongruous against the suave cream satin, Idabelle Lasher spread out certain small objects, touching them lingeringly.

"His little suit—he looked so sweet in yellow. Some pictures. A pink plush teddy bear. His little nursery-school reports—he was already in nursery school, Miss Dare—pre-kindergarten, you know. It was in an experimental stage then, and so interesting. And the calico dog, Miss Dare."

She stopped there, and Susan looked at the faded, flabby calico dog held so tenderly in those fat diamonded hands. She felt suddenly a wave of cold anger toward the man who was not Derek and who must know that he was not Derek. She took the pictures eagerly.

But they were only pictures. One at about two, made by a photographer; a round baby face without features that were at all distinctive. Two or three pictures of a little boy playing, squinting against the sun.

"Has anyone else seen these things?"

"You mean either of the two boys—either Dixon or Duane? No, Miss Dare."

"Has anyone at all seen them? Servants? Friends?"

Idabelle's blue eyes became vague and clouded.

"Long ago, perhaps," she said. "Oh, many, many years ago. But they've been in the safe in my bedroom for years. Before that in a locked closet."

"How long have they been in the safe?"

"Since we bought this apartment. Ten—no, twelve years."

"And no one—there's never been anything like an attempted robbery of that safe?"

"Never. No, Miss Dare. There's no possible way for either Dixon or Duane to know of the contents of this box except from memory."

"And Dixon remembers the calico dog?"

"Yes." The prominent blue eyes wavered again, and Mrs. Lasher rose and walked toward the door. She paused then and looked at Susan again.

"And Duane remembers the teddy bear and described it to me," she said definitely and went away.

There was a touch of comedy about it, and, like all comedy, it overlay tragedy.

Left to herself, Susan studied the pictures again thoughtfully. The nursery-school reports, written out in beautiful "vertical" handwriting. *Music*: A good ear. *Memory*: Very good. *Adaptability*: Very good. *Sociability*: Inclined to shyness. *Rhythm*: Poor (advise skipping games at home). *Conduct*: (This varied, with at least once a suggestive blank and once a somewhat terse remark to the effect that there had been considerable disturbance during the half-hours devoted to naps and a strong suggestion that Derek was at the bottom of it). Susan smiled there and began to like baby Derek. And it was just then that she found the first indication of an identifying trait. And that was after the heading *Games.* One report said: Quick. Another said: Mentally quick but does not coordinate muscles well. And a third said, definitely pinning the thing down: Tendency to use left hand which we are endeavoring to correct.

Tendency to use left hand. An inborn tendency, cropping out again and again all through life. In those days, of course, it had been rigidly corrected—thereby inducing all manner of ills, according to more recent trends of education. But was it ever altogether conquered?

Presently Susan put the things in the box again and went to Mrs. Lasher's room. And Susan had the somewhat dubious satisfaction of watching Mrs. Lasher open a delicate ivory panel which disclosed a very utilitarian steel safe set in the wall behind it and place the box securely in the safe.

"Did you find anything that will be of help?" asked Mrs. Lasher, closing the panel.

"I don't know," said Susan. "I'm afraid there's nothing very certain. Do Dixon and Duane know why I am here?"

"No," said Mrs. Lasher, revealing unexpected cunning. "I told them you were a dear friend of Christabel's. And that you were very much interested in their—my—our situation. We talk it over, you know, very frankly, Miss Dare. The boys are as anxious as I am to discover the truth of it."

Again, thought Susan feeling baffled, as the true Derek would be. She followed Mrs. Lasher toward the drawing room again, prepared heartily to dislike both men.

But the man sipping a cocktail in the doorway of the library was much too old to be either Dixon or Duane.

"Major Briggs," said Mrs. Lasher. "Christabel's friend

Susan, Tom." She turned to Susan. "Major Tom Briggs is our closest friend. He was like a brother to my husband, and has been to me."

"Never a brother," said Major Briggs with an air of gallantry. "Say, rather, an admirer. So this is Christabel's little friend." He put down his cocktail glass and bowed and took Susan's hand only a fraction too tenderly.

Then Mrs. Lasher drifted across the room where Susan was aware of two pairs of black shoulders rising to greet her, and Major Briggs said beamingly:

"How happy we are to have you with us, my dear. I suppose Idabelle has told you of our—our problem."

He was about Susan's height; white-haired, rather puffy under the eyes, and a bit too pink, with hands that were inclined to shake. He adjusted his gold-rimmed eyeglasses, then let them drop the length of their black ribbon and said:

"What do you think of it, my dear?"

"I don't know," said Susan. "What do you think?"

"Well, my dear, it's a bit difficult, you know. When Idabelle herself doesn't know. When the most rigid—yes, the most rigid and searching investigation on the part of highly trained and experienced investigators has failed to discover—ah—the identity of the lost heir, how may my own poor powers avail!" He finished his cocktail, gulped, and said blandly: "But it's Duane."

"What—" said Susan.

"I said, it's Duane. He is the heir. Anybody could see it with half an eye. Spittin' image of his dad. Here they come now."

They were alike and yet not alike at all. Both were rather tall, slender, and well made. Both had medium-brown hair. Both had grayish-blue eyes. Neither was particularly handsome. Neither was exactly unhandsome. Their features were not at all alike in bone structure, yet neither had features that were in any way distinctive.

Their description on a passport would not have varied by a single word. Actually they were altogether unlike each other.

With the salad Major Briggs roused to point out a portrait that hung on the opposite wall.

"Jeremiah Lasher," he said, waving a pink hand in that direction. He glanced meaningly at Susan and added, "Do you see any resemblance, Miss Susan? I mean between my old friend and one of these lads here."

One of the lads—it was Dixon—wriggled perceptibly, but Duane smiled.

"We are not at all embarrassed, Miss Susan," he said pleasantly. "We are both quite accustomed to this sort of scrutiny." He laughed lightly, and Idabelle smiled, and Dixon said:

"Does Miss Dare know about this?"

"Oh, yes," said Idabelle, turning as quickly and attentively to him as she had turned to Duane. "There's no secret about it."

"No," said Dixon somewhat crisply. "There's certainly no secret about it."

There was, however, no further mention of the problem of identity during the rest of the evening. Indeed, it was a very calm and slightly dull evening except for the affair of Major Briggs and the draft.

That happened just after dinner. Susan and Mrs. Lasher were sitting over coffee in the drawing room, and the three men were presumably lingering in the dining room.

It had been altogether quiet in the drawing room, yet there had not been audible even the distant murmur of the men's voices. Thus the queer, choked shout that arose in the dining room came as a definite shock to the two women.

It all happened in an instant. They hadn't themselves

time to move or inquire before Duane appeared in the doorway. He was laughing but looked pale.

"It's all right," he said. "Nothing's wrong."

"*Duane,*" said Idabelle Lasher gaspingly. "*What–*"

"Don't be alarmed," he said swiftly. "It's nothing." He turned to look down the hall at someone approaching and added: "Here he is, safe and sound."

He stood aside, and Major Briggs appeared in the doorway. He looked so shocked and purple that both women moved hurriedly forward, and Idabelle Lasher said, "Here—on the divan. Ring for brandy, Duane. Lie down here, Major."

"Oh, no—no," said Major Briggs stertorously. "No. I'm quite all right."

Duane, however, supported him to the divan, and Dixon appeared in the doorway.

"What happened?" he said.

Major Briggs waved his hands feebly. Duane said:

"The Major nearly went out the window."

"O-h-h-h—" It was Idabelle in a thin, long scream.

"Oh, it's all right," said Major Briggs shakenly. "I caught hold of the curtain. By God, I'm glad you had heavy curtain rods at that window, Idabelle."

She was fussing around him, her hands shaking, her face ghastly under its make-up.

"But how could you—" she was saying jerkily—"what on earth—how could it have happened—"

"It's the draft," said the Major irascibly. "The confounded draft on my neck. I got up to close the window and—I nearly went out!"

"But how could you—" began Idabelle again.

"I don't know how it happened," said the Major. "Just all at once—" A look of perplexity came slowly over his face. "Queer," said Major Briggs suddenly, "I suppose it was the draft. But it was exactly as if—" He stopped, and Idabelle cried:

"As if what?"

"As if someone had pushed me," said the Major.

Perhaps it was fortunate that the butler arrived just then, and there was the slight diversion of getting the Major to stretch out full length on the divan and sip a restorative.

And somehow in the conversation it emerged that neither Dixon nor Duane had been in the dining room when the thing had happened.

"There'd been a disagreement over—well, it was over inheritance tax," said Dixon, flushing. "Duane had gone to the library to look in an encyclopedia, and I had gone to my room to get the evening paper which had some reference to it. So the Major was alone when it happened. I knew nothing of it until I heard the commotion in here."

"I," said Duane, watching Dixon, "heard the Major's shout from the library and hurried across."

That night, late, after Major Briggs had gone home, and Susan was again alone in the paralyzing magnificence of the French bedroom, she still kept thinking of the window and Major Briggs. And she put up her own window so circumspectly that she didn't get enough air during the night and woke struggling with a silk-covered eiderdown under the impression that she herself was being thrust out the window.

It was only a nightmare, of course, induced as much as anything by her own hatred of heights. But it gave an impulse to the course she proposed to Mrs. Lasher that very morning.

It was true, of course, that the thing may have been exactly what it appeared to be, and that was, an accident. But if it was not accident, there were only two possibilities.

"Do you mean," cried Mrs. Lasher incredulously when Susan had finished her brief suggestion, "that I'm to say openly that Duane is my son! But you don't understand, Miss Dare. I'm not sure. It may be Dixon."

"I know," said Susan. "And I may be wrong. But I think it might help if you will announce to—oh, only to Major Briggs and the two men—that you are convinced that it is Duane and are taking steps for legal recognition of the fact."

"Why? What do you think will happen? How will it help things to do that?"

"I'm not at all sure it will help," said Susan wearily. "But it's the only thing I see to do. And I think that you may as well do it right away."

"Today?" said Mrs. Lasher reluctantly.

"At lunch," said Susan inexorably. "Telephone to invite Major Briggs now."

"Oh, very well," said Idabelle Lasher. "After all, it will please Tom Briggs. He has been urging me to make a decision. He seems certain that it is Duane."

But Susan, present and watching closely, could detect nothing except that Idabelle Lasher, once she was committed to a course, undertook it with thoroughness. Her fondness for Duane, her kindness to Dixon, her air of relief at having settled so momentous a question, left nothing to be desired. Susan was sure that the men were convinced. There was, to be sure, a shade of triumph in Duane's demeanor, and he was magnanimous with Dixon —as, indeed, he could well afford to be. Dixon was silent and rather pale and looked as if he had not expected the decision and was a bit stunned by it. Major Briggs was incredulous at first, and then openly jubilant, and toasted all of them.

Indeed, what with toasts and speeches on the part of Major Briggs, the lunch rather prolonged itself, and it was late afternoon before the Major had gone and Susan and Mrs. Lasher met alone for a moment in the library.

Idabelle was flushed and worried.

"Was it all right, Miss Dare?" she asked in a stage whisper.

"Perfectly," said Susan.

"Then—then do you know—"

"Not yet," said Susan. "But keep Dixon here."

"Very well," said Idabelle.

The rest of the day passed quietly and not, from Susan's point of view, at all valuably, although Susan tried to prove something about the possible left-handedness of the real Derek. Badminton and several games of billiards resulted only in displaying the more perfectly a consistent right-handedness on the part of both the claimants.

Dressing again for dinner, Susan looked at herself ruefully in the great mirror.

She had never in her life felt so utterly helpless, and the thought of Idabelle Lasher's faith in her hurt. After all, she ought to have realized her own limits; the problem that Mrs. Lasher had set her was one that would have baffled—that, indeed, had baffled—experts. Who was she, Susan Dare, to attempt its solution?

The course of action she had laid out for Idabelle Lasher had certainly, thus far, had no development beyond heightening an already tense situation. It was quite possible that she was mistaken and that nothing at all would come of it. And if not, what then?

Idabelle Lasher's pale eyes and anxious, beseeching hands hovered again before Susan, and she jerked her satin slip savagely over her head—thereby pulling loose a shoulder strap and being obliged to ring for the maid, who sewed the strap neatly and rearranged Susan's hair.

"You'll be going to the party tonight, ma'am?" said the maid in a pleasant Irish accent.

"Party?"

"Oh, yes, ma'am. Didn't you know? It's the Charity Ball. At the Dycke Hotel. In the Chandelier Ballroom. A grand, big party, ma'am. Madame is wearing her pearls. Will you bend your head, please, ma'am."

Susan bent her head and felt her white chiffon being slipped deftly over it. When she emerged she said:

"Is the entire family going?"

"Oh, yes, ma'am. And Major Briggs. There you are, ma'am—and I do say you look beautiful. There's orchids, ma'am, from Mr. Duane. And gardenias from Mr. Dixon. I believe," said the maid thoughtfully, "that I could put them all together. That's what I'm doing for Madame."

"Very well," said Susan recklessly. "Put them all together."

It made a somewhat staggering decoration—staggering, thought Susan, but positively abandoned in luxuriousness. So, too, was the long town car which waited for them promptly at ten when they emerged from the towering apartment house. Susan, leaning back in her seat between Major Briggs and Idabelle Lasher, was always afterward to remember that short ride through crowded, lighted streets to the Dycke Hotel.

No one spoke. Perhaps only Susan was aware (and suddenly realized that she was aware) of the surging desires and needs and feelings that were bottled up together in the tonneau of that long, gliding car. She was aware of it quite suddenly and tinglingly.

Nothing had happened. Nothing, all through that long dinner from which they had just come, had been said that was at all provocative.

Yet all at once Susan was aware of a queer kind of excitement.

She looked at the black shoulders of the two men, Duane and Dixon, riding along beside each other. Dixon sat stiff and straight; his shoulders looked rigid and unmoving. He had taken it rather well, she thought; did he guess Idabelle's decision was not the true one? Or was he still stunned by it?

Or was there something back of that silence? Had she underestimated the force and possible violence of Dixon's reaction? Susan frowned: it was dangerous enough without that.

They arrived at the hotel. Their sudden emergence from the silence of the car, with its undercurrent of emotion, into brilliant lights and crowds and the gay lilt of an orchestra somewhere, had its customary tonic effect. Even Dixon shook off his air of brooding and, as they finally strolled into the Chandelier Room, and Duane and Mrs. Lasher danced smoothly into the revolving colors, asked Susan to dance.

They left the Major smiling approval and buying cigarettes from a girl in blue pantaloons.

The momentary gayety with which Dixon had asked Susan to dance faded at once. He danced conscientiously but without much spirit and said nothing. Susan glanced up at his face once or twice; his direct, dark blue eyes looked straight ahead, and his face was rather pale and set.

Presently Susan said: "Oh, there's Idabelle!"

At once Dixon lost step. Susan recovered herself and her small silver sandals rather deftly, and Idabelle, large and pink and jewel-laden, danced past them in Duane's arms. She smiled at Dixon anxiously and looked, above her pearls, rather worried.

Dixon's eyebrows were a straight dark line, and he was white around the mouth.

"I'm sorry, Dixon," said Susan. She tried to catch step with him, for the moment, and added: "Please don't mind my speaking about it. We are all thinking of it. I do think you behave very well."

He looked straight over her head, danced several somewhat erratic steps, and said suddenly:

"It was so—unexpected. And you see, I was so sure of it."

"Why were you so sure?" asked Susan.

He hesitated, then burst out again:

"Because of the dog," he said savagely, stepping on one of Susan's silver toes. She removed it with Spartan composure, and he said: "The calico dog, you know. And the green curtains. If I had known there was so much money involved, I don't think I'd have come to—Idabelle. But then, when I did know, and this other—fellow turned up, why, of course, I felt like sticking it out!"

He paused, and Susan felt his arm tighten around her waist. She looked up, and his face was suddenly chalk white and his eyes blazing.

"Duane!" he said hoarsely. "I hate him. I could kill him with my own hands."

The next dance was a tango, and Susan danced it with Duane. His eyes were shining, and his face flushed with excitement and gayety.

He was a born dancer, and Susan relaxed in the perfect ease of his steps. He held her very closely, complimented her gracefully, and talked all the time, and for a few moments Susan merely enjoyed the fast swirl of the lovely Argentine dance. Then Idabelle and Dixon went past, and Susan saw again the expression of Dixon's set white face as he looked at Duane, and Idabelle's swimming eyes above her pink face and bare pink neck.

The rest of what was probably a perfect dance was lost on Susan, busy about certain concerns of her own which involved some adjusting of the flowers on her shoulder. And the moment the dance was over she slipped away.

White chiffon billowed around her, and her gardenias sent up a warm fragrance as she huddled into a telephone booth. She made sure the flowers were secure and un-revealing upon her shoulder, steadied her breath, and smiled a little tremulously as she dialed a number she very well knew. It was getting to be a habit—calling Jim Byrne, her newspaper friend, when she herself had reached an impasse. But she needed him. Needed him at once.

"Jim—Jim," she said. "It's Susan. Listen. Get into a white tie and come as fast as you can to the Dycke Hotel. The Chandelier Room."

"What's wrong?"

"Well," said Susan in a small voice, "I've set something going that—that I'm afraid is going to be more than I meant—"

"You're good at stirring up things, Sue," he said. "What's the trouble now?"

"Hurry, Jim," said Susan. "I mean it." She caught her breath. "I—I'm afraid," she said.

His voice changed.

"I'll be right there. Watch for me at the door." The telephone clicked, and Susan leaned rather weakly against the wall of the telephone booth.

She went back to the Chandelier Room. Idabelle Lasher, pink and worried-looking, and Major Briggs and the two younger men made a little group standing together, talking. She breathed a little sigh of relief. So long as they remained together, and remained in that room surrounded by hundreds of witnesses, it was all right. Surely it was all right. People didn't murder in cold blood when other people were looking on.

It was Idabelle who remembered her duties as hostess and suggested the fortune-teller.

"She's very good, they say," said Idabelle. "She's a professional, not just doing it for a stunt, you know. She's got a booth in one of the rooms."

"By all means, my dear," said Major Briggs at once. "This way?" She put her hand on his arm and, with Duane at her other side, moved away, and Dixon and Susan followed. Susan cast a worried look toward the entrance. But Jim couldn't possibly get there in less than thirty minutes, and by that time they would have returned.

Dixon said: "Was it the Major that convinced Idabelle that Duane is her son?"

Susan hesitated.

"I don't know," she said cautiously, "how strong the Major's influence has been."

Her caution was not successful. As they left the ballroom and turned down a corridor, he whirled toward her.

"This thing isn't over yet," he said with the sudden savagery that had blazed out in him while they were dancing.

She said nothing, however, for Major Briggs was beckoning jauntily from a doorway.

"Here it is," he said in a stage whisper as they approached him. "Idabelle has already gone in. And would you believe it, the fortune-teller charges twenty dollars a throw!"

The room was small: a dining room, probably, for small parties. Across the end of it a kind of tent had been arranged with many gaily striped curtains.

Possibly due to her fees, the fortune-teller did not appear to be very popular; at least, there were no others waiting, and no one came to the door except a bellboy with a tray in his hand who looked them over searchingly, murmured something that sounded very much like Mr. Haymow, and wandered away. Duane sat nonchalantly on the small of his back, smoking. The Major seemed a bit nervous and moved restlessly about. Dixon stood just behind Susan. Odd that she could feel his hatred for the man lolling there in the armchair almost as if it were a palpable, living thing flowing outward in waves. Susan's sense of danger was growing sharper. But surely it was safe—so long as they were together.

The draperies of the tent moved confusedly and opened, and Idabelle stood there, smiling and beckoning to Susan.

"Come inside, my dear," she said. "She wants you, too."

Susan hesitated. But, after all, so long as the three men were together, nothing could happen. Dixon gave her a sharp look, and Susan moved across the room. She felt a slight added qualm when she discovered that in an effort probably to add mystery to the fortune-teller's trade, the swathing curtains had been arranged so that one entered a kind of narrow passage among them, which one followed with several turns before arriving at the looped-up curtain which made an entrance to the center of the maze and faced the fortune-teller herself.

Susan stifled her uneasiness and sat down on some cushions beside Idabelle. The fortune-teller, in Egyptian costume, with French accent and a sibylline manner began to talk. Beyond the curtains and the drone of her voice Susan could hear little, although once she thought there were voices.

But the thing, when it happened, gave no warning.

There was only, suddenly, a great dull shock of sound that brought Susan taut and upright and left the fortune-teller gasping and still and turned Idabelle Lasher's broad pinkness to a queer pale mauve.

"*What was that?*" whispered Idabelle in a choked way.

And the fortune-teller cried: "It's a gunshot—out there!"

Susan stumbled and groped through the folds of draperies, trying to find the way through the entangling maze of curtains and out of the tent. Then all at once they were outside the curtains and staring at a figure that lay huddled on the floor, and there were people pouring in the door from the hall, and confusion everywhere.

It was Major Briggs. And he'd been shot and was dead, and there was no revolver anywhere.

Susan felt ill and faint and after one long look backed away to the window. Idabelle was weeping, her face blotched. Dixon was beside her, and then suddenly someone from the hotel had closed the door into the corridor. And a bellboy's voice, the one who'd wandered into the room looking for Mr. Haymow, rose shrilly above the tumult.

"Nobody at all," he was saying. "Nobody came out of the room. I was at the end of the corridor when I heard the shot and this is the only room on this side that's unlocked and in use tonight. So I ran down here, and I can swear that nobody came out of the room after the shot was fired. Not before I reached it."

"Was anybody here when you came in? What did you see?" It was the manager, fat, worried, but competently keeping the door behind him closed against further intrusion.

"Just this man on the floor. He was dead already."

"And nobody in the room?"

"Nobody. Nobody then. But I'd hardly got to him before there was people running into the room. And these three women came out of this tent."

The manager looked at Idabelle—at Susan.

"He was with you?" he asked Idabelle.

"Oh, yes, yes," sobbed Idabelle. "It's Major Briggs."

The manager started to speak, stopped, began again:

"I've sent for the police," he said. "You folks that were in his party—how many of you are there?"

"Just Miss Dare and me," sobbed Idabelle. "And—" she singled out Dixon and Duane—"these two men."

"All right. You folks stay right here, will you? And you, too, miss—" indicating the fortune-teller—"and the bellboy. The rest of you will go to a room across the hall. Sorry, but I'll have to hold you till the police get here."

It was not well received. There were murmurs of outrage and horrified looks over slender bare backs and the indignant rustle of trailing gowns, but the scattered groups that had pressed into the room did file slowly out again under the firm look of the manager.

The manager closed the door and said briskly:

"Now, if you folks will be good enough to stay right here, it won't be long till the police arrive."

"A doctor," faltered Idabelle. "Can't we have a doctor?"

The manager looked at the sodden, lifeless body.

"You don't want a doctor, ma'am," he said. "What you want is an under—" He stopped abruptly and reverted to his professional suavity. "We'll do everything in our power to save your feelings, Mrs. Lasher," he said. "At the same time we would much appreciate your—er—assistance. You see, the Charity Ball being what it is, we've got to keep this thing quiet." He was obviously distressed but still suave and competent. "Now then," he said, "I've got to make some arrangements—if you'll just stay here." He put his hand on the doorknob and then turned toward them again and said quite definitely, looking at the floor: "It would be just as well if none of you were to try to leave."

With that he was gone.

The fortune-teller sank down into a chair and said, "Good gracious me," with some emphasis and a Middle Western accent. The bellboy retired nonchalantly to a corner and stood there, looking very childish in his smart white uniform, but very knowing. And Idabelle Lasher looked at the man at her feet and began to sob again, and Duane tried to comfort her, while Dixon shoved his hands in his pockets and glowered at nothing.

"But I don't see," wailed Idabelle, "how it could have happened!" Odd, thought Susan, that she didn't ask who did it. That would be the natural question. Or why? Why had a man who was—as she had said, like a brother to her—been murdered?

Duane patted Idabelle's heaving bare shoulders and said something soothing, and Idabelle wrung her hands and cried again: "How could it have happened! We were all together—he was not alone a moment—"

Dixon stirred.

"Oh, yes, he was alone," he said. "He wanted a drink, and I'd gone to hunt a waiter."

"And you forgot to mention," said Duane icily, "that I had gone with you."

"You left this room at the same time, but that's all I know."

"I went at the same time you did. I stopped to buy cigarettes, and you vanished. I don't know where you went, but I didn't see you again. Not till I came back with the crowd into this room. Came back to find you already here."

"What do you mean by that?" Dixon's eyes were blazing in his white face, and his hands were working. "If you are accusing me of murder, say so straight out like a man instead of an insolent little puppy."

Duane was white, too, but composed.

"All right," he said. "You know whether you murdered him or not. All I know is when I got back I found him dead and you already here."

"You—"

"*Dixon!*" cried Idabelle sharply, her laces swirling as she moved hurriedly between the two men. "Stop this! I won't have it. There'll be time enough for questions when the police come. When the police—" She dabbed at her mouth, which was still trembling, and at her chin, and her fingers went on to her throat, groped, closed convulsively, and she screamed, "*My pearls!*"

"Pearls?" said Dixon staring, and Duane darted forward.

"Pearls—they're gone!"

The fortune-teller had started upward defensively, and the bellboy's eyes were like two saucers. Susan said:

"They are certainly somewhere in the room, Mrs. Lasher. And the police will find them for you. There's no need to search for them, now."

Susan pushed a chair toward her, and she sank helplessly into it.

"Tom murdered—and now my pearls gone—and I don't know which is Derek, and I—*I don't know what to do*—" Her shoulders heaved, and her face was hidden in her handkerchief, and her corseted fat body collapsed into lines of utter despair.

Susan said deliberately:

"The room will be searched, Mrs. Lasher, every square inch of it—ourselves included. There is nothing," said Susan with soft emphasis. "Nothing that they will miss."

Then Dixon stepped forward. His face was set, and there was an ominous flare of light in his eyes.

He put his hand upon Idabelle's shoulder to force her to look up into his face, and brushed aside Duane, who had moved quickly forward, too, as if his defeated rival had threatened Idabelle.

"Why—why, Dixon," faltered Idabelle Lasher, "you look so strange. What is it? Don't, my dear, you are hurting my shoulder—"

Duane cried: "Let her alone. Let her alone." And then to Idabelle: "Don't pay any attention to him. He's out of his mind. He's—" He clutched at Dixon's arm, but Dixon turned, gave him one black look, and thrust him away so forcefully that Duane staggered backward against the walls of the tent and clutched at the curtains to save himself from falling.

"Look here," said Dixon grimly to Idabelle, "what do you mean when you say as you did just now, that you don't know which is Derek? What do you mean? You must tell me. It isn't fair. *What do you mean?*"

His fingers sank into her bulging flesh. She stared upward as if hypnotized, choking. "I meant just that, Dixon. I don't know yet. I only said I had decided in order to—"

"In order to what?" said Dixon inexorably.

A queer little tingle ran along Susan's nerves, and she edged toward the door. She must get help. Duane's eyes were strange and terribly bright. He still clutched the garishly striped curtains behind him. Susan took another silent step and another toward the door without removing her gaze from the tableau, and Idabelle Lasher looked up into Dixon's face, and her lips moved flabbily, and she said the strangest thing:

"How like your father you are, Derek."

Susan's heart got up into her throat and left a very curious empty place in the pit of her stomach. She probably moved a little farther toward the door, but was never sure, for all at once, while mother and son stared revealingly and certainly at each other, Duane's white face and queer bright eyes vanished.

Susan was going to run. She was going to fling herself out the door and shriek for help. For there was going to be another murder in that room. There was going to be another murder, and she couldn't stop it, she couldn't do anything, she couldn't even scream a warning. Then Duane's black figure was outlined against the tent again. And he held a revolver in his hand. The fortune-teller said: "Oh, my God," and the white streak that had been the bellboy dissolved rapidly behind a chair.

"Call him your son if you want to," Duane said in an odd jerky way, addressing Mrs. Lasher and Derek confusedly. "Then your son's a murderer. He killed Briggs. He hid in the folds of this curtain till—the room was full of people—and then he came out again. He left his revolver there. And here it is. *Don't move.* One word or move out of any of you, and I'll shoot." He stopped to take a breath. He was smiling a little and panting. "Don't move," he said again sharply. "I'm going to hand you over to the police, Mr. *Derek.* You won't be so anxious to say he's your son then, perhaps. It's his revolver. He killed Briggs with it because Briggs favored me. He knew it, and he did it for revenge."

He was crossing the room with smooth steps, holding the revolver poised threateningly, and his eyes were rapidly shifting from one to another. Susan hadn't the slightest doubt that the smallest move would bring a revolver shot crashing through someone's brain. He's going to escape, she thought, he's going to escape. I can't do a thing. And he's mad with rage. Mad with the terrible excitement of having already killed once.

Duane caught the flicker of Susan's eyes. He was near her now, so near that he could have touched her. He cried: "It's you that's done this! You that advised her! You were on his side! Well—" He'd reached the door now, and there was nothing they could do. He was gloating openly, the way of escape before him. In an excess of dreadful triumphant excitement, he cried: "I'll shoot you first—it's too bad, when you are so pretty. But I'm going to do it." It's the certainty, thought Susan numbly; Idabelle is so certain that Derek is the other one that Duane knows it, too. He knows there's no use in going on with it. And he knew, when I said what I said about the pearls, that I know.

She felt oddly dizzy. Something was moving. Was she going to faint—was she—something *was* moving, and it was the door behind Duane. It was moving silently, very slowly.

Susan steeled her eyes not to reveal that knowledge. If only Idabelle and Derek would not move—would not see those panels move and betray what they had seen.

Duane laughed.

And Derek moved again, and Idabelle tried to thrust him away from her, and Duane's revolver jerked and jerked again, and the door pushed Duane suddenly to one side and there was a crash of glass, and voices and flashing movement. Susan knew only that someone had pinioned Duane from behind and was holding his arms close to his side. Duane gasped, his hand writhed and dropped the revolver.

Then somebody at the door dragged Duane away; Susan realized confusedly that there were police there. And Jim Byrne stood at her elbow. He looked unwontedly handsome in white tie and tails, but very angry. He said:

"Go home, Sue. Get out of here."

It was literally impossible for Susan to speak or move. Jim stared at her as if nobody else was in the room, got out a handkerchief, and wiped his forehead with it.

"I've aged ten years in the last five minutes," he said. He glanced around. Saw Major Briggs's body there on the floor—saw Idabelle Lasher and Derek—saw the fortune-teller and the bellboy.

"Is that Mrs. Jeremiah Lasher over there?" he said to Susan.

Mrs. Lasher opened her eyes, looked at him, and closed them again.

Jim looked meditatively at a revolver in his hand, put it in his pocket, and said briskly:

"You can stay for a while, Susan. Until I hear the whole story. Who shot Major Briggs?"

Susan's lips moved and Derek straightened up and cried:

"Oh, it's my revolver all right. But I didn't kill Major Briggs—I don't expect anyone to believe me, but I didn't."

"He didn't," said Susan wearily. "Duane killed Major Briggs. He killed him with Derek's revolver, perhaps, but it was Duane who did the murder."

Jim did not question her statement, but Derek said eagerly:

"How do you know? Can you prove it?"

"I think so," said Susan. "You see, Duane had a

revolver when I danced with him. It was in his pocket. That's when I phoned for you, Jim. But I was too late."

"But how—" said Jim.

"Oh, when Duane accused Derek, he actually described the way he himself murdered Major Briggs and concealed himself and the revolver in the folds of the tent until the room was full of people and he could quietly mingle with them as if he had come from the hall. We were all staring at Major Briggs. It was very simple. Duane had got hold of Derek's revolver and knew it would be traced to Derek and the blame put upon him, since Derek had every reason to wish to revenge himself upon Major Briggs."

Idabelle had opened her eyes. They looked a bit glassy but were more sensible.

"Why—" she said—"why did Duane kill Major Briggs?"

"I suppose because Major Briggs had backed him. You see," said Susan gently, "one of the claimants had to be an impostor and a deliberate one. And the attack upon Major Briggs last night suggested either that he knew too much or was a conspirator himself. The exact coinciding of the stories (particularly clever on Major Briggs's part) and the fact that Duane turned up after Major Briggs had had time to search for someone who would fulfill the requirements necessary to make a claim to being your son, seemed to me an indication of conspiracy; besides, the very nature of the case involved imposture. But there had to be a conspiracy; someone had to tell one of the claimants about the things upon which to base his claim, especially about the memories of the baby things—the calico dog," said Susan with a little smile, "and the plush teddy bear. It had to be someone who had known you long ago and could have seen those things before you put them away in the safe. Someone who knew all your circumstances."

"You mean that Major Briggs planned Duane's claim —planned the whole thing? But why—" Idabelle's eyes were full of tears again.

"There's only one possible reason," said Susan. "He must have needed money very badly, and Duane, coming into thirty millions of dollars, would have been obliged to share his spoils."

"Then Derek—I mean Dixon—I mean," said Idabelle confusedly, clutching at Derek, "this one. He really is my son?"

"You know he is," said Susan. "You realized it yourself when you were under emotional stress and obliged to feel instead of reason about it. However, there's reason for it, too. *He is Derek.*"

"He—is—Derek," said Idabelle, catching at Susan's words. "You are sure?"

"Yes," said Susan quietly. "He is Derek. You see, I'd forgotten something. Something physical that never changes all through life. That is, a sense of rhythm. Derek has no sense of rhythm and has never had. Duane was a born dancer."

Idabelle said: "Thank God!" She looked at Susan, looked at Derek, and quite suddenly became herself again. She got up briskly, glanced at Major Briggs's body, said calmly: "We'll try to keep some of this quiet. I'll see that things are done decently—after all, poor old fellow, he did love his comforts. Now, then. Oh, yes, if someone will just see the manager of the hotel about my pearls—"

Susan put a startled hand to her gardenias.

"I'd forgotten your pearls, too. Here they are." She fumbled a moment among the flowers, detached a string of flowing beauty, and held it toward Idabelle. "I took them from Duane while we were dancing."

"Duane," said Idabelle. "But—" She took the pearls and said incredulously: "They *are* mine!"

"He had taken them while he danced with you. During

the next dance you passed me, and I saw that your neck was bare."

Jim turned to Susan.

"Are you sure about that, Susan?" he said. "I've managed to get the outline of the story, you know. And I don't think the false claimant would have taken such a risk. Not with thirty millions in his pocket, so to speak."

"Oh, they were for the Major," said Susan. "At least, I think that was the reason. I don't know yet, but I think we'll find that he was pretty hard pressed for cash and had to have some right away. Immediately. Duane probably balked at demanding money of Mrs. Lasher so soon, so the Major suggested the pearls. And Duane was in no position to refuse the Major's demands. Then, you see, he had no pearls because I took them; he and the Major must have quarreled, and Duane, who had already foreseen that he would be at Major Briggs's mercy as long as the Major lived, was already prepared for any opportunity to kill him. After he had once got to Idabelle, he no longer needed the Major. He had armed himself with Derek's revolver after what must have seemed to him a heaven-sent chance to stage an accident had failed. Mrs. Lasher's decision removed any remaining small value that the Major was to him and made Major Briggs only a menace. But I think he wasn't sure just what he would do or how—he acceded to the Major's demand for the pearls because it was at the moment the simplest course. But he was ready and anxious to kill him, and when he knew that the pearls had gone from his pocket he must have guessed that I had taken them. And he decided to get rid of Major Briggs at once, before he could possibly tell anything, for any story the Major chose to tell would have been believed by Mrs. Lasher. Later, when I said that the police would search the room, he knew that I knew. And that I knew the revolver was still here."

"Is that why you advised me to announce my decision that Duane was my son?" demanded Idabelle Lasher.

Susan shuddered and tried not to look at that black heap across the room.

"No," she said steadily. "I didn't dream of—murder. I only thought that it might bring the conspiracy that evidently existed somewhere into the open."

Jim said: "Here are the police."

Queer, thought Susan much later, riding along the Drive in Jim's car, with her white chiffon flounces tucked in carefully, and her green velvet wrap pulled tightly about her throat against the chill night breeze, and the scent of gardenias mingling with the scent of Jim's cigarette— queer how often her adventures ended like this: driving silently homeward in Jim's car.

She glanced at the irregular profile behind the wheel and said: "I suppose you know you saved my life tonight."

His mouth tightened in the little glow from the dashlight. Presently he said:

"How did you know he had the pearls in his pocket?"

"Felt 'em," said Susan. "And you can't imagine how terribly easy it was to take them. In all probability a really brilliant career in picking pockets was sacrificed when I was provided with moral scruples."

The light went to yellow and then red, and Jim stopped. He turned and gave Susan a long look through the dusk, and then slowly took her hand in his own warm fingers for a second or two before the light went to green again.

WILLIAM IRISH, known equally well to mystery readers as Cornell Woolrich, was born Cornell George Hopley-Woolrich in 1906 and died in 1968. He spent part of his childhood in the revolution-torn Mexico of the early years of the century, also traveling with his family throughout South America. Returning to the United States, he became a student at Columbia College, during which time he began his writing career. Of his many short mystery stories, novelettes, and books, the two best known have "female" titles: *The Bride Wore Black* (1940) and *Phantom Lady* (1942, an "Irish" work). He also published books under the pseudonym George Hopley.

Though Jerry Wheeler, stage name "Honey Sebastian," admiringly nicknamed "Angel Face," is not to be found on previous lists of women detectives, she proves herself to be a first-rate sleuth as she determinedly sets about proving her brother innocent of a murder charge. This story predates by four years Gypsy Rose Lee's 1941 novel of sudden death in a burlesque house, *The G-String Murders*, in which another stripteaser turns amateur investigator.

Angel Face

by William Irish

I had on my best hat and my warpaint when I dug into her bell. You've heard make-up called that a thousand times, but this is one time it rated it; it was just that—warpaint.

I caught Ruby Rose Reading at breakfast time—hers, not mine. Quarter to three in the afternoon. Breakfast was a pink soda-fountain mess, a tomato-and-lettuce, both untouched, and an empty glass of Bromo Seltzer, which had evidently had first claim on her. There were a pair of swell ski slides under her eyes; she was reading Gladys Glad's beauty column to try to figure out how to get rid of them before she went out that night and got a couple more. A Negro maid had opened the door, and given me a yellowed optic.

"Yes ma'am, who do you wish to see?"

"I see her already," I said, "so skip the Morse code." I went in up to Ruby Rose's ten-yard line. "Wheeler's the name," I said. "Does it mean anything to you?"

"Should it?" She was dark and Salome-ish. She was mean. She was bad medicine. I could see his finish right there, in her eyes. And it hadn't been any fun to dance at Texas Guinan's or Larry Fay's when I was sixteen, to keep him out of the orphan asylum or the reformatory. I hadn't spent most of my young girlhood in a tinseled G-string to have her take apart what I'd built up, just to see what made him tick.

I said, "I don't mind coming right out with it in front of your maid—if you don't."

But evidently she did. Maybe Mandy was on a few other payrolls beside her own. She hit her with the tomato-and-lettuce in the left eye as preamble to the request: "Whaddo I pay you for, anyway? Take Foo-Too around the block a couple of times!"

"I tuk him once already, and he was a good boy," was the weather report she got on this.

"Well, take him again. Maybe you can kid him it's tomorrow already."

Mandy fastened something that looked like the business end of a floor mop to a leash, went out shaking her head. "You sho didn't enjoy yo'self last night. That Sto'k Club never do agree with you."

As soon as the gallery was out of the way I said, "You lay off my brother!"

She lit a cigarette, nosed the smoke at me. "Well, Gracie Allen, you've come to the wrong place looking for your brother. And, just for the record, what am I supposed to have done to him, cured him of wiping his nose on his sleeve or something?"

"He's been spending dough like wild, dough that doesn't come out of his salary."

"Then where does it come from?" she asked.

"I haven't found out. I hope his firm never does, either." I shifted gears, went into low—like when I used to sing "Poor Butterfly" for the customers—but money couldn't have dragged this performance out of me, it came from the heart, without pay. "There's a little girl on our street, oh not much to look at, thinks twelve o'clock's the middle of the night and storks leave babies, but she's ready to take up where I leave off, pinch pennies and squeeze nickels along with him, build him into something, get him somewhere, not spread him all over the landscape. He's just a man, doesn't know what's good for him, doesn't know his bass from his oboe. I can't stand by and watch her chew her heart up. Give her a break, and him, and me. Pick on someone your size, someone that can take it. Have your fun and more power to you—but not with all I've got!"

She banged her cigarette to death against a tray. "O.K., is the screen test about over? Now, will you get out of here, you ham actress, and lemme get my massage?" She went over and got the door ready for me. Gave a traffic-cop signal over her shoulder with one thumb. "I've heard of wives pulling this act, and even mothers, and in a pitcher I saw only lately, Camilly it was called, it was the old man. Now it's a sister!" She gave the ceiling the once-over. "What'll they think of next? Send grandma around tomorrow—next week East Lynne. Come on, make it snappy!" she invited, and hitched her elbow at me. If she'd touched me, I think I'd have murdered her.

"If you feel I'm poison, why don't you put it up to your brother?" she signed off. And very low, just before she walloped the door after me: "And see how far you get!"

She was right. I said, "Chick, you're not going to chuck your job, you're not going to Chicago with that dame, are you?"

He looked at me funny and he said, "How did you know?"

"I saw your valise all packed, when I wanted to send one of your suits to the cleaners."

"You ought to be a detective," he said, and he wasn't pally. "O.K.," he said, "now that you mention it," and he went in and he got it to show me—the back of it going out the door. But I got over there to the door before he did,

and pulled a Custer's Last Stand. I skipped the verse and
went into the patter chorus. And boy did I sell it, without
a spot and without a muted trumpet solo either! At the
El-Fay in the old days they would have all been crying into
their gin and wiring home to mother.

"I'm not asking anything for myself. I'm older than
you, Chick, and when a girl says that you've got her down
to bedrock. I've been around plenty, and 'around' wasn't
pretty. Maybe you think it was fun wrestling my way home
each morning at five, and no holds barred, just so—so . . .
Oh, I didn't know why myself sometimes; just so you
wouldn't turn out to be another corner lizard, a sharp-
shooter, a bum like the rest of them. Chick, you're just a
punk of twenty-four, but as far as I'm concerned the sun
rises and sets across your shoulders. Me and little Mary
Allen, we've been rooting for you all along; what's the
matter with her, Chick? Just because her face don't come
out of boxes and she doesn't know the right grips, don't
pass her by for something that ought to be shampooed out
of your hair with gasoline."

But he didn't have an ear for music; the siren song had
got to him like Ulysses. And once they hear that . . . "Get
away from the door," he said, way down low. "I never
raised a hand to you in my life, I don't want to now."

The last I saw of him he was passing the back of his
hand slowly up and down his side, like he was ashamed of
it; the valise was in the other one. I picked myself up from
the opposite side of the foyer where he'd sent me, the
place all buckling around me like seen through a sheet of
water. I called out after him through the open door:
"Don't go, Chick! You're heading straight for the eight-
ball! Don't go to her, Chick!" The acoustics were swell.
Every door in the hall opened to get an earful.

He just stood there a split-second without looking back
at me, yellow light gushing out at him through the
porthole of the elevator.

He straightened his hat, which my chin against his duke had dislodged—and no more Chick.

At about four that morning I was still sniveling into the gin he'd left behind him, and talking to him across the table from me—without getting any answer—when the doorbell rang. I thought it was him for a minute, but it was two other guys. They didn't ask if they could come in, they just went 'way around to the other side of me and then showed me a couple of tin-heeled palms. So I did the coming-in—after them; I lived there, after all.

They looked the place over like they were prospective tenants being shown an apartment. I didn't go for that; detectives belong in the books you read in bed, not in your apartment at four bells, big as life. "Three closets," I mentioned, "and you get a month's concession. I'm not keeping you gentlemen up, am I?"

One of them was kind of pash-looking; I mean he'd washed his face lately, and if he'd been the last man in the world, well, all right, maybe I could have overlooked the fact he was a bloodhound on two legs. The other one had a face like one of those cobblestones they dug up off Eighth Avenue when they removed the trolley tracks.

"You're Jerry Wheeler, aren't you?" the first one told me.

"I've known that for twenty-seven years," I said. "What brought the subject up?"

Cobblestone-face said, "Chick Wheeler's sister, that right?"

"I've got a brother and I call him Chick," I consented. "Any ordinance against that?"

The younger one said, "Don't be so hard to handle. You're going to talk to us and like it." He sat down in a chair, cushioned his hands behind his dome. He said, "What time'd he leave here this evening?"

Something warned me, "Don't answer that." I said, "I really couldn't say. I'm not a train dispatcher."

"He was going to Chicago with a dame named Ruby Rose Reading; you knew that, didn't you?"

I thought, "I hit the nail on the head, he did help himself to his firm's money. Wonder how much he took? Well, I guess I'll have to go back to work again at one of the hot-spots; maybe I can square it for him, pay back a little each week." I kept my face steady. I said, "Now, why would he go anywhere with anyone with a name like that? It sounds like it came off a bottle of nail polish. Come to the point, gentlemen. What's he supposed to have done?"

"There's no supposition about what he's done. He went to the Alcazar Arms at eight-fifteen tonight and throttled Ruby Rose Reading to death, Angel Face."

And that was the first time I heard myself called that. I also heard the good-looking one remonstrate, "Aw, don't give it to her that sudden, Coley, she's a girl after all," but it came from 'way far away. I was down around their feet somewhere sniffling into the carpet.

The good-looking one picked me up and straightened me out in a chair. Cobblestone said, "Don't let her fool you, Burnsie, they all pull that collapsible concertina act when they wanna get out of answering questions." He went into the bedroom and I could hear him pulling out bureau drawers and rummaging around.

I got up on one elbow. I said, "Burns, he didn't do it! Please, he didn't do it! All right, I did know about her. He was sold on her. That's why he couldn't have done it. Don't you see, you don't kill the thing you love?"

He just kind of looked at me. "You go to bat for the thing you love too," he murmured. He said, "I've been on the squad eight years now. We never in all that time caught a guy as dead to rights as your brother. He showed up with his valise in the foyer of the Alcazar at exactly twelve minutes past eight tonight. He said to the doorman, 'What time is it? Did Miss Reading send her baggage down yet? We've got to make a train.' Well, she had sent her baggage down and then she'd changed her mind, she'd had it all taken back upstairs again. There's your motive right there. The doorman rang her apartment and said through the announcer, 'Mr. Wheeler's here.' And she gave a dirty laugh and sang out, 'I can hardly wait.'

"So at thirteen past eight she was still alive. He went up, and he'd no sooner got there than her apartment began to signal the doorman frantically. No one answered his hail over the announcer, so he chased up, and he found your brother crouched over her, shaking her, and she was dead. At fifteen minutes past eight o'clock. Is that a case or is that a case?"

I said, "How do you know somebody else wasn't in that apartment and strangled her just before Chick showed up? It's got to be that!"

He said, "What d'you suppose they're paying that doorman seventy-five a month for? The only other caller she had that whole day was you yourself, at three that afternoon, five full hours before. And she'd only been dead fifteen to twenty minutes by the time the assistant medical examiner got to her."

I said, "Does Chick say he did it?"

"When you've been in this business as long as I have, you'd have their heads examined if any of them ever admitted doing anything. Oh, no-o, of course he didn't do it. He says he was crouched over her, shaking her, trying to restore her!"

I took a deep breath. I said, "Gimme a swallow of that gin. Thanks." I put the tumbler down again. I looked him right in the eye. "All right, I did it! Now how d'ye like that? I begged him not to throw his life away on her. When he walked out anyway, I beat him up to her place in a taxi, got there first, gave her one last chance to lay off him. She wouldn't take it. She was all soft and squashy and I just took a grip and pushed hard."

"And the doorman?" he said with a smile.

"His back was turned. He was out at the curb seeing some people into a cab. When I left, I took the stairs down. When Chick signaled from her apartment and the doorman left his post, I just walked out. It was a pushover."

His smile was a grin. "Well, if you killed her, you killed her." He called in to the other room, "Hey, Coley, she says she killed her!" Coley came back, flapped his hand at me disgustedly, said, "Come on, let's get out of here. There's nothing doing around here."

He opened the door, went out into the hall. I said, "Well, aren't you going to take me with you? Aren't you going to let him go and hold me instead?"

"Who the hell wants you?" came back through the open door.

Burns, as he got up to follow him, said offhandedly, "And what was she wearing when you killed her?" But he kept walking to the door, without waiting for the answer.

They'd had a train to make. I swallowed hard. "Well, I—I was too steamed up to notice colors or anything, but she had on her coat and hat, ready to leave."

He turned around at the door and looked at me. His grin was sort of sympathetic, understanding. "Sure," he said softly. "I guess she took 'em off, though, after she found out she was dead and wasn't going anywhere after all. We found her in pajamas. Write us a nice long letter about it tomorrow, Angel Face. We'll see you at the trial, no doubt."

There was a glass cigarette box at my elbow. I grabbed it and heaved, berserk. "You rotten, low-down—detective, you! Going around snooping, framing innocent people to death! Get out of here! I hope I never see your face again!"

It missed his head, crashed and tinkled against the doorframe to one side of him. He didn't cringe, I liked that about him, sore as I was. He just gave a long drawn-out whistle. "Maybe you did do it at that," he said. "Maybe I'm underestimating you," and he touched his hatbrim and closed the door after him.

The courtroom was so unnaturally still that the ticking of my heart sounded like a cheap alarm clock in the silence. I kept wondering how it was they didn't put me out for letting it make so much noise. A big blue fly was buzzing on the inside of the windowpane nearest me, trying to find its way out. The jurists came filing in like ghosts, and slowly filled the double row of chairs in the box. All you could hear was a slight rustle of clothing as they seated themselves. I kept thinking of the Inquisition, and wondered why they didn't have black hoods over their heads.

"Will the foreman of the jury please stand?"

I spaded both my hands down past my hips and grabbed the edges of my seat. My handkerchief fell on the floor and the man next to me picked it up and handed it back to me. I tried to say "Thanks" but my jaws wouldn't unlock.

"Gentlemen of the jury, have you reached a verdict?"

I told myself, "He won't be able to hear it, if my heart doesn't shut up." It was going bangetty-bangetty-bang!

"We have, your honor."

"Gentlemen of the jury, what is your verdict?"

The banging stopped; my heart wasn't going at all now. Even the fly stopped buzzing. The whole works stood still.

"We find the defendant guilty of murder in the first degree."

Some woman screamed out "No!" at the top of her lungs. It must have been me, they were all turning their heads to look around at me. The next thing I knew, I was outside in the corridor and a whole lot of people were standing around me. Everything looked blurred. A voice said, "Give her air, stand back." Another voice said, "His sister. She was on the stand earlier in the week." Ammonia fumes kept tickling the membranes of my nostrils. The first voice said, "Take her home. Where does she live? Anybody know where she lives?"

"I know where she lives. I'll take care of her."

Somebody put an arm around my waist and walked me to the creaky courthouse elevator, led me out to the street, got in a taxi after me. I looked, and it was that dick, Burns. I climbed up into the corner of the cab, put my feet on the seat, shuffled them at him. I said, "Get away from me, you devil! You railroaded him, you butcher!"

"Attagirl," he said gently. "Feeling better already, aren't you?" He gave the old address, where Chick and I had lived. The cab started and I couldn't get him out of it. I felt too low even to fight any more.

"Not there," I said sullenly. "I'm holed up in a cheap furnished room now, off Second Avenue. I've hocked everything I own, down to my vaccination mark! How d'you suppose I got that lawyer Schlesinger for him? And a lot of good it did him! What a washout he turned out to be!"

"Don't blame him," he said. "He couldn't buck that case we turned over to the State; Darrow himself couldn't have. What he should have done was let him plead guilty to second-degree, then he wouldn't be in line for short-circuiting. That was his big mistake."

"No!" I shrilled at him. "He wanted us to do that, but neither Chick nor I would hear of it! Why should he plead guilty to anything, even if it was only housebreaking, when he's innocent? That's a guilty man's dodge, not an innocent man's. He hasn't got half an hour's detention rightfully coming to him! Why should he lie down and accept twenty years? He didn't lay a hand on Ruby Reading."

"Eleven million people, the mighty State of New York, say that he did."

I got out, went in the grubby entrance, between a

delicatessen and a Chinese laundry. "Don't come in with me, I don't want to see any more of you!" I spat over my shoulder at him. "If I was a man I'd knock you down and beat the living hell out of you!"

He came on, though, and upstairs he closed the door behind him, pushing me out of the way to get in. He said, "You need help, Angel Face, and I'm crying to give it to you."

"Oh, biting the hand that feeds you, turning into a double-crosser, a turncoat!"

"No," he said, "no," and sort of held out his hands as if asking me for something. "Sell me, won't you?" he almost pleaded. "Sell me that he's innocent, and I'll work my fingers raw to back you up! I didn't frame your brother. I only did my job. I was sent there by my superiors in answer to the patrolman's call that night, questioned Chick, put him under arrest. You heard me answering their questions on the stand. Did I distort the facts any? All I told them was what I saw with my own eyes, what I found when I got to Reading's apartment. Don't hold that against me, Angel Face. Sell me, convince me that he didn't do it, and I'm with you up to the hilt."

"Why?" I said cynically. "Why this sudden yearning to undo the damage you've already done?"

He opened the door to go. "Look in the mirror sometime and find out," was all he said. "You can reach me at Centre Street, Nick Burns." He held out his hand uncertainly, probably expecting me to slap it aside.

I took it instead. "O.K., flatfoot," I sighed wearily. "No use holding it against you that you're a detective. You probably don't know any better. Before you go, gimme the address of that maid of hers, Mandy Leroy. I've got an idea she didn't tell all she knew."

"She went home at five that day. How can she help you?"

"I bet she was greased plenty to softpedal the one right

name that belongs in this case. She mayn't have been there, but she knew who to expect around. She may have even tipped him off that Ruby Rose was throwing him over. It takes a woman to see through a woman."

"Better watch yourself going up there alone," he warned me. He took out a notebook. "Here it is, One Hundred Eighteenth, just off Lenox." I jotted it down. "If she was paid off like you think, how you going to restore her memory? It'll take heavy sugar . . ." He fumbled in his pocket, looked at me like he was a little scared of me, finally took out something and shoved it out of sight on the bureau. "Try your luck with that," he said. "Use it where it'll do the most good. Try a little intimidation with it, it may work."

I grabbed it up and he ducked out in a hurry, the big coward. A hundred and fifty bucks. I ran out to the stairs after him. "Hey!" I yelled, "aren't you married or anything?"

"Naw," he called back, "I can always get it back, anyway, if it does the trick." And then he added, "I always did want to have something on you, Angel Face."

I went back into my cubbyhole again. "Why, the big rummy!" I said hotly. I hadn't cried in court when Chick got the ax, just yelled out. But now my eyes got all wet.

"Mandy doan live here no mo'e," the colored janitor of the 118th Street tenement told me.

"Where'd she go? And don't tell me you don't know, because it won't work."

"She done move to a mighty presumptuous neighborhood, doan know how come all of a sudden. She gone to Edgecomb Avenue."

Edgecomb Avenue is the Park Avenue of New York's darktown. Mandy had mentioned on the stand, without being asked, that Reading had died owing her two months' wages. Yet she moves to the colored Gold Coast right on top of it. She hadn't been paid off—not much!

Edgecomb Avenue is nothing to be ashamed of in any man's town. Every one of the trim modern apartment buildings had a glossy private car or two parked in front of the door. I tackled the address he'd given me, and thought they were having a housewarming at first. They were singing inside and it sounded like a revival meeting.

A fat old lady came to the door, in a black silk dress, tears streaming down her cheeks. "I'se her mother, honey," she said softly in answer to what I told her, "and you done come at an evil hour. My lamb was run over on the street, right outside this building, only yesterday, first day we moved here! She's in there daid now, honey. The Lawd give and the Lawd has took away again."

I did a little thinking.

Why just her, and nobody else, when she held the key to the Reading murder? "How did it happen to her? Did they tell you?"

"Two white men in a car," she mourned. " 'Peared almost like they run her down purposely. She was walking along the sidewalk, folks tell me, wasn't even in the gutter at all. And it swung right up on the sidewalk aftah her, go ovah her, then loop out in the middle again and light away, without nevah stopping!"

I went away saying to myself, "That girl was murdered as sure as I'm born, to shut her mouth. First she was bribed, then when the trial was safely over she was put out of the way for good!"

Somebody big was behind all this. And what did I have to fight that somebody with? A borrowed hundred and fifty bucks, an offer of cooperation from a susceptible detective, and a face.

I went around to the building Ruby Rose had lived in, and struck the wrong shift. "Charlie Baker doesn't come on until six, eh?" I told the doorman. "Where does he live? I want to talk to him."

"He don't come on at all any more. He quit his job, as soon as that—" he tilted his head to the ceiling—"mess we had upstairs was over with, and he didn't have to appear in court no more."

"Well, where's he working now?"

"He ain't working at all, lady. He don't have to any more. I understand a relative of his died in the old country, left him quite a bit, and him and his wife and his three kids have gone back to England to live."

So he'd been paid off heavily too. It looked like I was up against Wall Street itself. No wonder everything had gone so smoothly.

No wonder even a man like Schlesinger hadn't been able to make a dent in the case.

"But I'm not licked yet," I said to myself, back in my room. "I've still got this face. It ought to be good for something. If I only knew where to push it, who to flash it on!"

Burns showed up that night, to find out how I was making out.

"Here's your hundred and fifty back," I told him bitterly. "I'm up against a stone wall every way I turn. But is it a coincidence that the minute the case is in the bag, their two chief witnesses are permanently disposed of, one by exportation, the other by hit-and-run? They're not taking any chances on anything backfiring later."

He said, "You're beginning to sell me. It smells like rain."

I sat down on the floor (there was only one chair in the dump) and took a dejected half-Nelson around my own ankles. "Look, it goes like this. Some guy did it. Some guy that was sold on her. Plenty of names were spilled by Mandy and Baker, but not the right one. The ones that were brought out didn't lead anywhere, you saw that yourself. The mechanics of the thing don't trouble me a bit, the how and why could be cleared up easy enough—even by you."

"Thanks," he said.

"It's the who that has me buffaloed. There's a gap there. I can't jump across to the other side. From there on, I could handle it beautifully. But I've got to close that gap, that who, or I might as well put in the order for Chick's headstone right now."

He took out a folded newspaper and whacked himself disgustedly across the shins with it. "Tough going, kid," he agreed.

"I'll make it," I said. "You can't keep a good girl down. The right guy is in this town. And so am I in this town. I'll connect with him yet, if I've got to use a ouija board!"

He said, "You haven't got all winter. He comes up for sentence Wednesday." He opened the door. "I'm on your side," he let me know in that quiet way of his.

He left the paper behind him on the chair. I sat down and opened it. I wasn't going to do any reading, but I wanted to think behind it. And then I saw her name. The papers had been full of her name for weeks, but this was different; this was just a little boxed ad off at the side.

AUCTION SALE
Jewelry, personal effects and
furniture belonging to the late
Ruby Rose Reading
Monarch Galleries Saturday A.M.

I dove at the window, rammed it up, leaned halfway out. I caught him just coming out of the door.

"Burns!" I screeched at the top of my voice. "Hey, Burns! Bring that hundred and fifty back up here! I've changed my mind!"

•   •   •

The place was jammed to the gills with curiosity-mongers and bargain-hunters, and probably professional dealers too, although they were supposed to be excluded. There were about two dozen of those 100-watt blue-white bulbs in the ceiling that auction rooms go in for, and the bleach of light was intolerable, worse than on a sunny beach at high noon.

I was down front, in the second row on the aisle; I'd got there early. I wasn't interested in her diamonds or her furs or her thissas or her thattas. I was hoping something would come up that would give me some kind of a clue, but what I expected it to be, I didn't know myself. An inscription on a cigarette case, maybe. I knew how little chance there was of anything like that. The D.A.'s office had sifted through her things pretty thoroughly before Chick's trial, and what they'd turned up hadn't amounted to a row of pins. She'd been pretty cagey that way, hadn't left much around. All bills had been addressed to her personally, just like she'd paid her rent with her own personal checks, and fed the account herself. Where the funds originated in the first place was never explained. I suppose she took in washing.

They started off with minor articles first, to warm the customers up. A cocktail shaker that played a tune, a make-up mirror with a light behind it, a ship's model, things like that. They got around to her clothes next, and the women customers started "ohing" and "ahing" and foaming at the mouth. By the looks of most of them that was probably the closest they'd ever get to real sin, bidding for its hand-me-downs.

The furniture came next, and they started to talk real money now. This out of the way, her ice came on. Brother, she'd made them say it with diamonds, and they'd all spoken above a whisper too! When the last of it went, that washed up the sale; there was nothing else left to dispose of but the little rosewood jewel case she'd kept them in.

About ten by twelve by ten inches deep, with a little gilt
key and lock; not worth a damn but there it was. However,
if you think an auctioneer passes up anything, you don't
know your auctioneers.

"What am I offered for this?" he said almost apologeti-
cally. "Lovely little trinket box, give it to your best girl or
your wife or your mother, to keep her ornaments in or old
love letters." He knocked the veneer with his knuckles,
held it outward to show us the satin lining. Nothing in it,
like in a vaudeville magician's act. "Do I hear fifty cents,
just to clear the stand?"

Most of them were getting up and going already. An
overdressed guy in my same row, across the aisle, spoke up.
"You hear a buck."

I took a look at him, and I took a look at the box. "If
you want it, I want it, too," I decided suddenly. "A guy
splurged up like you don't hand a plain wooden box like
that to any woman that he knows." I opened my mouth
for the first time since I'd come in the place. "You hear a
dollar and a quarter."

"Dollar-fifty."

"Two dollars."

"Five." The way he snapped it out, he meant business.

I'd never had such a strong hunch in my life before but
now I wanted that box, had to have it, I felt it would do
me some good. Maybe this overdressed monkey had given
it to her, maybe Burns could trace where it had been
bought . . .

"Seven-fifty."

"Ten."

"Twelve."

The auctioneer was in seventh heaven. "You're giving
yourself away, brother, you're giving yourself away!" I
warned my competitor silently.

We leaned forward out of our seats and sized each
other up. If he was giving himself away, I suppose I was

too. I could see a sort of shrewd speculation in his snaky eyes, they screwed up into slits, seeming to say, "What's your racket?" Something cold went down my back, hot as it was under all those mazdas.

"Twenty-five dollars," he said inexorably.

I thought: "I'm going to get that thing if I spend every cent of the money Burns loaned me!"

"Thirty," I said.

With that, to my surprise, he stood up, flopped his hand at it disgustedly, and walked out.

When I came out five minutes later with the box wrapped up under my arm, I saw him sitting in a young dreadnaught with another man, a few yards down the street.

"So I'm going to be followed home," I said to myself, "to find out who I am." That didn't worry me any; I'd rented my room under my old stage name of Honey Sebastian (my idea of a classy tag at sixteen) to escape the notoriety attendant on Chick's trial. I turned up the other way and hopped down into the subway, which is about the best bet when the following is to be done from a car. As far as I could make out, no one came after me.

I watched the street from a corner of the window after I got home, and no one going by stopped or looked at the house or did anything but mind his own business. And if it had been that flashy guy on my tail, you could have heard him coming from a block away. I turned to the wrapped box and broke the string.

Burns's knock at my door at five that afternoon was a tattoo of anxious impatience. "God, you took long to get here!" I blurted out. "I phoned you three times since noon."

"Lady," he protested, "I've been busy, I was out on something else, only just got back to Headquarters ten minutes ago. Boy, you threw a fright into me."

I didn't stoop to asking him why he should be so worried something had happened to me; he might have given me the right answer. "Well," I said, "I've got him," and I passed him the rosewood jewel case.

"Got who?"

"The guy that Chick's been made a patsy for."

He opened it, looked in, looked under it. "What's this?"

"Hers. I had a hunch, and I bought it. He must have had a hunch too—only his agent—and it must have been his agent, he wouldn't show up himself—didn't follow it through, wasn't sure enough. Stick your thumb under the little lock. Not over it, down below it, and press hard on the wood." Something clicked, and the satin bottom flapped up, like it had with me.

"Fake bottom, eh?" he said.

"Don't be an echo. Read that top letter out loud. That was the last one she got, the very day it happened."

" 'You know, baby,' " Burns read, " 'I think too much of you to ever let you go. And if you ever tired of me and tried to leave me, I'd kill you first, and then you could go wherever you want. They tell me you've been seen going around a lot lately with some young punk. Now, baby, I hope for his sake, and yours too, that when I come back day after tomorrow I find it isn't so, just some more of my boys' lies. They like to rib me sometimes, see if I can take it or not.' "

"He gave her a bum steer there on purpose," I pointed out. "He came back 'tomorrow' and not 'day after,' and caught her with the goods."

"Milt," Burns read from the bottom of the page. And then he looked at me, and didn't see me for once.

"Militis, of course," I said, "the Greek nightclub king. Milton, as he calls himself. Everyone on Broadway knows him. And yet, d'you notice how that name stayed out of the trial? Not a whisper from beginning to end! That's the missing name all right!"

"It reads that way, I know," he said undecidedly, "but there's this: she knew her traffic signals. Why would she chuck away the banana and hang onto the skin? In other words, Milton spells real dough, your brother wasn't even carfare."

"But Militis had her branded—"

"Sure, but—"

"No, I'm not talking slang now. I mean actually, physically; it's mentioned in one of these letters. The autopsy report had it too, remember? Only they mistook it for an operation scar or scald. Well, when a guy does that, anyone would have looked good to her, and Chick was probably a godsend. The branding was probably not the half of it, either. It's fairly well known that Milton likes to play rough with his women."

"All right, kid," he said, "but I've got bad news for you. This evidence isn't strong enough to have the verdict set aside and a new trial called. A clever mouthpiece could blow this whole pack of letters out the window with one breath. Ardent Greek temperament, and that kind of thing, you know. You remember how Schlesinger dragged it out of Mandy that she'd overheard more than one guy make the same kind of jealous threats. Did it do any good?"

"This is the McCoy, though. He came through, this one, Militis."

"But, baby, you're telling it to me and I convince easy, from you. You're not telling it to the Grand Jury."

I shoved the letters at him. "Just the same, you chase out, have 'em photostatted, every last one of them, and put 'em in a cool, dry place. I'm going to dig something a little more convincing to go with them, if that's what's needed. What clubs does he own?"

"What clubs doesn't he? There's Hell's Bells—" He stopped short, looked at me. "You stay out of there."

"One word from you . . ." I purred, and closed the door after him.

"A little higher," the manager said. "Don't be afraid. We've seen it all before."

I took another hitch in my hoisted skirt, gave him a look. "If it's my appendix you want to size up, say so. It's easier to uncover the other way around, from up to down. I just sing and dance. I don't bathe for the customers."

"I like 'em like that," he nodded approvingly to his yes-man. "Give her a chord, Mike," he said to his pianist.

"The Man I Love," I said. "I do dusties, not new ones."

> *And he'll be big and strong,*
> *The man I love—*

"Good tonsils," he said. "Give her a dance chorus, Mike."

Mike said disgustedly, "Why d'ya wanna waste your time? Even if she was paralyzed from the waist down and had a voice like a frog, ain't you got eyes? Get a load of her face, will you?"

"You're in," the manager said. "Thirty-five, and buy yourself some up-to-date lyrics. Come around at eight and get fitted for some duds. What's your name?"

"Bill me as Angel Face," I said, "and have your electrician give me an amber spot. They take the padlocks off their wallets when I come out in an amber spot."

He shook his head, almost sorrowfully. "Hang onto that face, girlie. It ain't gonna happen again in a long time!"

Burns was holding up my locked room-door with one shoulder when I got back. "Here's your letters back; I've got the photostats tucked away in a safe place. Where'd you disappear to?"

"I've landed a job at Hell's Bells. I'm going to get that guy and get him good! If that's the way I've got to get the evidence, that's the way. After all, if he was sold on her, *I'll* have him cutting out paper dolls before two weeks are out. What'd she have that I haven't got? Now, stay out of there. Somebody might know your face, and you'll only queer everything."

"Watch yourself, will you, Angel Face? You're playing a dangerous game. That Milton is nobody's fool. If you need me in a hurry, you know where to reach me. I'm right at your shoulder, all the way through."

I went in and stuck the letters back in the fake bottom of the case. I had an idea I was going to have a visitor fairly soon, and wasn't going to tip my hand.

I stood it on the dresser top and threw in a few pins and glass beads for luck.

The timing was eerie. The knock came inside of ten minutes. I'd known it was due, but not that quick. It was my competitor from the auction room, flashy as ever; he'd changed flowers, that was all.

"Miss Sebastian," he said, "isn't it? I'd like very much to buy that jewel case you got."

"I noticed that this morning."

He went over and squinted into it.

"That all you wanted it for, just to keep junk like that in?"

"What'd you expect to find, the Hope diamond?"

"You seemed willing to pay a good deal."

"I lose my head easy in auction rooms. But, for that matter, you seemed to be willing to go pretty high yourself."

"I still am," he said. He turned it over, emptied my stuff out, tucked it under his arm, put something down on the dresser. "There's a hundred dollars. Buy yourself a real good one."

Through the window I watched the dreadnaught drift away again. "Just a little bit too late in getting here," I smiled after it. "The cat's out of the bag now and a bulldog will probably chase it."

The silver dress fitted me like a wet compress. It was one of those things that break up homes. The manager flagged me in the passageway leading back. "Did you notice that man all by himself at a ringside table? You know who he is, don't you?"

If I hadn't, why had I bothered turning on all my current his way? "No," I said, round-eyed, "who?"

"Milton. He owns the works. The reason I'm telling you is this: you've got a date with a bottle of champagne at his table, starting in right now. Get on in there."

We walked on back.

"Mr. Milton, this is Angel Face," the manager said. "She won't give us her right name, just walked in off Fifty-Second Street last Tuesday."

"And I waited until tonight to drop around here!" he laughed. "What you paying her, Berger?" Then before the other guy could get a word out, "Triple it! And now get out of here."

The night ticked on. He'd look at me, then he'd suddenly throw up his hands as though to ward off a dazzling glare. "Turn it off, it hurts my eyes."

I smiled a little and took out my mirror. I saw my eyes in it, and in each iris there was a little electric chair with Chick sitting strapped in it. Three weeks from now, sometime during that week. Boy, how they were rushing him! It made it a lot easier to go ahead.

I went back to what we'd been talking about—and what are any two people talking about, more or less, in a nightclub at four in the morning? "Maybe," I said, "who can tell? Some night I might just feel like changing the scenery around me, but I couldn't tell you about it, I'm not that kind."

"You wouldn't have to," he said. He fooled with something below table-level, then passed his hand to me. I took it and knotted my handkerchief around the latchkey he'd left in it. Burns had been right. It was a dangerous game, and bridges were blazing and collapsing behind me.

The doorman covered a yawn with a white kid glove, said, "Who shall I announce?"

"That's all been taken care of," I said, "so you can go back to your beauty sleep."

He caught on, said insinuatingly, "It's Mr. Milton, isn't it? He's out of town tonight."

"You're telling me!" I thought. I'd sent him the wire that fixed that, signed the name of the manager of his Philly club. "You've been reading my mail," I said, and closed the elevator in his face.

The key worked, and the light switch worked, and his Filipino had the night off, so the rest was up to me. The clock in his two-story living room said four-fifteen. I went to the second floor of his penthouse and started in on the bedroom. He was using Ruby Rose Reading's jewel case to hold his collar buttons in, hadn't thrown it out. I opened the fake bottom to see if he'd found what he was after, and the letters were gone, probably burned.

I located his wall safe but couldn't crack it. While I was still working at it, the phone downstairs started to ring. I jumped as though a pin had been stuck into me, and started shaking like I was still doing one of my routines at the club. He had two phones, one downstairs, one in the bedroom, which was an unlisted number. I snapped out the lights, ran downstairs, picked it up. I didn't answer, just held it.

Burns's voice said, "Angel Face?" in my ear.

"Gee, you sure frightened me!" I exhaled.

"Better get out of there. He just came back, must have tumbled to the wire. A spotter at Hell's Bells tipped me off he was just there asking for you."

"I can't, now," I wailed. "I woke his damn doorman up getting in just now, and I'm in that silver dress I do my numbers in! He'll tell him I was here. I'll have to play it dumb."

"D'ja get anything?"

"Nothing, only that jewel case! I couldn't get the safe open but he's probably burned everything connecting him to her long ago."

"Please get out of there, kid," he pleaded. "You don't know that guy. He's going to pin you down on the mat if he finds you there."

"I'm staying," I said. "I've got to break him down tonight. It's my last chance. Chick eats chicken and ice cream tomorrow night at six. Oh, Burns, pray for me, will you?"

"I'm going to do more than that," he growled. "I'm going to give a wrong-number call there in half an hour. It's four-thirty now. Five that'll be. If you're doing all right, I'll lie low. If not, I'm not going to wait, I'll break in with some of the guys, and we'll use the little we have, the photostats of the letters, and the jewel case. I think Schlesinger can at least get Chick a reprieve on them, if not a new trial. If we can't get Milton, we can't get him, that's all."

"We've got to get him," I said, "and we're going to! He's even been close to breaking down and admitting it to me, at times, when we're alone together. Then at the last minute he gets leery. I'm convinced in my own mind he's guilty. So help me, if I lose Chick tomorrow night, I'm going to shoot Milton with my own hands!"

"Remember, half an hour. If everything's under control, cough. If you can get anywhere near the phone, cough! If I don't hear you cough, I'm pulling the place."

I hung up, ran up the stairs tearing at the silver cloth. I jerked open a closet door, found the cobwebby negligee he'd always told me was waiting for me there whenever I felt like breaking it in. I chased downstairs again in it, more like Godiva than anyone else, grabbed up a cigarette, flopped back full length on the handiest divan, and did a Cleopatra—just as the outside door opened and he and two other guys came in.

Milton had a face full of storm clouds—until he saw me. Then it cleared and the sun came up in it. "Finally!" he crooned. "Finally you wanted a change of scenery! And just tonight somebody had to play a practical joke on me, start me on a fool's errand to Philly! Have you been here long?"

I couldn't answer right away because I was still trying to get my breath back after the quick-change act I'd just pulled. I managed a vampish smile.

He turned to the two guys. "Get out, you two. Can't you see I have company?"

I'd recognized the one who'd contacted me for the jewel case, and knew what was coming. I figured I could handle it. "Why, that's the dame I told you about, Milt," he blurted out, "that walked off with that little box the other day!"

"Oh, hello," I sang out innocently. "I didn't know that you knew Mr. Milton."

Milton flared, "You, Rocco! Don't call my lady friends dames!" and slapped him backhand across the mouth. "Now scar-ram! You think we need four for bridge?"

"All right, boss, all right," he said soothingly. But he went over to a framed "still" of me, that Milton had brought home from Hell's Bells, and stood thoughtfully in front of it for a minute. Then he and the other guy left. It was only after the elevator light had flashed out that I looked over and saw the frame was empty.

"Hey!" I complained. "That Rocco swiped my picture, right under your nose!"

He thought he saw a bowl of cream in front of him; nothing could get his back up. "Who can blame him? You're so lovely to look at."

He spent some time working on the theory that I'd finally found him irresistible. After what seemed years of that, I sidestepped him neatly, got off the divan just in time.

He got good and peeved finally.

"Are you giving me the runaround? What did you come here for anyway?"

"Because she's double-crossing you!" a voice said from the foyer. "Because she came here to frame you, chief, and I know it!"

The other two had come back. Rocco pulled my picture out of his pocket. "I traced that dummy wire you got, sending you to Philly. The clerk at the telegraph office identified her as the sender, from this picture. Ask her why she wanted to get you out of town, and then come up here and case your layout! Ask her why she was willing to pay thirty bucks for a little wood box, when she was living in a seven-buck furnished room! Ask her who she is! You weren't at the Reading trial, were you? Well, I was! You're riding for a fall, chief, by having her around you. She's a stoolie!"

He turned on me. "Who are you? What does he mean?"

What was the good of answering? It was five to five on the clock. I needed Burns bad.

The other one snarled, "She's the patsy's sister. Chick Wheeler's sister. I saw her on the stand with my own eyes."

Milton's face screwed up into a sort of despairing agony; I'd never seen anything like it before. He whimpered, "And you're so beautiful to have to be killed!"

I hugged the negligee around me tight and looked down at the floor. "Then don't have me killed," I said softly. It was two to five, now.

He said with comic sadness, "I got to if you're that guy's sister."

"I say I'm nobody's sister, just Angel Face that dances at your club. I say I only came here 'cause—I like soft carpets."

"Why did you send that fake telegram to get me out of town?"

He had me there. I thought fast. "If I'm a stoolie I get killed, right? But what happens if I'm the other kind of a double-crosser, a two-timer, do I still get killed?"

"No," he said, "because you were still a free-lance; your option hadn't been taken up yet."

"That's the answer, then. I was going to use your place to meet my steady, that's why I sent the queer wire."

Rocco's voice was as cracked as a megaphone after a football rally.

"She's Wheeler's sister, chief. Don't let her ki—"

"Shut up!" Milton said.

Rocco just smiled a wise smile, shrugged, lit a cigarette. "You'll find out."

The phone rang. "Get that," Milton ordered. "That's her guy now. Keep him on the wire." He turned and went running up the stairs to the floor above, where the other phone was.

Rocco took out a gun, fanned it vaguely in my direction, sauntered over.

"Don't try nothing, now, while that line's open. You may be fooling Milton, you're not fooling us any. He was always a sucker for a twist."

Rocco's buddy said, "Hello?"

Rocco, still holding the gun on me, took a lopsided drag on his cigarette with his left hand and blew smoke vertically. Some of it caught in his throat, and he started to cough like a seal. You could hear it all over the place.

I could feel all the blood draining out of my face.

The third guy was purring, "No, you tell me what number you want first, then I'll tell you what number this is. That's the way it's done, pal." He turned a blank face. "Hung up on me!"

Rocco was still hacking away. I felt sick all over. Sold out by my own signal that everything was under control!

There was a sound like dry leaves on the stairs and Milton came whisking down again. "Some guy wanted an all-night delicatess—" the spokesman started to say.

Milton cut his hand at him viciously. "That was Centre Street, police headquarters. I had it traced! Put some clothes on her. She's going to her funeral!"

They forced me back into the silver sheath between them. Milton came over with a flagon of brandy and dashed it all over me from head to foot. "If she lets out a peep, she's fighting drunk. Won't be the first stewed dame carried outa here!"

They had to hold me up between them, my heels just clear of the ground, to get me to move at all. Rocco had his gun buried in the silver folds of my dress. The other had a big handkerchief spread out in his hand held under my face, as though I were nauseated—in reality to squelch any scream.

Milton came behind us. "You shouldn't mix your drinks," he was saying, "and especially you shouldn't help yourself to people's private stock without permission."

But the doorman was asleep again on his bench, like when I'd come in the first time. This time he didn't wake up. His eyelids just flickered a little as the four of us went by.

They saw to it that I got in the car first, like a lady

should. The ride was one of those things you take to your grave with you. My whole past life came before me, in slow motion. I didn't mind dying so terribly much, but I hated to go without being able to do anything for Chick. But it was the way the cards had fallen, that was all.

"Maybe it's better this way," I said to myself, "than growing into an old lady and no one looks at your face any more." I took out my mirror and I powdered my nose, and then I threw the compact away. I'd show them a lady could die like a gentleman!

The house was on the Sound. Milton evidently lived in it quite a bit, by the looks of it. His Filipino let us in.

"Build a fire, Juan, it's chilly," he grinned. And to me, "Sit down, Angel Face, and let me look at you before you go." The other two threw me into a corner of a big sofa, and I just stayed that way, limp like a rag doll. He just stared and stared. "Gosh, you're swell!" he said.

Rocco said, "What're we waiting for? It's broad daylight already."

Milton was idly holding something into the fire, a long poker of some kind. "She's going," he said, "but she's going as my property. Show the other angels this, when you get up there, so they'll know who you belong to." He came over to me with the end of the thing glowing dull red. It was flattened into some kind of an ornamental design or cipher. "Knock her out," he said. "I'm not that much of a brute."

Something exploded off the side of my head, and I lost my senses. Then he was wiping my mouth with a handkerchief soaked in whiskey, and my side burned, just above the hip, where they'd found that mark on Ruby Rose Reading.

"All right, Rocco," Milton said.

Rocco took out his gun again, but he shoved it at the third guy hilt first. The third one held it level at me, took the safety off. His face was sort of green and wet with sweat. I looked him straight in the eyes. The gun went down like a drooping lily. "I can't, boss, she's too beautiful!" he groaned. "She's got the face of an angel. How can you shoot anything like that?"

Milton pulled it away from him. "She double-crossed me just like Reading did. Any dame that double-crosses me gets what I gave Reading."

A voice said softly, "That's all I wanted to know."

The gun went off, and I wondered why I didn't feel anything. Then I saw that the smoke was coming from the doorway and not from Milton's gun at all. He went down at my feet, like he wanted to apologize for what he'd done to me, but he didn't say anything and he didn't get up any more. There was blood running down the part of his hair in back.

Burns was in the room with more guys than I'd ever seen outside of a police parade. One of them was the doorman from Milton's place, or at least the dick that Burns had substituted for him to keep an eye on me while I was up there. Burns told me about that later and about how they followed Milt's little party but hadn't been able to get in in time to keep me from getting branded. Rocco and the other guy went down into hamburger under a battery of heavy fists.

I sat there holding my side and sucking in my breath. "It was a swell trick-finish," I panted to Burns, "but what'd you drill him for? Now we'll never get the proof that'll save Chick."

He was at the phone asking to be put through to Schlesinger in the city. "We've got it already, Angel Face," he said ruefully. "It's right on you, where you're holding your side. Just where it was on Reading. We all heard what he said before he nose-dived anyway. I only wish I hadn't shot him," he glowered, "then I'd have the pleasure of doing it all over again, more slowly."

GEORGE DOUGLAS HOWARD COLE (1890–1959) was a Fabian economist and a leading light of the British Labour Party. His wife, Margaret (1893–   ), sister to mystery novelist Raymond Postgate, shared his socialist interests and herself wrote a history of the Fabian Society and a biography of Beatrice Webb. Together, they collaborated on over thirty detective novels, a few of which are *Murder at Crome House* (1927), *End of an Ancient Mariner* (1934), *Off with Her Head* (1938), and *The Murder at the Munitions Works* (1940). The Coles explained to curious interviewers that writing fictional crime provided them with a diversion.

Mrs. Elizabeth Warrender made her first appearance in a collection entitled *A Lesson in Crime and Other Stories* (1933). The following vignette was used to introduce this "elderly lady of respectable family and small means" in *Mrs. Warrender's Profession* (1939), which contains four long tales of her problem-solving adventures. (The titular allusion to Shaw must have been irresistible.) Mrs. Warrender admits herself that she has no literary or artistic taste—she is not even terribly interested in crime. What she does enjoy are gardens, holiday vacations, and observing the people around her.

The Mother of the Detective

by G. D. H. and M. Cole

It cannot be pleasant for an eminent private detective to be the victim of an unsolved mystery in his own home; it must be as humiliating as for a Harley Street specialist to suffer from an unexplained catarrh. So it is not altogether surprising that when Mrs. Warrender, after a very pleasant weekend spent in the company of an old friend of her girlhood, alighted one Monday morning at the garden gate of her house she kept for her son James, she should find the aforesaid son in what can only be described as a fit of the sulks.

James Warrender was a very well-known detective indeed. He was in very close relationship with some of the highest officials at Scotland Yard, who had often admitted that his imagination was as useful, at times, as their elaborate and complete organisation. But at the moment he did not look at all eminent or imaginative; to his mother's practised eye, in fact, he bore the appearance of a man whose best dress-shirt has been irretrievably torn by the Perfect Sanitary Steam Laundry or one of its kin, and it was under this apprehension that she first addressed him.

"Nonsense! Nothing of the sort!" said the irate public

man, whose nerves had been additionally frayed by the visits of several bright young pressmen, anxious to provide him with a quite unwanted advertisement. "The silver's been stolen!"

"What? The silver stolen? I knew it!" said his mother, causing her son to start and look up with a suspicious glance. "No, James, don't be silly. Of course I didn't steal it. Why should I want to steal it, when it will all belong to me if you die suddenly—not that I want you to die, of course, dear—I should be very sorry indeed . . . I only meant that something always does happen when I go away. You remember that time when I only went to a garden party—Mrs. Hughes's, I believe it was—and you let that man sell you a cat he said was a tom, and it had kittens almost at once . . . Yes, dear, of course it's very annoying. But you'll get it all back, won't you? You surely know all about thieves and who they are, and that nice inspector—the one who doesn't take milk in his tea, or else he does, but I can never remember—he'll arrest them for you."

"But I don't!" the exasperated detective cut in at last. "There's no way I can track him! Not a single trace. The pantry window was forced; so was the door of the silver cupboard; but there isn't a single footprint or fingerprint about. He simply walked in and walked out, as cool as a cucumber!"

"Through the *pantry window*," Mrs. Warrender interrupted. "James, dear, he couldn't. Not carrying all those spoons and forks and things. It's quite a jump from the window. He'd be certain to drop some of them."

"I didn't say he went out through the pantry," Warrender snapped. "He didn't. He walked out through the hall door, just as cool as—as a cucumber!" he finished, with a certain lack of effect. "And if that maid of yours—Gladys—hadn't been God's own fool, we'd have caught him!"

"*Gladys?* But—never mind, dear," seeing that he was on the verge of apoplexy. "Tell me all about it. What did Gladys do?"

"She didn't do anything! At least," Warrender said, "what happened was this. Gladys heard a noise in the night, and instead of calling me, she crept to the head of the stairs to see what it was. Then she saw a shadow moving, which looked like a man in the hall. And he must have heard her, because at once he sprang to the hall door, and let himself out. And she, the idiot! instead of coming and waking me she must needs creep down to the front door and shriek. By the time she'd got there the man was through the gate and out of sight, but all she could do was to go on shrieking. I heard a row, and came down, and there she was, yelling Blue Murder on the front doorstep, and half the neighbours were awake and wanting to know what the devil we were making such a row about on a Sunday morning. But there was not a sign of the chap, of course."

"But, dear," said his mother mildly, "if he was running away so fast with a great load of silver, surely somebody must have seen him?"

"Well, they didn't. You know what a nice quiet sabbath-keeping suburb we are! They were all in bed and asleep. And the constable was up the other end of the main road, so *he* didn't see. There wasn't anybody about at all. It's too bad!" finished James fiercely.

"Yes, dear. I wonder if Gladys has been having toothache, poor girl. I think I'll just trot along and see. They're so careless about not going to the dentist when they ought to, but I suppose one can't blame them, they've never been taught that a little pain at once saves such a lot later—"

"It isn't her teeth, it's her brains that are wrong. I wish you would get servants with a little more intelligence."

"I do try to, dear; but it isn't very easy, you know.

And I don't think one really wants servants to be *too* clever, does one? They get such curious ideas," said Mrs. Warrender. "I think I'll just ask Gladys now, if you wouldn't mind taking up my bag, dear. There's no time like the present. And then if you don't want me, I must have a look at the garden. I'm sure you've none of you had time to do anything to it, and I've been worrying about those autumn sunflowers all the weekend. They look so dreadful if they aren't cut regularly." There was the sound of a knock.

"That'll be Hennessy," said James gloomily. Hennessy was the inspector.

"Oh, how nice! Be sure you let me give him a glass of sherry when you've finished your talk, dear. It's such a nice habit. I'll just run along and be out of your way, as soon as I've got my old pinafore on. Now, where are my gardening gloves?" She softly fussed her way out of the room, just before a warm police inspector, obviously worried by the publicity which failure to find Mr. Warrender's burglar would bring to his department, was ushered in.

"Mother! Mother! Where are you? The inspector is just going!"

"Here, dear!" a faint voice came from the bottom of the garden. "There's just something here I can't quite manage to reach."

The inspector hurried politely down the path, followed by Warrender, to find the little old lady standing in the corner of the garden by the wall, gazing plaintively at something caught in the branches of a tree.

"Oh, how kind of you, Mr. Hennessy! How do you do? It's just—I can't quite reach this . . . If you wouldn't mind . . ." The inspector made a long arm and brought down the little parcel. Then his jaw dropped and he gave a gasp, for what it contained was a number of Georgian silver forks wrapped in green baize and tissue paper.

"What the—I beg your pardon, ma'am. But—are these yours?"

"Why, yes. Aren't they, James?"

"But Mr. Warrender was telling me the thief got away by the front door!"

"Oh, yes, but of course he didn't. I was quite sure he didn't. He went this way. And I told you he'd never be able to climb without dropping some of the things, didn't I, James? But wasn't it fortunate they caught in the tree, like this?" She looked round with a pleasant smile.

"But . . . but . . . " Warrender seemed "struck all of a heap," and none too pleased. He tried sarcasm. "If you know all about this, mother, perhaps you won't mind telling Hennessy the name of the thief."

"I'm afraid I don't know his name," Mrs. Warrender said, regretfully. "But I'm sure Inspector Hennessy can find out who Gladys's young man is, if he asks people round about here."

"Gladys's young man!"

"Well, it mayn't be her young man, of course, but I don't think she's got any brothers or anything like that in the neighbourhood. Of course, she might have more than one young man; some girls are really dreadful in that way. But you could find out, couldn't you, inspector?"

"Mother! Will you kindly explain? What do you mean about Gladys? and how do you know?"

"Why," said the old lady, "I guessed, as soon as you told me about it."

"Why?"

"Why, it was so absurd about Gladys. You see, James, you know a great deal about criminals and how they behave, what you call psychology, but it's all about people you don't know at all, really. I'm sure you don't know anything about me"—and indeed the eminent criminologist did not look as though he did—"and of course you'd never dream of knowing anything about anybody like

Gladys. But, you see, I know Gladys, and she's a very quick girl when anything happens, not a bit likely to have a fit when she saw a burglar or scream instead of calling you. So when you told me, I thought, why on earth was Gladys screaming at the front door? And, of course, the easiest answer was, to let somebody get away by the back door, and have you all running the wrong way. Then she'd have plenty of time to cover up the tracks or anything, if he made them, before you ever thought of looking in the garden. And, besides, there was her waking up."

"Why on earth shouldn't she wake up?"

"There, you see! If you knew about Gladys, you wouldn't ask. Nothing will ever wake her, either in the morning or any other time. Why, James, you *know* I have to wait up for you, if you're going to be late, because Gladys never heard, even when we put a bell in her bedroom. Of course, she *might* have had toothache or something like that, that kept her awake, so I asked her if she wanted something for it. But she hadn't got the sense to make up a lie and say she had—of course I didn't tell her why I wanted to know, but she might have guessed. But she isn't really very intelligent, as you said, James; though I think it's rather a good thing when servants aren't. Don't you, Mr. Hennessy?" She addressed the inspector, who was still standing lost in surprise.

"Well, but . . . you mean she told him where the stuff was, and helped him pinch it?"

"And lent him my gardening gloves." Mrs. Warrender nodded vigorously.

"At least, they weren't in the proper place, and I'm sure nobody's been gardening while I've been away. Don't you say criminals always forget some little thing, James, like that?"

"Well, if that's so, and anyway it looks pretty much as if your maid's lying, sir," said the inspector, "I'd better be getting on with the job. I'd best have a word with her first."

"Oh, you let James bully Gladys, Mr. Hennessy." Mrs. Warrender smiled at him. "I'm sure he'll get the truth out of her. James can be really terrible when he likes; I should be afraid of him myself, if I wasn't his mother. And then you could go and look for Gladys's young man."

"I wish you could tell me who he is, ma'am," the inspector said.

"I'm so sorry I can't. But, you see, I make a point of never interfering with my servants' private affairs. I don't think it's right."

"Not even," James enquired with heavy sarcasm, "if their young men are criminals?"

"Certainly not!" said Mrs. Warrender. "I'm sure if you were engaged to a girl who was a thief, James, you wouldn't want people asking you questions about it!" Both men gasped.

"But," Inspector Hennessy protested faintly, "that seems a bit overconfident, ma'am, if I may say so. When you get your house burgled through it."

"Oh, but it wouldn't have been burgled if I'd been at home, you see."

"May one ask why not?" James enquired.

"Because I should have woken, of course; and I should have looked out of the back window. Gladys isn't so stupid as not to know that. But men always sleep heavily in their own homes, and wake up all in a muddle. Won't you have a glass of sherry before you go, Mr. Hennessy?" said Mrs. Warrender.

GLADYS MITCHELL, though of Scots ancestry, was born in Cowley, Oxford, in 1901. For most of her professional career, she has combined the writing of detective stories—over three dozen to date—with teaching English and history, doubling sometimes as a games mistress. She has also written under the names Stephen Hockaby and Malcolm Torrie, besides producing numerous children's books. Her first mystery novel was *Speedy Death* (1929); her latest, *A Javelin for Jonah* (1974), featuring the incomparable Beatrice Adela Lestrange Bradley.

In this rural adventure, the twice-married Mrs. Bradley, a consulting psychiatrist to the Home Office, has not yet been made a Dame of the British Empire; nor is she accompanied by her secretary, Laura Gavin, who is the wife of a Scotland Yard inspector. A woman of indefinite latish middle age throughout most of the series, Mrs. Bradley has a consistently disarming manner which ranges from the offhand to the whimsical, masking an impressive omniscience that stems from her sharp observations of character. She is described as resembling "a benign lizard" and as having "her own peculiar sense of fun." A follower of Freud's, she maintains her own London clinic. She is also wont to pursue an interest in witchcraft, which stems from her fond belief that some of her ancestresses were burned at the stake.

Daisy Bell

by Gladys Mitchell

Daisy, Daisy, give me your answer, do!
I've gone crazy, all for the love of you!
It won't be a stylish marriage—
We can't afford a carriage—
But you'll look neat upon the seat
Of a bicycle made for two.

In the curved arm of the bay the sea lay perfectly still. Towards the horizon was reflected back the flashing light of the sun, but under the shadow of huge cliffs the dark green water was as quiet as a lake at evening.

Above, riding over a ridge between two small villages, went the road, a dusty highway once, a turnpike on which the coach had changed horses three times in twenty miles. That dusty road was within the memory of the villagers; in the post office there were picture postcards, not of the coaches, certainly, but of the horse-drawn station bus on the shocking gradients and hairpin bends of the highway.

The road was now slightly wider—not much, because every extra foot had to be hacked from the rocky hillside, for on one side the road fell almost sheer to the sea. A humped turf edge kept this seaward boundary (insufficiently, some said, for there had been motoring accidents, especially in the dark), and beyond the humped edge, and, treacherously, just out of sight of motorists who could see the rolling turf but not the danger, there fell away a Gadarene descent of thirteen hundred feet.

George took the road respectfully, with an eye for hairpin bends and (although he found this irksome) an occasional toot on the horn. His employer, small, spare and upright, sat beside him, the better to admire the rolling view. Equally with the moorland scenery she admired her chauffeur's driving. She was accustomed to both phenomena, but neither palled on her. In sixteen crawling miles she had had not a word to say.

At the County Boundary, however, she turned her head slightly to the right.

"The next turning, George. It's narrow."

His eyes on the road ahead, the chauffeur nodded, and the car turned off to the left down a sandy lane, at the bottleneck of which it drew up courteously in face of a flock of lively, athletic, headstrong moorland sheep. The shepherd saluted Mrs. Bradley, passed the time of day with the chauffeur, said it was a pity all they motors shouldn't have the same danged sense, and urged his charges past the car, and kept them within some sort of bounds with the help of a shaggy dog.

At the bottom of the slope, and wedged it seemed in the hollow, was a village with a very small church. Mrs. Bradley went into the churchyard to inspect the grave of an ancestress (she believed) of her own who had died in the odour of sanctity, but, if rumour did not lie, only barely so, for she had enjoyed a reputation as a witch.

Mrs. Bradley, looking (with her black hair, sharp black eyes, thin hands and beaky little mouth) herself not at all unlike a witch, spent an interesting twenty minutes or so in the churchyard, and then went into the church.

Its architectural features were almost negligible. A fourteenth-century chancel (probably built on the site of the earliest church), a badly restored nave, a good rood screen, and the only remaining bit of Early English work mutilated to allow for an organ loft, were all obvious. There seemed, in fact, very little, on a preliminary investigation, to interest even the most persistent or erudite visitor.

In the dark south wall, however, of what had been the Lady Chapel, Mrs. Bradley came upon a fourteenth-century piscina whose bowl had been carved in the likeness of a hideous human head. She took out a magnifying glass and examined the carving closely. Montague Rhodes James, with his genius for evoking unquiet imaginings and terrifying, atavistic fears, might have described the expression upon its horrid countenance. All that Mrs. Bradley could accomplish was a heathenish muttering indicative of the fact that, in her view, the countenance betrayed indications of at least two major Freudian complexes and a Havelock Ellis regression into infantile criminology.

"A murderer's face, mam," said a voice behind her. "Ay, as I stand, that be a murderer's face."

She turned and saw the verger with his keys. "Ay, they do tell, and vicar he do believe it, as carver was vouchsafed a true, just vision of Judas Iscariot the traitor, and carved he out for all to look upon."

He smiled at her—almost with the sinister leer of the carving itself, thought Mrs. Bradley, startled by the change in his mild and previously friendly expression. He passed on into the vestry, dangling his keys.

Shaking her head, Mrs. Bradley dropped some money into the offertory box on the pillar nearest to the porch, and took the long sloping path between the headstones of the graves to the lych-gate. Here she found George in conversation with a black-haired woman. George had always given himself (with how much truth his employer had never troubled herself to find out) the reputation of being a misogynist, and on this occasion, seated on the step of the car, he was, in his own phrase, "laying down the law" with scornful masculine firmness. The girl had her back to the lych-gate. She was plump and bareheaded, and was wearing brown corduroy shorts, a slightly rucked-up blouse on elastic at the waist, and—visible from the back view which Mrs. Bradley had of her—a very bright pink vest which showed between the rucked-up blouse and the shorts. For the rest she was brown-skinned and, seen face to face, rather pretty.

A tandem bicycle, built to accommodate two men, was resting against the high, steep, ivy-grown bank of the lane. The young woman, seeing Mrs. Bradley, who had in fact strolled round to get a view of her, cut short George's jeremiads by thanking him. Then she walked across the road, set the tandem upright, pushed it sharply forward, and, in spite of the fact that the slope of the road was against her, mounted with agility and ease on to the front saddle. Then she tacked doggedly up the hill, the tandem, lacking any weight on the back seat, wagging its tail in what looked to Mrs. Bradley a highly dangerous manner as it zigzagged up to the bend in the lane and wobbled unwillingly round it.

George had risen to his feet upon the approach of his employer, and now stood holding the door open.

"A courageous young woman, George?" suggested Mrs. Bradley, getting into the car.

"A foolish one, madam, in my opinion," George responded primly, "and so I was saying to her when she was asking the way. Looking for trouble I call it to cycle one of them things down these roads. Look at the hill she's coming to, going to Lyndale this route. Meeting her husband, she says; only been married a month, and having their honeymoon now and using the tandem between them; him having to work hereabouts, and her cycling that contraption down from London, where she's living with her mother while he gets the home for her. Taken three days to do it in, and meeting him on top of Lyndale Hill this afternoon. More like a suicide pact, if you ask me what I think."

"I not only ask you, George, but I am so much enthralled by what you think that I propose we take the same route and follow her."

"We were due to do so in any case, madam, if I can find a place to turn the car in this lane."

It took him six slow miles to find a suitable place. During the drive towards the sea, the big car brushing the summer hedgerows almost all the time, Mrs. Bradley observed,

"I don't like to think of that young woman, George. I hope you advised her to wheel the bicycle on all dangerous parts of the road?"

"As well advise an errand boy to fit new brake-blocks, madam," George austerely answered. "I did advise her to that effect, but not to cut any ice. She fancies herself on that jigger. You can't advise women of that age."

"Did you offer her any alternative route to Lyndale?"

"Yes, madam; not with success."

At the top of the winding hill he turned to the left, and then, at the end of another five miles and a quarter of wind and the screaming seabirds, great stretches of moorland heather, bright green tracks of little peaty streams, and, south of the moor, the far-off ridges and tors, he engaged his lowest gear again and the car crept carefully down a long, steep, dangerous hill. There were warning notices on either side of the road, and the local authority, laying special emphasis on the subject of faulty brakes, had cut a parking space from the edge of the stubborn moor. The gradient of the steepest part of the hill was one in four. The car took the slant like a cat in sight of a bird.

"What do you think of our brakes, George?" Mrs.

Bradley enquired. George replied, in the reserved manner with which he received her more facetious questions, that the brakes were in order, or had been when the car was brought out of the garage.

"Well, then, pull up," said his employer. "Something has happened on the seaward side of the road. I think someone's gone over the edge."

Her keen sight, and a certain sensitivity she had to visual impressions, had not deceived her. She followed the track of a bicycle to the edge of the cliff, crouched, lay flat, and looked over.

Below her the seagulls screamed, and, farther down, the sea flung sullenly, despite the brilliant day, against the heavy rocks, or whirlpooled, snarling, about the black island promontories, for the tide was on the turn and coming in fast. Sea-pinks, some of them brown and withered now, for their season was almost past, clung in the crevices or grew in the smallest hollows of the cliff-face. Near one root of them a paper bag had lodged. Had it been empty, the west wind, blowing freshly along the face of the cliff (which looked north to the Bristol Channel), must have removed it almost as soon as it alighted, but there it perched, not wedged, yet heavy enough to hold its place against the breeze. To the left of it, about four yards off, was a deep, dark stain, visible because it was on the only piece of white stone that could be seen.

"Odd," said Mrs. Bradley, and began to perform the feat which she would not have permitted to anyone under her control—that of climbing down to reach the dark-stained rock.

The stain was certainly blood, and was still slightly sticky to the touch. She looked farther down (having, fortunately, a mountaineer's head for heights) and thought that, some thirty feet below her, she could see a piece of cloth. It was caught on the only bush which seemed to have found root and sustenance upon the rocky cliff. It resembled, she thought, material of which a man's suit might be made.

She left it where it was and scrambled across to the bag.

"George," she said, when she had regained the dark, overhanging lip of the rough turf edge of the cliff and had discovered her chauffeur at the top, "I think I saw a public telephone marked on the map. Somebody ought to search the shore below these cliffs, I rather fancy."

"It would need to be by boat, then, madam. The tide comes up to the foot," replied the chauffeur. He began to walk back up the hill.

Mrs. Bradley sat down at the roadside and waited for him to return. While she was waiting she untwisted the top of the screwed-up paper bag and examined the contents with interest.

She found a packet of safety-razor blades, a tube of toothpaste half-full, a face flannel, a wrapped cake of soap of the dimensions known euphemistically in the advertisements as "guest-size," a very badly worn toothbrush, a set of small buttons on a card, a pipe-cleaner, half a bicycle bell, two rubber patches for mending punctures, and a piece of wormlike valve-rubber.

"Calculated to indicate that whoever left the bag there was a cyclist, George," she observed, when her chauffeur came back from the telephone. "Of course, nobody may have fallen over the cliff, but—what do you make of the marks?"

"Palmer tires, gent's model—not enough clearance for a lady's—see where the pedal caught the edge of the turf?"

"Yes, George. Unfortunately one loses the track a yard from the side of the road. I should have supposed that the bicycle would have left a better account of itself if it had really been ridden over. Besides, what could have made anybody ride it over the edge? The road is wide enough, and there does not seem to be much traffic. I think perhaps I'll retrieve that piece of cloth before we go."

"I most seriously hope you will not, madam, if you'll excuse me. I've no head for heights myself or I would get it. After all, we know just where it is. The police could get it later, with ropes and tackle for their men, if it *should* be required at an inquest."

"Very true, George. Let us get on to the village to see whether a boat has put out. How much farther is it?"

"Another three miles and a half, madam. There's another hill after this—a smaller one."

The car descended decorously. The hill dropped sheer and steep for about another half-mile, and then it twisted suddenly away to the right, so that an inn which was on the left-hand side at the bend appeared, for an instant, to be standing in the middle of the road.

So far as the black-haired girl on the smashed and buckled tandem was concerned, that was where it might as well have stood, Mrs. Bradley reflected. The tandem had been ridden straight into a brick wall—slap into it as though the rider had been blind or as though the machine she was riding had been completely out of her control. Whatever the cause of the accident, she had hurtled irrevocably to her death, or so Mrs. Bradley thought when first she knelt beside her.

"Rat-trap pedals, of all things, madam," said George. The plump large feet in the centre-seamed cycling shoes were still caught in the bent steel traps. George tested the brakes.

"The brakes don't act," he said. "Perhaps a result of the accident, madam, although I shouldn't think so." He released the girl's feet and lifted the tandem away. Mrs. Bradley, first delicately and then with slightly more firmness, sought for injuries.

"George," she said, "the case of instruments. And then go and get some cold water from somewhere or other."

The girl had a fractured skull. Her left leg was slightly lacerated, but it was not bruised and the bone was not broken. Her face was unmarked, except by the dirt from the roadside. It was all a little out of the ordinary, Mrs. Bradley thought, seizing the thermos flask full of icy water which the resourceful George had brought from a moorland stream.

"She's alive, George, I think," she said. "But there have been some very odd goings-on. Are the tandem handlebars locked?"

"No, madam. They move freely."

"Don't you think the front wheel should have been more seriously affected?"

"Why, yes, perhaps it should, madam. The young woman can't go much less than ten or eleven stone, and with the brakes out of order . . ."

"And although her feet were caught tight in the rat-trap pedals, her face isn't even marked. It was only a little dirty before I washed it."

"Sounds like funny business, madam, to me."

"And to me, too, George. Is there a hospital near? We must have an ambulance if possible. I don't think the car will do. She ought to lie flat. That skull wants trepanning and at once. Mind how you go down the hill, though. I'll stay here with her. You might leave me a fairly heavy spanner."

Left alone with the girl, Mrs. Bradley fidgeted with her case of instruments, took out gouge forceps, sighed, shook her head, and put them back again. The wound on the top of the head was extremely puzzling. A fracture of the base of the skull would have been the most likely head injury, unless the girl had crashed head-first into the wall, but, from the position in which the body had been lying, this seemed extremely unlikely. One other curious point Mrs. Bradley noticed which changed her suppositions into certainty. The elastic-waisted white blouse and the shorts met neatly. It was impossible to believe that they could do so unless they had been pulled together after the girl had fallen from the saddle.

Mrs. Bradley made a mental picture of the girl leaning forward over the low-slung sports-type handlebars of the machine. She must, in the feminine phrase, have "come apart" at the back. That blouse could never have over-lapped those shorts.

Interested and curious, Mrs. Bradley turned up the edge of the soiled white blouse. There was nothing underneath it but the bare brown skin marked with two or three darker moles at the waist. Of the bright pink vest there was no sign; neither had the girl a knapsack or any kind of luggage into which she could have stuffed the vest supposing that she had taken it off for coolness.

"Odd," said Mrs. Bradley again, weighing the spanner· thoughtfully in her hand. "I wonder what's happened to the husband?"

At this moment there came round the bend an A.A. scout wheeling a bicycle. He saluted as he came nearer.

"Oh dear, madam! Nasty accident here! Poor young woman! Anything I can do?"

"Yes," said Mrs. Bradley very promptly. "Get an ambulance. I'm afraid she's dead, but there might be a chance if you're quick. No, don't touch her! I'm a doctor. I've done all that can be done here. Hurry, please. Every moment is important."

"No ambulance in the village, madam. Couldn't expect it, could you? I might perhaps be able to get a car. How did you get here? Was you with her when she crashed?"

"Go and get a car. A police car, if you like. Dead or alive, she'll have to be moved as soon as possible."

"Yes, she will, won't she?" said the man. He turned his bicycle, and, mounting it, shot away round the bend.

Mrs. Bradley unfolded an Ordnance Survey map of the

district and studied it closely. Then she took out a reading glass and studied it again. She put out a yellow claw and traced the line of the road she was on, and followed it into the village towards which first George and then the A.A. scout had gone.

The road ran on uncompromisingly over the thin red contour lines of the map, past nameless bays on one side and the shoulder of the moor on a rising hill on the other. Of deviations from it there were none; not so much as the dotted line of a moorland track, not even a stream, gave any indication that there might be other ways of reaching the village besides crossing the open moorland or keeping to the line of the road. There was nothing marked on the map but the cliffs and the shore on the one hand, the open hilly country on the other.

She was still absorbed when George returned with the car.

"The village has no ambulance, madam, but the bus has decanted its passengers on to the bridge and is getting here as fast as it can. It was thought in the village, madam, that the body could be laid along one of the seats."

"I hope and trust that 'body' is but a relative term. The young woman will live, George, I fancy. Somebody has had his trouble for nothing."

"I am glad to hear that, madam. The villagers seem well-disposed, and the bus is the best they can do."

He spoke of the villagers as though they were the aboriginal inhabitants of some country which was still in process of being explored. Mrs. Bradley gave a harsh little snort of amusement and then observed,

"Did the A.A. scout stop and speak to you? Or did you ask him for information?"

"No, madam, neither at all. He was mending a puncture when I passed him."

"Was that on your journey to the village or on the return here?"

"Just now, madam. I saw no one on my journey to the village."

"Interesting," said Mrs. Bradley, thinking of her Ordnance map. "Punctures are a nuisance, George, are they not? If you see him again you might ask him whether *Daisy Bell* met her husband on top of the hill."

Just then the bus arrived. Off it jumped a police sergeant and a constable, who, under Mrs. Bradley's direction, lifted the girl and placed her on one of the seats, of which the bus had two, running the whole of the inside length of the vehicle.

"You take the car to the hotel, George. I'll be there as soon as I can," said his employer. "Now, constable, we have to hold her as still as we can. Sergeant, kindly instruct the driver to avoid the bumps in the road, and then come in here and hold my coat to screen the light from her head. Is there a hospital in the village?"

"No, mam. There's a home for inebriates, though. That's the nearest thing. We're going to take her there, and Constable Fogg is fetching Doctor MacBain."

"Splendid," said Mrs. Bradley, and devoted herself thenceforward entirely to her patient.

One morning some days later, when the mist had cleared from the moors and the sun was shining on every drop of moisture, she sent for the car, and thus addressed her chauffeur:

"Well, did you give the scout my message?"

"Yes, madam, but he did not comprehend it."

"Indeed? And did you explain?"

"No, madam, not being instructed."

"Excellent, child. We shall drive to the fatal spot, and there we shall see—what we shall see."

George, looking haughty because he felt befogged, held open the door of the car, and Mrs. Bradley put her foot on the step.

"I'll sit in front, George," she said.

The car began to mount slowly to the bend where the accident had come to their notice. George was pulling up, but his employer invited him to go on.

"Our goal is the top of the hill, George. That is where they were to meet, you remember. That is the proper place from which to begin our enquiry. Is it not strange and interesting to consider all the motives for murder and attempted murder that come to men's minds? To women's minds, too, of course. The greater includes the less."

She cackled harshly. George, who (although he would have found it difficult to account for his opinion) had always conceived her to be an ardent feminist, looked at the road ahead, and did not relax his expression of dignified aloofness.

Prevented, by the fact that he was driving, from poking him in the ribs (her natural reaction to an attitude such as the one he was displaying), Mrs. Bradley grinned tigerishly, and the car crawled on up the worst and steepest part of the gradient.

George then broke his silence.

"In my opinion, madam, no young woman losing her brakes on such a hill could have got off so light as *she* did, nor that tandem neither."

"True, George."

"If you will excuse the question, madam, what put the idea of an attempt on her into your mind?"

"I suppose the piscina, George."

George concluded that she was amusing herself at his expense and accepted the reply for what it was worth, which to him was nothing, since he did not know what a piscina was (and was habitually averse to seeking such information). He drove on a little faster as the gradient eased to one in seven and then to one in ten.

"Just here, George," said his employer. "Run off on to the turf on the right-hand side."

George pulled up very close to the A.A. telephone which he had used before. Here the main road cut away from the route they had traversed and an A.A. scout was on duty at the junction.

" '*Behind the barn, down on my knees,*' " observed Mrs. Bradley, chanting the words in what she fondly believed to be accents of their origin, " '*I thought I heard a chicken sneeze*'—and I did, too. Come and look at this, George."

It was the bright pink vest. There was no mistaking it, although it was stained now, messily and rustily, with blood.

"Not *her* blood, George; *his*," remarked Mrs. Bradley. "I wonder he dared bring it back here, all the same. And I wonder where the young woman the first time fell off the tandem?" She looked again at the blood-stained vest. "He must have cut himself badly, but, of course, he had to get enough blood to make the white stone look impressive, and he wanted the vest to smear it on with so that he need use nothing of his own. Confused thinking, George, on the whole, but murderers do think confusedly, and one can feel for them, of course."

She sent George to fetch the A.A. scout, who observed, "Was it the young woman as fell off bottom of Countsferry? Must have had a worse tumble just here by the box than Stanley seemed to think. He booked the tumble in his private log. Would you be the young woman's relatives, mam?"

"We represent her interests," said Mrs. Bradley, remarking afterwards to George that she thought they might consider themselves as doing so since they had saved her life.

"Well, he's left the log with me, and it do seem to show the cause of her shaking up. Must have been dazed like, and not seen the bend as was coming, and run herself into the wall. And Stanley, they do say, must have gone over the cliff in trying to save her, for he ain't been back on duty any more. Cruel, these parts, they be."

"Did her fall upset both her brakes, then?" Mrs. Bradley enquired. She read the laconic entry in the exercise book presented for her inspection, and having earned the scout's gratitude in the customary simple manner, she returned to the car with the vest (which the scout had not seen) pushed into the large pocket of her skirt.

"Stop at the scene of the accident, George," she said. "She seemed," said George admiringly later on to those who were standing him a pint in exchange for the story, "like a bloodhound on the murderer's trail."

"For a murderer he was, in intention, if not in fact," continued George, taking, without his own knowledge, a recognized though debatable ecclesiastical view. "She climbed up the bank and on to the moor as if she knew just what to look for, madam did. She showed me the very stone she reckoned he hit the young woman over the head with, and then where he sunk in the soft earth deeper than his first treads, because he was carrying the body back to the tandem to make out she crashed and fell off."

"And didn't she crash?" his hearers wanted to know.

"Crash? What, her? A young woman who, to give her her due (although I don't hold with such things), had cycled that tandem—sports model and meant for two men—all the way down there from London? No. He crashed the tandem himself after he'd done her in. That was to deceive the police or anybody else that found her. He followed her on his bike down the hill with the deed in his heart. You see, he was her husband.

"But he didn't deceive me and madam, not by a long chalk he didn't! Why, first thing I said to her, I said, 'Didn't it ought to be buckled up more than that if she came down that hill without brakes?' 'Course, that was his little mistake. That, and using her vest. I hope they give him ten years!

"Well, back we went up the hill to where madam found the paper bag and its etceteras. The only blood we could see was on the only white stone."

The barmaid at this point begged him to stop. He gave her the horrors, she said.

"So what?" one listener enquired.

"Well, the whole bag of tricks was to show that *someone,* and that someone a man and a cyclist, had gone over the cliff and was killed, like the other scout said. That was going to be our scout's alibi if the police ever got on his track, so madam thinks, but he hoped he wouldn't need to use that; it was just his stand-by, like. The other A.A. man had seen him go off duty. That was his danger, or so he thought, not reckoning on madam and me. He'd fixed the head of the young woman's machine while she stood talking to him at the A.A. telephone, so that when she mounted it threw her. That was to show (that's why he logged it, see?) as she mightn't have been herself when she took the bend. Pretty little idea."

Three days later Mrs. Bradley said to him,

"They will be able to establish motive at the trial, George. Bell—I call him that—was arrested yesterday evening. He had insured her life, it appears, as soon as they were married, and wished to obtain possession of the money."

"But what I would still like to know, madam," George observed, "is what put the thought of murder into your mind before ever we saw the accident or even the bag and the blood."

"The bag and the blood, for some reason, sounds perfectly horrible, George."

"But, madam, you spotted the marks he'd made on that edge with his push-bike as though you'd been *waiting* to spot them. And you fixed on him as the murderer, too, straight away."

"Ah, that was easy, George. You see, he never mentioned that he'd seen you go by in the car, and you told me that on your journey to the village to find assistance you had not seen him either. Therefore, since he must have been somewhere along that road, I asked myself why, even if he should have left the roadside himself, his bicycle should not have been visible. Besides, he was the perfect answer to several questions which, up to that time, I had had to ask myself. One was: why did they choose to meet at the top of that hill? Another was: why did he risk bending over the injured girl to fix her feet back in those rat-trap pedals we saw and out of which, I should imagine, her feet would most certainly have been pulled if she'd had such a very bad crash?"

"Ah, yes, the A.A. box and the A.A. uniform, madam. In other words, Mr. G. K. Chesterton's postman all over again."

"Precisely, George. The obvious meeting place, in the circumstances, and the conspicuous yet easily forgotten uniform."

"But, madam, if I may revert, what *did* turn your mind to murder?"

"The piscina, George," Mrs. Bradley solemnly reminded him. George looked at her, hesitated, then over-rode the habit of years and enquired,

"What *is* a piscina, madam?"

"A drain, George. Merely a drain.

> " 'Now, body, turn to air,
> Or Lucifer will bear thee quick to hell!
> O soul, be chang'd into little water drops,
> And fall into the ocean, ne'er be found!' "

STUART PALMER (1905–1968) was a native of Wisconsin. He attended the University of Wisconsin and the Chicago Art Institute. He was one of four editors of an anthology of Wisconsin writing and, besides his solo mystery efforts, collaborated with Craig Rice on *The People vs. Withers and Malone* (1963), which combined their two sleuth-creations (hers, in this case, being the lawyer John J. Malone) in one book. He adopted as his personal emblem the drawing of a tiny penguin, often with a spyglass in hand, owing to the success of an early Hildegarde Withers title, *The Penguin Pool Murder* (1931). This Stuart Palmer is sometimes confused with another one—Stuart H. Palmer, who wrote academic studies of the criminal mind.

Miss Hildegarde Withers is given to wearing monstrous hats and to bursting in unexpectedly on Inspector Oscar Piper, a gentleman with whom she has had "a long and sometimes stormy association." When she is not walking her equally strong-minded apricot poodle Talleyrand, she can be found listening to police calls on her radio. Three actresses portrayed this spinster schoolteacher on the screen, most notably Edna May Oliver, followed by Helen Broderick and Zasu Pitts.

Snafu Murder

by Stuart Palmer

"I suppose," muttered the sergeant belligerently, "that *you* think you know all about women?"

Mike Maloney, the bartender, mopped thoughtfully at the damp mahogany of the bar. "Only from hearsay, soldier. My weakness is horses."

"Well, how is anybody going to figure a dame who drops a guy cold just because he's got permanent duty right here in little old New York, and turns him down for a sad-sack buck private who's going to be shipped out overseas any day, where he won't be no good to her whatever? It don't make sense."

Mike brightened. "Oh, you mean the mouse who was in here with you Saturday, the one who always wants a Manhattan with two cherries, and half the time she eats them and leaves the drink?" He drew another beer. "She plays the field, I guess. Maybe she likes saying goodbye."

"It'll be goodbye for that sad sack if I run into them tonight," the sergeant promised. Then he put twenty cents down on the bar and went out.

"Trouble, looking for a place to happen," Mike diagnosed. "Well, as long as it don't happen in here—"

"Naturally," said Miss Hildegarde Withers, "I'm more than flattered at being called upon for help by the Federal Bureau of Investigation." She beamed. "Now anything I can do—"

"It wasn't exactly advice that I was looking for," admitted the pleasant if somewhat gimlet-eyed young man who sat on the edge of Miss Withers' best chair. "Just information. You see, there was a disturbance of the peace at the Longacre Bar and Grill last Thursday night, with two soldiers fighting over a girl. What do you know about it?"

The maiden schoolteacher blinked, and then a wry smile cracked her somewhat equine features. "I? Why, my dear young man, you flatter me! But I have an alibi; I was in the auditorium at Public School 38, at a Parent-Teachers' meeting. So the soldiers weren't battling for my favors. As a matter of fact, even in my heyday—"

Mr. McCabe of the FBI had no sense of humor. "I just wanted you to explain something, ma'am. This girl who was the cause of the trouble, she slipped away while the soldiers were being held for the military police. But the cop on the beat got her name, and it was Hildegarde Withers, address 232 West Ninety-Sixth Street, which happens to be a warehouse."

"I suppose it has occurred to you that the girl, to avoid publicity, gave a false name?"

"Yeah. But why yours?"

"I know," countered the schoolteacher, "that it isn't polite to answer a question with another one. But tell me, why is the FBI so interested in a ginmill fracas?"

He hesitated. "It is just possible that there are some other angles. We were tipped off that this girl—the bartenders of the bright-light section call her 'Cherries' because she always asks for two in her drinks—well, she hangs out in the bars where servicemen congregate. Sometimes she picks one up, in a genteel sort of way. But one of the first things she always wants to know is whether he is shipping out overseas or not."

"Now I begin to see," Miss Withers said. "You think she might be a Mata Hari?"

He winced. "Naturally we are suspicious of anyone who shows an interest in troop movements. Too bad we have such a poor description of her—just that she is medium-sized, brownish-blond hair, and young. A quiet type."

"In spite of the Manhattans?"

"She usually just eats the cherries and leaves the drink. Anyway, we believe that she knows you, because your name came to her mind when she had to think of an alias in a hurry."

Miss Withers frowned. "Young man, I have had hundreds of pupils—"

"Ever have one named Mazda? One of the soldiers said she had told him that was her first name. And her last name begins with V, because on another date she carried a handbag with big block initials MV."

"Mazda V. Unusual name. No, Mr. McCabe, I never had a pupil named Mazda anything. I think she got it off a light bulb. But I'll think about the problem, and if I have the slightest inspiration I'll call you."

"That won't be necessary—"

"It's no trouble at all. I'll be delighted to help. You see, they wouldn't let me enlist in the WACs, and I don't feel that I can entertain the troops as a dancing partner at the USO, but a problem like this is right up my alley. I'll report to you tomorrow—"

"I bet she will," Mr. McCabe muttered to himself, after her door had closed upon him. "I should never have mentioned the whole thing." He departed, shoulders sagging.

But Miss Hildegarde Withers was in the seventh heaven. She made herself a strong cup of orange pekoe, washed her hair, and then spent some time studying the inhabitants of her tank of tropical fish—all three being usual sources of inspiration. Finally she dug out a well-worn loose-leaf notebook from her desk drawer, and fell to checking it with a determined grimness.

"Oh, it's you," said Inspector Oscar Piper somewhat later that day, as he pushed aside the remains of his dinner.

Miss Withers surveyed the liverwurst sandwich and container of coffee, and sniffed. "Oscar, you ought to let the Homicide Squad run itself for long enough to go out and get a good hot meal for yourself."

The wiry little Irishman looked at her quizzically. "You didn't come down to Headquarters to discuss my diet. Sit down and get it off your chest."

"You needn't be indelicate. Oscar, you'll be surprised to hear that I am doing some special work for the FBI, and I need your help. I want you to have some of your detectives locate a Miss Mina Vance."

"Why?" asked the Inspector, not unreasonably.

She told him of her interview with McCabe. "Of course it is obvious, Oscar, that the whole thing revolves on the fact that this mysterious Mata Hari person gave my name when she had to think of something quick."

"She might have picked it out of the phone book."

"Which she happened to be carrying under her arm? Don't be silly."

"So what? Maybe she's an old pupil of yours. Anyway, it is departmental policy to let the FBI do their own work, and I advise you to take the same attitude. Besides, the girl is probably just trying to do something for the boys. We get a lot of juvenile delinquents who are khaki-happy."

"This girl is no juvenile. From her description she is between nineteen and twenty-three. That means, since she would have been eight or nine in third grade, that if she was ever a pupil of mine it would have been between the years 1929 and '34. As you know, I keep a file of the names of my pupils. Many of them I could eliminate at once, because I've kept in touch with them. Besides, there are very few surnames beginning with V."

"You're working on the theory that the girl, like most amateurs mixed up in monkey-business, kept her own initials?"

"Except for Thursday night, yes. She departed from tradition then. But you've explained it often enough—it simplifies monograms and things. Anyway, I found that in the years mentioned I had twelve pupils with the initials MV. I could eliminate seven of the twelve at once, either because I know where they are now or because of physical peculiarities which would presumably prevent them from growing up to be sirens. Then I turned to the back copies of the Manhattan telephone book, which I manage to retain for reference, and found just one of the names listed there—and that was only for the summer issue for 1942. 'Vance, Mina, 444 Barrow, PA 5-6763.' No listing for her in later issues, so she evidently moved or didn't pay her phone bill or both. That is why I want you to help me trace her."

The Inspector picked up a dead dank cigar and set it methodically afire. "Look, Hildegarde, this is strictly needle-in-a-haystack. Just because for a few months a long time ago an ex-pupil of yours lived somewhere down in the Village doesn't mean that we have any interest—"

As he spoke, the Inspector was casually shuffling over a stack of routine reports from the precinct homicide men, which was his usual way of signifying that the interview was closed. Suddenly he stopped and whistled—something of a feat since he whistled without disturbing the cigar clamped in his jaws. He whirled suddenly to face his visitor. "Hildegarde, just *where* was it you said that Mina Vance lived?"

"Four-forty-four Barrow. Why?"

"I'll tell you why." There was a wild gleam in the Inspector's eye. "Because you've gone and stumbled into something again! See this report that just came in ten minutes ago? It says there was a homicide in the Ninth Precinct, reported at five-thirty P.M. today, name PFC Ralph Henning, cause of death, strangulation. And the address is 444 Barrow!"

"Oh, my prophetic soul!" quoted Miss Withers. "Oscar, this must be something more than coincidence."

"It's the long nose of Hildegarde Withers," he retorted unkindly. "Just when everything was nice and quiet, you had to come along—"

"I'm coming along to Barrow Street, too. So let us go."

The address specified turned out to be a four-story remodeled brownstone at the end of a narrow street a few blocks from Sheridan Square, in the heart of Greenwich Village. On the surface it didn't appear to be much of a case, or so the precinct boys thought. They were quite obviously surprised and uneasy that Centre Street was taking so much interest in an ordinary mugging.

The body had been discovered by some neighborhood urchins who claimed to have been scouting for waste paper but who were suspected to be in the hot baby-buggy racket. It had been jammed most unceremoniously into the narrow nook beneath the stairs on the first floor of the apartment, at the rear of the hall.

"Around four o'clock this afternoon," was the guess of the medical examiner's assistant. The victim, now awaiting the arrival of the Board of Health truck with its grim wicker basket, turned out to be a thin, wiry young man, dressed in the winter uniform of an Army private, first class. In addition to the heavy G.I. overcoat, fastened neatly on the left-hand buttons, he wore a woman's silk stocking tied cruelly tight around his neck.

The precinct detective said, "So some come-on dame

lured the kid in here with the promise of the old you-know-what, and—"

"And took off her stocking and strangled him with it?" Miss Withers interrupted.

"She probably had a boyfriend waiting. The doors in these old apartment buildings are always on the latch, and they're pretty deserted during the day. If you wanta see his stuff, it's back here."

The detective gestured, and Miss Withers turned willingly away from the deeply purpled face of the victim to gaze upon the contents of his pockets, now turned out upon the windowsill at the end of the hall.

There was a cheap metal watch, still ticking. There was a leather wallet, empty except for a wad of airmail stamps. There was a Zippo lighter, a crumpled pack of cigarettes, a Scout jackknife, a rabbit's-foot key chain with no key, and a small green pamphlet entitled "So You're Shipping Out" and containing facts, figures, and advice over the imprint of the Morale Services Division, Army Service Forces.

"Typical mugging," the Inspector agreed. "Nothing missing but the money."

"Nothing?" inquired Miss Withers with meaning.

"Oh, you mean his Army identification and dogtags? We got those, that's how he was identified. We turned 'em over to the Provost Marshal's office at the Fort."

"I didn't mean that. Look, Oscar. If Private Henning came to the city on leave or on a furlough or whatever they call it, then where are his papers—or his pass?"

"Huh? Well, maybe he was AWOL, how do I know?"

"And his shoes are so unshined, and his uniform so rumpled, and his overcoat buttoned wrong—" Miss Withers shook her head dubiously. "I suppose you're going to interview all the residents of the house?"

"In a way. We're going to have them all down to look at the body, to see if any of them know the poor guy or show any reaction. Psychological stuff, you know."

"I know," said Miss Withers. She watched, from the background, while the residents of the building were paraded before the stiffening exhibit in the hall. Most of the people, she decided, were obviously respectable, honestly shocked at what they had to see, and glad to get back to their little apartments and their private lives.

But not all. There was the stiff, clipped young Navy lieutenant j.g. who held his wife's plump arm tightly in his grasp and stared at the corpse for what seemed and probably was an unnecessarily long time before shaking his head. There were three young men who shared an apartment in which they made lampshades and printed linoleum-cut Christmas cards. They thought for a little while, or pretended to think, that the deceased looked a little like somebody known as "Helmuth," but finally decided it wasn't, after all.

There were two girls, barely out of the bobby-sock stage, who wore Air Corps insignia in defiance of Army regulations, and who went pale and then blushed furiously as they looked at the remains. There was a tall, expensive-looking girl in black hat and silver-fox cape, who gave her name as Miss Andrea Winton. Andrea, Miss Withers noted, looked at the dead man's shoes instead of at his face, which hardly showed any sincere desire to aid in his identification.

"Did you notice, Oscar," she whispered, "that the young lady who just left had very unusual hands? They were rough and reddened, as if she had been washing them over and over again in cold water."

He grinned. "Maybe she just doesn't use the stuff on the right radio program."

"Perhaps. But remember—'All the perfumes of Araby will not sweeten this little hand.' Macbeth."

"I'll make a note of it," the Inspector said wearily.

The remainder of the tenants were even less interesting, and Miss Withers quietly detached herself from the group and slipped forward along the hall into the foyer, where she spent some time in studying the list of tenants' names on the wall. There were, she discovered, no girls living here who had the initials MV. There was no girl living alone here at all, except for Miss Andrea Winton, although the second floor front appeared to be vacant.

The curious schoolteacher also paused briefly near the front door, unlocked as usual, to study the large amount of recent but unclaimed mail which rested on a table there. Most of it was advertising or bills, and all of it addressed to names not now listed among the tenants. Evidently this building was a place favored by people who moved often and left no forwarding address.

Miss Withers went out, past the uniformed cop at the portal, and then hesitated. There had been a card in the hall, underneath the list of tenants, which read *For Manager, ring basement bell.* Like Alice with the bottle marked *Drink Me,* the schoolteacher felt a compulsion to obey. So she turned and went down a narrow stair, the steps of which had been covered with rough boards which creaked dismally under her feet. She found the bell button, and leaned against it.

There was a light within, and the sound of voices, but no answer. She pressed again, and then the door opened and a swarthy young man appeared, hastily and modestly adjusting his suspenders. His would have been a pleasant face if he had been smiling, which he was not.

"Sorry ma'am, we got no vacancies."

Behind him, in a crowded narrow room, Miss Withers could see a table set for supper, and there was the smell of cooking.

"I wasn't looking for an apartment," Hildegarde explained hastily. "I'm just trying to locate a friend of mine who used to live here. Her name was Vance, Mina Vance."

The man scowled. "I don't think we got anybody by

that name. They come and go so fast, though—want to come inside?"

Miss Withers already was in. The place seemed barely to have room for a visitor, it was so crowded with furniture, with mahogany bookcases full of gift editions, with a baby grand piano, with a mammoth radio-phonograph, with heavy rugs and fringed lamps and end-tables and gimcracks.

There were ivory billikins from Alaska, a Japanese flag and two curved swords, plaster pottery from Pompeii, a grass skirt, and even a hideous little *tsanta*, one of the shrunken heads faked by enterprising Canal Zone curio dealers.

"My wife's brother sends that stuff home," offered the host. "He's in the Army. Crowds the place up some, don't it—a little hole like this. But what are you going to do nowadays? Only way to get an apartment was to take the job of managing the place. And we get rent free. Just a minute. About this friend of yours, I'll ask the wife, because she keeps the books." He turned and raising his voice, called "Baby!"

There was a sudden clatter of pans from the kitchen. "You will have to excuse us," the man said, "for having dinner so late. But there was an accident upstairs, and the cops have been running us ragged . . ."

A girl, face flushed red from cooking, came into the room, drying her hands on a dish towel. She looked pleasant, small-townish, and pretty, although there was flour on her cheek and damp curls of reddish hair stuck to her forehead.

"This is Mrs. Tewalt," said the man, a faint note of pride in his voice. "Baby, meet Mrs.—?"

"Miss Withers," said the schoolteacher.

"She's come to ask some questions about a Mina Vance who used to live here," Tewalt went on.

The girl stood solidly upon her flat bedroom slippers,

and knotted the towel. She was a tiny thing, Miss Withers realized, and she was deeply frightened.

"I—" she began. Then she caught her breath. "But—"

"She's all upset," the man said. "The body and all. We were the first ones to see it—after the kids, I mean. Sit down, honey."

But the girl didn't sit. She stared at Miss Withers accusingly. "*That* isn't why you're here! You're not worrying about anybody who used to live here!" She whirled on her husband. "Max, she's a detective! She's with the police!"

There was an uncomfortable pause. "I'm afraid you have seen some misleading publicity," Miss Withers said. "I'm not very close to the police, especially not at the moment. It's really as I said. I'm trying to locate Mina Vance, who once lived here, because I think there is just a faint chance that she may be involved with this murder."

The couple looked at each other. "You do want to see it solved, don't you?" the schoolteacher pressed.

Tewalt spoke. "Of course. We were just—Baby, get the book. We'll look it up."

Silently, the girl went over to a shelf above the fireplace and took down a large account book. "If anybody named Vance ever lived here it must have been a long time ago," she said. "I'll see."

"It was the summer of 1942," Miss Withers said.

"Here it is," the girl said. She showed the record, which proved that from May 15th to December 15th of that year, Mina Vance had occupied the third-floor apartment, paying her rent very irregularly indeed. "She moved out owing three months. I bet I know why it ran so long, too. Before I married him, Max was what you call susceptible, especially for tramps."

Tewalt laughed easily, as if somehow flattered. "She wasn't any tramp, Baby. Had a job as an accountant or something. I never knew where." He shrugged. "Baby here figures she reformed me when we got married last year."

"I wonder—" began Miss Withers, and then cocked her head. "Don't look now," she said softly, "but I just heard somebody come softly down those outside steps. And that same somebody hasn't rung the bell."

She turned and crossed the room, flinging open the door. Inspector Oscar Piper stood outside, looking sheepish. "What," cried Miss Withers, "are you doing here?"

"I'm asking the same question," he barked back. Then he came in, displaying his badge. The young wife gave her husband an "I told you so" look.

"Relax," said the Inspector. "I just wanted to ask some routine questions, but I see somebody beat me to it."

Hastily Miss Withers filled in on what had happened. "I was just about to ask," she continued pleasantly, "if Miss Vance, who once lived here, had left a forwarding address?"

The manager and his wife looked, and found that she hadn't. People who moved without paying three months' rent rarely did.

"Yes," said Mrs. Tewalt bitterly, "and I'll bet—" Suddenly she stiffened. "Oh, heavens, the steaks!" She turned and ran out of the room.

After some more crashing of pans in the kitchen she returned, bearing a platter on which two luscious T-bones were steaming. Another trip, and she produced baked potatoes, broiled mushrooms, a salad, and bread and butter.

"Oscar, we needn't keep this young couple from their dinner," Miss Withers reminded him. "One last question and we're off. Mr. Tewalt, can you tell me if any of your feminine tenants run around a good deal with servicemen?"

"Huh? Why, all of them do, the single ones, I mean. There aren't many of us 4Fs left, you know. There's Miss Chandler and Miss Carlsen on the third floor, and Miss

Winton on the fourth—they all usually have dates with
soldiers and sailors."

His wife added, gently, "But we don't pay a lot of
attention to other people's business, do we, Max?"

The Inspector looked at Miss Withers, with meaning
in his glance. "Well, Hildegarde?"

"Yes, Oscar. I was going to ask if any of the tenants
here had shown any sudden signs of prosperity, but we
won't linger for that now. Good night, Mr. and Mrs.
Tewalt, and thank you."

The girl went to the door with them. "I don't mind
answering that," she said. "Nobody has struck it rich
around here. Oh, I mean a lot of people are making more
money than they used to, but that's one of the bright spots
about a war, isn't it?"

"Good night!" said Miss Withers, with what seemed to
the Inspector unnecessary firmness. They went up the
creaky stairs together. Oscar Piper suggested a hamburger,
but the schoolteacher said she was anxious to get home.

Once back in her little apartment on West Seventy-
Fourth Street, she made herself a cup of tea and then
settled down on a stool before her aquarium. For a happy
hour she lost herself in that glowing wonderland, in that
marine jungle peopled by jeweled neon tetras, by smooth
dark mollies, bulging guppies, and fanciful, delicate bettas
out of a Dali painting.

She even liked watching one of the big river snails,
which had determined to get a breath of air and was
inching its way toward the surface of the tank. She waited,
feeling that her progress in this murder case was slower
even than his, until the greenish-black gastropod reached
the top, took his snifter of air through one sucker, blew it
out gustily, and then let go and floated peacefully down to
the bottom, bubbling a little.

"An excellent idea, relaxation," observed Miss Withers
to herself. She turned out the light over the tank, and

immediately her wonderland became a plain glass box full of murky water peopled with colorless minnows. But it turned out to be easier for the snail to let go than it was for the maiden schoolteacher. She turned and tossed most of the night, and when she finally slept she dreamed of hiking through the snow, and of going back mile after mile along her own trail, looking for something she had lost and could never find again.

Nor could she find it upon wakening. Her first thought was one of guilt at the lateness of the hour, and then she remembered that this was vacation week, and that she need not make her first class today. The day was free—free for worry about the case of the strangled soldier. Somehow she had counted upon her subconscious to come up with the answer to the whole problem in her sleep, but she was right where she had started.

A phone call from the Inspector, arriving as she loaded her percolator for action, did not help. "Just thought you might like to know that we broke the Henning case," he informed her.

"Say no more. I'll be right down."

She arrived at Centre Street twenty minutes later, to find the Inspector in one of his happier moods. "Don't feel bad," he advised her. "This was no job for fancy sleuthing. Nothing you could have done. The case was washed up by pure routine. We just checked with the Army, and—"

"And what?"

"They're bringing the killer in this morning. Stick around, I'll give you the picture..This Henning, he was due to ship out overseas, only he got delayed. And he didn't like sitting around in the staging area, so he tried to make a break for it, without a pass. He ran up against a tough MP, an old-timer who never made a mistake or wouldn't admit it if he had, a guy named Rapf, Sergeant Rapf. Anyway he was taking Henning to the clink, and the soldier broke away from him. Made a clean getaway, I guess he was dying for New York's bright lights.

"But the sergeant figured he knew where his escaped prisoner was heading, so he got some time off, grabbed a taxi, and beat the train here. It was a point of pride with him, see? He hung out in Penn Station, figuring that Henning would have to come through there. Sure enough he saw him, and made the pinch. But he was off duty, and before he could get the regular military police in the station to back him up, Henning had clipped him a judo smack and got away again. So he followed him down in the Village—"

"How much of this is a confession, Oscar?"

"Most of it. All of it, except he says he lost Henning on the subway, and gave it up. We figure, and so does Military Intelligence, that the sergeant, who has had twenty years in the service without ever losing his man, went off the deep end when he caught up with him—hit him too hard, and then tried to cover it up to look like a regular mugging."

"I'd like to meet the prisoner," Miss Withers said dryly. "Especially if he carries silk stockings around with him."

"We got an answer to that too. Men who have served in Central and South America—and the sergeant was in the Canal Zone for a while—had a chance to buy stuff like that. They like to cart it home for their lady friends. Well, we figure Sergeant Rapf had a pair of silk stockings with him that he was saving for some girl, and when he found he had to cover up a murder, he used one to try and make it look like a woman's job."

"I'm still not satisfied," the schoolteacher objected. "Why did Henning come to 444 Barrow?"

"I can answer that one, too," announced Piper triumphantly. "Look, we even checked and found that about four weeks ago a license was issued at City Hall for Ralph

Henning and Miriam Voorhis. And *she* gave that address! I don't know why, maybe she once lived there and didn't want to give her real location. Anyway, Henning was only trying to locate his missing bride, and the MP he had got away from tagged after him and erased him. In spite of the attempt to cover the thing up, I think the killer ought to get off with a plea of manslaughter."

"How nice for him!" said Miss Withers without conviction. That was all she had a chance to say before the prisoner, a tanned, tubby man in his fifties, with a heavy jaw and a pair of dogged, bewildered eyes, was brought in by two MPs and a stiff young captain.

"Your prisoner," said the officer. "As long as you have a warrant, the Army is willing to let you have him. However—" his voice trailed away. It was evident that the captain wanted no part of this.

"How about it, Rapf?" challenged the Inspector. "Make it easy for yourself."

The grizzled sergeant wiped his nose on his sleeve, hashmarks of service notwithstanding, and shook his head. "Look, I'm a family man with three kids at Fort Bragg. The Army's my life. Do you think—?"

"The Army's your life, and you knew you'd be busted for letting a prisoner escape. So you followed him, tangled with him, and finally killed him. We know all about that."

The prisoner licked his lips. "Excuse me, sir, but that ain't it. I'm not saying I wouldn't have liked to beat some sense into his thick head, him trying to bust out of a staging area just to see a dame. But why should I snafu everything up by bumping him—"

"Why should you what?" Miss Withers cut in, blankly.

The men looked at her, all annoyed.

"Army talk," the Inspector said. "Snafu means *situation normal: all fouled up*, or something like that."

The young captain nodded. "By the way, Inspector, this man has an excellent record."

"And he had to keep it perfect, even if it meant killing. Sorry, we're holding him for first-degree murder. Maybe, since overzealousness was the motive, the D.A. will accept a lesser plea, I don't know."

Sergeant Rapf was led away.

Miss Withers buttonholed the Inspector. "Oscar, that phrase fits your case admirably—*situation normal: all fouled up.* Because that sergeant didn't kill anybody, and if he did he wouldn't strangle them with a silk stocking."

"Oh, you can tell the innocent from the guilty just by looking at 'em, huh? Like they wore a mark on their face?"

The schoolteacher's eyes widened. "The Mark of Cain! Yes, Oscar, I mean just that. Sometimes, anyway. And to think that it was right in front of me all the time . . ."

"What was right in front of you? Look, I'm busy—I've got to see the D.A."

"Very well. But as a personal friend, I advise you to book the sergeant on some minor charge, such as being a material witness. And I also advise you to send a telegram, at once."

Piper rubbed his thinning hair. "A telegram to who?"

"To *whom*, please. Well, I really don't know. It will take a trip to City Hall to find that out. However, I can give you the body of the telegram. It should read 'DARLING HAVE THIRTY DAYS FURLOUGH ARRIVE TONIGHT' . . ."

"And signed what?"

"I don't know that either," she said. And hastily departed.

When the telegram was finally dispatched, somewhat against the Inspector's better judgment, it was addressed to a party who, up to this time, had not appeared in the case at all. A Mrs. Robert Ballentyne was the recipient, address 444 Barrow Street, and it was simply signed "Bob." Moreover, the messenger had instructions to leave it on the hall table.

"I still don't get it," the Inspector protested. "Why not just pick a name out of the phone book?"

"Wait and see," Miss Withers retorted. "Oscar, you don't get the significance of the Mark of Cain—nor of the fact that a Corporal Robert Ballentyne married Mavis Vidor at City Hall last June."

"Still barking up that same tree about the mysterious lady spy with the initials MV?"

"Somewhat vulgarly phrased, but essentially correct. By the way, Oscar, if an officer is still stationed in the hallway where the body was found, I want him taken away."

"I sometimes wish somebody would take you away," said the Inspector wearily. "But I suppose I've got to play along, just to give you rope enough—"

"Rope enough to hang a murderer," she concluded crisply. "And now, if you'll excuse me, I'll summon the FBI."

"Why them?" demanded the Inspector.

He was still asking questions at eight o'clock that evening when he met Miss Withers by appointment at the Sheridan Square subway stop. "At least you're on time," the schoolteacher said. "I wish—oh, there he is."

She made the Inspector wait for a moment, and then they walked down the street, a few dozen paces behind the young man in Army uniform, who carried a bulging canvas case and had his overseas cap at a jaunty angle. He finally turned into the doorway of 444 Barrow. As they came inside he was going quickly up the stairs.

The Inspector, intrigued in spite of himself, started to follow, but Miss Withers caught his arm. "Look, Oscar," she whispered. "The telegram's gone—and if you'll notice—" She pointed to the clean new card, neatly lettered, which had appeared somehow on the bulletin board. It read *Ballentyne, 2nd Floor Front.*

They went up the stairs, arriving in time to see the soldier they had been following press his thumb against the bell of the second floor front. Then the door opened, and a girl stood there. Without hesitation she flung her arms around the neck of the soldier, crying "Bob! Bob darling!"

She was held tight and firm, but not lovingly. And the young man who embraced her suddenly became very cold and gimlet-eyed indeed.

"The name isn't Bob. I'm McCabe, of the FBI. You're under arrest, Mrs. Ballentyne . . ."

"Alias Mrs. Max Tewalt, alias Cherries, alias a dozen other names, but originally Mina Vance," put in the schoolteacher, as she and the Inspector came closer. "Thank you, Mr. McCabe, for the impersonation. I was certain that a young lady who made a profession of marrying soldiers for their allotment checks wouldn't be sure of the faces of all her victims."

The girl said something unprintable.

"You should have your mouth washed out with soap," Miss Withers told her. "Yes, I remember you, Mina. You used to cheat in your quizzes, and when we had the Christmas party you went through the line three times and got three bags of candy. As the twig is bent—"

The Inspector had heard enough. "I'm afraid I'll have to take over, Mr. McCabe," he said. "We have a murder rap against this girl."

"And we want her for espionage. So—"

Miss Withers managed to shoo them all back into the small, neat little apartment, into a living room obviously not too lived-in. The two men were politely wrangling over their prisoner, who snarled at both of them. But Miss Withers quietly found the girl's handbag on a dresser, took a ring of keys from it, and then tiptoed out of the room.

Five minutes later she was back, white and shaken. The

argument was still going on, with both McCabe and the Inspector standing on their rights.

"If you'll just listen to me—" she began.

The Inspector waved her to silence. "I'm sorry, Mr. McCabe, but in a case of this kind . . ."

"Neither of you knows what kind of case this is!" Miss Withers burst forth. "There's no espionage—Mina simply wanted to know about troop movements so she could be sure her husbands would be leaving immediately. She married the manager of the building so she could keep an apartment always available in case one of her husbands came home—and so the allotment checks could come in and be thrown on the hall table with the other mail."

McCabe was stubborn. "I still think I have a better case against her than you have. After all, it's pretty likely that the murder was committed by this Tewalt fellow . . ."

"It's pretty unlikely," Miss Withers cut in. "Because Max Tewalt is lying downstairs in the middle of the living room, with a silk stocking knotted around his neck. He was interrupted in the midst of burning the files in which this precious couple kept their records of the names and description of the men Mina married, and copies of her letters to them."

The girl sagged suddenly, so that the Inspector and McCabe had to catch her and ease her into a chair.

"She evidently planned to drop Tewalt and the whole business and go away somewhere as Mrs. Ballentyne," Miss Withers said. "Oscar, you should have known that no matter how wonderful a soldier her brother was, he would not have sent back Japanese swords and pottery from Pompeii and Central American souvenirs and Alaskan ivory. The curios downstairs proved that she was in touch with a lot of soldiers in *different* theaters of war."

"Yeah, but—"

"And one husband, a man she thought was safe on his

way overseas, came back unexpectedly and had to be put away. She killed Ralph Henning—*because only a woman buttons her coat as his was buttoned.* It was all as plain as the nose on your face—remember what I said about the Mark of Cain?"

"Yeah, what about that?" The Inspector and McCabe were both waiting, but it was not to either of them that Miss Withers gave the answer.

"It was the flour on your cheek, dearie," she told the writhing prisoner. "An artistic touch—but much *too* artistic. Because I saw the dinner you cooked last night and *there was nothing in it which required the use of flour!* So you got caught cheating, just as you used to get caught in P. S. 38."

That was it. The girl was taken away, and Mr. McCabe shook hands with the Inspector and then with Miss Withers. "It's been a pleasure being one of your pupils, ma'am," he said.

The Inspector promised to bring her a red apple someday soon.

The Women Detectives
A Chronological Survey

This idiosyncratic and informal bibliography is not, in the strictest sense, scholarly, for lack of space prevents me from giving complete title listings and from including variant editions —English, American, reprint, and so forth. Rather, my purpose is to give interested readers, detective-story addicts, and second-hand-bookstore browsers an inventory of names with which they can familiarize themselves should they wish to pursue further the exploits of the many women detectives. My descriptions are intended to indicate the wide variety of these heroines and thus to supplement my introduction.

The research I have done is a combination of fifteen years of reading and collecting, plus several months of intensive poking around in card catalogues. I have, of course, relied greatly on the standard authorities in the field, such as Howard Haycraft, Ellery Queen, Dorothy Glover, and Graham Greene (the last-named pair for Victorian detective fiction), and I have had many good leads supplied by enthusiastic scholar-collectors who were aware of my project. Still, it is not impossible or unlikely that others will have, or will discover, additions to this list. Moreover, I have had to eliminate (regretfully) those heroines about whom I could turn up no first hand or verifiable information: creations with tantalizing names like *Mura, the Western Lady Detective; Lady*

Kate, the Dashing Female Detective; and *The Bobbed-Hair Detective.*

I have tried to avoid the inclusion of HIBK female characters who do incidental detection in books that are more romance or romantic mystery than they are straight detective fiction. This eliminates the novels of Mabel Seeley, for one, and also the major part of the output of Mary Roberts Rinehart and Mignon G. Eberhart. Cataloguing these heroines is better left to the person who wishes to chronicle the "damsel-in-distress" school from Mrs. Radcliffe through the dime novels to the current "Gothic" phenomenon.

I have left out most of the female halves of the many popular sleuthing couples: Nora Charles, Pam North, Haila Troy, Jane Brown, Helene Justus, Suzy Marshall, Betty Jones, Tuppence Beresford, Jean Abbott, Elsie Mae Hunt. Excluded too are such secondary figures as Della Street, Isis Klaw, Nikki Porter, Lucy Hamilton, Polly Burton, and Peter Wimsey's own Miss Climpson. In regard to such important personalities as Harriet Vane and Agatha Christie's Mrs. Ariadne Oliver (both detective-story writers and both, to some extent, author surrogates), it becomes more and more difficult to make the necessary arbitrary distinctions. I have reluctantly drawn the line and left them out also.

The last omission I wish to specify is that of the girl detectives: Nancy Drew, the Dana Girls, and the other ageless teen-agers who drove roadsters and found clues in crumbling castles and skeletons in the neighbor's cupboards. The proliferation and sameness of these titles is so great that to include them would unbalance the roster too heavily in their favor.

With some of the earliest heroines, I have allowed greater latitude, following the lead of those critics and historians who have labeled many doubtful characters "women detectives."

In each case, the places and dates given are intended to indicate the original publication. However, it must be remembered that many of these works appeared initially, in story or serial form, in magazines or newspapers before they were issued in book form. Where possible, I have indicated this.

ABBREVIATIONS

ss   short story/short stories

EQ '43   Ellery Queen, ed., *The Female of the Species* (Boston: Little, Brown & Co., 1943). An anthology of the great women detectives and criminals.

VDF   *Victorian Detective Fiction.* A catalogue of the collection made by Dorothy Glover and Graham Greene. Bibliographically arranged by Eric Osborne and introduced by John Carter (London Bodley Head, 1966).

For further information on other works cited, see Selected Bibliography, on pages 379–80.

The Late 19th and Early 20th Century

MRS. PASCHAL. "Anonyma." *The Experiences of a Lady Detective* (London, 1861? 1884?); *The Revelations of a Lady Detective* (London, 1864?). See Introduction, pages xvi–xix.

THE FEMALE DETECTIVE. Andrew Forrester, Jr. *The Female Detective* (London, 1864). See Introduction, pages xvii–xviii.

VALERIA BRITTEN WOODVILLE. Wilkie Collins. *The Law and the Lady* (London, 1875). Dorothy Sayers, in her introduction to *The Omnibus of Crime*, considers Valeria Woodville and an earlier Collins heroine—Magdalen Vanstone in *No Name* (London, 1862)—to be attempts at the woman detective, resulting from Collins' fascination with the strong-minded female character. *The Law and the Lady* is described briefly on page xx of my own introduction; *No Name* is simply a story of revenge and of Miss Vanstone's search for a lost "Secret Trust."

CLARICE DYKE. Harry Rockwood. *Clarice Dyke, the Female Detective* (New York, known only in an 1883 reprint edition). The book jacket says of her: "As the wife and confidante of one of the most skillful detectives living, she had become an enthusiast in the profession. More than once had her wit and forethought proven themselves equal to Donald Dyke's, and more than once had she rendered him substantial aid in the ferreting out of mysterious crimes."

DOLL RAINBOW. Thomas Wright. *The Mystery of St. Dunstan's* (London, 1892). Doll Rainbow is listed in *VDF*, where she is described as "a pickpocket."

LAURA KEEN. C. Little. "Laura Keen, the Queen of Detectives" (New York, 1892). Printed in *The New York Detective Library*. Fearlessly, she packs two pistols and a bowie knife. In this hair-raising, melodramatic series of episodes, she is accompanied by a "darky bootblack" and an Indian.

LOVEDAY BROOKE. Catherine Louisa Pirkis. *The Experiences of Loveday Brooke, Lady Detective* (London, 1894). See story introduction, page 3.

CORALIE URQUHART. M. E. Braddon. *Thou Art the Man* (London, 1894). Coralie Urquhart is listed in *VDF*, where she is described simply as "a lady's companion." Mary Elizabeth Braddon was the author of one of the most famous mystery and sensation novels of the nineteenth century, *Lady Audley's Secret* (1862).

"THE SQUIRREL." Carlton Strange. *The Beechcourt Mystery* (London, 1894). In *VDF*, "The Squirrel" is described as "a poacher's daughter."

ANNIE CORY. Mrs. George Corbett. *When the Sea Gives Up Its Dead, A Thrilling Detective Story* (London, 1894). Listed in *VDF*, where it is explained that Annie Cory does her detecting in conjunction with her father. The same author wrote *Adventures of a Lady Detective* (London, about 1890).

ROSE CORTENAY. Milton Danvers. *The Fatal Finger Mark, Rose Cortenay's First Case* (London, 1895). Listed in *VDF*. She is the "principal lady agent" of Robert Spicer, who is the leading detective in other titles by the same author.

FLORENCE ATWATER RENWICK. Richard Henry Savage. *Checked Through Missing, Trunk No. 17580: A Story of New York Life* (New York, 1896). Listed in *VDF*. She is a happily married, very rich young woman who hires detectives to find a missing friend. Only near the end does she do a spot of investigating herself, in disguise.

DORCAS DENE. George R. Sims. *Dorcas Dene, Detective: Her Adventures* (London, 1897). A second series appeared in 1898. See story introduction, page 34.

LAURA METCALF. Headon Hill, pseud. of Francis Edward Grainger. *By a Hair's-Breadth* (London, 1897). Listed in *VDF*. All that Miss Metcalf does, in this tale of an unsuccessful plot to assassinate the Tsar of Russia, is attempt to keep a friend's fiancé from being exposed as the lovesick tool of a seductive nihilist princess.

MISS AMELIA BUTTERWORTH. Anna Katharine Green (Mrs. Charles Rohlfs). *The Affair Next Door* (New York, 1897); *Lost Man's Lane* (New York, 1898). See Introduction, pages xxi–xxii.

MISS VAN SNOOP. Clarence Rook. "The Stir Outside the Café Royal" (London, 1898). Listed in *VDF*. This appeared originally as a *ss* in the September issue of *The Harmsworth Magazine*. See story introduction, page 62.

MISS LOIS CAYLEY. Grant Allen. *Miss Cayley's Adventures* (London, 1899). As the title indicates, Miss Cayley is more of an intrepid adventuress than a sleuth. A graduate of Girton College, Cambridge, she considers herself a "modern woman." In the course of an around-the-world jaunt, she rides a camel, hunts tigers, races bicycles, and goes mountain climbing. She also rescues a fellow Englishwoman from forced entry into a harem, foils a jewel thief, and proves the authenticity of a lost will in order to restore the honor of her fiancé.

MRS. MOLLIE DELAMERE. Beatrice Heron-Maxwell. *The Adventures of a Lady Pearl-Broker* (London, 1899). She is a widow who dabbles in journalism and who, in order to support herself, consents to act as an appraiser and secret go-between for a pearl merchant. She is informed by her employer that "ladies seem to become expert without any training at all." Mrs. Delamere sustains a great deal of physical abuse while thwarting the activities of various burglars and kidnappers.

HAGAR STANLEY. Fergus Hume. *Hagar of the Pawn-Shop* (London, 1899). A gypsy pawnbroker of considerable spirit, she is more of a problem-solver than a detective. Though she is untaught, her Romany heritage makes her naturally shrewd and quick-witted, and her adventures follow the appearance of unusual pawned objects.

FLORENCE CUSACK. L. T. Meade and Robert Eustace. Listed in *VDF*. Four *ss* which appeared in *The Harmsworth Magazine:* "Mr. Bovey's Unexpected Will" (April 1899); "The Arrest of Captain Vandaleur" (July 1899); "A Terrible Railway Ride" (July 1900); and "The Outside Ledge—A Cablegram Mystery" (October 1900). See story introduction, page 70.

HILDA WADE. Grant Allen. *Hilda Wade: A Woman with Great Tenacity of Purpose* (London, 1900). A nurse, she is portrayed as a "natural" detective because of her photographic memory and because she possesses "in so large a measure the deepest feminine gift—intuition." An interesting historical footnote to this book is that the last chapter was finished by Conan Doyle as a gesture to his late neighbor.

DORA MYRL. Matthias McDonnell Bodkin. *Dora Myrl: The Lady Detective* (London, 1900). She is a professional detective-consultant, working on her own rather than employed by an agency.

GEORGIE NAPPER. Sarah Folsom Ennebuske. *"A Detective in Petticoats"—A Comedy in Three Acts for Female Characters Only* (Boston, 1900). Published in pamphlet form four years after the original performance at Radcliffe College. Miss Napper is a crude parody of the "lady sleuth" who, in this farce of mistaken identity, is determined to get her man, a crook named Burglar Bill.

BELLA THORN. Tom Gallon. *The Girl Behind the Keys* (London, about 1903). She is a typist whose employment with the Secretarial Supply Syndicate, Ltd., involves her in her investigative exploits.

KITTY CLOVER. Ella Wheeler Wilcox. "Detective Kitty" (New York, 1903). A *ss* in the September 5 issue of Street & Smith's *New York*

Weekly. When the popularity of an obviously determined flirt threatens her sister's romance, Kitty delves into the past life of this stranger to their circle, and her skillful amateur detection turns up a variety of scandalous activities to discredit the vamp.

MISS FRANCES BAIRD. Reginald Wright Kauffman. *Miss Frances Baird, Detective: A Passage from her Memoirs* (Boston, 1906). The reader is told, in the author's dedication, that this case is based on one of many related to him by a dear friend who is a real-life, professional female sleuth. Miss Baird falls in love with the accused after she has made a case against him, then attempts to prove his innocence. (An unusual touch of period color has her frequenting a New York City Turkish bath.)

LADY MOLLY. Baroness Emmuska Orczy (Mrs. Montagu Barstow). *Lady Molly of Scotland Yard* (London, 1910). See story introduction, page 90.

JUDITH LEE. Richard Marsh. *Judith Lee, Some Pages from Her Life* (London, 1912); *The Adventures of Judith Lee* (London, 1916). She is a teacher of the deaf-and-dumb and is an adept at lip-reading. Because of this skill, she stumbles on a variety of crimes and is able to solve them.

MISS MADELYN MACK. Hugh C. Weir. *Miss Madelyn Mack, Detective* (Boston, 1914). See story introduction, page 112.

VIOLET STRANGE. Anna Katharine Green. *The Golden Slipper and Other Problems for Violet Strange* (New York, 1915). See story introduction, page 152.

CONSTANCE DUNLAP. Arthur B. Reeve. *Constance Dunlap—Woman Detective* (New York, 1916). See story introduction, page 172. This is the first book edition of this series of stories; apparently their initial appearance was in *Pearson's Magazine*, during the years 1913–1914.

MILLICENT NEWBERRY. Jeanette Lee. *The Green Jacket* (New York, 1917); *The Mysterious Office* (New York, 1922); *Dead Right* (New

York, 1925). Millicent Newberry is a small woman who dresses entirely in gray. As head of a consulting agency named after herself, she specializes in a gentle omniscience and refers to herself as a "mind nurse." She will undertake to solve cases personally only if the criminal, when caught, is turned over to her for rehabilitation.

EVELYN TEMPLE. Ronald Gorell Barnes (Lord Gorell). *In the Night* (London, 1917). Dorothy Sayers considers Evelyn Temple a good example of the amateur woman detective whose involvement stems from her being a member of the family or houseparty. She does scientific detection and deductive reasoning but, unhappily, follows the footprints and fingerprints to the *wrong* conclusion. She learns from the inspector in charge of the case that "the same facts can often be explained in several different ways," though he tells her that she does have "a real gift."

LUCILLE DARE. Marie Connor Leighton. *Lucille Dare, Detective* (London, about 1919). She is a mistress of disguise and has a "sleuth-hound instinct." When a friend's betrothed is accused of murdering his father-in-law-to-be, she steps in to prove him innocent and herself falls passionately in love with him. Throughout the story, many of her past cases are referred to.

The 20s, 30s, and 40s

DAPHNE WRAYNE. Valentine, pseud. of Archibald Thomas Pechey. *The Adjusters* (London, 1922). Also in many other books written by Pechey under the pen name of Mark Cross. With an obvious debt to Edgar Wallace's *The Four Just Men*, Daphne Wrayne and her four debonair young men comrades have dedicated themselves to "the adjustment of the inequalities that at present exist between the criminal and the victim." Though she seems to be playing Maid Marion to a group of modern-day Robin Hoods, an observer notes that she has the "criminal life of London at her slim fingers' ends." A story entitled "The Man Who Scared the Bank" is included in *EQ '43*.

MISS BALMY RYMAL. Arthur Stringer. *The Diamond Thieves* (Indianapolis, 1923). A publisher's blurb calls this "a detective story with an innovation," the novelty being that a woman is placed "in the role of huntress of a band of desperate criminals." Balmy is employed by Security Alliance, whose main client is the Jewelers' Protective Union. She is forced to hide her sentimental nature behind a tough exterior in order to survive what she terms "a treadmill of crime."

SYLVIA SHALE. Mrs. Sydney Groom. *Detective Sylvia Shale* (London, 1923). She is employed by a New York detective bureau. At the age of twenty-five, her consuming ambition is to crack a really big case, and she states her desire to forgo marriage in order to devote her life to her work. She is described as looking very refined, with "nothing in the least mannish about her appearance."

ELINOR VANCE. Frederic A. Kummer. "Diamond Cut Diamond" (1924). Included in *EQ '43*. She is an independently rich young woman who enjoys solving curious problems and helping people who are in trouble.

RUTH KELSTERN. Edgar Jepson and Robert Eustace. "The Tea Leaf" (1925). This is one of three *ss* chosen to represent the woman detective in Ellery Queen's mammoth collection *101 Years' Entertainment: The Great Detective Stories 1841–1941*. Ruth Kelstern uses her scientific knowledge to clear her lover of the charge of murdering her father.

"MISS PINKERTON." Mary Roberts Rinehart. "The Buckled Bag" and "Locked Doors," included in *Mary Roberts Rinehart's Crime Book* (New York, 1925), mark the first appearance of Nurse Hilda Adams, whose nickname was bestowed upon her affectionately by a police inspector who makes use of her talents. (The famous Allan Pinkerton, a private inquiry agent who wrote many books, had become an eponym for "detective.") Subscribing to the belief that "illness follows crime," Miss Pinkerton recognizes the worth of becoming an "invisible" spy in a household where a misdeed has occurred. She satisfies her scruples by remembering that she is "a nurse first, a police agent second." *Miss Pinkerton* (New York, 1932) and *The Haunted Lady* (New York, 1942) are book-length treatments. A 1932 film featured Joan Blondell in the role of Miss Adams/"Pinkerton."

MADAME ROSIKA STOREY. Hulbert Footner. *The Under Dogs* (New York, 1925); *Madame Storey* (New York, 1926); *The Velvet Hand: New Madame Storey Mysteries* (New York, 1928); *The Almost Perfect Murder: A Case Book of Madame Storey* (Philadelphia, 1937); *The Casual Murderer: More Cases from Madame Storey's File* (Philadelphia, 1937). The first-listed is a novel, the rest collections of long stories which probably began appearing separately as early as 1922. Other book-length titles include *The Doctor Who Held Hands* (New York, 1929) and *Dangerous Cargo* (New York, 1934). For further information, see story introduction, page 192.

LESLIE MAUGHAN. Edgar Wallace. *The Square Emerald* (London, 1926). American title: *The Girl from Scotland Yard*. The daughter of a former assistant commissioner, she has no need to earn her living, but police investigation is in her blood and she works her way up in the Criminal Investigation Department. The general consensus is that "there never was a woman better fitted to hold down a high position at the Yard." Yet a typical piece of Wallace prose has another character think to herself, upon meeting Miss Maughan, "A detective—this slip of a girl!" Another Wallace creation is Mrs. Jane Ollerby, a high-ranking Yard detective who appears in *Traitor's Gate* (London, 1927).

NURSE SARAH KEATE. Mignon G. Eberhart. *The Patient in Room 18* (New York, 1929); *From This Dark Stairway* (New York, 1931); *Wolf in Man's Clothing* (New York, 1942); *Man Missing* (New York, 1954); others. She is "a spinster of uncertain age, unromantic tendencies, sharp eyesight, and an excellent stomach." With regard to Nurse Adams, the similarities are greater than the differences, though Eberhart has a sprightlier style.

MISS MAUD SILVER. Patricia Wentworth, pseud. of Dora Amy Dillon Turnbull. Among the numerous Miss Silver titles are *The Grey Mask* (Philadelphia, 1929), *Miss Silver Deals with Death* (Philadelphia, 1943), and *The Alington Inheritance* (Philadephia, 1958). Having abandoned "the scholastic profession for the much more lucrative work of private detection," she depends upon her shrewdness to keep her in her chosen "shabby Victorian" splendor. Like Miss Marple, whom she resembles, she plays "her part in restraining the criminal and protecting the innocent" throughout the villages and country houses of England.

MISS JANE MARPLE. Agatha Christie. *Murder at the Vicarage* (London, 1930). The collection *The Thirteen Problems* (London, 1932) contains the earliest Miss Marple stories, which date from 1928. As most everyone knows, she is a "white-haired old lady with a gentle, appealing manner," whose unerring knowledge of human nature leads her to suspect that the worst is usually the truth. Other novel-length Miss Marples include *The Body in the Library* (London, 1942), *A Murder Is Announced* (London, 1950), *At Bertram's Hotel* (London, 1965), and *Nemesis* (London, 1971). During the sixties, Miss Marple was portrayed on screen by Margaret Rutherford, who acted the part with great zest though with little resemblance to the original.

KYRA SOKRATESCU. Gilbert Frankau. Four *ss:* "Who Killed Castelvetri?" and "Misogyny at Mougins" from *Concerning Peter Jackson* (London, 1931); "Christmas with Kyra" from *Wine, Women, and Waiters* (London, 1932); "Tragedy at St. Tropez" from *Experiments in Crime and Other Stories* (London, 1937), which is included in *EQ '43*. Kyra is a Rumanian playgirl who considers detection an intellectual exercise and a good way to stave off boredom.

SOLANGE FONTAINE. F. Tennyson Jesse. *The Solange Stories* (London, 1931). The daughter of a consultant to the French Sûreté, she solves crimes by combining her talent for scrutinizing character and her peculiar gift for "feeling" the presence of evil.

HILDEGARDE WITHERS. Stuart Palmer. *The Penguin Pool Murder* (New York, 1931); *Miss Withers Regrets* (New York, 1947); *The Green Ace* (New York, 1950); others. Many of the early Hildegarde Withers novels have the word "puzzle" in the title. *The Riddles of Hildegarde Withers* (New York, 1947) is a collection of some of the many Miss Withers *ss.* For further information, see story introduction, page 334.

BARONESS CLARA LINZ. E. Phillips Oppenheim. *Advice, Ltd.* (London, 1932). See story introduction, page 218. When some of these stories appeared in the *Woman's Home Companion* (1933–1934), the character of Clara Linz was transformed inexplicably into that of a young Englishwoman, Elizabeth Martin.

OLGA KNARESBROOK. Hazel Campbell. *Olga Knaresbrook: Detective* (London, 1933). She is a young woman who pursues a career as a professional detective.

MRS. WARRENDER. G. D. H. and M. Cole. A *ss* in *A Lesson in Crime* (London, 1933). Also, *Mrs. Warrender's Profession* (London, 1939). See story introduction, page 308.

GWYNN LEITH. Viola Brothers Shore. "The MacKenzie Case" (1934). Originally appeared in *Mystery League Magazine*. One of three *ss* representing the woman detective in Queen's *101 Years' Entertainment*. She is an attractive amateur sleuth very similar to the Lockridges' Mrs. North.

GRACE LATHAM. Leslie Ford, pseud. of Mrs. Zenith Jones Brown. Novels featuring this widowed Washington socialite began appearing in the early part of the thirties. Titles include *The Strangled Witness* (New York, 1934), *Ill Met by Moonlight* (New York, 1937), *The Murder of the Fifth Columnist* (New York, 1941), and *The Philadelphia Murder Story* (New York, 1945). Mrs. Latham exudes Southern gentility, gushes a great deal, and inevitably winds up confronting the murderer, usually with the aid of the stoically handsome Colonel John Primrose.

SUSAN DARE. Mignon G. Eberhart. *The Cases of Susan Dare* (New York, 1934). See story introduction, page 243.

SALLY CARDIFF. Vincent Starrett. "The Bloody Crescendo" (1934). Taken from *Real Detective Tales and Mystery Stories* and retitled "Murder at the Opera" for inclusion in *EQ '43*. A young woman with an impersonal curiosity, she prefers the excitement of the chase to the meting out of justice.

MATILDA PERKS. Ralph C. Woodthorpe. *Death in a Little Town* (London, 1935); *The Shadow on the Downs* (London, 1935). Miss Perks is the antithesis of Jane Marple. A plump little woman with a prominent hooked nose and a pronounced mustache, she has a deep, gruff voice which misleads strangers into believing her bark is worse than her bite. Actually, she is consistently acid-tongued and wholly formidable. The sleuthing instincts of this former schoolteacher stem from an academic fondness for the strictest truth.

LUCIE MOTT. E. Phillips Oppenheim. *Ask Miss Mott* (London, 1936). Miss Mott is the advice columnist for a London newspaper. While she is deciding whether or not she wants to be wooed by a gentleman crook named Violet Joe, she lets him rescue her from a number of scrapes. Her uncle is a detective superintendent at Scotland Yard. Yet another Oppenheim heroine was *Miss Brown of XYO* (1927).

ETHEL THOMAS. Cortland Fitzsimmons. *The Whispering Window* (New York, 1936); *The Moving Finger* (New York, 1937); *Mystery at Hidden Harbor* (New York, 1938); *The Evil Men Do* (New York, 1941). Miss Thomas is "one of the New York Thomases . . . born to wealth and a position in society." She is also a self-described old maid who has outlived the rest of her family. She opines that a murder is "like a good fire—if they must happen I want to be where I can see them and be a part of the activity." In all respects, she is a direct descendant of Amelia Butterworth.

MRS. PALMYRA EVANGELINE PYM. Nigel Morland. Some of the many titles featuring Mrs. Pym are *The Clue of the Bricklayer's Aunt* (London, 1936), *The Corpse on the Flying Trapeze* (London, 1941), *Sing a Song of Cyanide* (London, 1953), and *So Quiet a Death* (London, 1960). A deputy commissioner at Scotland Yard, she is stern, dispassionate, and tough. Her one weakness is her powerful motorcar, which she drives at top speed.

ROSE GRAHAM. Karl Detzer. "Murder in the Movies" (1937). Taken from *The American Legion Monthly* and included in *EQ '43*. Rose Graham is a professional script girl who solves a murder on a Hollywood set.

ADELAIDE ADAMS. Anita Blackmon. *Murder à la Richelieu* (New York, 1937). Her fellow residents of the sedate Hotel Richelieu refer to this amateur sleuth affectionately as "old battle-ax." A marvelous piece of HIBK has her saying, "Nor at any time could any power on earth have convinced me that I should find myself late one terrible night, sans my dress and false hair, dangling from the eaves of the Richelieu Hotel in pursuit of a triple slayer."

BEATRICE ADELA LESTRANGE BRADLEY. Gladys Mitchell. Among the many Beatrice Bradley titles are *Come Away, Death* (London, 1937), *Tom Brown's Body* (London, 1949), *Watson's Choice* (London, 1955), *Pageant of Murder* (London, 1965), and *A Javelin for Jonah* (London, 1974). See also story introduction, page 316.

SALLY "SHERLOCK" HOLMES LANE. Paul Gallico. "Solo Job" (1937). Originally published in *Cosmopolitan* Magazine and included in *EQ '43*. She "was the best girl reporter on the *Standard*, and probably the best man, too. She had a fantastic nose for news and a lot of theories." She exhibits an extraordinary amount of courage when she unwittingly stumbles upon a baby-killing racket.

THEODOLINDA BONNER. Rex Stout. *The Hand in the Glove* (New York, 1937). With a woman partner, Dol Bonner runs a detective agency on Park Avenue. In a 1938 novel featuring Nero Wolfe, *Too Many Detectives*, she makes an appearance along with another female operative named Sally Colt, causing Archie Goodwin to deliver a resentful, chauvinist soliloquy on "she-dicks." Also, see Introduction, page xxvii.

JANE AMANDA EDWARDS. Charlotte Murray Russell. Among the Jane Edwards stories, which began appearing in the middle of the thirties, are *Tiny Diamond* (New York, 1937), *Murder on the Pathway* (New York, 1938), and *Ill Met in Mexico* (New York, 1948). She is an unmarried woman in her forties, unemployed and of independent means. It is generally in Midwestern settings that she indulges what her sister terms her "preoccupation with murder mysteries."

EMMA MARSH. Elizabeth Dean. *Murder Is a Collector's Item* (New York, 1939); *Murder Is a Serious Business* (New York, 1940); *Murder a Mile High* (New York, 1944). Emma Marsh is an attractive young woman with a pronounced fondness for night life. Her job as an assistant in a Boston antique shop involves her in murder, thus developing in her a taste for amateur detection.

MISS RACHEL MURDOCK. D. B. Olsen, pseud. of Dolores Hitchens. *The Cat Saw Murder* (New York, 1939); *Cats Don't Need Coffins* (New York, 1946); *The Cat Walks* (New York, 1953); others. Miss Rachel is a spinster in her seventies who lives in Los Angeles with her sister, Miss Jennifer, and her cat, Samantha. Her grandmotherly mien is misleading, for there is nothing she enjoys more than a lurid movie mystery, and she is able to look down the barrel of a gun with calm relish.

BERTHA COOL. A. A. Fair, pseud. of Erle Stanley Gardner. The long series of books featuring Bertha Cool and her assistant, Donald Lam, began with *The Bigger They Come* (New York, 1939). Although technically they qualify as a sleuthing couple, the name of the agency is BERTHA COOL—CONFIDENTIAL INVESTIGATIONS. She is described as "profane, massive, belligerent, and bulldog."

JANE CARBERRY. Beryl Simons. *Jane Carberry: Detective* (London, 1940); others. She is a society woman who becomes involved with crime, initially through a mysterious jewel theft and murder.

AMANDA AND LUTIE BEAGLE. Torrey Chanslor. *Our First Murder* (New York, 1940); *Our Second Murder* (New York, 1941). They are a pair of elderly sisters who inherit their brother Ezekiel's New York detective agency. After moving from their home in East Biddicutt, they tackle with prim enthusiasm cases involving a headless corpse and a murdered debutante.

SISTER URSULA. H. H. Holmes, pseud. of Anthony Boucher (pseud. of William Anthony Parker White). Sister Ursula appears in five ss and two novels. "Coffin Corner" was written especially for *EQ '43*. The two books are *Nine Times Nine* (New York, 1940) and *Rocket to the Morgue* (New York, 1942). She is a nun-detective who, in one tale, reminds the culprit that "one doesn't joke about murder in the confessional."

HANNAH VAN DOREN. Dwight V. Babcock. *The Gorgeous Ghoul* (New York, 1941); *A Homicide for Hannah* (New York, 1941). She is an angelic-looking, hard-drinking writer for true crime and detective magazines. Another character describes her: "Downtown around city hall and the county courts she's known as 'Homicide Hannah, the Gorgeous Ghoul.' She's bloodthirsty. She just goes around hoping for a homicide to happen to someone. The gorier the better, and with a sex angle if possible."

LACE WHITE. Jeanette Covert Nolan. *Final Appearance* (New York, 1943), *I Can't Die Here* (New York, 1945), and *Sudden Squall* (New York, 1955) are three of the Lace White titles. She describes herself as a middle-aged spinster, "by profession a writer of what is often called escape literature. Also, and quite incidentally, an honorary lieutenant of State Police, an anomalous position devoid of rewards, emoluments, or specified duties." The stories take place in and around Dugger County, Indiana.

DESDEMONA "SQUEAKIE" MEADOW. Margaret Manners. "Squeakie's First Case" (1943) was taken from *Ellery Queen's Mystery Magazine* and used in *EQ '43*. Others include "Squeakie's Second Case" (1945) and "Matter for a May Morning" (1946). She is a wide-eyed, talkative gamine who startles her husband by coming up with the solutions to crimes.

AMY BREWSTER. Sam Merwin, Jr. *Knife in My Back* (New York, 1945); *Message from a Corpse* (New York, 1945); *A Matter of Policy* (New York, 1946). A three-hundred-pound, cigar-smoking, blue-blooded lawyer-*cum*-financier, Amy Brewster has "all the deft grace of a Pershing tank." She can never resist coming to the rescue of young friends who have gotten themselves in trouble. In one book, she downs the villain with the spray from a seltzer bottle.

DR. MARY FINNEY. Matthew Head, pseud. of John Canaday. *The Devil in the Bush* (New York, 1945); *Congo Venus* (New York, 1950); others. She is a medical missionary in Africa. A large, dowdy woman with red hair and freckles, she uses her scientific intellect plus her sturdy common sense to solve several exotic murders.

MISS LUCY PYM. Josephine Tey, pseud. of Elizabeth Mackintosh. *Miss Pym Disposes* (London, 1946). Having written, much to her surprise, a best-selling book on psychology, Miss Pym is invited to lecture at a women's college of physical culture. When confronted with a student murder, she attempts to put her theories into practice and is dismayed to learn that not all solutions are clear-cut.

MISS JULIA TYLER. Louisa Revell. *The Bus Station Murders* (New York, 1947); *See Rome and Die* (New York, 1958); *A Party for the Shooting* (New York, 1960); others. Miss Tyler is an elderly Southern gentlewoman, a retired Latin teacher who adores equally traveling and reading detective stories; she winds up combining sightseeing with sleuthing.

GALE GALLAGHER. Gale Gallagher, pseud. of Will Oursler. *I Found Him Dead* (New York, 1947); *Chord in Crimson* (New York, 1949). She is the head of her own agency, the Acme Investigating Bureau. For more information, see Introduction, page xxviii.

EVE GILL. Selwyn Jepson. *Man Running* (London, 1948); *The Black Italian* (London, 1954); *The Laughing Fish* (London, 1960); others. The first title was made into the Alfred Hitchcock film *Stagefright*, with Jane Wyman playing Eve Gill, a young woman who is unable to resist intruding in police affairs.

MIRIAM BIRDSEYE. Nancy Spain. *Poison for Teacher* (London, 1949); *Out, Damned Tot* (London, 1952); others. Miriam is an ex-actress turned detective who, when not in her flat, leaves a placard on the door which reads "Out—Gone to Crime."

The 50s, 60s, and 70s

MARION PHIPPS. Phyllis Bentley. Since 1952 there have been many *ss* in *Ellery Queen's Mystery Magazine* featuring this English detective novelist who happens upon crimes and proceeds to solve them.

SALLY DEAN. Leonard Gribble and Geraldine Laws. *Sally of Scotland Yard* (London, 1954). A member of the Yard's famed Ghost Squad, Sally works on undercover cases.

ANNETTE KERNER. Annette Kerner. *Woman Detective* (London, about 1954). This is a nonfiction memoir of a real-life female sleuth, head of the Mayfair Detective Agency and an investigator for over twenty years.

SOEUR ANGÈLE. Henri Catalan, pseud. of Henri Dupuy-Mazuel. *Soeur Angèle and the Embarrassed Ladies* (London, 1955); *Soeur Angèle and the Ghosts of Chambord* (London, 1956); *Soeur Angèle and the Bell-Ringer's Niece* (London, 1957). Another nun-detective, this time a French one.

MARION KERRISON. Edward Grierson. *The Second Man* (New York, 1956). See Introduction, page xxviii.

MISS HOGG. Austin Lee. *Call in Miss Hogg* (London, 1956); *Miss Hogg and the Brontë Murders* (London, 1956); *Miss Hogg's Last Case* (London, 1963); others. Another ex-school-mistress turned private investigator.

HONEY WEST. G. G. Fickling. *A Gun for Honey* (New York, 1958); *Blood and Honey* (New York, 1961); others. A short-lived television series in the early sixties starred Anne Francis as this California private eye. Besides a debt to such male characters as Brett Halliday's Mike Shayne, the style of Honey West seems to owe something to radio's "Candy Matson," a detective series which lasted from the end of the forties to 1951. For further information on Honey, see Introduction, page xxix.

MARLA TRENT. Henry Kane. *Private Eyeful* (New York, 1959). Marla is a blonde with a voluptuous figure and a doctorate in abnormal psychology, a lethal combination for unwary criminals.

DAYE SMITH. Frank Usher. *Death in Error* (London, 1959); *Who Killed Rosa Gray?* (London, 1962); others. Daye is a painter and an amateur detective.

THE HON. VICTORIA PUMPHREY. H. C. Bailey. "A Matter of Speculation." First published in *Ellery Queen's Mystery Magazine* in 1961. After solving the mystery of a strange impersonation, this benevolent, aristocratic young amazon determines to set herself up as a professional "Friend of the Family: relatives discovered or destroyed; domestic quarrels settled; mysteries solved—family skeletons a specialty." Bailey, the creator of Mr. Reggie Fortune, was one of the star authors of the Golden Age.

CHARMIAN DANIELS. Jennie Melville. *Come Home and Be Killed* (London, 1962); *A New Kind of Killer* (London, 1970). A member of the Deerham constabulary, she represents the new breed of trained police persons. The stories are low-key, and Charmian performs throughout in a highly competent and sensitive manner.

KATE FANSLER. Amanda Cross, pseud. of Carolyn Heilbrun. *In the Last Analysis* (New York, 1964); *The James Joyce Murder* (New York, 1967); *Poetic Justice* (New York, 1970); *The Theban Murders* (New York, 1972). She is a professor of English literature who begins her extracurricular career by masterminding an investigation in order to clear an innocent friend of a murder charge. She is adroit both at following clues and at capping quotations.

MODESTY BLAISE. Peter O'Donnell. *Modesty Blaise* (London, 1965); *A Taste for Death* (London, 1969); *The Impossible Virgin* (London, 1971); others. *Pieces of Modesty* (London, 1972) is a collection of ss. With her origins in a comic strip, this kinky pop heroine is a far cry from Loveday Brooke. Her exploits contain many of the bizarre trappings of radio's "Lady in Blue," and a 1966 film starred Italian actress Monica Vitti as Modesty. A similar heroine is television's Emma Peel, of "The Avengers."

MADAME DOMINIQUE AUBRY. Hugh Travers, pseud. of Hugh Travers Mills. *Madame Aubry and the Police* (New York, 1966); *Madame Aubry Dines with Death* (New York, 1967). An attractive and sophisticated widow, she is a trained lawyer and a handwriting expert. It is said of her that "no woman had ever occupied such an extraordinary position vis-à-vis the French police."

MRS. POLLIFAX. Dorothy Gilman. *The Unexpected Mrs. Pollifax* (New York, 1966); *A Palm for Mrs. Pollifax* (New York, 1973); others. She is a middle-aged widow who, in the course of irregular duty, forsakes the calm life of the suburbs to act as an unofficial agent of the CIA. There has been one Mrs. Pollifax film, starring Rosalind Russell.

CHRISTIE OPARA. Dorothy Uhnak. *The Bait* (New York, 1968); *The Witness* (New York, 1969); *The Ledger* (New York, 1970). Besides these novels about the widow of a New York City policeman who is a member of the force in her own right, the author wrote of her experiences as a detective of the New York City Transit Authority in a 1963 nonfiction book, *Policewoman.*

MISS SEETON. Heron Carvic. Among the Miss Seeton titles are *Picture Miss Seeton* (New York, 1968) and *Miss Seeton Draws the Line* (New York, 1970). She is an elderly English gentlewoman who is equally skillful at wielding her umbrella or handling a drawing pencil. Her talent for sketching portraits enables her to aid Scotland Yard in apprehending killers.

HILARY QUAYLE. Marvin Kaye. *A Lively Game of Death* (New York, 1972); *The Grand Ole Opry Murders* (New York, 1974). Hilary is a Manhattan public relations agent whose clients seem to end up as homicides. Unfortunately, she is a bit high-handed and sulks when the clues don't come her way. A much more acceptable character who also combined PR with amateur detection was Kathleen Moore Knight's Margot Blair, who appeared in the 1940s.

MOLLY MELLINGER. Kin Platt. *Dead as They Come* (New York, 1972). She is an editor of mystery novels who solves the murder of one of her authors. The setting is the world of New York publishing; Molly's firm is named Puddingstone & Dow.

NORAH MULCAHANEY. Lillian O'Donnell. *The Phone Calls* (New York, 1972); *Don't Wear Your Wedding Ring* (New York, 1973); *Dial 577 R-A-P-E* (New York, 1974). She is a detective attached to the Fifth Homicide and Assault Squad of the New York City Police. For more information, see Introduction, page xxix.

THE HON. CONSTANCE ETHEL MORRISON-BURKE. Joyce Porter. *A Meddler and her Murder* (London, 1973); others. The "Hon. Con.," as she is referred to, is a strident, self-opinionated, bull-like, overgrown tomboy. Yet, despite her bumbling, she is "one of nature's private detectives."

CORDELIA GRAY. P. D. James. *An Unsuitable Job for a Woman* (London, 1972). See Introduction, page xxix.

NICOLE SWEET. Fran Huston. *The Rich Get It All* (New York, 1973). She is the daughter of a cop who has chosen to follow in his footsteps by being a private eye. The incestuous complexity of her debut case, set in California, makes her seem little more than a female counterpart of Ross Macdonald's Lew Archer.

Selected Bibliography

Barzun, Jacques, and Taylor, Wendell Hertig. *A Catalogue of Crime*. New York: Harper & Row, 1971.

Everson, William K. *The Detective in Film*. Secaucus, N.J.: Citadel Press, 1972.

Hagen, Ordean A. *Who Done It? A Guide to Detective, Mystery, and Suspense Fiction*. New York: R. R. Bowker Co., 1969.

Haycraft, Howard. *Murder for Pleasure: The Life and Times of the Detective Story*. New York: D. Appleton-Century Co., 1941. Reprint ed. New York: Biblo & Tannen, 1972.

————, ed. *The Art of the Detective Story*. New York: Simon & Schuster, 1946.

Kabatchnik, Amnon. "Retrospective Review." *The Armchair Detective* (February 1974): 131–2.

LaCour, Tage, and Mogensen, Harald. *The Murder Book: An Illustrated History of the Detective Story*. New York: Herder & Herder, 1971.

Macgowan, Kenneth, ed. *Sleuths: Twenty-Three Great Detectives of Fiction and Their Best Stories*. New York: Harcourt, Brace & Co., 1931.

Murch, A. E., *The Development of the Detective Novel*. London: Peter Owen, 1958. Reprint ed. Port Washington, N.Y.: Kennikat Press, 1968.

Owings, Chloe. *Women Police: A Study of the Development and Status of the Women Police Movement*. New York: Frederick H. Hitchcock, 1925.

Queen, Ellery. *The Detective Short Story: A Bibliography.* Boston: Little, Brown & Co., 1942. Reprint ed. New York: Biblo & Tannen, 1969.

————. *In the Queen's Parlor, and Other Leaves from the Editors' Notebook.* New York: Biblo & Tannen, 1969.

————, ed. *101 Years' Entertainment: The Great Detective Stories 1841–1941.* Boston: Little, Brown & Co., 1941.

————, ed. *Twentieth Century Detective Stories.* Cleveland: World Publishing Co., 1948.

Sayers, Dorothy L., ed. *The Omnibus of Crime.* New York: Payson & Clarke, 1929.

Symons, Julian. *Mortal Consequences: A History from the Detective Story to the Crime Novel.* New York: Harper & Row, 1972.

Thomson, H. Douglas. *Masters of Mystery: A Study of the Detective Story.* London: Wm. Collins Sons, 1931.

Watson, Colin. *Snobbery with Violence: Crime Stories and Their Audience.* London: Eyre & Spottiswoode, 1971.

About the Editor

Michele B. Slung was born in Louisville, Kentucky, in 1947. After college she worked in bookstores in Philadelphia. She now does free-lance reading and writes a column entitled "Mystery Tour," which appears in *Ms.* Magazine. She employs her own sleuthing talents in secondhand bookshops and thrift shops. She lives in the same corner of New York as did Amelia Butterworth and Madame Storey, two women detectives.